JOSIE TOWNSEND

Shadow Bear

First published by Josie Townsend 2024

First edition

This book was professionally typeset on Reedsy.
Find out more at reedsy.com

Contents

Chapter 1

It comes from the universal shadows. You cannot bargain with it, you cannot reason with it, it's not a human being, it's not a beast, it's an entity, not of this earth, it is known as a skin-changer.

The adolescent boy's eyes were transfixed on the hot bowl of soup that had been placed in front of him as he listened to the other children's spoons clank against the deep dishes, while they hungrily slurped in unison, devouring the coffee-colored liquid. The broth did nothing to stir the boy's appetite, he had eaten a similar meal the night before and as he secretly observed the other children, all he craved was something more substantial like a plate of steamy rice and vegetables. He was exhausted from the sensation of waking up every morning with an empty stomach and as he stared at the solitary piece of carrot, suspended in the brown fluid, he heaved a long displeasing sigh.

"Is there something wrong Master Kane?" The old monk asked

"No, it's fine" Kane answered respectfully, his voice soft in a submissive manner. "Well then don't just stare at it.....eat it. Willful waste makes woeful want....you know this Master Kane now eat" The monk continued as he stood directly behind the boy and the moment he began walking away, at a slow relaxed pace, he gave Kane a swift clip over the ear.

The young man did not react to the strike. Instead, he reluctantly picked up the spoon that lay beside the bowl and began mimicking the sucking noises that the other children were making, without swallowing a drop of the disgusting brew.

"You don't need to eat any food, fat boy, you're already bigger than a house," one of the adjacent teenagers quipped.

"And hairier than a bear," another added, laughing behind his hand.

"Shut up Isamu" Kane mouthed quietly towards the spiteful young man, while some of the other teens giggled.

Kane briefly glanced up at the governing monk, whose footsteps made no sound, like a piece of wood quietly drifting along a slow stream, he effectively glided around the large table, glaring down at each child as he passed by, but thankfully, he didn't notice the boy's short quarrel.

With relief swathing him, Kane waited until the monk gave the command for everyone to leave the table. As the others uniformly departed, walking to their respective dormitories, Kane deliberately lagged behind them, leaving the uneaten bowl of soup right where it had been originally placed.

His decision to reject the meager offering wasn't just a defiance against the monotony of their meals; it was a small act of rebellion against the suffocating routine of the monastery. With each step he took away from the dining hall, he felt a sense of liberation, a fleeting taste of freedom amidst the structures of their daily lives. Though he knew there would be consequences for his actions, for now, the simple act of leaving behind the bowl of soup was enough to lift his spirits and remind him that even in the most regimented of environments, he still retained a measure of autonomy.

"Master Kane" the monk shouted in a demanding tone from the far side of the vast dining room.

Kane stopped in his tracks and instantly bowed his head in defeat and as he slowly turned around to face the distant bellowing, he was confronted by the monk who stood right in front of him, his rutted nose protruding an inch away from Kane's face. Startled by the monk's quick approach, Kane jumped backward and wondered how the old buzzard could move so quickly.

"Hai father," Kane replied in a faint voice. "You did not finish your soup"

"I wasn't hungry" he continued

"Humpf" the monk groaned with disfavor, then continued with what he really wanted to say.

"It has been brought to my attention that you're talking in your sleep again" He glared at the teenager with his small dark beady eyes.

"Have I? What's wrong with that?" Kane answered boldly and was tersely replied with an unexpected slap in the face.

"There's a lot wrong with that, you throw away child. You are keeping the others awake with your incessant babbling. Who are you talking to? The other boys are telling me that you're answering questions.....who is it? The old monk was resolute.

The lingering throb on the side of his face began to fade and combined with the initial shock of the slap, caused him to stammer and he hesitated to answer.

"I...I...I don't know father.....I...I...I am asleep.....I must be having nightmares" Kane tried to justify his late-night tirades.

"No, I don't think they are nightmares, your brothers tell me that the ramblings involve complicated dialogues and that you speak in forgotten ancient tongues. Are you talking to a deity?" The monk queried.

"I'm sorry father, I don't know what that means" Kane lied

"I'm asking you if you're talking to a supreme divinity.....the creator?"

"No I don't know any celestial beings" He replied with impudence and even though he thought his mouthy retort was smart, he was given another whack in the face.

The old monk squinted his beady eyes as he studied the young man, scrutinizing him with doubt and suspicion. Kane's stoic facade did little to deter the monk's penetrating gaze; if anything, it seemed to fuel his skepticism further. With a subtle tilt of his head, the monk continued to assess Kane, as if searching for any sign of weakness or deception lurking beneath the surface.

Despite the intensity of the old monk's scrutiny, Kane remained unmoved, his expression a mask of unwavering stubbornness. He knew that winning the hoary man's trust would be no easy feat, but he was determined to prove himself, to show that he was more than just the sum of the monk's doubts. With each passing moment, the tension between them grew obvious, a silent battle of wills playing out beneath the monastery's hallowed halls.

"There's something about you boy that I don't trust. You remind me of a cunning serpent, artfully hiding in the grass waiting to strike" He finally stated.

Without reacting to the monk's ongoing abuse, Kane stood there firmly, his jaw clenched and his eyes burning with restrained fury. Though the old man's words cut deep, Kane refused to give him the satisfaction of a reaction. Instead, he met the monk's gaze with a riveted, blank stare that could have penetrated stone.

Inside, a storm raged within Kane's mind, thoughts of revenge and retribution swirling like dark clouds. He imagined countless ways to silence the offensive bastard, each scenario more satisfying than the last. But amidst the chaos of his thoughts, a glimmer of control held him back, reminding him of the consequences of acting on his impulses.

With every insult hurled his way, Kane's will power only strengthened. He would endure the monk's abuse for now, biding his time until the perfect moment presented itself, and when it did, the old man would regret the day he ever crossed paths with him.

"Go.....get out of my sight boy, but if I hear of any more about your nightly gibberish, you will suffer the consequences, five days in prayer and meditation to return your virtue" He added, his voice carrying a hint of mockery, as Kane turned away from him and walked out of the mess hall with despondency filling his heart. The weight of the monk's words hung heavy on Kane's shoulders, adding to the burden of his already troubled thoughts. With each step he took, the walls of the monastery seemed to close in around him, strangling him with their oppressive presence.

Outside, the air was rich with the scent of incense and the distant sound of chanting hummed through the courtyard. Kane's footsteps echoed against the stone walls as he made his way through the winding hallway, his mind consumed by a whirlwind of emotions. Anger, frustration, and despair warred within him, each fighting for dominance as he struggled to make sense of the turmoil brewing inside.

As he emerged into the cool evening air, Kane paused for a moment, his gaze drifting upwards towards the darkening sky. In that fleeting moment of solitude, he felt a flicker of hope ignite within him, a tiny spark amidst the darkness. Feeling the renewed determination, he squared his shoulders, knowing that despite the challenges ahead, he would not falter in his quest for freedom.

Just like Kane, the staunch, decrepit old monk was an orphan. He had been found by a group of passing villagers, lying in a fetal position under an elevated house that reeked of mold. Starving and beaten, he was dying in his own excrement and he had been repeatedly sodomized by other vagrants so he bled frequently from his anus.

The watchful townspeople rescued him from his foul existence and transported him directly to the monastery where he began residing there in 1844 at the tender age of six. The difference between Kane and himself was that he valued the monasteries' rigid spiritual enforcement so much, that he eventually became part of the institution and devoted his entire life to serving all other living beings, spending his time dedicated to prayer and contemplation; something he believed

Kane was incapable of doing. He couldn't accept that the insolent boy possessed the discipline or had the right way of thinking to be a blessing to the convent.

The irritable monk's name was Gideon.

During his youth, he had spent many years in the abbey, toiling on the surrounding land, farming vegetables for the other monks. He washed their clothes, cooked their food, and applied his crafty skills to repairing the monastery's deteriorating structure. But as the years passed, he elevated to the supreme honor of a scribe, where he would spend his days copying sacred manuscripts and producing books from them. In the quiet solitude of the scriptorium, Gideon found solace and purpose.

Surrounded by the timeless wisdom contained within the pages of ancient texts, he felt a profound connection to something greater than himself. Each stroke of his quill was a prayer, a testament to his devotion to the divine and his commitment to preserving the knowledge of generations past.

Despite the hardships he endured in his childhood, Gideon's tireless faith sustained him, guiding him along the path of service and enlightenment. He meticulously transcribed the words of the holy scriptures, and found fulfillment in knowing that his

labor was a small but essential contribution to the legacy of the monastery and the spiritual journey of all who lived in its ancient chambers.

His daily ritual consisted of rising at 4 am, still not completely awake, he'd stumble down the main staircase, braving the sharp morning air. Carrying a jug down the candle-lit passageway to the hot water tap, he'd fetch water and return to his room where he washed, shaved, and dressed for another day.

The flickering candlelight cast dancing shadows on the walls as he moved through the dim corridors, the only sound his footsteps piercing the silence of the early morning. The air was crisp and cool against his skin, invigorating him despite his groggy state.

In the solitude of his room, he performed his bathing with practiced efficiency, the ritual grounding him in the present moment as he prepared himself for the tasks that lay ahead. With each splash of water on his face and stroke of the razor against his skin, he felt the drowsiness of sleep begin to dissolve, replaced by a quiet sense of purpose that propelled him forward into the new day.

As the early morning broke the peaceful darkness, Gideon attended the first service. Psalms flowed from one side to the other of the altar, as the monks chanted stories, illuminating the history of God's long centuries of vigil watching, before the birth of the creator's brilliance and his coming into a world that was immersed in hostility, ignorance, and sin.

The twinkling light cast a warm glow over the faces of the worshippers, their voices rising and falling in harmony with the ancient verses. Gideon closed his eyes, letting the familiar words wash over him, filling him with a sense of peace and appreciation. As the service drew to a close, Gideon felt a restored touch of purpose stirring within him. The sound of the psalms lingered in the air, a reminder of the stable power of faith and the unfaltering presence of God in the midst of life's trials and tribulations. With a heart full of gratitude, Gideon bowed his head in prayer, ready to face whatever challenges the day ahead might bring, fortified by the strength of his beliefs and the fellowship of his brothers.

Two hours later, Gideon receives a pot of tea, a piece of bread, butter, and jam, which ignites some life into his listless body as he contemplates the next service he must attend in the rectory. Distracted by his inner thoughts, Gideon finishes his breakfast while the sunbeams break through the temple windows, the white and yellow rays penetrating the shoddy brown and orange bricks, as they soak up the advancing warmth of the day.

By lunchtime, Gideon had attended four of the monastery's services and looked forward to consuming the dish of chicken and potato mash. As he reads an inspiring manuscript, he has no difficulty attending to both his food and the riveting parchments in front of him. After his meal, he is allowed to relax a little with the other monks, but the surrounding conversations soon turn to the problems of the convent's ongoing renovations. After a while, the older monks, bored with the same old chit chat, nod off and fall asleep next to the blazing, crackling fire.

Gideon finds himself lost in the comforting warmth of the flames, the glimmering light whirling across the worn pages of the manuscripts scattered around him. Despite the chatter of his companions fading into the background, Gideon's mind remains active, pondering the mysteries of faith and the timeless wisdom contained within the ancient texts. In these moments of quiet contemplation, he finds solace and renewal, his spirit replenished by the timeless truths that have guided generations of worshipers before him.

The monastery was an isolated and remote sanctuary, seldom visited by the outside world. As Gideon entered the library, he pushed through the heavy, solid doors with one arm, papers stuffed haphazardly under the other. His eyes immediately darted to the small, confined window that offered a glimpse of the expiring cornfields and the majestic, snow-capped mountains beyond.

He enjoyed the solitude and seclusion of the heavily mahogany room, and while he advanced into it, his eyes had to adjust to the shadiness. Thousands of stacked books and scrolls were neatly arranged and aligned back to back on the dark shelves, their confidential insides disguised by their covers. They sat patiently on the wooden shelves, every supporting mantle the color of arterial blood.

The scent of aging parchment and leather bound volumes hung thick in the air, mingling with the faint aroma of incense that wafted in from the chapel nearby. Gideon's walked softly across the polished floor as he made his way deeper into the library, his fingers grazing over the spines of the ancient books that held the accumulated knowledge of centuries past.

In this sacred space, time seemed to stand still, and Gideon felt a feeling of reverence come over him as he immersed himself in the wisdom contained within the pages of the books. Here, amidst the hushed whispers of forgotten voices and the weight of centuries-old knowledge, he found a sanctuary from the tumult of the outside world—a place where he could lose himself in the pursuit of truth and insight. Approaching another maze of shelves, he walked parallel to them, softly touching each book in admiration, caressing their delicate shields.

He stops in front of a particular book that jutted out of line with the others, as if hastily shoved amongst them. This one, he hadn't noticed before.

His forehead wrinkled and his eyes blinked with curiosity. Reaching for the unfamiliar journal, he cautiously pulled it from its hiding place.

Gently cradling the strange hefty book, Gideon placed it on his usual desk and as he sat down to examine it, the pungent smell of mold and earth penetrated his nostrils. The cover of the journal was weathered and worn, its pages yellowed with age and frayed at the edges.

The stench was so strong that Gideon immediately slipped his hand into his pocket, pulled out a handkerchief, and placed it over his mouth while he began heaving from the stench. With the hanky still masking his face, he carefully examined the obscure book and instantly noticed a prominent mark on the front. Where the lock was fastened, an indentation was present, resembling the ghoulish likeness of a human belly button, stretched to its full capacity. There was also a declaration embedded into the macabre human skin at the top of the cover, and with his extensive knowledge of scribing ancient languages, he was able to translate what it said.

"In his pitiful life he did not serve mankind with honor. Now he can be of service in death."

The translation sent a shiver down Gideon's spine, and he felt a sense of unease settle over him like a heavy cloak. What kind of book was this, and who was its mysterious author? As he stared at the book, he couldn't shake the feeling that he had stumbled upon something far more sinister than he'd ever imagined. Despite the ominous warning on the cover, curiosity got the better of him, and he vowed to unravel the secrets hidden within the ancient book, no matter the cost.

The monk sat there motionless, his face white as chalk, stupefied at the insidious discovery. He struggled with increasing trepidation in his mind on whether to open it, as every essence of his Buddhist faith warned him not to.

Gideon's hands trembled as he reached for the book, his fingers hovering over the ancient lock. A voice deep within him whispered a warning, urging caution and restraint. He knew that to open the book would be to invite unknown dangers into his life, to tread upon forbidden ground that could never be uncharted. So, with profound uncertainty gnawing at his soul and with his infinite wisdom, he didn't pursue it.

Gideon grabbed the book and carefully replaced it on the shelf, its secrets remaining hidden for now. Though his curiosity burned bright, he understood that some mysteries were best left undisturbed, their dark truths lurking in the shadows of the unknown.

Deep down, he knew that he had made the right choice—to honor his faith, to consider the potential danger of the ancient book, and to protect himself and those he loved from the perils that could lay within its pages.

In the far dormitory wing of the monastery, Kane sat on the flimsy bed with his back to the wall, exhausted from the incessant taunting the other orphans inflicted on him. He couldn't understand why everyone hated him so much and concluded that it must be a result of his enormous size and the fact that he babbled loudly every night while he slept.

He felt a surge of bitterness and discrimination, his sense

of self-pity escalating with each passing moment. Yet, as his emotions churned, he experienced a profound realization. Despite his suffering, he was grateful that he had not been condemned to the harsh fate of imprisonment or forced into labor, unlike some of the other unfortunate boys he had once known.

Very few of the orphans were adopted into the monastery, but he felt as though this secluded lifestyle was a punishment for surviving the war. He just wanted to be a normal boy with a loving family, but instead, with every waking moment, he felt hopeless and alone, yet another day void of a hug or any token of kindness. The lack of any human affection and the incessant bullying he received made Kane's heart petulant and resentful towards those who found pleasure in his gawkiness, and the revenge he visualized grew and consumed his thoughts.

In the dim light, Kane's eyes burned with anger and frustration. He longed for a way out of this cycle of suffering, a way to escape the abuse of his peers and find solace in a world that seemed determined to reject him. As the pressure of his loneliness pressed down upon him, he knew that the road ahead would be long and fraught with challenges. With a forlorn heart, he resigned himself to another sleepless night, the sounds of laughter and taunts ringing in his ears.

As he stared blankly at the entrance of his room, with the door slightly ajar, he heard it obscurely scrape open, but nothing appeared in his direct line of sight. Leaning forward to identify what had just entered, he saw Gideon's cat discreetly gliding inside. When it discovered Kane peering back, it let out a spine-chilling hiss as its body instantly arched up and twisted into a ball, attempting to escape Kane's presence.

"Even the cat hates me," he muttered to himself miserably as he watched the animal scuttle out the door like its tail was on fire. Then, in a huff, he accordingly slumped back to his original position.

The rejection from even the smallest creatures felt like another blow to Kane's already bruised ego. He longed for companionship, for acceptance, but it seemed that even the animals of the monastery shunned his presence. With much saddness, he locked himself to the solitude of his room, and in the darkness of the dormitory, he felt completely alone, a solitary figure adrift in a sea of indifference.

An impressive grandfather clock sat at the end of the long, dim corridor where Kane's bedroom was situated. Its craftsmanship dated back to the 1600s and skillfully boasted a dark walnut veneer and crested top. The pendulum eternally swayed back and forth while the hands pointed to its square brass dials, indicating the time of day with a loud booming sound each and every hour—a stark contrast to the customary silence of the monastery. It was midmorning when the clock resonated its pulsating bang as it vibrated down the hallway, announcing it was 10 am, rudely informing the boys it was time for their martial arts compound training in the quadrangle.

Kane casually stood up and ambled over to his wardrobe, gathering his ninja-yoroi, the traditional dark and mysterious outfit worn by these stealthy warriors, and proceeded to dress.

As he fastened the straps of his uniform, Kane's mind drifted to the training ahead. Despite the challenges he faced within the monastery, the martial arts compound offered him a brief respite from the torment of his peers—a chance to focus his energy and hone his skills in the ancient art of combat. With each piece of armor he donned, he felt a sense of purpose stirring within him, a bravery to prove himself worthy of the title of ninja, despite the odds stacked against him.

With a final adjustment to his attire, Kane made his way to the quadrangle, his steps steady and sure. As he entered the training grounds, he cast aside the worry of his troubles, allowing the rhythm of his movements to guide him into the flow of the martial arts, where for a fleeting moment, he could forget the pain of his past and present, embracing the possibility of a brighter future.

He didn't mind the rigorous training, as his size and strength far exceeded the other boys' physical capabilities, and he relished in the acquired skills he was learning to be a stealthy and effective ninja. The suitably colored dark red yoroi ensured that it was an asset to his stealth, as all ninja exploits were well-rehearsed to go unnoticed, and if the blood from his gashes and gouges were to spill on his claret uniform, it wouldn't be visible to any of the spectators or his opponent.

Once everyone had gathered in the quadrangle, like automated robots, they organized themselves into designated lines and stood perfectly silent until the three ninja masters arrived to command their ritualistic training. The minute the grandmasters set foot on the ancient pavement, the entire entourage of students bowed, acknowledging that their duty was to learn and listen to the best of their ability, demonstrating respect towards the superior monks.

Kane stood among his fellow students, his posture erect and his gaze focused, ready to absorb the wisdom of his masters and apply it to his training. As the grandmasters

began to speak, their voices reverberating through the courtyard, Kane listened intently, committing each instruction to memory with a fierce determination to excel. Under the watchful eye of the ninja masters, Kane and his fellow students embarked on a series of drills and exercises designed to test their agility, speed, and stealth.

With each movement, Kane felt a surge of exhilaration coursing through his veins, the thrill of the chase and the rush of adrenaline driving him to push himself to his limits.

The sun belted down upon the courtyard, but Kane threw himself into his training with unwavering dedication, compelled to prove himself worthy of the title of ninja. He loved to move through the exercises with precision and grace, knowing that with each passing moment, he was one step closer to realizing his dreams of becoming a true master of the shadows.

The middle Sensei stepped forward, breaking away from the other monks, standing composed and mutely for twenty minutes as he surveyed his students with a cold and calculated stare, before bellowing out his first order.

"Find your inner chi and execute the horse stance," he commanded, and at the precise moment he finished speaking, the twenty-strong crowd answered in unison, yelling out the word "Hai" and simultaneously crouched in a low squatting position. With legs burning like hot iron, they remained there motionless for what seemed like a decade.

Kane didn't mind squatting for such a lengthy amount of time. His legs were stocky and muscular with thick, coarse black hair, and while some of the other students began to collapse under the intensity of the stance, Kane remained insistent and steadfast. Those who succumbed to the severity of the torture were punished with an intense blow from the master's staff as he casually walked around with his hands clasped behind his back, holding the disciplinary stick.

As Kane held the horse stance, he focused on channeling his inner energy, feeling the burn in his muscles intensify with each passing moment. Despite the pain, he remained rooted in place, his mind clear and focused on the task at hand. With each passing second, he felt himself drawing closer to the elusive state of inner peace and harmony that the Sensei had instructed them to find.

The minutes stretched on,and Kane's fortitude only grew stronger, his resilience unshaken by the physical discomfort or the harsh discipline of his master. He knew that in order to truly master the art of the ninja, he would need to endure far greater challenges than a simple horse stance. With that knowledge driving him forward, he remained strong in his commitment to excellence, ready to face whatever trials lay ahead on his path to greatness.

"Now execute the deep grass rabbit walk," The Sensei finally demanded as the crowd answered "Hai" and crouched down, placing the balls of their feet on top of their hands and began walking effectively on the palms of their hands, constantly moving back and forth covering a very long distance.

Kane moved with a serene confidence, his mastery of the intricate technique a testament to countless hours of dedicated practice. Though it was exceedingly difficult, he knew that this relentless effort would one day pay off. Honing his skills inched him closer to his ultimate goal of becoming the elusive, silent assassin he so desperately aspired to be. With each fluid movement, he felt himself growing closer to his goal, his body flowing with the precision and grace of a seasoned warrior.

"Now execute the floating foot," the Sensei continued as the students began to walk entirely on the tips of their toes, with neither their heels nor flat feet touching the ground.

"This is an ancient technique and essential for a good ninja to move closely and silently up to your opponent," he announced with pride.

Kane focused intently as he shifted his weight onto the balls of his feet, feeling the strain in his calves and ankles as he lifted his heels off the ground. With every step, he moved with the lightness and precision of a cat stalking its prey, his movements barely making a sound as he glided across the courtyard.

This was the essence of ninja training—the ability to move with stealth and grace, to become one with the shadows and strike with deadly precision. As he continued to perfect his technique under the watchful eye of his grandmasters, he understood that he was becoming the ultimate silent assassin.

Kane felt himself growing stronger and more confident in his abilities. He knew that mastering the floating foot technique would be essential for his future as a ninja, allowing him to move undetected through the darkness and strike fear into the hearts of his enemies.

"Now execute the walk of the fox," he persisted, lecturing in a strident and powerful manner.

"Ninjas are masters of strength, stealth, and silence. You must train these techniques day and night to make sure you are experts in the art of being unseen and unheard. You must learn how to hide, remain invisible, and be silent in any habitat. You must wear nothing but your ninja-yoroi, gloves, and weapons as this will maximize your stealth and enable you to roam in a distinctive mix of situations and environments... we are elite ninjas and must uphold our ancient reputation as specialized assassins,

saboteurs, and secret agents.... do you understand?" The Master continued to bellow.

"Hai," the students answered as Kane mumbled brazenly under his breath....

"You must do this and must do that, always must, must, must."

Despite his outward compliance, Kane felt a surge of frustration rising within him. Again, the constant barrage of orders and expectations from his superiors naturally grated on his nerves, their harsh demeanor a relentless reminder of the strict, rigid hierarchy of the monastery.

He was young, with a lifetime ahead of him, and the thought of spending his days growing into an old man at the monastery filled him with dread. Kane longed to break free from the constraints of tradition and forge his own path, to escape the stifling predictability of monastic life. Yet, he knew that as a ninja, obedience was paramount, a bitter irony that kept him tethered to a destiny he desperately wanted to escape.

As he moved through the walk of the fox, Kane couldn't help but feel rebellion stirring within him. He was tired of being told what to do and how to do it, tired of living under the watchful eye of his masters. For now, he would bide his time, sharpening his skills and waiting for the opportunity to strike out on his own.

Kane strived to prove himself worthy of the title of ninja, not just through his compliance, but through his skill and cunningness.

The commanding Sensei had not always lived at the monastery. Unlike Kane and the old monk Gideon, he wasn't orphaned. He began his cultivated journey of ninja mastery as a child living in his native village, and later in his adult years, he worked as a covert agent in feudal Japan. He came from a lower-class family who were generational rice farmers, and all the men in the village were actually feared warriors, cleverly disguised as simple peasants carrying out their daily work. Their weapons resembled farm tools, but they could dismantle them quickly, exposing vicious and barbaric sickles and shears, instantly ready to kill and disfigure any menacing intruder.

Growing up in this environment, the Sensei learned the art of stealth and deception from a young age. He trained tirelessly with his family, gaining skills in combat and mastering the art of blending in with his surroundings. As he grew older, he took on missions as a covert agent, using his expertise to gather intelligence, sabotage enemy operations, and eliminate threats to his village and country.

Despite his humble beginnings, the Sensei rose through the ranks of the ninja hierarchy, earning a reputation as one of the most competent and feared warriors in feudal Japan. His effeciency in espionage and assassination made him a valuable asset to his superiors, and his loyalty to his village and country was steadfast.

But as time went by, the Sensei began to question the morality of his actions. He saw the devastation and suffering caused by the endless cycle of violence and war, and he longed for a life of peace and tranquility. That's when he decided to retire from active duty and seek refuge at the monastery, where he could pass on his knowledge and skills to the next generation of warriors.

Now, as he stood before his students, teaching them the ancient techniques of the ninja, the Sensei reflected on his own journey and the lessons he had learned along the way. He knew that the path of the ninja was not an easy one, but he also knew that with dedication, discipline, and a strong sense of purpose, his students would be able to overcome any obstacle and become true masters of the shadows.

Even though his Buddhist faith was deep, the high ninja had successfully completed many missions and had perpetrated brutal executions according to his directive.

Unfortunately, these experiences, over time, had developed an unshakable pomposity about him.

The separation between his spiritual beliefs and his actions in the past played on the Sensei's mind. While he had once believed that he was serving the greater good by carrying out his murderous missions with ruthless efficiency, he now found himself questioning his virtue. The violence and bloodshed that he had inflicted nagged at him, leaving a stain on his soul that he could not easily wash away.

Despite his inner regrets, the Sensei remained committed to his Buddhist principles, seeking redemption through meditation and prayer. He now dedicated himself to a life of peace and tranquility, using his skills as a ninja to protect the monastery and its inhabitants from harm.

As he trained his students, the Sensei imparted not only martial techniques but also the importance of mercy. He hoped that by passing on his knowledge and wisdom, he could help his students avoid the same mistakes that he had made and know the importance of enlightenment and inner peace, even when fulfilling their duty as a trained assassin.

Though the scars of his past may never fully heal, the Sensei remained hopeful that through his teachings, he could make amends for the violence he had inflicted on others and find redemption in the eyes of the Buddha. He continued on his journey of spiritual growth and self-discovery, and he knew that the path to ultimate mindfulness was long and arduous, but ultimately worth the effort.

"Now, reform your lines and begin the ninja magical signs with your fingers. These will assist you with self-control during times of danger, restoring your confidence and giving you inner strength in moments of desperation.... these techniques hypnotize

your enemy into inaction and are similar to casting the evil eye on them.... at the same time I want you to chant your Buddhist sutras and maxims from the scriptures." "Have your wits about you at all times, sharpen your perception and insights. If you master these skills, your instincts will evolve to a point where you'll become accomplished shadow warriors and appear superhuman to the average person. You must learn to be mysterious and cause confusion to your enemies," he barked out loudly as he continually strolled around the aligned, regimented students.

As the Sensei's words bellowed through the training ground, the young men listened intently, their minds focused on mastering the ancient techniques. With each gesture and chant, they felt a sense of empowerment flowing through them, a feeling of being connected to something greater than themselves.

For Kane, the Sensei's teachings struck a chord deep within him. He knew that in order to become the ultimate warrior, he would need to master not only the physical skills of combat but also the mental and spiritual aspects of the art. As he performed the magical signs with his fingers and chanted the Buddhist sutras, he felt a calm and clarity wash over him, like he was tapping into a hidden reservoir of inner strength.

The training session continued, and Kane focused all of his attention on mastering the techniques that the Sensei had taught him.

From the high, compact window that illuminated the monastery library, Gideon stood there motionless, peering down at the students, singling out a burly young man and scrutinizing his endeavors with distaste. Kane instinctively felt the monk's ominous presence and looked up to observe his menacing scowl as he cradled and stroked his beloved cat.

Kane stared directly back at him, his gaze fixed, and as he did, Gideon noticed something unsettling happening in the distance, far beyond the young man.

Storm clouds began billowing and transforming into the distinct likeness of a severed skull. The curious apparition hung in the air, its sawtoothed mouth and empty eye sockets dripping with blackness. Gideon felt a chill run down his spine as he stared at the threatening sight.

While he looked into the skull's dark shadows, an overwhelming dread swept over him, and he instantly absorbed the brooding fear the skull vigorously discharged. It was as if the very essence of evil had taken form in the swirling clouds, and Gideon couldn't shake the feeling that something malevolent was watching them from beyond.

For a moment, he considered warning the students of the impending danger, but a touch of foreboding held him back. He knew that whatever was coming, they would need to face it on their own. Deep down, Gideon feared that the storm was just the

beginning, an indicator of even greater darkness to come. He sensed that they would need to prepare themselves for whatever trials lay ahead, but he couldn't shake the feeling of dread that clung to him like a stifling veil.

Feeling as though he'd been struck by a powerful force or some supernatural entity, Gideon stumbled backward, his balance lost in an instant. He accidentally flung the cat high toward the ceiling before landing hard on his buttocks, the impact jarring him as he struggled to comprehend what had just happened.

He sat there petrified from the encounter, trying desperately to shake off the lingering sense of fear that grasped him like enveloping fog. No matter how hard he tried, he couldn't erase the skull image from his mind.

Sensing that he was under attack, Gideon eased his way off the floor, his heart pounding in his chest like a drum. Every instinct screamed at him to flee, to escape the malevolent presence that seemed to be closing in on him from all sides.

Unconsciously, he found himself reciting the words "Hell

is empty..... the devil is here" under his breath, a mantra of protection against the encroaching darkness he felt.

With trembling hands, Gideon reached for the library door, his fingers fumbling with the latch in his haste to escape. As he swung the door open, a rush of icy wind whooshed past him, sending a shiver down his spine. He didn't hesitate. Taking one last glance over his shoulder, he stepped out into the corridor, his mind racing with thoughts of what horrors awaited him.

After witnessing the reaction his cold hard stare had on the snooping Gideon and watching him with delight, fall away from the library window, Kane remained cool and composed as he focused his attention back on Jonin's (high ninja) teachings with a more determined passion than ever before.

"Remember your five elements when engaging with the enemy," Jonin instructed, his voice steady and authoritative.

Kane listened intently, his mind sharp as he absorbed every word of wisdom from his mentor. The teachings of the high ninja were like a beacon of light in the darkness, guiding him on the path to mastery.....for he was Kane, the shadow warrior, and nothing would stop his destiny.

"Earth, Water, Fire, Wind and Void. Through study and practice, you will become instinctive, and automatic with your unconscious responses. Remain grounded in your thinking to repel attempts to distract or deceive you. Shift and move fluidly to confuse your attackers to put them off balance. Stay light on your feet and move nimbly to evade attempts to trap you, all of these are the elements you have to master, so you can become effectively employed as assassins.

Your assignments will not only involve executions but the gathering of sensitive information for government intelligence, so remember to use your techniques of non-detection, avoidance and misdirection powerfully"

This is the way of the ninja....Hai?" He screamed "Hai" the students loudly responded.

"Master Kane and Master Hiro, step forward and begin hand-to-hand combat. Show the others how it is done" Jonin ordered.

The men moved out of their lines, first bowing respectfully to Jonin and then to each other as they prepared to face off. Unlike the precise, well-executed forms and disciplines that had been imprinted into the boys' minds through practiced katas, the actual physical confrontation was hard to control.

They squared off against each other, their movements were erratic and uncoordinated, fueled by adrenaline and instinct. Kane could feel the heat of battle coursing through his veins, his senses on high alert as he anticipated his opponent's every advance.

He moved cautiously to the left, observing Hiro, and contemplated his first strike. Forming his hands as if he was gripping imaginary racket balls, he launched himself at Hiro, ducking under his rival's swing, and snapped himself into the mindset of invisibility, strength and assertiveness. There was no holding back.

One direction, always forward, towards the challenger.....all offensive.

With each clash of fists and feet, Kane pushed himself harder, testing the limits of his strength and skill. He could hear Jonin's voice in his head, urging him to stay watchful and disciplined, but the havoc of the fight threatened to overwhelm him.

Despite the frenzy, Kane tried to remain calm and composed,

his training kicking in as he fought with precision. He could see his opponent's weaknesses, exploiting them with calculated strikes and maneuvers.

Grabbing Hiro's attempted strike, Kane dug his fingers into the bicep of his swinging arm, feeling the muscles tense beneath his grip, and ripped at the flesh with savage force. At the same time, he struck Hiro's forearm with the full force of his fist, aiming to weaken his opponent's offensive stance.

Hiro responded in kind, retaliating with a vicious assault of his own. His fingers raked across Kane's face, leaving painful scratches along his nose and mouth. Kane refused to back down, channeling his fury into a relentless barrage of strikes and kicks.

With swift motion, Kane drove his elbow upwards, aiming for Hiro's abdomen.

The blow landed with a satisfying thud, momentarily stunning his rival. Seizing the opportunity, Kane followed up with a stab kick to Hiro's groin, evoking a gasp of pain.

But Kane wasn't finished yet. Channelling lightning speed, he unleashed a spinning hook kick followed by a rising elbow strike to the underside of Hiro's chin, sending a shockwave of agony through his body.

Hiro jerked violently, his arms thrashing around as he fell, unable to muster the

self-control to counterattack. Seizing the advantage, Kane moved swiftly, forcing the aggressor to stumble into his next flying strike head-on.

The impact was brutal, blood splattering from Hiro's nose and mouth as he staggered backward and Kane could feel the satisfaction of vengeance coursing through him, driving him forward with relentless tenacity.

As Hiro wobbled about completely in shock, Kane delivered another punishing blow, this time targeting his throat. The pain rippled through Hiro's body, leaving him gasping for air as he finally fell to the ground, struggling to remain conscious.

Blood poured from the various facial lacerations, mixing with the vomit that spilled from his lips.

As the remnants of their brutal confrontation faded away, Kane stood over his fallen opponent, victorious but weary. He knew that their personal battle was far from over, but now, he allowed himself a brief moment of triumph, knowing that he had emerged victorious against his most formidable foe.

This is the dark underbelly of the ninja way.

Kane's chest heaved with exertion. He had emerged the champion, proving once again that he was a true ninja and a master of the art of combat.

There had been no wasted movements, Kane's motions were designed to roll naturally into the next, creating a grabbling effect and to the observer. It had been a typhoon of blinding speed movements, a haze, too fast for the eye to follow.

Defeated and dispirited, Hiro lay in the dirt, still coughing and spitting up blood from his mouth injuries. Meanwhile, Kane returned to his appointed position in the line, feeling proud and masterfully skilled. He watched as Hiro squirmed with shame in front of the other students, his gaze filled with loathing and resentment.

The intensity of Hiro's glare, didn't worry Kane. He knew that he had emerged triumphant through his strength and superior mastery, and he refused to let Hiro's hatred affect him. Instead, he stood tall and resolute, his confidence growing in the face of adversity.

As the other students looked on, Kane could sense their admiration and respect. *"Hate begets hate Hiro, taste your own medicine you bully"* Kane secretly thought to himself.

"Get up Master Hiro. What are you to do? Stay in the dirt? Jonin (high ninja) screamed, continuing to humiliate him

"Get up, there are hardships and there are delights in life Master Hiro. After the rain comes fair weather, no pain, no gain, now stop slithering around in the dirt like a worm and get up"

Hiro gingerly looked up at Jonin, his expression a mix of pain and resentment. With great effort, he began lifting his aching body off the ground, gritting his teeth against the agony as he slowly reclaimed his position in the line.

Although he lost, Hiro refused to be defeated in spirit. He knew that setbacks were a part of the journey, and he was determined to learn from this experience and come back stronger, and beat Kane.

As he stood among his fellow students, his body battered and bruised but his spirit unbroken, Hiro silently vowed to redouble his efforts and train even harder and defeat his nemisis.

He may have been knocked down this time, but he was not out. He proudly took his place in the line once more, but he was now ready to face anything Kane could dish out.

"Training is over, you may leave and go to your dormitories. Hai?" Jonin concluded "Hai. Thank you Sensei" the men answered in unison.

The students bowed respectfully to the three ninja masters as they finally departed, their figures disappearing through the convent's doorway. With their departure, the atmosphere in the courtyard shifted, the tension of the training session dissipating like smoke in the wind.

As the students dispersed, some exchanging words of encouragement or sharing knowing glances, a sense of camaraderie filled the air. Despite the intensity of their training and the challenges they faced, they knew that they were united in their brotherhood.

Having the lessons of the day still fresh in their minds, they dispersed to tend to their duties or enjoy a moment of respite.

Kane started to exit the quadrangle, but he couldn't shake the feeling of Hiro's resentful glare burning into his back. Just as he was walking away, he heard the undignified rival yell after him, his voice tinged with bitterness and frustration. "Kane! This isn't over between us. Watch your back!" Hiro's words repeating across the courtyard, filled with a venomous promise of future conflict.

Kane paused for a moment, considering his response. But then, with a calm demeanour he continued on his way, refusing to be drawn into Hiro's petty provocations. He knew that their rivalry was far from over, but he was confident in his abilities.

"I'll get you for this fat boy" Hiro screamed

Holding his head high, Kane walked away, leaving Hiro's taunts behind him. The true test of a ninja wasn't in the words they spoke, but in the actions they took, so to irritate Hiro further, he just smirked and ignored him, walking into the monastery and retiring to his room.

He flopped down onto his bed. His thoughts simmering;

completely devoured by irritating questions about the ever-intrusive, constantly spying Gideon and then, just like it was sent a directive, the old monks cat wandered in.

Kane stood up and visually inspected the animal with curiosity and as he bent down to stroke its tail, the cat turned around and swiped at him with its long, razor-sharp claws, opening up two deep gashes along his right arm as the blood instantly surged from the unnecessary injuries.

Instinctively Kane grabbed a folded blanket from the end of his bed and after shutting the door and successfully cornering the vindictive beast, he threw the bed cover over its body and grabbed it by the neck, wrapping it entirely within the quilt. His anger was at boiling point and with the agitated cat hissing, wildly fighting and scratching, he grabbed its head and using all of his powerful strength, he yanked at it, breaking its neck and ripping its head entirely off with his bare hand.

For a brief moment, Kane felt a rush of guilt and remorse wash over him. He didn't intend on harming the cat, but in a fit of anger and frustration, he had lashed out without thinking, a passionate outburst. He looked down at the lifeless body hanging from his fist as blood dripped from his arm where the cat had slashed him, mingling with the crimson stain of its own demise.

"You didn't like me anyway, you spoilt pain in the arse" He concluded with deviant pleasure.

"You're Gideon's precious pet.....then let's see how the old turkey deals with this" While he sniggered as he revelled in nasty thoughts of pulling a vile prank, a searing image of the puzzling human skinned book flashed into his mind, forever piercing his psyche.

He stumbled around with terror, dropping the decapitated cat on the floor and as he struggled to interpret what the hell was going on, the elusive book, which sat abandoned in the library, began to pulsate, its belly button lock glowing blood red, but oozing a thick, black substance as it marginally unsealed itself.

Kane's world began to twist and distort. The murmuring voices grew louder, more insistent, each one whispering horrors and dark secrets, feeding his paranoia and low self esteem. He clutched at his head, trying to shake off the rasping, but the voices only grew stronger, more pervasive.

"You are alone," they hissed. *"No one cares for you. You are nothing but a tool, a weapon. You will never find peace."*

Kane's heart pounded, his breath quickened. Sweat poured down his face as he fought to regain control, but the demonic whispers burrowed deeper, wrapping around his mind like constricting vines.

"They will all turn against you," the voices continued. *"Even those who pretend to care. They despise you, fear you. You must strike first. You must survive."*

His body trembled, muscles tensing painfully. His vision blurred, and the ceiling seemed to warp and pulse as if alive. The fright and rage inside him swirled into a vortex of pure vexation and despair. He wanted to scream, to lash out, but he was trapped within his own mind, a prisoner of the demonic onslaught.

"Embrace the darkness," the voices urged. *"Become what you are meant to be. Only then will you find power. Only then will you be free."*

Kane's hands clawed at the bed, his nails raking furrows into the fabric as if trying to escape the crushing confinement.

The room seemed to constrict around him, its oppressive smallness pressing down with a stifling weight that threatened to suffocate him.

He felt a burning sensation in his chest, a mix of terror and a perverse thrill at the idea of giving into the darkness within.

Somewhere deep inside, a flicker of resistance remained. A small, stubborn spark of his former self fought against the overwhelming tide of madness. With every ounce of willpower he could muster, Kane focused on that spark, trying to drown out the voices, to push back against the encroaching darkness.

"No," he muttered through gritted teeth. "I won't let you control me."

The voices snarled in frustration, their hold on him momentarily weakening. Kane seized the opportunity, forcing himself to take slow, deliberate breaths, grounding himself in the present. He latched onto any thought of hope, any slight memory of love and kindness, using them as a lifeline to pull himself back from the brink.

Gradually, the voices began to recede, their whispers fading into the background noise of his mind. Kane's vision cleared, and he found himself once again staring at the ceiling, but this time with a sense of clarity. The intense feelings still simmered beneath the surface, but he had regained a facade of self control.

He realised the new, growing darkness within him would always be there, lurking, waiting for a moment of weakness. But for now, he had pushed it back. For now, he was still himself. Kane took one last deep breath and vowed to find a way to confront and conquer the demons that were trying to control him.

Outside, a strong wind began howling, growing louder, shaking the old monastery's walls and windows. Its chilling gusts seemed to mirror the confusion within Kane's mind, a relentless force seeking to tear apart the peace and order of the sanctuary.

Gideon's frantic cries pierced through the storm's noise, a desperate plea filled with worry and dread.

"Whiskers! Whiskers, where are you?" His voice bounced off the stone walls, growing more urgent with each shout.

Kane could hear the old monk's footsteps approaching, the sound of his sandals slapping against the cold floors. Panic began to bubble within him as he glanced at the bloody blanket in the corner, the brutal evidence of his wrath concealed beneath its folds. The voices in his mind had subsided, but the aftermath of their influence lay glaringly before him.

Eventually, Gideon found himself at Kane's bedroom door and a penetrating chill infiltrated his soul as he approached the solid wooden entrance. He cautiously pressed his ear against the door, attempting to listen for any commotion from within, but there was only silence, so he spied through the two way peephole of the door and when he gained his focus, what he saw spiraled him into extreme terror.

Gideon stumbled back from the door, his heart pounding and breath coming in ragged gasps. The sight of that unblinking, bloodshot eye haunted his mind. He could feel a malevolent presence behind the door, something dark and twisted. The wind howled louder, as if reflecting the unrest within Gideon's own soul, fuelling his suspicions of Kane.

Exhaling a heavy, unnatural sigh, revealing his unfamiliar

anxiety and worry, Gideon scurried back down the corridor and retreated to his room, bolting the door at lightning speed behind him as he attempted to flee from the menacing threat; the feeling of trepidation smothering and questioning every fibre of his reality.

He sat for some time deep in thought, wondering if he should report the unnatural events, then after determining it was the safest thing to do, he summoned a passing novice monk to hastily deliver a sealed letter to the Abbots office which was located near the other end of the monastery. It was too far for an old man like himself to transport the note to its destination as quickly as possible.

The note read.

Namo Buddhya, "I bow before the Buddha"

I need to speak with you about something of great concern Master Kane is showing unholly traits

I've witnessed first-hand demonic episodes from him.

I believe that he's currently in his room because I've just come from there and I saw something evil

This needs to be discussed urgently

Gideon signed off.

At dinner time, the dining room buzzed with a vibrant energy, the air thick with the rich, enticing aroma of the congregation's evening meal.

The clatter of utensils and the murmur of conversation filled the air, creating a warm and inviting atmosphere. The boys had been at supper for thirty minutes by now, so Gideon made his way to the dining room. As he approached the entrance, his steps slowed and he hesitated briefly before entering, eventually standing unflinching in the doorway.

Trying desperately to spot Kane, Gideon strained his neck to get a better look at the crowd of boys, their heads down as they hungrily devoured the food and periodically chatted to one another. The dull light cast playful shadows across the room, and the occasional burst of laughter punctuated the general hum of contentment.

Gideon's eyes scanned the room, searching for the familiar figure of Kane.

The events of the day lingered vividly in his mind, leaving him with a gnawing sense of apprehension. Despite his unease, he knew he had to check on Kane, to make sure he was alright. At the same time, he couldn't shake the feeling that he needed to keep a vigilant eye on the enigmatic boy, whose presence seemed to hold unsettling, unexplained depths.

At last, Gideon spotted Kane sitting at the far end of one of the long wooden tables, his back hunched and his movements slow. Kane's plate was barely touched, and he seemed more interested in pushing his food around than eating it. Gideon noted a bandage that had been crudely wrapped around his arm.

"Is everything alright?" The presiding monk asked, noticing Gideon conspicuously gawking around the dining room.

"Hello, Master Fuji. You're on prefect duty this evening? Can you tell me if Master Kane has been here in the dining room since the bell rang?" Gideon questioned "Hai, I think he's been here ever since the dinner bell rang but they all arrived in such large groups so I can't be sure. I didn't actually see him walk in"

Kane knew that Gideon was searching for him, so he deliberately hid between the other boys, while his bloodshot eyes twitched uncomfortably as he embellished a deceitful, evil grin.

His nerves were a tangled web of fear and exhilaration, a potent cocktail that surged through him as he savored the thrill of having momentarily outwitted the old monk with his prank. The whispers in his mind had faded, leaving him with a lingering sense of devilry, as if he had briefly danced on the edge of mischief and sin.

Gossipy banter started to emerge as the boys, one by one, noticed Gideon looking nervously around the room.

"What's he doing here? It's not his night supervising dinner. Who's he looking for?" Where some of the whispers

Clutching the crucifix that hung around his neck, Gideon walked further into the room.

"He's sitting over there and was when the food came out" Fuji nodded discreetly towards Kanes direction.

"Is there a problem?" He continued

"I see him.....No, I'm just keeping a watchful eye on his whereabouts for the moment.....nothing to worry about Master Fuji. Thank you" Gideon replied and with scepticism invading his entire being, he automatically walked out of the dining room.

As Gideon strolled down the corridor heading back to his dormitory, his mind raced with both fury and terror, trying desperately to comprehend how Kane managed to transport himself from his bedroom to the dining area without being seen. He replayed the events in his mind, searching for any clue or explanation that might make sense of the boy's uncanny abilities.

Random shadows moved along the stone walls, adding to the eerie atmosphere that now permeated the monastery. The storm outside continued to rage, the wind howling through the ancient hallways, amplifying Gideon's sense of unease. He felt as though he were being watched again, not just by the unseen eyes of the storm, but by something far more sinister.

As he turned a corner, he paused, catching his breath. His heart thumped erratically, and he couldn't shake the image of Kane's bloodshot, maniacal eyes staring back at him through the peephole. The boy's deceitful grin he'd just seen in the dining room obsessed him, a chilling reminder of the darkness that seemed to be taking hold of Kane

Gideon knew he had to act, but he was torn. His Buddhist faith preached compassion and understanding, yet the growing threat posed by Kane could not be ignored. He needed to find a way to help the boy without causing further harm. The thought of confronting Kane filled him with dread, but he also realised that ignoring the problem could lead to even greater consequences.

As he continued down the corridor, Gideon made a silent vow to uncover the truth behind Kane's transformation.

"Is it his ninja training? He seemed to be advancing with his lessons much quicker than the other students.......or is it because he is possessed by a demon and has the supernatural powers that come with it....and then there's the mysterious book that just appeared out of thin air?"

"I must be hyper-vigilant, this fear I'm feeling is unnatural and uncomfortable.......

I can feel the coldness spreading within me like a virus" He rambled to himself as he fumbled around with the keys in his pocket, when he eventually arrived at his room.

Unlocking the entrance, he pushed open the heavy wooden door with speed and just as he was about the close it, he heard a voice cry out his name.

"Master Gideon" The returning novice monk shouted "Hai"

"Master Gideon, the Abbot has responded to your note.....I have his letter and I found your dinner on the kitchen table. It had a note with your name on it. I thought I'd bring it to you as well" The young monk boasted, proud of his thoughtfulness and obedience.

"Thank you Master Hoi. I appreciate your kindness" Gideon smiled while he took the note.

"Can you place the tray on my table over there please" He continued

"Hai Master Gideon" The juvenille monk eagerly complied and after he left the room, Gideon abruptly secured the door behind him.

The familiar scent of sandle wood and fresh linen greeted him, offering a brief respite from his troubled thoughts. He sat down on the edge of his bed, his mind still racing. The commotion of the storm outside seemed to copy his anguish, a constant reminder of the potential trouble at hand. In the stillness of his room, Gideon closed his eyes and began to meditate. He focused on his breath, seeking to still the worry within his mind. As he did, a sense of clarity began to emerge. He knew that the decisions ahead would be difficult, but he also knew that he could not face it alone.

He realized he needed the support of his fellow monks, the wisdom of the ancient texts, and perhaps most importantly, the strength of his own faith.

Turning around to face the rest of the room, Gideon approached the dining table where the silver tray sat, with its polished, shiny dome covering the food. He exhaled a groan of some relief, while he removed his coat and leisurely pulled out the chair, sitting down at the table to eat. After performing the ritual dinner prayer, he casually opened the sealed letter and began reading what the Abbot had wrote.

It said

"Namo Buddhya"

Master Gideon, I have faith in your judgements. Your extensive spiritual experience, thorough knowledge, loyalty and Buddhist faith is unshakable. I trust that you're suspicions about Master Kane are valid. After dinner, come to my quarters to discuss the situation further and tell me your concerns"

Calmly folding the note back to its original shape, he shoved it in his pocket, and began arranging the cutlery. As he removed the silver dome, gradually exposing the food underneath, what he saw made him launch in his chair, crashing hard onto the floor. He remained there for some time, trying to fathom what he'd just seen.

Underneath the dome lay the severed head of Gideon's beloved cat, Whiskers, its eyes still open and its mouth twisted into a grimace of pain. The amount of blood that pooled around it, was enough to quickly spill onto Gideons once-pristine white tablecloth when he lifted the silver dome. The sight was horrifying, a macabre reminder of the evil presence that had taken root within the monastery.

Gideon's breath became erratic as he struggled to process the gruesome scene before him.

Slowly, he forced himself to his feet, his legs shaking beneath him. He glanced around the room, half-expecting to see Kane lurking in the shadows, but there was no one. He had to remain calm, he told himself. He needed to think clearly and act decisively.

His first instinct was to seek out the other monks. They needed to be warned, and they needed to come together to confront this growing darkness.The monastery was no longer a sanctuary; it had become a battleground.

Gideon's beliefs hardened. He could not allow fear to paralyze him. There was a malevolent force at work, and it was up to him to uncover it.

Finding the courage to look at the savagery again, Gideon stood frozen, staring at the revulsion, as the stench of death rose in the air like invisible gas. Perched in the center of his dinner plate was the severed head, fur matted with blood, stiff and ugly, its sharp dead eyes reflecting the agony it had endured.

"KANE!.......this is his doing! I know it is." Gideon blurted out loudly and swiftly replaced the dome over the severed head. Floating like a hovercraft, he briskly drifted down the hallway towards the Abbotts chambers, carrying the entire tray. This time he was satisfied that he had the evidence needed to verify Kane's depravity. As he approached the main hall, he could hear the distant chanting of the monks, their voices rising and falling in a soothing rhythm. It was a stark contrast to the panic raging within him.

Pounding frantically on the Abbots door, Gideon heard a faint voice reply. "Come in" The Abbot directed

Gideon struggled to open the hefty door with one hand but determination aided his strength.

"Hai Gideon, have you come to discuss the matters regarding Master Kane?" He casually said, looking up from his desk

"I've already eaten dinner thank you" He continued, quickly noticing the dinner tray "Hai I understand Abbot, this isn't your dinner though it was supposed to be mine

and look at what was dished up to me" Gideon said respectfully then, placed the tray on Abbot's desk and uncovered it, exposing the hideous contents. The Abbot sat there dumbstruck as he visually surveyed the cat's head. Its petrified eyes stared back at him, void of life, and the blood-stained mouth gaped wide open. His mind spun in a whirlpool of disbelief and horror, struggling to comprehend the atrocity.

He felt a cold sweat break out across his forehead as he tried to piece together the implications of this gruesome discovery. The monastery, a place of peace and refuge, was now tainted by a malevolent force that had claimed its first victim. "Who would do such an evil thing?" Abbot questioned

"Is this the cat you loved so much.....Whiskers?" He continued.

"Hai it is. I've been looking for him all day, then Master Hoi delivered my dinner tray with your note.....I believe this is Kane's doing"

"Did you see him do this? You mentioned earlier that you've witnessed something demonic about Master Kane. Can you please elaborate?"

The Abbot sat behind the imposing table with his arms folded across his chest waiting intently for a reasonable explanation. Gideon outlined in detail the experiences he had seen. He spoke about the clouds turning into a severed skull right behind Kane, the complaints about his nightly ramblings is ancient languages and the bulging swollen eye that peered at him from behind the boy's door now this spiteful deed his cat.

He deliberately chose to withhold the discovery of the human-skinned book, intent on delving deeper into its sudden appearance in the library and unraveling its true significance. This calculated omission was designed to give him the upper hand, a strategic advantage in his quest to uncover the mysteries it might hold.

Rising shakily to his feet, the Abbot turned to Gideon, who had been standing nearby, equally stunned.

"Gideon, you are an old and reliable friend. I believe that you don't exaggerate and that you know your scriptures well. I respect your opinion. If this is true what you've told me, then I will need further proof that Master Kane is becoming possessed.

Show me solid evidence and we will take the next step in regards to our beliefs and the monasteries strategy for demonic exorcism. Leave your cat with me. I will get one of the junor monks to bury it, under strict confidence of course"

"Hai, Abbot I fully understand. I will get you the proof" Gideon nodded, his face pale and he left the Abbots office. As he stood motionless outside the closed door, Gideon deliberated how he could get the proof without Kane's knowledge, so he devised an explicit way to completely expose him and he was going to use

himself as the bait.

Chapter 2

Nightfall engulfed the evening with a whisper of perfect darkness, while a juvenile monk individually lit the hallway candles. As he moved along after each successful flare-up, Kane sat alone in his room, fully aware that Gideon would have discovered his tragic gift by now.

He could see the illuminating glow of light from beneath his door, and as he stared at the seeping glimmer, he heard footsteps approaching. Anticipating a knock, Kane sat on the edge of his bed, but instead of the figure beckoning to come in, the footsteps suddenly stopped, and all he could see was the shadow of someone's feet just standing at the doorway. They remained there, fixed, only to move on after a couple of minutes.

Kane stood up and moved towards the door, pressing his ear against it. He heard the footsteps retreating, fading into the distance, and he smiled to himself, knowing that the mysterious feet must have belonged to Gideon. He felt triumphant that his cunningly swift plan had worked, and with his recently acquired vitality, he'd successfully unnerved the abusive old monk. The intoxicating reverence made him feel all-powerful.

As the footsteps vanished into the silence, Kane's room felt suddenly colder. He stepped back from the door, a smirk still playing on his lips. He had waited for this moment, for the chance to strike fear into the heart of the man who had tormented him for years. His newfound power, dark and terrible, pulsed within him like a second heartbeat.

He moved to the small mirror hanging on the wall, examining his reflection. His eyes, once dull and lifeless, now glowed with a sinister light. The gift, as he had come to call it, was both a blessing and a curse. It had given him strength, but at a cost.

He turned away from the mirror and moved to the window, looking out into the night. The monastery grounds were shrouded in darkness, the only light coming from its scattered windows. He felt invincible, ready to take on anything or anyone. But then suddenly, the whispering voices came back and grew louder, more insistent. It was as if the very walls of his room were alive, speaking to him in hushed, urgent tones. He tried to focus, to make out the words, but they eluded him, slipping through his mind like smoke.

The newly released blossoms cascaded gently down, swaying side to side like butterfly wings on a summer breeze, vivid and soft, landing on the little boy who lay beneath the cherry tree. The warm breath of the tranquil wind kissed his face as he dreamt he was the son of an Emperor. In his mind's eye, he mastered poetry, painting, and calligraphy, and envisioned himself as a skilled horseman, riding a magnificent stallion. He galloped past targets, hitting the bullseye with expert precision, and his father's prideful gaze made his heart race.

In reality, his name was Eito, the second eldest son of a poor farmer and his wife, Akito and Sara. His essential family unit consisted of three brothers, his parents, and his grandparents. Yet, the vivid dreams hinted at a hidden destiny, an untold secret buried deep within him.

"Eito, Eito, where are you?" He could hear his mother calling.

"I'm here" He replied, jumping up and brushing down the leaves and cherry petals that clung to his threadbare trousers.

"Come quickly, you have work to do" Sara informed

As Eito returned home, he entered the kitchen and noticed a monk sitting at the table talking with his father.

"Eito, sit down. This is Master Minato. He is here to speak with you about joining the monastery and learning their Buddhist ways and ninja tactics. As you know your older brother is going to inherit this farm one day, so that leaves you with no honorable future. You will learn obligation, obedience and loyalty at the monastery and we think this will be good for you"

"But father, I am not disobedient or disloyal so why are you sending me away?" Eito protested

"It is your calling Eito. Master Minato will take good care of you. You will be adopted by the monks and live at the monastery. It will cultivate in you a positive sentiment, the art of ninjitsu and the Buddhist faith. This will be your destiny Eito" His father stipulated

The middle aged monk sat quietly and listened intently to Akito instruct his son, then he motioned to speak.

"Eito, you will be accepted, loved and taught the disciplines and moral values of the Buddhist and ninja ways. You won't be alone. There are other boys at the monastery, just like you" He spoke directly but in a gentle manner.

"When am I supposed to leave?" Eito questioned

"Today go and pack your belongings" Akito guided, but he

didn't look into his
son's eyes.

Eito began crying as he entered his room, and as tears ran down his tiny face, he finally re-emerged with his meager haversack slung over his shoulder.

"Good luck, my son, and remember that this journey you are about to undertake is for your own good," his father asserted. With his mother weeping at the door, the monk paid his parents a sum of money, and then Eito kissed his family goodbye.

The arduous journey took four days to complete. Trekking eight hours every waking moment, Eito endured the journey in complete silence, not wishing to speak to the strange monk who escorted him to the remote temple. With his head hung low, they hiked their way up a steep mountainside. When Eito eventually looked up from the ground, he noticed a sheer cliff with his impending accommodation perched high on the edge of a plateau, overlooking a deep gorge below. The formidable structure revealed the riches and power it had accrued over the thousands of years since its construction.

The sight of the temple sent a chill down Eito's spine. Its towering presence, with ancient stone walls etched with enigmatic symbols, seemed to whisper secrets of the past. As they approached, the wind howled through the gorge, amplifying the monk's silent steps on the rocky path. Eito's heart pounded with a mix of fear and curiosity, wondering what awaited him within those imposing walls.

"Here is your new home" Were Minato's first and only words that he'd spoken since the journey began.

Eito didn't reply. Instead, he marveled at the monastery's exquisite architecture, with its sturdy towers, elegant chapels, grand stained glass windows, and the scenic canyon below. The remarkable structure seemed to defy nature, standing proudly on the precipice of the sheer cliff.

Finally reaching and entering the monastery, Eito was greeted at the door by another monk, who he later found out was the presiding Abbot at the time. The Abbot, a tall figure with a serene yet authoritative presence, observed Eito with a keen, almost penetrating gaze.

"Welcome, young Eito," the Abbot said in a calm, measured voice. "You have embarked on a path that will test your spirit and mold your destiny."

Eito nodded obediently, as he stepped into the dimly lit hallway. The air inside was cool, filled with the familiar scent of cherry blossoms. As he followed the Abbot through the labyrinthine corridors, the walls adorned with ancient tapestries and intricate carvings, Eito felt a mix of awe and trepidation.

The monk who had escorted him remained silent, his presence a constant reminder of the life the little boy had left behind, so together they led him to a small, sparsely furnished room.

"This will be your quarters," he said, opening the door. "Rest now. Your training begins at dawn."

"We will give you a formal induction once you have settled in" He continued "What does induction mean?" Eito innocently asked

"The chanting ceremony will be led by me, your Eminence, and will ultimately cleanse you from your old life and transform you into a new one. You will be given another name during the ordinance. You will have your head shaven to symbolize your renunciation of worldly ego and fashion"

Left alone in the quiet room, Eito unpacked his modest belongings and sat on the simple straw mattress that served as his bed. He gazed out of the narrow window, the vast canyon stretching out before him. The wind blew softly, carrying with it the faintest moans of ancient secrets and untold stories.

As night fell, Eito lay down, his thoughts stirring with uncertainty and anticipation. He knew his journey had just begun, and the path ahead was fraught with challenges.

Tired and disheartened, he fretted after his family and as he reflected on why his father was paid money to sell him like a piece of furniture, he began to cry.

The induction ritual lasted three hours, during which Eito was formally ordained into the monastery. In the ancient communion, Eito was touched with a burning incense stick, leaving a permanent mark on his forehead as a reminder of his vow to uphold the five principles of their faith. It was then that he was given the Buddhist name Eshin, meaning "understanding mind and wisdom."

During his two-year apprenticeship, Eshin struggled with the discipline and dedication expected of him.

His conflicting thoughts constantly clashed as he grappled with the strict commandments of the Buddhist faith, the rigorous and grueling ninja training regimen, and a deep-seated longing for the life he might have had.

He lay awake most nights, suffering from delayed onset muscle soreness, persistently tired yet expected to face each new day with contentment and perseverance. The strategies and tactics of ninja battles included daily training in guerrilla warfare and espionage. The students were expected to operate as spies and scouts, disguising and concealing themselves to assassinate their targets in secrecy for a price.

Eshin's heart was innately kind, often sacrificing himself to help others when they should have been caring for themselves. As his faith grew, he sometimes ached with spiritual overflow and struggled to see his own worth, rarely aware of his own vulnerability, as he tried to create a positive atmosphere and enhance the well-being of those around him.

He continually suffered from distress, missing his family and the moments spent lying under the cherry tree with the warm breeze caressing his face. He felt deeply cheated, burdened by the inability to choose his own destiny.

After five years of ninja training, Eshin was appointed to his first mission. He was taken down to a dim, earthen room far below the monastery's base floor, where the Master Sensei re-affirmed the ninja's commitment to obedience and responsibility.

"This client is an important person who holds our way of life very close and dear to their heart, so I want the respect and faithfulness that is expected of you for this assignment," the Sensei drilled as he walked slowly around the warrior. Eshin, dressed in his ninja armor—a black jacket, black trousers, light sandals, and a hooded cowl—stood silently, listening intently to his Master's instructions with his head bowed.

"There are dangers, but the client has paid handsomely, so this mission will be executed to the perfection you have been trained for.... Hai?"

"Hai, Master," Eshin obeyed.

"I know that this is your first assignment, but I am obligated to tell you that failure will bring very harsh consequences, and aborting the assassination will result in you performing Seppuku. Your short sword will ensure a slow and agonizing death, but it will be an honorable one.... Hai?"

"Hai, Master."

"Here are your instructions, and you will begin your mission at sundown.... Hai?" "Hai," Eshin answered as the Master Sensei dematerialized into the shadows of the dark basement.

After the sun retreated behind the spectacular mountains, Eshin left the monastery and headed towards the nominated village where his victim resided. His swift pace brought him to his destination within a day.

Once night had fully descended, Eshin stealthily approached the house. He stood by the porch, listening as he pressed his back against the wall, blending seamlessly with the climbing jasmine that adorned the residence. Suddenly, he heard voices. "Were they upstairs or downstairs?" he wondered, observing intently before tactfully opening the door. The voices emanated from the kitchen.

Moving as quietly as a mouse, Eshin climbed the stairs and slipped into the main bedroom and waited patiently behind the door for his victim, his heart pounding faster than a cat lapping milk.

"Good night," a man's voice resonated. With the darkness swallowing his presence, the ninja delayed his attack, listenining intently until the rhythmic sounds of snoring filled the air. With calculated precision, he approached the cot, his dagger poised for the kill.

As the man lazily rolled over, his mind still tethered to the realm of dreams, he suddenly jolted awake, as if sensing the looming shadow of death. Eyes wide with terror, he whispered a feeble "No" as Eshin's blade sliced through the silence, plunging deep into his throat with a chilling finality.

With the deed done, Eshin swiftly retreated, his figure melting into the night like a ghostly specter, leaving behind only a haunting silence and the echo of his victim's last breath.

After experiencing his first taste of bloodshed, Eshin committed himself for many decades to his faith, assassin missions, and the monastery. His dedication, saw him ascend through the ranks of the religious orders, eventually claiming the mantle of the presiding Abbot. He was a stern leader, now monarching over Gideon and Kane with an iron fist, his authority marked by discipline, uncompromising resolve, and staunch precision.

* * *

In the expansive library, Gideon delved intentionally into scriptures detailing satanic possession and exorcisms. Though he initially looked for the repulsive

human-skinned book he had hidden away, it had vanished without a trace. Undeterred, he immersed himself in studying the disciplines of defeating Kane.

As the tutorials grew increasingly unnerving and grotesque,

Gideon poured himself a cup of tea, sinking back into his chair. His mind wandered to the Abbot's remark about proving Kane's demonic possession, stirring memories of his childhood encounters.

Recollections of his lonely beginnings at the monastery flooded back—uncertainty and fear shadowed everywhere. Weak and malnourished from his time on the foul streets of the outlying village, Gideon's emotions churned.

Refocusing, he finished the cup of tea, and returned to the sacred writings of expulsion and purification, his mind still consumed by thoughts of how to unearth the evidence needed to convince the Abbot of Kane's demonic possession. Finally, he concluded that he would draw out Kane's demon by challenging him to a fight—a combat that would be supervised and witnessed by the Abbot Eshin himself.

Meanwhile, the warm rays of the sun caressed Kane's skin as he tilted his face towards the sky, watching the clouds dance above him. In that moment, he felt a sense of longing, as if the clouds were calling him to sprout wings and soar into the sky, away from the dramas below. Nestled in a secluded courtyard behind the monastery, Kane found solace from the bullying and abuse inflicted upon him by Hiro's gang of thugs and the malevolent Gideon.

Kane drew a deep breath, letting the warmth of the sun seep into his body as he closed his eyes in meditation. In the stillness, he envisioned a life beyond the confines of his current reality. He placed his trust in the forces of destiny and chance, hoping that his karma would align with the greater spiritual universe to manifest his deepest desires—worthiness, approval, love, and freedom.

Despite the challenges he faced, Kane's hope burned bright, fueled by the courage of his heroic spirit. With a solemn wish, he longed for a path to a better existence, knowing it would be fraught with obstacles yet sensing the promise of a new exciting journey ahead.

Within him, Kane grappled with a persistent struggle between his Buddhist faith and a malevolent force that lurked deep within. At times, he could feel the unsettling presence of a distinct paranormal entity surging within him, its antagonistic nature threatening to overwhelm his inner peace.

Lowering his head, Kane gazed down at the new discovery cradled in his lap, marveling at its mysterious allure. His mind raced with questions, wondering what secrets lay hidden within its depths and why it had beckoned him to find it. Suddenly, he felt a soft tapping on his right arm, drawing his attention away from the object in his hands.

As Kane looked down, he was met with the sight of a large moth perched beside him on the wooden bench. Its size was so imposing that it resembled a small bird, and its iridescent wings glowed in the sunlight. Mesmerized by the creature's ethereal beauty, Kane felt a strange energy wash over him, as if he had been ensnared in an ecstatic trance.

Studying the moth intently, Kane noticed markings on its bulky head and back that strangely resembled a human skull. The symbol's head was as white as snow, its eyes as black as night. Entranced by the mystical pattern, Kane reached out to touch the moth, his hand moving slowly towards it. But just as he drew closer, the birdmoth suddenly took flight, ascending effortlessly into the sky.

As he watched the creature disappear into the horizon, he felt a sense of clarity. In that moment, he knew what he had to do.

"Just like the moth," he whispered to himself, his voice filled with determination, "I will be free."

Gently caressing his hands over the book on his lap, Kane felt a shiver run down his spine as its texture stirred a weird sense of familiarity within him. It didn't take long for him to realize what it was—a human-skinned book. As the realisation dawned upon him, a sudden hypnotic intimacy penetrated him, shrouding him in its eerie embrace.

"You called for me and I found you. We're connected," Kane whispered to the book, his voice barely audible in the quiet of the courtyard. With a sense of urgency, he quickly camouflaged the book under his coat, determined to keep its secrets safe. While he discreetly made his way back into the monastery, Kane couldn't shake the feeling of being watched. Upon reaching his room, he noticed Gideon standing motionless in the far corner of the long hallway, his expression twisted in open disdain.

The intensity of Gideon's gaze sent an icy shiver through Kane, kindling a profound sense of foreboding that seeped into the very depths of his soul.

"Good morning Master Gideon" He gestured with a nod of polite recognition. "Master Kane, I need to speak with you" He replied and as Kane glanced down to unlock the door, he suddenly found Gideon standing right beside him as quick as a flash.

"Hai Master Gideon, how can I help you?" He nervously asked as he registered it was probably something to do with the decapitated cat.

"As a result of your success defeating Master Hiro in unarmed combat the other day, the Abbot and I would like to test your skills and challenge you to another fight" He smirked

"Hai Master Gideon, that will be alright. Who will be my opponent?" Kane agreed unwittingly

"It will be me" Gideon studied the young man's expression upon conveying the news. "You Master Gideon? Why? It's not customary to fight our superiors" He added, startled by the request.

"Hai, I know it's unconventional but Abbot and I believe you have the talent to learn higher abilities that aren't normally taught to the other students. After your success overpowering Master Hiro, I saw something in you that I believe needs individual nurturing" He fabricated.

"It would be my honor but when?" Kane asked as he held on tightly to the concealed human-skinned book under his jacket.

"I will let you know when.....I just thought I would inform you of our intentions" Gideon replied as he glided effortlessly past Kane and down the passageway, disappearing around the corner.

Kane entered his room, and carefully hid the book in a well-disguised alcove, ensuring its secrets remained hidden from prying eyes. Turning his attention to the window, he observed the bustling activity outside with a mix of curiosity and detachment.

It was the traditional monthly visit of the merchant wagons, a welcome sight for the monastery as they brought much-needed supplies of candles, razors, spindles, sugar, flour and other essentials, along with luxury items such as leather, silk, cologne, jewels, and glassware. In exchange for their goods, the monastery paid in

cash and provided lodging, food, and care for any merchants

who had fallen ill during their journey to the temple.

Settling himself on a cushion by the window, Kane watched as the stream of men unloaded their wares under the watchful gaze of Abbot Eshin, Gideon, and the High Ninja Master. The air was filled with the sounds of labor as tasks were delegated and carried out with precision.

Amidst the commotion, a rustic old storekeeper approached the three presiding monks, who stood off to the side, clad in their simple grey habits of undyed wool. As they engaged in conversation, Kane couldn't help but wonder about the merchants travelling secrets hidden beneath their solemn exterior.

"Good day Masters, we have been blessed with a beautiful day" the leader greeted, bowing respectfully to the monks.

"Good day Botan, it is nice to see you again. What have you brought this month? Were you able to obtain everything on the list I gave you last time?" Abbot enquired "Hai, it's all there," Botan answered, constantly bowing his head up and down as he spoke.

"Thank you, Botan," Abbot Eshin said, his voice warm with gratitude. "Here's the money for this month's stock and the list for next month. I see you managed to secure the cocoa and chocolate I requested—excellent. I hope you'll enjoy similar success next time as well." He chuckled softly, amused by his own comment and visibly pleased with Botan's success in procuring the elusive chocolate.

"How long will your caravan people be staying with us? And do you have anyone who's ill?" Gideon added.

"Hai, Hai, there are two men, one has a broken ankle and the other has a pain in his stomach, he must have eaten something bad I think" Botan rambled

"Bring them to the abbey. I will see that they receive proper medicine" Abbot directed and the three monks casually re-entered the monastery as they followed their ushered patients inside.

Botan stood watching them for a moment, his gaze lingering on the laboring merchants before he returned to his task of organizing the unloaded merchandise. With practiced efficiency, he sorted through the goods, ensuring each item found its rightful place.

The accompanying merchants unhitched the bullocks and began setting up their caravans for a two-day stopover. Botan's honest and kind-hearted nature shone through his every action. Despite the hustle and bustle around him, he approached his work with a sense of quiet dedication, a steadfast presence amidst the chaos of the merchant's arrival.

His personality was a learned role, molded by a lifetime of giving and generosity.

Even though he was elderly, Botan had a youthful spark in his eyes, a rascally twinkle that belied his years.

His withered face continually peered from beneath a well-worn conical Asian hat which covered his patchy balding scalp and as he tilted his head back to survey his traveling companions, Botan's eyes struggled to open wide, weighed down by folds of wrinkled skin. To the inexperienced, he appeared to be asleep until his voice boomed out like a seasoned colonel, commanding attention with its power and authority.

Botan's mobile home had been passed down from his family, wandering traders who had instilled in him a familiarity with the trek to the remote monastery. As a child, he had accompanied his father on these journeys, navigating the rugged terrain and dealing with the fastidious monks.

"Remember, we leave the day after tomorrow," he called out to his companions, his voice cutting through the air with certainty.

"Make sure your oxen are well fed and watered—it's a long journey back."

His companions busied themselves with their tasks, as Botan stood there pleased with himself while he counted the money. He was a stable figure amidst the uncertainty of camp life, his presence a reassuring anchor to his clan.

Kane had noticed Gideon and Abbot standing outside earlier.

His mind buzzed with questions as he pondered why they had singled him out for special training. Rather than feeling a sense of pride or importance, an unfamiliar nervousness gnawed at him, unsettling his usual rational demeanor. It was as if he couldn't quite grasp the significance of their attention.

Lost in his thoughts, Kane was abruptly yanked back to reality by the sharp sound of a knock at the door. The unexpected interruption sent a jolt through him, causing a flutter of anxiety to rise in his stomach and intensifying the unease that had already taken hold.

With a hesitant breath, he approached the door, his hand trembling slightly as he reached for the handle, unsure of what awaited him on the other side.

"Hai" He feebly answered, gingerly opening it.

"Master Gideon?" He continued with a surprised tone in his voice when he saw who it was.

"Master Kane, I just want to confirm that your first personalized session with Abbot and myself will be the day after tomorrow. We had arranged it for this afternoon but with the merchant's arrival and having to do inventory for our items, it's been postponed.....Hai?"

"Hai, Master Gideon" Kane obeyed

"It will be around noon after Abbot Eshin has conducted his solitary prayers and sacred readings but I will inform you later about the precise time. Make sure that you're available. That is all"

"Hai, Master Gideon" Kane repeated his compliance and accordingly closed the door behind him.

After a few moments of hesitation, Kane found himself drawn to his locker. With a sense of urgency that surprised him, he retrieved the book from its hidden alcove. Holding it in his hands, he studied the cover intently, turning it over and over again in search of answers.

As his fingers traced the inscription, Kane's eyes fell upon a distinctive mark on the bottom right-hand corner of the back cover. His breath caught in his throat as recognition dawned—it was a birthmark, just like the one that marred his own skin. A sickening sense of dread overwhelmed him as he realized the truth—the mark on the book matched the disfigured sickle-shaped birthmark that adorned his chest.

Kane lifted his shirt, his hands shaky as he compared the two marks. To his disbelief, they were identical, mirroring each other in every detail.

Fear gripped him as he realized the implications of this chilling discovery.

"What is this? and why do we have the same birthmark?" He muttered under his breath and with his grip so firmly on the book, he abruptly sat down on his bed, like someone had pulled

the rug out from under his feet.

Debilitating exhaustion surrounded Kane, dragging him down into the depths of darkness. Collapsing onto his bed, his eyes, once vibrant with life, now resembled two stones of polished onyx—cold, empty, and void of light.

As he closed his eyes, they seemed to hold an endless abyss of sorrow and pain, as if they harbored the mournful cries of a thousand lost souls, each one desperate to be heard.

In the depths of his subconscious, Kane found himself trapped in a haunting dream. Before him stood a figure cloaked in radiant white, its form tall and skeletal, devoid of any discernible facial features. Surrounded by an oppressive murkiness, the figure emanated an aura of malevolence that made Kane's blood run cold.

A primal instinct surged within Kane at the sight of the ethereal being, igniting a primal need to cause harm, to unleash the pent-up rage and bitterness that simmered beneath the surface. A bitter chill crept up his spine, causing him to tremble uncontrollably as the figure spoke—a voice as hideous and macabre as the depths of hell itself. In its words, Kane could sense the depravity that lurked within, a darkness that threatened to consume him whole.

"You tread upon the pathway of magnificence," the figure's voice echoed through the darkness, petrifying Kane to the core.

"Your true journey has only just begun. You will use torture as your tool, power and greed as your guiding stars. For you are a descendant of darkness, and the sick and twisted deeds you shall inflict upon your victims will invoke disgust in all who dare to gaze upon you, my son."

The words hung heavy in the air, dripping like syrup with venomous intent. Kane's mouth ran dry with dread as he realized the depths of corruption that awaited him on this malevolent path. He was but a pawn in a sinister game, a vessel for darkness to reign unchecked upon the world. It appeared that the phantom sought comfort in Kane's anguish and as the figure's voice faded into the void, Kane knew that his descent into corruption had begun.

His attempted scream was stifled by a muffled breath, a pitiful whisper that sounded hollowly in the oppressive room. But instead of finding release in his agony, his cries seemed to fuel the malevolent phantom that haunted his nightmares. With a chilling howl, it surged forth, its roar a grotesque symphony of torment, reminiscent of a snarling wolf as it devours its prey.

The howl reverberated through Kane's mind, filling him with a primal terror that threatened to consume him entirely. He was trapped, ensnared in the grip of his own nightmares, with no hope of escape from the evil that loomed all around him. The phantom's howls repeated into the abyss, and Kane knew that he was utterly alone, lost in a real nightmare from which he may never awaken.

"Who are you?" His voice croaked out, strained with distress and confusion, as he confronted the apparition before him. But before he could receive an answer, the figure began to turn away, its form glowing with an otherworldly brilliance.

In a booming voice that seemed to shake the very foundations of reality, the apparition responded,

"You embrace me in your arms, and you wear my symbol.... I am your forefather." The words lingered in the air, thick with a burden of ancestral legacy and forbidden knowledge.

"The book you possess has been handed down through universal generations. It holds many secrets and magic. I am your kin, and now it is yours.... In the end, all will know who you are."

With those ominous words, a sense of evil penetrated Kane, a foreboding certainty that he was bound to a destiny far darker and more sinister than he could have ever imagined.

A crisp evening had befallen and the breeze outside was fresh and restful when Kane aroused from his nightmare. He felt depleted and mentally battered from the experience and rolled onto his side, facing the wall with the human skinned book still clasped to his chest and as he recollected the villainess man and his depraved

message, he let out a painful shriek that resonated throughout his bedroom and down the hallway and within minutes he heard a knock at the door.

"Master Kane, are you alright?" The voice investigated "Hai, I'm fine" Kane lied

"What was that sound? Can you open the door please?" It communicated "I just hurt myself and I'm not feeling well, can you come back later?" "You must come to the dining room, it's dinner time"

"I don't want anything to eat, I'm not hungry, please leave me alone" Kane appealed and waited for the voice to respond but instead he only caught the sound of hurried footsteps retreating down the corridor.

* * *

The long-awaited day had finally dawned, the day when Kane would face off against Gideon in the ninja tournament and unlock the higher levels of skill he had been promised. But as the hour drew near, a gnawing anxiety gripped him like a vise, trapping him in a cage of nervousness. Desperate to break free from the panic that threatened to consume him, Kane summoned every ounce of bravery within him, determined to forge ahead and fulfill his mission, to achieve his goals and prove himself worthy of victory.

While he dressed for the tournament, Kane's gaze drifted to the window, where he observed the bustling activity of the merchants preparing to depart. The sight of them, moving about with purpose, filled him with a sense of envy. They seemed to possess a freedom that Kane could only dream of, the freedom to chart their own course without the anxiety of restraint bearing down upon them.

The merchants chattered amongst themselves, each focused on their own tasks and goals, and Kane couldn't help but long for the same autonomy in his own life.

The energetic group of people brought life to the monastery grounds that would normally be so quiet you could hear the church mice scurrying about their daily routines.

He turned his gaze away from the window and prepared to face the challenge that lay ahead.

He knew that today wasn't about envy or longing—it was about seizing the opportunity before him and carving out his own fate. It was about proving to the man who tormented him that he was a worthy opponent, capable of standing his ground. *"That will be me one day.....I will choose my own destiny, not Gideon, not the monastery and not the sinister poltergeist in my dreams"* He secretly vowed, just as a note slipped under his door. Studying it for a moment, Kane casually walked over to the creased piece of paper, picked it up and read:

"Arrive in the principal dojo at 1.00 pm, dress in your customary ninja-yoroi and bring your Nunchaku, blowgun, ninja stars and Kunai Knife" So Kane did exactly what the note told him to do.

His footsteps repeated loudly on the timber floor as Kane made his way towards the underground Dojo, each step matching the pounding rhythm of his heart. With a creak of protest, he pushed open the massive door, its tarnished hinges groaning with objection as if warning him of the trials that lay ahead. On the other side, Abbot Eshin and Gideon stood in silence, their presence casting a chilling aura over the room.

Kane glanced at the stained glass windows, their vibrant hues shimmering with a colourful glow that seemed to mock the gravity of the situation. With a respectful bow, he approached the Masters, his pulse quickening with a mix of anticipation and fear.

"Master Kane," the Abbot Eshins voice cut through the heavy silence,

"You have been chosen to engage in advanced hand-to-hand combat with Master Gideon. Are you prepared for the battle ahead?"

Only a single word escaped Kane's lips, laden with purpose. "Hai."

Across from him, Gideon stood with an air of arrogance, clad in his traditional ninja-yoroi and wearing a smirk that sent a cautionary warning.

The stage was set for a showdown of epic proportions, and Kane knew that the outcome would shape his destiny in ways he could scarcely imagine.

He was physically and mentally prepared for what was about to transpire. He moved to the center of the dojo, with Gideon shadowing right behind him. Both opponents bowed, then began circling each other, each anticipating who would strike first.

Without warning, Gideon swiftly pounced, initiating the fight.

He launched a roundhouse kick with such force that it smashed into the side of Kane's head, sending him sprawling backward onto the ground. The impact forced the air from Kane's lungs in a rushing gasp. As he lay there, struggling to regain his composure, Gideon orbited him like a predator circling its prey, ready to deliver the next blow. But instead of attacking, Gideon began to insult him, his words sharp and mocking, adding a psychological edge to the physical battle.

"Get up, I thought you'd be tougher than this Master Kane. Where are the skills you've been taught?" He laughed

Kane slowly picked himself up off the floor and turned to face Gideon. With a burst of determination, he lunged at his opponent, but the old monk was too fast and nimble.

Blocking Kane's assault with ease, Gideon countered with a powerful strike to Kane's ribs, causing his chest to tighten. Kane staggered back, the pain radiating through his body as he struggled to remain centred, knowing he had to push through the agony to have any chance of victory.

Horror flooded Kane's veins as panic set in, realizing the full extent of Gideon's proficiency. The sheer skill and precision displayed by his opponent sent a cold wave of fear crashing over him.

He weaved and ducked the ruthless onslaught from the old man, trying to find an opening. Just as he began to regain his balance, Gideon slid into a leg sweep, knocking Kane's foundation out from under him. He crashed to the floor, the impact sending searing pain radiating through his body. Struggling to breathe, Kane fought to stay conscious, the relentless assault pushing him to his limits.

"You are pathetic, a big lump of nothingness?" Gideon provoked as Kane became increasingly agitated. He could feel the resentment rising up and the continual insults infuriated him.

"You are nothing but dirt" Kane screamed back as he stood up, leaning in he spat at Gideon's feet.

"If I am dirt, then what does that make you? I know that you are beneath me in every way" Gideon chuckled

Resuming his fighting stance, Kane unleashed a flurry of blows, his arms vibrating with each strike. His face twisted with anger as he fought back with all his might.

With every successful punch from Gideon, the old man continued to slander him, each insult cutting deeper than the blows. The relentless taunts fueled Kane's rage, driving him to fight harder despite the pain coursing through his body.

"You lack discipline, you lack focus, you lack ferocity, what kind of ninja are you? A strange, weak boy with no friends"

Finally regaining his composure, Kane pushed on with arms and legs moving at a fierce speed, successfully hitting Gideon right between the eyes, delivering a powerful blow and as his rival stumbled backward, blood began streaming from his nose.

"You are pitiful and you are a disgrace to the ninja way" Gideon immediately taunted and swiftly wiped away the blood.

"Master Gideon, you pretend to practice virtue, good conduct and morality, but you are vile and when you die I hope you rot in hell" Kane tried intimidating him back.

"I can smell your fear Master Kane and it will be your ultimate downfall. You think you can defeat me.....then think again you stupid fat boy. You are not like the others.

There's something wrong with you" Gideon humiliated

A searing, frigid indifference surged within Kane, exploding from his core with an unstoppable force. Hatred for Gideon spiraled wildly, igniting an uncontrollable transformation. Kane's human form contorted, twisted, and mutated into a demonic

entity thirsting for vengeance. He felt the incubus spirit rip itself from his consciousness, sidestepping the inevitable shame for the sin he was on the brink of committing. His hot, blistering rage demanded retribution, intensifying to a fever pitch. Kane's overwhelming desire to inflict unimaginable harm on Gideon consumed him entirely.

In total disbelief, Abbot Eshin and Gideon watched as Kane's right hand morphed into a massive bear's paw, talons growing to grotesque lengths. A wild urge to unleash disturbing violence rushed through him. Seizing the moment, Gideon lunged to attack, but Kane, acutely aware of the old man's movements, was ready.

As Gideon approached, Kane's mutated claws slashed through the air, ripping open the flesh on the left side of Gideon's face, tearing through his eye with terrifying precision.

Gideon clutched his hands over the gaping lacerations, an ungodly scream tearing from his throat. He staggered backward, eyes wide with horror as blood gushed into his palms, before collapsing onto the floor. Kane loomed over his victim, eyes blazing red with fury, deliberating whether to continue the brutal onslaught.

He was just about to deliver another devastating blow to the writhing, obnoxious old man when Abbot Eshin leaped forward, shielding his fallen friend with a desperate, fearless defense. Kane stumbled backward, staring at his mutated bear paw in disbelief, the sheer shock of it momentarily paralyzing him.

"So it is true.... Gideon was right, you are a demon!" Abbot Eshin shrieked, then launched himself into the air with a flying kick that struck Kane's head, taking him by surprise. Abbot Eshin's foot connected with the force of a hammer, smashing into Kane's skull like the hoof of a wild beast. Kane crumpled to the ground, and the Abbot continued his relentless assault, each blow more forceful and deliberate than the last. The searing pain eradicated any remnants of humanity in Kane, and as he struggled to his feet, he retaliated with a powerful kick to the Abbot's chest, sending the ninja master flying. But Abbot Eshin recovered quickly, counterattacking with ferocious intensity. In a swift, covert motion, he drew his Kunai knife and lunged at Kane, driving the steely blade deep into the demon's grotesquely transformed right arm.

Their eyes locked for a fleeting, intense moment as Kane fell to his knees, the agony from the knife injury compelling him to swipe viciously at his assailant.

His elongated claws tore through the Abbot's throat, leaving a gaping wound and Abbot Eshin instinctively clutched at his neck, desperately trying to stem the torrent flow of blood.

Gideon, still conscious on the floor, watched in horror as his dear friend collapsed beside him, bleeding out. Summoning the last of his strength, he cried out,

"What are you?!"

His voice trailed off while he watched the murderer, drenched in butchery, retreating through the door in a frenzied panic, leaving a gruesome trail of blood in his wake. Horrified, Kane clutched his wrist and watched in disbelief as the bear's arm and foot pad morphed back into a human form. Wracked with pain, he skulked into his room, tearing a shirt into strips to fashion a makeshift bandage for his bleeding arm.

Quickly, he changed out of the blood-soaked ninja-yoroi, donning another set of armor. He swiftly grabbed the human-skinned book from its hiding place and pulled on a clean tunic. Glancing outside his window, he observed the convoy of merchants slowly making their way down the mountainside.

"This is my chance," he whispered, the words barely escaping his lips.

Dressed in his customary ninja uniform, armed with the weapons he was ordered to bring to the Dojo, Kane opened the window and slipped out, vanishing down the trail. He shadowed the procession of caravans as they meandered along the dirt road, eventually disappearing around a bend.

His mind was a whirlwind of thoughts, his focus laser-sharp on his escape. He could already envision the horrifying discovery of the Abbot's body and the mutilated Gideon. Fear clawed at his heart as he contemplated the inevitable repercussions of his brutal actions, the weight of his deeds pressing heavily on his mind.

As dusk descended, a canvas of peach-colored hues painted the pathway Kane followed, transforming the weary day into a scene of breathtaking majesty. In the fading light, he felt the ancient souls of creatures that once inhabited the nearby forest envelop him, while the symphony of cascading water and melodious birdcalls inundated his senses.

Thick, verdant trees arched over the path, casting shadows with their mottled darkness, their interwoven branches concealing the trail as it wound its way through the mountainous terrain. Kane moved with purpose, blending seamlessly into the enveloping darkness, his silhouette melding with the natural surroundings as he silently pursued the convoy, determined not to be detected.

Closing the distance, Kane observed the merchants while they halted their journey for the day, their weary forms setting up campfires beside their caravans. Hiding behind a sizable boulder, he watched intently, his gaze fixed on the group as they went about their evening rituals.

With practiced patience, he waited for them to complete their tasks, knowing that soon they would retire into the safety of their wagons. His eyes narrowed with tenacity while he prepared to make his move, every moment spent in observation, a vital piece of the puzzle in his quest for freedom.

In the quiet of the night, Kane retrieved the human-skinned book from beneath his jacket, his fingers tracing the matching birthmark with a sense of foreboding. As he examined the book, he realized the latch was unsealed, and with a cautious breath, he opened it, revealing pages that seemed to hold secrets long forgotten.

Though the earliest pages were blank, he could feel the faint impressions of previously etched scripts beneath his fingertips. In the dim light, he struggled to discern the contents, only able to make out crude drawings of astrological symbols and numbers scattered across the pages. With a sense of frustration, he closed the book, his mind swirling with unsolvable questions.

Recalling his dream and the cryptic message from the apparition, Kane lifted his right hand, studying it intently. The memory of its transformation into a bear's claw lingered, prompting him to ponder the origins of his heritage and his lack of a clan title. In that moment of realization, he understood that he knew himself only as Kane, a solitary figure navigating a world without direction.

Around midnight, the weary pilgrims had sought refuge in their wagons, seeking solace in the embrace of much-needed rest. This was the moment Kane had been waiting for, the perfect opportunity to advance his plan. With silent footsteps, he made his way towards the rearmost wagon, pausing intermittently to listen for any signs of activity.

But the night remained eerily quiet, except for the occasional rumble of his own stomach and the soft snores of the sleeping men. Hunger gnawed at him, a familiar companion that seemed to sap not only his physical strength but also his very essence. It was a cruel reminder of the deprivation he had grown accustomed to, a constant thief of his vitality.

Spotting a cast-iron stewpot hanging over a dwindling fire, Kane wasted no time in rushing over, his heart pounding with excitement. Silently, he peered into the vessel, his eyes widening with anticipation as he discovered a few leftover chicken legs nestled in the casserole.

With eager hands, he snatched each succulent chunk, devouring them hungrily, savoring every yummy bite. As he polished off the last piece, his gaze turned to his surroundings, scouring the area for any sign of peasant clothing. His search was rewarded when he uncovered a larger-sized pair of earth-colored trousers, a matching shirt, a traditional Japanese farmer's hat, and a knapsack.

Quick as lightning, Kane retreated to the shelter of the boulder, his fingers flying as he shed his ninja uniform and donned the peasant attire. Stuffing his discarded garments, weapons and book into the knapsack, he disappeared down the steep and rugged track, blending seamlessly into the dense forest.

Instantly, he felt a sense of belonging soak into him, the somehow familiar scents of earth, wood, and leaf swathing him like a comforting cuddle.

With each step, he embraced his newfound disguise, disappearing into the wilderness with a renewed sense of motivation and independence.

As Kane ventured deeper into the dense vegetation, the encroaching frost gnawed at his skin, the icy tendrils of impending cold pressing in on him like a pressing vice.

Alarm swept through him as the temperature plummeted, his breath coming in frantic, visible puffs.

Desperation drove him to seek shelter, and he stumbled upon an unoccupied cavern hidden within the tangled undergrowth. The entrance loomed before him, dark and foreboding, but he had no choice.

With a shudder of disgust, he pressed inside, the damp, moss-covered walls slimy against his skin. The musty smell of decay filled his nostrils, and he gagged, fighting the urge to retch.

Nestling himself in the filth, he tried to calm his racing heart, forcing his mind to empty, to find a semblance of peace.

But the oppressive darkness and the cold, clammy surroundings made it impossible to relax. Every drip of water, every rustle echoed in the cavern, amplifying his sense of fear. Kane struggled to meditate, to exist in this horrific refuge, fighting the overwhelming desire to flee, yet knowing he had nowhere else to go.

Chapter 3

The golden rays of a new morning brought a gush of vigor to Kane's first day of liberation. Despite the bitter cold of the previous night, he felt an unusual warmth, noticing ice crystals clinging to his shirt and trousers from the frost. As he rolled up his sleeve to examine the knife puncture wound, his heart thrashed with shock.

Thick, bristly hair covered his arm, resembling the shaggy fur of a large woolly animal and he frantically explored the rest of his body, discovering that the wiry pelt covered him entirely. Desperation flooded his mind as the dual horrors of his situation overwhelmed him: the brutal slaughter at the monastery and his uncontrollable transformation into a bear.

His thoughts raced, the reality of his monstrous change and the bloodshed he left behind colliding in a torrent of fear and confusion. The awareness of his predicament consumed him, each breath a struggle as he grappled with the terrifying knowledge of what he was becoming.

Gathering his belongings, Kane resumed his escape down the mountain, navigating the excessively bush-covered track while picking various mulberries to eat along the way. As he floundered through the dense jungle, pushing back overgrown branches, he suddenly found himself face to face with a wild boar. Both stood frozen like statues, staring at one another in a tense, silent standoff.

Kane's senses were heightened, his hearing especially acute. He could detect the faintest movements in the forest, discerning every sound with startling clarity. The rustling of leaves, the distant scurry of squirrels in the canopy, their squeaks, and the repeated scraping as they gnawed on objects—each noise amplified in his ears. The forest came alive around him, every sound a reminder of his raw, primal connection to the wild as he pressed on, the suspense of the encounter lingering in the air.

Simultaneously, he could hear red foxes snuffling the ground, their distant,

high-pitched ow-wow-wow-wows echoing like blood-curdling screams through the forest.

Refocusing on the boar before him, Kane scrutinized it with fierce concentration, his senses honing in on the rapid thrashing of its heart. The intensity of his gaze bore into the creature, every detail of its movement captured in his attention.

The animal sensed the hostility in his gaze. Suddenly, as if someone had shouted "Ready, set, go," the boar bolted into the scrub, faster than a speeding bullet, with Kane hot on its heels. His enhanced speed and cruel emotional indifference fueled the chase.

Kane's transformation began, his abilities becoming extraordinarily heightened. As he tailed the boar, he moved through the dense forest with unyielding precision, his enhanced senses and agility allowing him to weave effortlessly through the underbrush, every movement executed with flawless accuracy.

As the gap closed, he finally captured the boar, his fanged jaws locking around its throat. The warm, sour blood trickled into his mouth, igniting a primal thrill within him. With his prey slowly fading beneath him, he felt an exhilarating rush, as if an electrical storm was charging through his brain. The raw power and excitement of the hunt consumed him, leaving him breathless and alive with savage intensity.

Kane was now blooded, and the intoxicating sensation made him cry out a bestial, hideous wail that resonated through the outlying valley. The primal scream filled with an eerie, chilling intensity, reverberating off the trees and rocks, announcing his transformation to the silent wilderness around him.

Two miles away, the entire caravan of merchants froze at the isolated carnal roar. It was a sound that pierced the early morning, stopping them dead in their tracks. As the occupants jumped from their wagons, they scurried around Botan's wagon, their nerves on edge as they nervously babbled amongst themselves.

"Did you hear that, Botan? What was it?" one man interrogated, his voice trembling with fear.

"I'm not sure.... It could be a bear.... but it sounded more primeval," Botan answered, his tone uneasy.

"In all my years traveling these roads, I've never heard something so vile before." Botan exited the wagon and joined the congregation, their eyes fixed on the direction from where the terrifying sound had come. Breaking the uneasy silence, Botan spoke, his voice carrying a hint of trepidation.

"When we set up camp tonight, keep close together. Don't let the oxen graze openly..... gather them near and have larger fires encircling us"

The congregation remained suspended in the tension, their senses on high alert as they cautiously waited for another roar from the wild animal. But all that filled the air was the soothing warble of forest birds, a stark contrast to the previous terrifying sound. Yet, the absence of the threatening roar only heightened their unease, leaving them feeling exposed and vulnerable in the darkness of the forest. "Everyone, back to your wagons," Botan instructed, his voice trembling with urgency. "We must keep moving towards the city and put as much distance between us and whatever made that sound."

With a sense of unease gnawing at their hearts, everyone scurried back onto their carriages, their movements quick and panicked. They commanded their beasts of burden to make haste, slapping the reins hard against their tough rumps with

unexpected insistence. The caravan lurched forward, the sound of hooves pounding against the earth as they fled from the unknown terror lurking in the shadows.

Deep in the forest, Kane stood beside the carcass of the exterminated pig, his stomach churning with disgust at the gruesome scene before him. Most of the animal's internal organs had been devoured, and he wiped his blood-stained mouth and chin with a grimace of revulsion. As he withdrew his hand, he examined the amount of blood that covered it, his appetite sickened at the sight.

Excruciating pain radiated from his jaw, causing him to wince as he stroked his fingers over his teeth. He could feel the fangs that had ultimately killed the boar, but to his surprise, they began gradually withdrawing into his gums, reshaping back to their natural human form.

Exhausted from the chase and his unrestrained metamorphosis, Kane realized with a sinking feeling that he must gain control over these mutating episodes before venturing further into the uncertainties of the world. The thought of unintentionally harming innocent people filled him with worry, urging him to find a way to master and control the dark forces that threatened to consume him.

"I will live here in the forest for a while until I can learn how to control my skin changing. But I cannot remain here too long because I know for certain that the monks will send their most brutal and merciless ninjas after me to avenge the murders. They will want their retribution"

Muttering to himself with persistence, Kane made a firm decision. He huddled against the cornerstone of a towering rock face and wrapped his jacket tightly around him. Pulling down the large farmer's hat, he shielded his face from the elements.

Gradually, exhaustion overcame him, and he sank into a deep slumber, his breathing slow and steady, like a hibernating bear. In the embrace of sleep, he sought refuge from the turmoil of his inner struggles, hoping to find comfort and clarity in the depths of his dreams.

Absolute chaos gripped the monastery as news of Abbot Eshin's demise and Master Gideon's defiled assault spread like wildfire, eliciting pity and support from all their brothers and cloistered students.

For centuries, their Christian monasticism had been devoted to the practice of peace and compassion, their lives steeped in worship and scripture. The etiquette of enlightenment and restraint had been their guiding principles, shaping every aspect of their existence.

As the horrifying details of the attack emerged, it devastated those who had dedicated their lives to the monastery's order and remained steadfast in their beliefs. The sanctity of their haven had been shattered, and the foundation of their faith shaken to its core. The once tranquil halls now recited with cries of disbelief and anguish, as the monks grappled with the harsh reality of violence encroaching upon their sacred sanctuary.

The other students were instructed to gather in the refectory as the Abbot's second-in-command made the sorrowful announcement to everyone present.

"It is with deep regret and despair that I must inform you.... yesterday, our beloved Abbot Eshin passed away, and his faithful Brother Gideon was viciously attacked during a premeditated onslaught," he articulated, his voice trembling with emotion. Instantly, the assembly erupted into a quiet murmur as the students exchanged shocked whispers among themselves, struggling to comprehend the gravity of the news.

"Quiet, please.... You will be informed of any further developments or changes," the second-in-command continued, attempting to restore order.

"I will be acting as the new Abbot in the meantime and will be available for anyone who needs counseling. Can everyone please form two lines and proceed to the main prayer hall, where we will conduct the funeral service and listen to spiritual readings from the Tipitaka. Hai?"

His words hung in the air, the heaviness of their grief and disbelief obvious as they prepared to bid farewell to their fallen leader and find support in their shared faith. "Hai, Master Akio," the students obediently replied, quietly walking towards the chapel with four monks leading the way. The scent of burning incense filled the air as they advanced, purifying the space and casting a tranquil atmosphere over the somber procession.

As the novice monks disappeared down the corridor, Master Akio turned to face his brother monk standing beside him.

"Has anyone found Master Kane?" he inquired with a furrowed brow.

"No one has seen him since yesterday afternoon," the brother monk responded solemnly.

"Brother Yuki heard him scream from his room, but when he checked on him, Master Kane claimed he wasn't feeling well. He was also absent from dinner in the refectory, and there's a dried blood trail leading to his room."

"Search it, but keep it confidential," Master Akio ordered firmly.

"Hai," the brother monk affirmed, bowing to the newly appointed Abbot before swiftly retreating to carry out his task.

The gravity of the situation cast a shadow over the monastery's already grieving heart, deepening the sense of sorrow and despair.

Master Akio had been a fixture in the monastery for close to forty years, his presence commanding respect from all who knew him. His loyalty to the Buddhist Brotherhood was unwavering, a testament to his tireless commitment to his faith.

His journey to the monastery had been fraught with hardship. Fleeing his village during the tumultuous Edo Period, he had struggled to find acceptance and a sense of belonging in a world torn apart by conflict. Masking his emotions, he clung to his courage in the face of despair, determined to stay connected to his convictions.

The trials of his youth, spent scrounging for his next meal in the grimy streets of war-torn villages, had taught him invaluable lessons. Akio learned to appreciate the simplest of things—food, shelter, sanitation—and he carried those lessons with him throughout his life.

He believed that forgiveness, even in the face of the Samurai's disregard for human life, held the key to finding divinity and inner peace. And so, he devoted himself to his spiritual journey, seeking solace and enlightenment within the walls of the monastery.

On a bitterly cold winter day, Akio stood at the entrance of the Buddhist monastery, his body battered and malnourished after enduring months of extreme poverty and hardship. Desperate to escape the ceaseless oppression of his circumstances, he had fled the ravaged villages and sought refuge in the rugged countryside.

In the mountains, he lived in constant fear, hiding from the marauding Samurai who scoured the land, mercilessly slaughtering anyone they deemed a threat. The sight of death and destruction surrounded him, a grim reminder of the brutality of war. Akio recoiled in horror at the inhumanity of it all, struggling to comprehend how those in power could inflict such unspeakable atrocities upon their own people.

Jinxed by the specter of violence and death, Akio's spirit was battered, his faith tested by the relentless cruelty of the world around him. And yet, as he stood at the threshold of the monastery, a glimmer of hope flickered within him, a fragile beacon of light amidst the darkness of despair.

Huddled in the corner of the monastery entrance, Akio heard the creak of a door as a compassionate monk stepped out, his eyes falling upon the ravaged figure curled up like a frightened kitten.

"My son, please come inside. We can offer you food, shelter, and protection," the Brother urged, extending his hand in a gesture of kindness.

Akio gazed up at the tender-hearted monk, his eyes filled with a mixture of misery and longing. Slowly, he withdrew his hand from the tattered coat wrapped around him, accepting the offered help.

With the monk's guidance, he embarked on a journey of spiritual awakening, dedicating himself to the Buddhist faith and the service of all living beings. Through prayer and contemplation, he found relief and purpose, his troubled past gradually fading into the background as he embraced a new path of enlightenment and compassion.

In the prayer hall, the monks congregated for the Abbot's meditation service, seeking reassurance and tranquility amidst their grief. The air was thick with the scent of incense and the soft glow of candles illuminated the solemn space. Offerings of flowers and fruit adorned the altar, alongside an image of Buddha and a picture of the late Abbot Eshin, their presence a reminder of the spiritual journey that lay ahead.

As the sermon began, the monks bowed their heads in reverence, their hearts heavy with sorrow. The officiating monk poured water from a vessel into an overflowing cup, symbolizing the transfer of merit and blessings to the departed soul. Offerings were made to the divine, a gesture of gratitude for the Abbot's life and teachings.

Clad in traditional white cloth and headbands, the monks chanted the sacred sutras in unison, their voices rising and falling with the rhythm of the gong. Each syllable reverberated through the hall, filling the space with a sense of solemnity and devotion. In the midst of their mourning, they found peace in the timeless rituals of their faith, drawing strength from the collective prayers of the community.

Despite the solemnity of the ceremony, the monks understood that death was not the end, but merely a transition from one form to another. They focused on the impermanence of life and their own mortality, recognizing the importance of making their existence meaningful through acts of kindness and compassion. Their ultimate goal was to help the deceased individual achieve a better position in the next life through their collective prayers and good deeds.

Abbot Eshins body, covered in a white sheet, lay in his bedroom, a serene presence amidst the quietude of the monastery. Washed and dressed in his traditional tunic, he rested on his own futon for one final night, surrounded by the familiar items of his earthly home. Throughout the night, his brothers paid their respects, offering condolences and prayers as if he were still among them. Their message was clear: a promise of paradise awaiting him at the end of his earthly journey, a testament to the eternal cycle of life and death embraced by his devotion.

The following day dawned with a discouraged heart as the monks gathered for the final ceremony, their grief noticeble as they leaned on sticks for support, burdened by the heaviness of their sorrow. Together, they made their way to the site of the cremation, their steps slow and deliberate, each movement a dignified tribute to their departed Abbot.

Throughout the night, they had labored to construct a wooden platform adorned with the sacred symbols of their faith: a white parasol, a conch shell, a treasure vase, a victory banner, a pair of golden fish, an endless knot, and a lotus flower. Now, as they approached the funeral podium in a courtly procession, Akio poured water over the body mounted on the pulpit, the final act of purification and reverence.

The monks, holding candles and burning incense, chanted in unison, their voices piercing the tranquility of the morning air. In their midst, the newly appointed Abbot held a flaming torch, his presence a symbol of leadership and guidance in the face of loss.

With earnest grace, he lowered the torch, igniting the logs with a blaze of intensity. In a voice heavy with emotion, he spoke the words that marked the end of the ceremony:

“This shrine is closed. May it keep out impure spirits and guide our valued Eshin to paradise.” As his words faded into the stillness, the congregation erupted into song, their voices mingling with the crackle of flames and the scent of incense, a closing farewell to their beloved Abbot Eshin.

* * *

Gideon lay motionless in the infirmary, his face obscured by thick bandages that concealed the extent of his injuries. The Abbey's medics hovered anxiously around him, their hands moving with practiced precision as they administered ancient herbal remedies and whispered prayers for his recovery.

The scent of medicinal herbs filled the air as the monks worked tirelessly to save their fallen brother. Gideon had lost a dangerous amount of blood, and his condition remained precarious as he drifted in and out of consciousness.

It was a novice monk who had discovered him, his usual task of delivering the Abbot's evening meal leading him to the Dojo where he stumbled upon the scene of carnage. Shocked and horrified, he raised the alarm, setting off a frenzy that ended with the grim news of Gideon and Abbot Eshin lying injured and bloodied on the floor. As they worked to save Gideon's life, the monks prayed fervently for his swift recovery, their faith profound in the face of such senseless violence.

"Do you think he will heal from the attack?" The new Abbot asked one of the doctors "Yes I believe so, although he won't get the sight back in his left eye and there will be dreadful scars from whatever struck him" He confessed

"Who do you think did this gruesome crime" The doctor continued

"We're not sure brother but we will eventually find the offender and bring him to justice" Abbot Akio replied

"Continue your good work and let me know when Master Gideon regains consciousness" He added, placing his hand on the medic's shoulder, as a sign of his support and compassion

"Hai" The doctor agreed, bowing respectfully

Abbot Akio wandered through the silent cloister as he made his way to the cellar Dojo, his mind consumed by thoughts of the recent tragedy. As he entered the dimly lit room, his gaze fixated on the claret-stained floorboards before him, searching for any sign of what had transpired.

Lost in his thoughts, he was startled when the monk assigned to search Kane's room appeared silently behind him. Without turning, Akio acknowledged the presence with a slight nod before returning his attention to the floor.

Carefully, he knelt down and began to examine the stained wood, his eyes sharp as he scanned for any clues that might shed light on the events that had unfolded. It was then that he noticed it—a single chunk of brown fur, partially coated with desiccated blood.

Instinctively, he reached out to retrieve it, his fingers closing around the coarse strands with a sense of grim intention. This small piece of evidence could be the key to unraveling the mystery that had gripped the monastery, and Abbott Akio was determined to uncover the truth, no matter who he had to track down.

"Hai Brother.....did you find anything?" He requested, examining the fragmented flesh he held in his fingers.

"No Abbot I didn't find anything but some of Master Kane's belongings are missing" "What kind of belongings?"

"All of his weapons and his ninja uniform" the monk revealed "Have you found Master Kane himself?"

"No Abbot.....he hasn't been located"

"Assemble the ninjas' scholars in the quadrangle immediately" The Abbot ordered "Hai" the monk replied and briskly scurried out of the room.

Once the students had congregated, the Abbot with the three ninja Masters exited the monastery and stood motionless in front of them.

"Masters pick your six best warriors" He instructed

"Hai" the ninja masters consented "Hikaru.....Itsuo.....Naoki.....Shusuki.....Taichi.....and Hiro step forward"

"Hai" The men answered together, promptly bowing with a spirited eagerness.

"The rest of you can return to the dormitory" The ninja master dictated and after the group had retreated through the doors, the Abbot gave his instructions

"It is your duty to find Master Kane and bring him back here to me. You will prepare for the journey tonight and leave when the sun rises.....Bring him back alive so he can pay for what he has done.....Understood?"

"Hai" The six warriors agreed, then the Abbot turned on his heels and retired into the monastery.

The six ninjas gathered in a tight circle, their voices hushed as they discussed their strategies for apprehending Kane as quickly as possible. Time was of the essence, and they knew they couldn't afford to waste a moment.

"We'll split into two teams," one of the ninjas suggested, his tone decisive.

"Three of us will track Kane's movements while the others gather information from the locals."

Nods of agreement rippled through the group as they quickly formulated their plan of action. Each ninja knew their role and understood the importance of working together to bring Kane to justice.

"There was always something strange about him, he never interacted or made friends with any of us" One of the men admitted

"Don't forget that he's stronger than any normal man.....I experienced his power the day when I was ordered to fight him" Hiro added

"How could he overthrow the Abbot and Master Gideon at the same time? They were martial art experts and I heard the injuries he'd inflicted on them were sickening"

Taichi declared

"He must have used weapons that they weren't familiar with" Hiro rationalized "Did you ever hear him babbling in other languages or screaming from his room at night?" Naoki asked

"Hai.....I used to share a room with him and his incessant ramblings kept me awake most nights, so I requested to be moved. I didn't care if they bunked me here in the quadrangle... ..I just had to get away from Kane's eerie behavior.....he sounded demonic.....he wasn't a true Buddhist monk" Itsuo protested

"With his unusual strength, we'll have to be hyper-vigilant hunting him down. We must use our craft proficiently and assist each other when the time comes to arrest him. This is our chance to prove we are superior warriors.....to bring honor to Master Gideon, our murdered Abbot Eshin and our Brotherhood. We will eliminate him" Hiro concluded

"But Hiro, the Abbot ordered us to bring him back alive"

"Hai.....but whatever happens out there will only be known by us and we won't tell anyone the truth about his demise" Hiro commanded, so the clan retreated to their quarters and assembled the arsenal needed for the hunt of the mutinous

Kane.

Hiro seethed with anger, his temper as sharp as his blade. A brutal ninja through and through, he cared only for his own glory and had little regard for the teachings of the Buddhist faith. Unlike the monks who sought enlightenment and humility, Hiro was driven by a toxic mix of arrogance and pride.

He considered himself superior to everyone around him, his power and skill making him a force to be reckoned with. But above all, he harbored a burning hatred for Kane, a hatred that consumed him with every passing moment.

The recent events had provided Hiro with the perfect opportunity to exact his revenge on Kane for the humiliating defeat he had suffered at his hands. With the Abbot's orders to capture the murderer, Hiro saw a chance to dish out his own form of justice, one that had nothing to do with fairness or righteousness. For Hiro, vengeance was all that mattered, and he would stop at nothing to see Kane pay for his crime.

As the first vibrant rays of the morning sun cast their warming glow, the ninjas assembled, poised and ready for action. At the entrance, the Abbot stood, an example of wisdom and guidance.

"Before you embark on this battle with Master Kane," he began, his voice grave yet resolute, "remember the gravity of his actions against our brotherhood. He is a formidable opponent, possessed of strength and stamina beyond that of a mere mortal. But do not be swayed by fear. Remember your training, and tap into your inner Feng Shui."

With a formal wave of his hand, the Abbot blessed the ninjas, invoking protection and victory upon their journey. As they dispersed into the mountainous countryside and dense woodlands, he offered a silent prayer for their safety.

"May the divine guide you as you confront pure evil," he whispered, his words carried away on the morning breeze.

As Kane journeyed through the wilderness, his stubbornness grew with each passing mile. Despite the constant threat of pursuit, he found a sense of belonging in the encircling woodland. With every step, he felt a newfound strength coursing through his veins, the untamed landscape fueling his resolve and sharpening his instincts.

His senses sharp, Kane moved with a swiftness and agility he had never known before. The forest seemed to saturate him with a vitality he had long thought lost, fueling his resolve to escape the grasp of his pursuers.

With the monastery's ninjas hot on his trail, Kane knew he had to stay one step ahead. This chase was more than just a battle for survival; it was a quest for freedom, a chance to break free from the control that had restricted him for so long.

As he pushed forward, Kane felt a glimmer of hope ignite within him. For the first time in years, he dared to believe in a future filled with possibility. Leaving the monastery behind was his first step towards self-preservation, a bold declaration of his promise to carve out a new path for himself and with each minute that passed, Kane felt himself growing stronger, more resilient, and ever more hopeful for the days that lay ahead.

Moving quickly down the mountainside, Kane eventually reached the forest river and as the fog danced upon the surface, and with his hunters advancing, Kane knew he had to think fast. As he reached the water, its tranquil beauty beckoned to him, offering a pathway to freedom. Without hesitation, he seized upon the idea.

Grabbing a large fallen log from the banks, Kane heaved it into the frigid waters, the cold spray awakening his senses. With practiced agility, he leapt onto the rolling surface, his heart pounding with exhilaration.

Balancing himself against the rushing current, Kane felt a surge of adrenaline as he rode the river's force like a wild stallion. The fog danced upon the water's surface, shrouding him in a mystical aura as he swiftly propelled himself downstream, leaving no trace behind.

As he disappeared around the bend, Kane's spirit soared with the thrill of his daring escape. With each twist and turn of the river, he felt a renewed sense of victory driving him ever onward.

As Kane continued his journey down the river, the once tumultuous waters gradually transformed into a serene and silent expanse. The mist, now a ghostly grey, clung to the surface with a bone-chilling silence, its tendrils caressing the embankment with a spectral touch.

With a steely mindfulness, Kane scanned the shoreline, his senses on high alert for any sign of danger. It was then that the mist revealed its sinister secret: rows of large stakes jutted out from the water, each adorned with a putrefied human head.

A shiver ran through Kane as he beheld the macabre sight, his instincts screaming at him to flee. Yet, he remained composed, his human form holding steady despite the surge of fear coursing through him. He was learning to temper his primal urges, to control the savage beast.

With a grim acceptance, Kane knew that mastering this inner

demon was essential for his survival in the civilized world he sought to reach, and as he continued on his journey, he vowed to keep his transformation in check, lest he become consumed by the unwanted darkness.

The mist coiled and writhed around the partially submerged tree trunks, adding to the eerie atmosphere of the riverbank. Kane's senses tingled with alertness as he caught a glimpse of movement behind the dense forest. Suddenly, primal arrows whizzed past him, but they merely glanced off his resilient form, like twigs bouncing off an elephant's hide.

Straining to see through the dense foliage, Kane squinted towards the tree line, where the whites of unseen eyes stared back at him. Then, as if acknowledging his presence, the natives emerged from the shadows, their figures stark against the misty backdrop.

Standing motionless on the riverbank, they exuded an aura of impenetrable isolation. Kane drifted past them, his gaze lingering on their afflictions: deformities wrought by disease and hardship. Some bore contorted, emaciated faces, while others suffered from missing noses or disfigured features. Their eyes drooped unevenly, and gaping holes marred their once-human visages, a testament to the harshness of their existence in the heart of the unforgiving wilderness.

Moving like a spectral apparition, Kane locked eyes with the grotesque tribespeople, their putrid forms emitting hissing and growling sounds. Some even dared to mimic the roar of a bear, a chilling reminder of the dominant forces that governed their existence.

Yet, as Kane stared back at them, a transformation occurred within him. The initial horror and disgust melted away, replaced by a newfound empathy for their plight. He recognized their torment as a reflection of his own, and a sense of kinship blossomed in his heart.

Sensing the increasing danger, Kane decided to abandon the floating log and plunged into the water, swimming swiftly to the other side. With mindfulness fueling his every stroke, he continued to follow the river, knowing that its winding path would eventually lead him to a city, where new adventures and challenges awaited.

* * *

Hiro stood on the edge of the road leading away from the monastery, his gaze sweeping across the rugged terrain. His comrades had already disappeared into the distant forest, their forms swallowed by the dense trees. But Hiro remained rooted to the spot, his instincts telling him that Kane was cunning enough to mislead the posse. Someone needed to stay behind, and Hiro's sharp logic and ironclad

self-control made him the ideal candidate.

His eyes narrowed as he peered into the vast expanse, a burning hatred simmering within. Dark, ruthless thoughts flickered across his mind, thoughts of how he would

deal with Kane once he caught him. In a flash, Hiro spun on his heels and sprinted down the dusty highway, his speed unmatched, his stamina unyielding.

Miles flew by beneath his feet until he finally spotted a group of roaming merchants in the distance. His heart pounded, not from exertion, but from the anticipation of the hunt. Kane's trail might be faint, but Hiro was relentless, and nothing would stand between him and his prey.

He moved with the stealth of a shadow, his form practically invisible as he crept up to the last trailing wagon. It was as if he wore an invisibility cloak, each step precise and silent. Hugging the side of the wagons, he advanced methodically, his eyes sharp and focused. Reaching Botan's carriage, he slipped into the rear, navigating over a clutter of boxes and duffle bags without a sound.

As Botan urged the bullocks onward along the trail, Hiro slithered up beside him. The moment Botan caught sight of the ninja fully clad in his dark uniform, he recoiled in terror, his body jerking sideways. The unexpected arrival of Hiro, with his cold, steely gaze, sent a wave of fear crashing through Botan. Hiro's presence was an sign, a silent omen of the danger that loomed.

"Hai, Master ninja," Botan greeted, his voice trembling.

"Did you come from the monastery?" He continued, hoping the ninja was a friend, not a foe.

"Hai," Hiro replied, withholding his name. "How can I help you, Master ninja?"

"Have you seen or heard anything unusual on your travels, Botan?" "Like what?"

"A solitary monk on his travels?" Hiro probed.

"No, we haven't seen anything, but the other night, we all heard a blood-curdling scream or howl coming from deep within the forest," Botan briefed.

"Which direction did it come from?" Hiro quizzed.

Botan shifted in his seat and turned around, pointing straight behind him, in the opposite direction from where they were heading.

"Do you believe it was an animal?"

"I'm not sure, Master ninja... but I've never heard such a hideous shriek before... it didn't sound human."

"Thank you. Keep to the roads, do not deviate for any reason, and stay close together at all times."

"Is that creature the one you're hunting?"

"It would be safer if you don't know anymore," Hiro cautioned. As he jumped from the driver's seat, a dark thought crossed his mind.

"Of course.....Kane must be heading towards the city.... I will make your dream of running away your worst nightmare."

Dusk descended abruptly, swallowing the remnants of daylight and shrouding the landscape in total darkness. The forest, once vibrant and alive, transformed into a realm of eerie stillness. Trees loomed like silent sentinels, their towering forms casting long, spooky shadows that masked the moon's feeble attempts to illuminate the night. In this cloak of obscurity, Kane moved with ghostly grace, his black eyes gleaming with a predatory intensity, surveying every corner of his surroundings. He blended effortlessly into the enveloping darkness, a phantom lurking unseen, his presence foreboding.

A movement in the shadows jolted Kane to a standstill. His eyes widened as he witnessed a grotesque figure scavenging nearby. Its back hunched at a sharp angle, forming a disfiguring hump, and Kane, hyper-aware, felt his heart pounding in his chest like a drum of dread.

The figure shuffled through the underbrush, clutching a bundle of dead plants, oblivious to Kane's presence. It moved with an unsettling gait, methodically sifting through leaves and twigs with a gnarled walking stick.

The makeshift bandages that once covered Kane's stab wound had been lost in the river, leaving him vulnerable and in discomfort from the festering sore. Despite the pain, his curiosity was aroused by the bizarre creature. He trailed it cautiously through the darkened forest until they arrived at a dilapidated hut. Faint candlelight flickered in the small windows, casting eerie shapes on the decrepit walls.

As Kane approached stealthily, the strange person spoke, its voice ancient and warped by years of solitude.

"I know you are there," the creature rasped without turning, its voice cutting through the silence like a rusty blade. It spoke slowly, each word resonating with the weight of years.

Kane approached cautiously, drawn by a mixture of desperation and curiosity. "Hello, I am injured and would appreciate your help with my wound," he said tentatively.

"I don't usually help people, but come," the elderly figure replied, her voice strained yet strangely inviting. She shuffled into the dimly lit hut, leaving the door slightly open. With reluctance, Kane followed, stepping into the musty interior.

"Sit down here sit, sit," the woman commanded with agitation in her gravelly voice.

Kane complied, placing his knapsack by the door and settling onto a rickety chair. He watched her closely, concern etched on his face as she moved about the room.

"Who are you?" the woman finally asked, her back still turned towards him as she tended to a bubbling cauldron over the crackling fireplace.

"I am a traveling monk, on my way to deliver an important message," Kane replied smoothly, his words masking the unease gnawing at him.

"What kind of message, friar?" The old woman's voice cracked through the dimly lit room, her tone laced with skepticism.

"Just a message to the monastery's superiors.... it's a Christian message," Kane replied, his voice steady but tinged with concern. He avoided meeting her gaze, sensing an undercurrent of suspicion in her attitude.

As soon as the words left his lips, the old woman abruptly turned to face him. Kane's breath caught in his throat at the sight of her grotesque face, twisted and weathered by time and hardship. Her features were a mosaic of scars and wrinkles, her eyes gleaming with a piercing intensity that seemed to strip away his defenses.

The air thickened with tension as Kane found himself staring into the abyss of her gaze, unsure of what lay behind those ancient eyes.

Her long, matted hair clung in patches to her scalp, resembling strands of rotting straw as they cascaded over her shoulders. Hooded eyes, sharp as a serpent's gaze, fixed on Kane with unsettling intensity. Her nose, vulturous and hooked like a raptor's beak, added to her menacing appearance. As she spoke, her words resonated through a mouth filled with gapped, blackened teeth, some broken into jagged stubs. Each feature seemed to magnify the repulsiveness of her presence, turning the dimly lit hut into a chamber of horrors. Kane fought to maintain his composure, but every glance at her contorted face sent a wave of revulsion and dread coursing through him.

"I don't like monks," the witch blurted out suddenly in her sickly, grainy voice.

"I'm just a messenger. That's my only task at the monastery running errands,"

Kane defended himself, his voice tense with irritation and apprehension.

"If you're just an errand boy, then how did you get that stab wound?" she probed, her tone dripping with doubt.

"I fell into the river by accident slipped down the embankment and a branch

embedded itself into my arm, like a knife," Kane explained, hoping to pacify her. "You're an idiot," the witch slandered, her words like venom as she approached Kane, disregarding his discomfort. She lifted his farmer's shirt abruptly and scrutinized the wound with a grimace.

"If you're a monk, then why do you wear these peasants' clothing? Hmmm? I know you are lying!" she wheezed heavily, turning away to attend to the furnace with a dismissive air.

The cauldron simmered malevolently over the crackling flames, emitting a foul, hellish stench that made Kane's stomach churn. His eyes scanned the decrepit hut, horror gripping him as he noticed scattered pieces of animal limbs and entrails strewn across the filthy floor. The sight alone threatened to turn his insides.

With a scowl, the witch tore herbs, leaves, and offal with her bare, gnarled hands, each motion accompanied by a macabre dexterity.

She added the ingredients to the bubbling brew, muttering arcane words that caused a cold sweat to bead on his forehead.

Her eyes, savage and wild, ignited with an unholy fervor as she worked her dark craft.

Turning slowly, she held up a moldy, fossilized horse hoof, its putrid smell mingling with the rancid mixture. With arthritic fingers like claws, she approached Kane, her movements akin to a spider weaving a sinister web in the darkness.

"Pull up your sleeve," the witch instructed with a twisted smile, her voice dripping with malice. She grabbed the pulpy blend and pressed it onto Kane's infected stab wound, forcing it deep into the laceration, causing Kane to grit his teeth against the excruciating pain. Even in her supposed act of kindness, she reveled in cruelty. "Stop!" Kane shouted, shoving the hag away from him. The witch stumbled backward on her spindly legs, her gaze fixing on him with an eerie intensity.

As the Wiccan glared at Kane with her dead fish eyes, he braced himself for a spell or curse, but instead, she unleashed a disturbing, unrepentant cackle. Her thin, bloodless lips curled into a mocking grin.

"See you later!" was the last thing Kane heard before his vision blurred and he collapsed, consciousness slipping away as he hit the floor with a heavy thud. The witch hobbled over to the unconscious man, her movements slow and deliberate. Unbeknownst to her, a faint scratching noise emanated from his

knapsack as she passed by it. Curiosity aroused, she turned back and studied the bag, noticing its sporadic movements.

With a huff, she bent down, her skinny, withered arms reaching to pick it up.

Flicking back the cover, she peered inside with a mixture of intrigue and anticipation. Her eyes widened with excitement as they landed on the human-skinned book nestled within. With eager fingers, she withdrew the grim book from the bag, holding it close as if it were a prized treasure unearthed from the depths of darkness.

Admiring the book's dark brown exterior, the witch ran her extended fingers over the surface, relishing the grotesque texture of human skin. A twisted smile played on her lips as she chuckled with delight at the macabre artifact before her. The latch on the book was tightly sealed, but her interest and stubborness drove her to pick at the lock with her long, gnarled fingernails, intent on unraveling its secrets.

However, the enchanted journal seemed to resist her efforts. The lock remained steadfast, thwarting her attempts to pry it open. Frustration mingled with fascination on the witch's face as she realized the book held secrets beyond her immediate reach.

Her eyes narrowed with renewed determination, a glint of dark ambition dancing in their depths, as she turned the object over from front to back, scrutinizing every detail.

Without warning, the book erupted into flames, engulfing the witch's arms in a sudden inferno. With a piercing scream, she instinctively released the book, horror carved on her face as she watched her hands burn with agonizing ferocity.

Rushing to the cauldron, desperation driving her movements, she plunged her arms into the simmering brew, hoping to extinguish the flames. But when she withdrew them, a wave of devastation engulfed her. Blood and melting flesh dripped down her forearms, her fingers completely disintegrated, leaving only liquefied stumps where her fists had once been.

Overwhelmed by shock and pain, extreme anger and a thirst for revenge surged through her. Hysterically screaming at the motionless book, her voice reverberated with wild fury. The witch began to weave a spell, her incantation building in power until the air crackled with wild electrical discharges, filling the room with a bitter energy.

Bright flashes sliced through the air like jagged lightning bolts as the witch wielded the fiery lances with her arms, swirling them in a frenzied dance. The searing energy coalesced into a glowing red ball, hissing with intense heat that turned the air around it into a stifling furnace.

With a final, vengeful howl, the hag unleashed the fiery storm towards the cursed book. But just as the burning orb hurtled towards its target, it abruptly halted mid-air, hovering weirdly above the malevolent book. In an instant, the fiery projectile reversed course with ferocious speed, hurtling back towards the witch with unstoppable force.

The witch shrieked in agony as the blazing orb struck her with brutal impact. Flames engulfed her entire body, consuming her in a fiery inferno. Frantically racing about the shack, she screamed and writhed in unbearable pain, her ancient form unable to withstand the force of the magical backlash.

Minutes passed in a horrifying spectacle until finally, with a final, anguished wail, the revolting old witch was reduced to a pile of blackened ashes, her spiteful, evil power extinguished and her dark presence vanquished from the world.

The following morning, Kane awoke with a pounding headache, his hand instinctively reaching to clutch his right arm where the witch had applied the strange pomace to his wound. Memories of the bizarre encounter flashed through his mind as he

carefully surveyed the room. His primary concern was the fate of the witch who had shared the shanty with him.

As his eyes scanned the room, they settled on a large charcoal mound in the center of the floor. The pile of ashes was all that remained, a solemn testament to the witch's existence. With cautious steps, Kane approached the heap, his heart pounding with a mixture of relief and unease.

Upon closer inspection, he noticed a solitary object amidst the charcoal—a solid gold tooth resting on the edge of the mound. It gleamed faintly in the morning light, a surreal and eerie artifact left behind from the horrifying events of the previous night. Kane's thoughts raced as he processed the implications of what he had witnessed.

The witch, with all her malevolent power, had met her end in a fiery demise, leaving behind only this cryptic souvenir of her existence.

With a deep breath, Kane reached down and picked up the gold tooth, a tangible reminder of the supernatural forces that had entwined his fate with hers.

"I wonder what happened to her last night?" He questioned

Picking up the hefty tooth, Kane felt its weight, realizing its considerable value—it was heavier than a lump of lead. Understanding its potential worth, he carefully stowed the nugget into his pocket, his mind already calculating its worth in town. Next, he swiftly retrieved the book from the ground, tucking it securely into his knapsack.

Just as he prepared to leave, his eyes fell upon a sword resting beside a chair. Without hesitation, he seized the weapon, feeling its weight and balance in his grip, an essential addition to his arsenal.

The night spent in the witch's cabin had not been in vain; it had provided Kane with crucial advantages as he continued his pursuit. Aware of the precious time lost, he quickened his pace, urgency fueling every step. Each passing minute brought his pursuers closer, and Kane knew that every moment counted in his race to stay ahead of them.

For the next few days, Kane pressed on through the rugged mountain terrain, his journey punctuated by frequent pauses to catch his breath. Gazing up at the towering peaks with a mix of awe and reverence for their crypt-like stillness, he found calm in the solitude of the wilderness. Yet, on this fateful day, the tranquility was shattered by the distant echo of voices reverberating through the woods.

Instinctively sensing the approaching men following his trail, fear gripped Kane's heart. Acting swiftly, he plunged into a muddied bog, smearing the pungent filth across his face and hands to mask his scent. With calculated urgency, he sought refuge in a natural hollow in the ground, camouflaging himself under leaves and fallen branches until he became nearly invisible.

Fifteen tense minutes passed before the voices materialized into the two ninjas he had anticipated. They moved with silent peristance, scouring the ground for any

trace of Kane's passage. Days earlier, they had stumbled upon the witch's secluded hut, now reduced to a charred remnant with her ashes scattered carelessly about. The ninjas kicked at the blackened remains, sending them swirling through the gaps in the floorboards, searching in vain for clues.

Hidden mere feet away, Kane held his breath, heart pounding in his chest as he prayed they would overlook his trail. Every rustle of leaves and whispered word intensified the weight of the wilderness around him, the mountain's solemnity bearing witness to his perilous game of evasion.

From his concealed vantage point, Kane held his breath as the two ninja brothers halted just inches away from his hidden hollow. With bated breath, he observed them closely, recognizing them as they finally exchanged words.

"Look.... here's something," whispered Shusuki, his voice barely audible in the still mountain air.

"What is it?" replied Naoki, his tone tinged with skepticism.

"It's a footprint heading south towards Kyoto," Shusuki answered, pointing decisively along the track.

"This could be anyone's," Naoki countered.

"No, look at the size of it. That's Master Kane's footprint; it's much larger than an average man's. Let's keep going, Naoki. It's our best chance of catching that murderous bastard," Shusuki asserted with determination.

"Hai," they agreed in unison, their common goal obvious as they continued down the treacherous mountain path, soon disappearing from Kane's view.

Relief flooded through Kane as he watched them depart, knowing his manoeuvre had bought him precious time. Yet, a knot of apprehension tightened in his stomach as he grasped the relentless pursuit that now lay ahead, realizing just how close they were getting.

He waited until the sounds of their footsteps faded into the mountain's expanse before cautiously emerging from his hiding place, steeling himself for the next leg of his perilous journey.

Reluctant to let his pursuers slip away, he began to trail the two ninjas, observing their every move with calculated precision. In this twist of fate, the hunters had unwittingly become the hunted.

As they ventured deeper into the terrain, the pathway narrowed ahead, vanishing gradually under a blanket of snow. The alpine conditions played to Kane's advantage, rendering the black-clad ninjas starkly visible against the pristine white landscape. This stark contrast facilitated Kane's cunning plan to draw closer to them, a task that seemed more achievable than he had initially anticipated.

With each step, Kane closed the distance, moving stealthily and strategically. His senses heightened, he calculated his approach carefully, mindful of every rustle of snow underfoot. The thrill of the hunt surged through him as he prepared to turn the tide, now poised to seize the upper hand in this perilous game of hunt and kill.

The slope steepened sharply, making each step a laborious climb for Kane. He waited patiently as twilight descended, the dim light providing him with the confidence to confront Shusuki and Naoki alone. His readiness mirrored that of a dedicated ninja, until he spotted a faint glow in the distance—a small fire where the two warriors had settled for the night.

Moving with impeccable stealth, Kane maneuvered towards the makeshift camp. The isolated flicker of their campfire served as an unwitting signal, casting long shadows that Kane used to his advantage. As Shusuki and Naoki scanned their surroundings in turns, Kane advanced methodically, finally positioning himself atop a vertical rock face just above their camp.

Summoning the strength he had before the stabbing incident, Kane launched himself from the overhanging cliff. His descent triggered a small avalanche of snow, engulfing the unsuspecting warriors below. In the chaos of the snowslide, Kane freed himself swiftly and regained his footing, poised to confront the assassins one by one. The night air was thick with tension as Kane moved with lethal intent, his senses sharp and focused. With the element of surprise on his side, he prepared to engage in a high-stakes battle against formidable opponents, driven by vengeance and the determination to emerge victorious from this perilous encounter.

Coughing and spluttering, Shusuki clawed his way out from beneath the icy debris, his breath ragged in the cold night air. As he cautiously lifted his gaze, he was met with the chilling sight of Kane standing above him, a long blade glinting in his grasp. Kane's presence seemed to loom larger than life in the eerie moonlight, casting a spectral glow around him that made him appear colossal and otherworldly. The shadows danced around his figure, enhancing the intensity of his stare and the sharpness of his features.

Shusuki's heart nearly stopped as he struggled to comprehend the perilous situation. The night had turned against them, and Kane, fueled by his thirst for retribution, now held the upper hand. Fear gripped Shusuki's throat like a claw, his mind racing with the sudden realization of their vulnerability in the face of Kane's relentless pursuit.

Each passing moment made the moonlight intensify the tension in the air, casting an eerie, surreal glow over the unfolding scene in the desolate mountain pass.

Shusuki's thoughts raced as he braced himself for the inevitable confrontation, knowing that their survival depended on their ability to outwit and outmaneuver Kane in this deadly game of cat and mouse.

"Stay on your knees and don't move" Kane demanded

"You have been sent by the Abbot to hunt me haven't you Shusuki?" "Hai" he answered softly, keeping his head bowed

"How many of you?" "Six brother Kane"

"Shut up.... I am not your brother, I never was.... you bullied me for years. Feeling all powerful as part of Hiro gang. You know I have to kill you," Kane's voice cut through the frozen air with disturning finality.

At that exact moment, Shusuki lifted his head to respond, but before any words escaped his lips, Kane swung his double-edged sword downward with brutal precision. The blade cleaved through flesh and bone, severing Shusuki's head from his shoulders in a swift, merciless strike.

Standing over the lifeless body, Kane flicked the blood off his blade with a sharp snap. His eyes scanned the snowy battlefield, adrenaline coursing through his veins. He remained alert, every sense heightened as he circled the crimson-stained snow, searching for his next target.

Suddenly, Naoki sprang into action from behind, launching a roundhouse kick aimed squarely at Kane's back. The impact reverberated through Kane's body, sending a jolt of pain through his spine. Reacting swiftly, Kane staggered forward, narrowly avoiding the full force of another blow.

With a snarl of a bulldog spirit, Kane's eyes were ablaze with fury. The dance of death had begun, each move calculated and lethal in the unforgiving wilderness. As they clashed amidst the swirling snow and shadows, the night bore witness to a relentless battle where survival demanded ferocity, skill, and the willingness to spill blood.

Suddenly, Kane whirled around to face Naoki, his grip on the sword tightening as he pointed it directly at his adversary. A vicious growl twisted Kane's face, his mouth elongating and distorting into a horrifying shape. His teeth extended into sharp fangs, glistening with saliva that dripped from their razor-sharp tips.

Naoki stood frozen, transfixed by the grotesque transformation unfolding before him. The sight of Kane's mutating features sent a chilling wave of terror through him, a disfiguration that seemed to defy all reason and logic. Fear gripped Naoki's heart as he realized the true nature of the foe he faced.

With a primal roar, Kane lunged forward, the elongated fangs driving deep into Naoki's chest with a sickening crunch. Pain seared through Naoki's body as the sharp points punctured his lung, stealing his breath and leaving him gasping for air in the freezing snow.

The taste of fresh blood flooded Kane's senses, sending a surge of savage exhilaration through his veins. He bellowed triumphantly into the darkness, consumed by the ecstasy of his conquest over his once-formidable opponent. Meanwhile, Naoki lay sprawled in the numbing cold, his strength ebbing away with each labored breath. The icy air stung his lungs, and with every exhale, he felt life slipping further from his grasp. Despite the agony, Naoki summoned the last remnants of his willpower to utter a few final words into the unforgiving night.

"Evil has its price, Kane.... others will come and condemn your soul," Naoki gasped, his voice strained with defiance even as his strength waned.

Kane's eyes narrowed with a cold purpose, unmoved by Naoki's final words. With a swift and merciless motion, he drove the blade deep into Naoki's heart. There was no hesitation, no hint of remorse in Kane's actions as he ended Naoki's life.

The snowy landscape bore witness to the grim tableau, the silence broken only by the harsh sound of Naoki's last breath escaping into the frigid air. Kane stood over his fallen foe, the weight of his deeds penetrating the stillness.

As he withdrew the sword from Naoki's lifeless body, Kane's expression remained stoic, hardened by the trials of his relentless stalking.

Naoki's final warning lingered in the air, and he knew others would come seeking vengeance, driven by the specter of his dark deeds. But in that moment, amidst the desolate terrain stained with blood and snow, Kane was unshaken in his conviction to survive at any cost.

In the early morning light, Kane retraced his steps along the snowy path, his mind set on exploring a less-traveled route. By midday, the trail led him to a well-worn dirt road, where the sounds of nature were soon joined by the approaching rumble of oxen and carts.

Positioning himself behind a massive oak tree, Kane waited with anticipation as two caravans rolled into view, their oxen laboring under heavy loads. He strained to see if it was Botan and his merchants, but as the wagons passed, he realized it was a different group entirely. Relieved, Kane stepped out from his concealment and seamlessly joined the convoy from the rear.

With his weathered farmer's hat pulled low to obscure his features and a sturdy wooden branch serving as his walking stick, Kane assumed the guise of an elderly wanderer. He blended effortlessly into the procession, falling into step behind one of the pilgrims, ready to journey onward with this new company.

As they continued down the road, Kane's senses were heightened with the thrill of adventure. Every stride brought him closer to new encounters, unknown destinations, and the unfolding chapters of his solitary quest.

"Hello" He greeted the man who jumped with surprise from the unexpected voice. "Oh you scared me" Answered the scruffy retailer

"Where are you headed?" Kane probed "Kyoto.....who are you?" The man asked "Just a traveler, like yourself"

"I am a trader thank you, so where did you come from? We did not pass you on the road"

"I've come from a monastery many days from here and I became lost when I veered off the road by mistake" Kane deluded the man

"Well that was a stupid thing to do.....it can be very dangerous traveling through the forest on your own" He warned

"Hai, I experienced that when I came across a foraging bear" Kane discreetly chuckled to himself.

"You are a lucky man then"

"Would it be alright if I travel with you until we reach Kyoto? I'll feel safer" "Hai" The man agreed, permitting Kane to carry on with them.

"But we must keep a vigilant watch for bandits, there has been gossip of criminals looting trailers along this road, but you're a stocky fellow, you will be an asset if we encounter any problems"

"I am happy that the monasteries and monks have brought Zen Buddhism to the Samurai. Instead of slaughtering innocent villagers, they are now focusing on their personal enlightenment through discipline and meditation" The man continued "You said that you've just come from a monastery.....are you a monk?.....you don't look like one" He quickly added

"I'm not a monk, I only visited the monastery for a short time for spiritual guidance" "Did you find it?"

"I'm not sure, I'm still searching for my purpose and honor in life" Kane insightfully disclosed.

"What is your name?" The old man inquired "I have no name" Kane replied

"Pffft" Was the only comment the merchant expressed and as they continued the rest of the journey in silence, Kane's well-worn Tabi sandals embraced each onward step, and provided him with the thirst for a better future, a life that others would not gaze upon as worthless.

In the intricate tapestry of Japanese society, traders found themselves relegated to the lowest rung. Perceived as parasites who contributed little while benefiting from others' toil, they became prime targets for bandits seeking validation for their illicit acts of theft.

Amidst periods of famine and economic turmoil, these outlaws emerged as a product of necessity rather than choice. For them, banditry wasn't just a means of survival

but a bold defiance against societal norms and economic

constraints. They navigated a harsh world with ruthless grit , showing no mercy as they pursued their own form of justice in an unforgiving landscape.

Late in the afternoon, after a full day's journey, the convoy encountered a man and a young boy ambling along the road. As the wagons maneuvered to one side to pass them, Kane noticed the boy's curious gaze fixed upon him.

Their eyes locked in an unexpected moment of connection. Kane's gaze, warm and engaging, seemed to captivate the child, who felt an instant bond with the towering stranger. Unable to contain his joy, the boy broke into the widest smile imaginable, and Kane responded with a wink, returning the smile with equal warmth.

In that fleeting exchange, amongst the dust and noise of the road, a simple gesture bridged the gap between two souls, leaving an indelible mark of kindness and camaraderi on them both.

As twilight descended, casting its soft glow over the weary travelers, the caravan veered off the road to make camp. The merchants swiftly set about their tasks: the cook wrestling with a stubborn fire, others tending to the oxen, and allowing them to graze on the hay.

Meanwhile, Kane had slipped into the forest earlier and returned with a bounty of rabbits, pheasants, and squirrels cradled in his arms. The group greeted him with astonishment and heartfelt appreciation as he presented his unexpected gift—a feast from the wilderness that promised warmth and sustenance.

"Here throw these in your stew" He chuckled, placing the game beside the cooking pot.

"Thank you so much.... we don't know your name," the cook declared, breaking the awkward silence that had settled over the group.

"His name is No Name!" shouted Kane's initial friend from the caravan. "Is that right, mister?" the cook inquired with a hint of curiosity.

"Hai, it is... Until I find my purpose and destiny determines my future, I shall be known as 'No Name,'" Kane proclaimed, throwing his arms up dramatically towards the heavens.

The caravan erupted in laughter, appreciating Kane's jest and the lighthearted moment amidst their evening preparations. It seemed the mysterious wanderer had found not just a name, but a bit of humor to carry along on his journey.

Once dinner was cooked, everyone gathered eagerly around the campfire and savored the hearty rabbit, pheasant, and squirrel stew, letting out satisfied sounds with every mouthful. The flavors mingled with the warmth of the fire, creating a cozy atmosphere that felt like home.

After they had licked their bowls clean, they crudely rinsed the dishes in a basin of water, sharing stories and laughter as they cleaned up together. With bellies full and spirits high, they retired for the night under the watchful sky, grateful for the warmth of the fire and the companionship of their journeying companions.

The morning dawned brightly, casting a renewed sense of optimism over Kane as he took in a deep breath and stretched out the remnants of last night's slumber.

His arms extended higher than the wagon beside him, prompting a few merchants to gather around and marvel at his towering stature.

"You would make a fierce warrior, No Name," remarked one of them.

"Hai, and you couldn't miss him in a crowd either," added the other man with a chuckle.

"I've heard that most of my life... my size runs in the family," Kane replied with a smile, feeling a sense of friendship with the convoy as they set off on their final day's journey towards the city of Kyoto. The day ahead held promises of new adventures and perhaps even uncovering more about his mysterious origins.

As the metropolis loomed closer, Kane found himself captivated by the beauty of the surrounding countryside. Well-manicured orchards stretched out before him, their blossoming flowers filling the air with a sweet fragrance. His anticipation grew as they approached the ancient city, its gates beckoning with promises of bustling markets and vibrant culture.

Just outside the city limits, Kane observed two crowded farmer's markets vibrant with activity. Passing through the majestic gates, he was immediately struck by the sight and sound of the lively urban center. A public flogging in the main courtyard caught his attention, a stark reminder of the city's law enforcement practices.

Amidst the commotion, Kane's eyes darted from one intriguing scene to another.

A vendor enthusiastically hawked bolts of silk from his shop, their striking colors catching the sunlight. Nearby, monks went door-to-door seeking donations for a new monastery bell, their serene presence contrasting with the buzzing city life. A group of samurais rode past with an air of importance towards Nijo Castle, adding to the city's aura of history and tradition.

On another corner, Kane spotted a mother assisting her child, a simple yet poignant moment amidst the city's hustle. Each sight and sound filled Kane with a mix of curiosity and wonder, eager to explore the depths of this ancient city.

"This is the best place for you, No Name. It's a clean boarding house, good food too.....you can stay here. Do you have any money? His friend asked, simultaneously pulling up in front of a guest house.

"No I don't" Kane admitted, then instantly thought of the witch's gold tooth still hiding in his pocket....."*Should I sell it?"* He thought long and hard as his traveling pal shoved a few dollars into his hands.

"Here, this is for the rabbits and pheasants, we still have plenty of meat left, so this is for your trouble. If you want work, go to the Izakayas Bar and ask for Goro. Keep out of harm's way... ..not everyone here is a good person, ok No Name? Good luck.....

I hope the journey brings you closer to your destiny" Waving goodbye, the merchant and his wagon moved down the street and further into the city, eventually disappearing amongst the dust and throngs of activity.

Kane settled into the Japanese Inn, securing a cozy tatami-matted room for himself. After making himself comfortable, he decided to unwind and rejuvenate at the communal bath, where the air was fragrant with the scent of orange blossoms. The warm water eased his aches and soreness, allowing him a moment of relaxation.

As he soaked, thoughts of Shusuki's revelation lingered in his mind. He pondered the proximity of the other four ninjas and strategized on how to evade their capture.

Kane began formulating a plan, considering his next moves

carefully in this unfamiliar yet intriguing city.

Chapter 4

The medics moved around the infirmary with a hushed urgency, their footsteps barely making a sound as they tended to Gideon's injuries. He had stirred from unconsciousness but remained disoriented, his mind clouded by the potent concoctions administered by the doctor.

With every gentle approach, Gideon's grip tightened around each medic's arm, his eyes blazing with desperate intensity as he anxiously demanded news about Eshin.

"How is the Abbot?" he asked, his voice a mix of worry and desperation. The medics exchanged worried glances, not sure how to break the news to him. They needed to focus on his recovery, but they also understood the deep bond between the two friends. It was a delicate balance, reassuring him while keeping his hopes grounded. "I saw him fall to the floor and there was a lot of blood. Is he alright?" Gideon's voice trembled with concern, his eyes pleading for reassurance.

"Sshh, just rest, Master Gideon," the friars murmured softly, trying to soothe him. "Where is he? I want to know what happened to him," Gideon demanded, his tone urgent and filled with worry.

“He passed away from his injuries.... The funeral ceremony was held last week,” the friar’s voice carried a heavy burden of sorrow.

Upon learning that his beloved Eshin had died, Gideon let out a horrific scream, a raw expression of grief and disbelief. Tears streamed down his face as the reality of his friend’s death shattered him, the vivid memory of Eshin’s final moments haunting him relentlessly.

“It was Kane.....he is the one who murdered Eshin. I saw him partially mutate into a demon bear” He weeped

“It’s ok, please calm yourself, Master Gideon. I will let the residing Abbot know that you’re awake and you can discuss the experience with him”

“It’s not ok. Kane is a cold-blooded murderer and no one knows what he’s capable of. He’s not human. I want to talk to the Abbot now” Gideon shouted, as he attempted to convince the friar that he wasn’t delusional.

“Hai, I will summon him right away” The friar conceded and swiftly walked out of the room.

With Gideon’s anxiety slightly relieved by the promise of clarity regarding the tragic incident, he settled into a restless wait for the Abbot, who arrived within the hour. The Abbot’s approach was deliberate, his footsteps measured as he approached Master Gideon with concern.

“Master Gideon, it’s good to see you conscious and attentive. It was touch and go with you for a while. The doctors have been taking care of you” The Abbot began the conversation with a mild greeting.

"Abbot.....oh I'm so glad you're here. I must tell you that Master Kane did all of this, he's the devil incarnate and he was the one who killed Eshin.....you have to find him and punish him for what he has done" Gideon spoke with a rising shrill in his voice. "Yes, we understand that Master Kane is the perpetrator of this immoral act"

"What are you doing about it Abbot? Where is the demon now? Have you captured him? Is he imprisoned yet?" Gideon blurted out one question after the other.

"No, we haven't been able to find him. He ran off into the valley after the attack.

I have sent six of our best ninja warriors to hunt him down, but as yet, there's been no news of his whereabouts" Abbot Akio reassured, as he didn't want Gideon to escalate his already intensified demeanor.

"Who did you send.....which warriors did you choose? Because I can honestly say from personal experience that the incubus within Kane is all-powerful and not of this earth. The ones who pursue him have to be the best in stealth and endurance, plus their mindset has to be sharp. You truly don't know what we're dealing with" Master Gideon warned with a frantic look on his face.

"Hai, some of our best ninjas, like Hiro and Naoki are tracking him as we speak.

I am confident that they will bring Master Kane back here to face judgment in due time"

"Please tell me in detail what happened that fateful afternoon. I need to know" The Abbot continued as he pulled up a chair and sat beside the patient, while Gideon began outlining in detail what he had witnessed.....he even included his discovery of the freakish human-skinned book.

"Where is this book now?" The Abbot enquired

"It's in the library.....don't worry I hid it in a special place" Gideon reassured Once the Abbot had acquired knowledge of the whole story, he asked to see the

ninja Master and proposed that they send an additional warrior to act as a scout..... His mission was to gather information about how far the original troupe had advanced and to immediately report back, so they chose Miko, a steward, but one of the more experienced brothers in tracking, and he departed soon after collecting his instructions.

As Gideon relaxed knowing that he had candidly disclosed the terrible events, he laid back down onto the pillow just as the doctor walked in.

"Master Gideon, we need to change your bandages" He directed "Please sit up for me"

"Can I look at my reflection doctor?" Gideon requested

"I don't think that's a good idea at this stage. Your injuries are still quite raw and they are very prominent" The doctor warned

"Just let me look, it's my face" Gideon challenged willfully

"Alright then" The doctor conceded, so as he removed the last piece of gauze, the doctor asked one of the friars to collect the "white bronzed" mirror.

Handing it to Gideon, both medics watched as he slowly raised it in front of him, revealing his altered face. He stared in disbelief at the deep gouges that marred his once unmarked skin, a testament to the ferocity of Kane's attack. He realized with a jolt that he was now branded, forever changed by the encounter—a survivor of a deadly confrontation with an evil beast.

Raising his hand to touch the brutal scars, Gideon felt a surge of shock and awe at the power it took to survive. Yet, alongside his relief, a profound sadness settled in. *"These wounds will heal,"* he thought, *"but the loss of Eshin will follow me forever."*

The scars, stretching from his temple to his jaw, served as a stark reminder of the price of vengeance and the deep bond he shared with his fallen friend.

His left eye had suffered severe damage during the attack.

Despite the doctors' heated discussions and the glint of rudimentary surgical tools at the ready, they ultimately decided against the risky procedure.

Now, it remained in his socket—a white sphere with a distinctive black jagged line running down the middle, splitting the eyelid and dividing his pupil. The eye bore a striking resemblance to a distorted goat's eye, its unsettling appearance catching the attention of anyone who looked upon it.

Gideon wasn't disgusted by his reflection, instead, he believed that it gave him the appearance of a victorious warrior and the story he would tell in the future about battling the devil would be the stuff legends are made of.

* * *

Miko raced through the forest track like lightning, halting occasionally to scrutinize any signs of recent travelers. A day into his journey, he came upon the decaying remains of Kane's partially devoured boar. Its belly was torn open, intestines spilling out, and nearby lay a deep imprint of a large paw in the soft mud. Miko concluded it must have been a wild bear and continued his pursuit.

Crossing the river downstream, he encountered no sign of the grotesque, deformed tribespeople but soon passed by the witch's dilapidated cabin.

Peering inside through the open doorway, he saw only scattered ashes on the ground and dilapidated furniture, leading him to believe it was an abandoned shack. Without hesitation, he pressed forward.

By the third day, Miko had reached the alpine region. As he climbed the steep, elevated path, he heard the frantic flapping of bird wings and spotted something ahead, lying next to a large mound of snow.

Drawing closer, he stumbled upon the mangled bodies of Shusuki and Naoki. Shock coursed through him as he beheld the gruesome aftermath of slaughter. The stark red stains contrasted vividly against the pristine snow, and the metallic scent of blood hung heavy in the air, leaving him reeling with disbelief at the brutality before him.

He deliberated whether to continue his quest for the surviving ninjas or return to the monastery, so he chose the latter, accepting that the Abbot would want to know that two of his most aggressive warriors had been overpowered and lay dead in the wilderness. After closely inspecting his brother's traumatic injuries, immediately cringing at the brutality and the frozen mortified expression on Naoki's face, Miko reversed his journey and turned back towards the abbey to communicate his macabre discovery with the superior monks.

Breathless as he entered the monastery doors, Miko promptly confronted Abbot Akio, who was sitting next to Gideon's convalescent bed.

"I didn't expect to find you back here so soon, what have you learned?" The Abbot queried

"I found Shusuki and Naoki dead in the mountains. Shusuki was dismembered, his head laid two feet from his body and the grisly look on Naoki's face will be stamped in my memory forever. Also, I think Kane is heading for Kyoto" He confessed "See? I told you Abbot.....this is the diabolical work of that Kane, he's the devil's spawn. Running away like a guilty coward" Gideon blurted out

"Are you going to deploy any more ninjas?" He continued

"No, the remaining four will be sufficient. They are experienced lethal warriors and it wouldn't be spiritually pure sending amateur ninjas to meet certain death"

"When I regain my strength, would you allow me to join the hunt?" Gideon pleaded "We will decide on that when you are fully healed my friend" Expressed the concerned Abbot.

He grasped Gideon's animosity towards Kane but felt uneasy about what Gideon planned to do once he found him. Each passing day saw Gideon gaining strength, encouraged to explore more of the monastery. His fellow monks would step aside reverently, bowing in respect as he walked past, honoring the man who had confronted pure malevolence and lived to tell the tale.

On a particular day, Gideon entered the columbarium, where Eshin's remains were enshrined atop a pillar. He knelt solemnly before the funerary urn, deep in meditation and prayer. With a heavy heart, he made an oath of retribution for Eshin's death—a vow that conflicted deeply with the teachings of the Buddhist faith.

His loathing for the murderer also extended to the beheading of his innocent cat and the two butchered ninjas lying discarded in the mountains and promised that a more atrocious fate was waiting for Kane.

Even though he was a peaceful man, Gideon vowed that he would have the predator dragged by a horse to his place of execution, bound to a stake and whipped with rods until his flesh erupted. Finally, he would decapitate him like the mongrel dog that he was.

Gideons confidential decision on Kane's demise was resolute and his vindictiveness ached for the day he'd be strong enough to carry out the sadistic punishment, as far as he was concerned Kane deserved everything that was coming to him.

As he lay back down in his hospital bed, his thoughts fixated on the human-skinned book he believed still resided in the library. Determined to find it, he used his allotted free time the next day to venture into the scriptorium.

He went straight to the secret spot where he'd hidden it, but it wasn't there. Panic rising, he began a meticulous search, pulling every book from its place, leaving no corner unexamined.

"Where is it?" he muttered repeatedly to himself.

The old monk spent hours searching even the most unlikely spots. When his hunt yielded nothing, he reached a disturbing conclusion: that Kane must have taken it. In that moment, Gideon realized the profound connection between the book and the demon.

Kane had lived at the monastery for most of his young life.

Besides being a sneaky troublemaker, known for his occasional insolence and constant nightly outbursts, his demonic behavior had not emerged until the mysterious book appeared. With this realization, Gideon gathered the Abbot and the three ninja Masters to discuss his concerns.

"I've thoroughly searched the library for the book and it's nowhere to be found, so I believe that Kane has taken it with him" Gideon declared

"Why would he do that?" One of the ninja Masters asked "The two are linked, that's why"

"How do you know this Master Gideon?" Abbot Akio cooly asked

"Because when the book emerged, that's when I noticed Kane altering into the monster, he'd always been a weird kid but his metamorphosis didn't exist until the book turned up. I'm absolutely sure he's got it"

"When will I be able to leave the infirmary, I feel fine and my injuries are quickly healing, please release me from the infernal hospital bed" He pleaded

"Hai, you may leave tomorrow. You seem to have more knowledge of what's going on than anyone else, so I think we could use your expertise, Gideon. We also need to retrieve the bodies of Shusuki and Naoki and give them an honorable burial as soon as possible. Please fetch the steward Miko" He ordered

"Thank you, Abbot" Then the four monks left to further discuss their plans as the summoned guide approached.

Miko stood at attention in front of the Abbot, as he listened intently to his instructions to escort hand-picked monks to the frozen graves of his brothers and bring them home.

"Select four ninjas and go to the mountain where our deceased brothers rest and bring them back here" Abbot directed

"Hai" Miko obeyed and after choosing his companions they headed off into the challenging forest with Miko leading the way, eventually reaching their fallen brothers a few days later as evening veiled the day with darkness.

The night was cloudy, but a full moon cast its eerie glow through the breaks in the clouds, illuminating the snow-covered ground. Staring down at the remnants of two mutilated bodies, they were overwhelmed with disgust. The presence of evil was obvious, and panic surged through them as they heard weird scratching and panting sounds from behind.

About fifty yards away, in the middle of the path, a grotesque figure emerged.

It resembled a large bear, but its front limbs were twisted and noodle-like, with clenched fists hovering two inches above the ground. The creature's deformed body bore human hands and feet, and it fixed its unnatural, glowing red eyes upon them. The gaze was the most terrifying they had ever seen, freezing them in sheer horror. A thick, dirty brown coat covered its emaciated body. When the ninjas stood their ground, unsheathing their swords, the beast charged towards them on its hind legs, moving with inhuman speed. Its spine-chilling scream, eerily similar to that of a traumatized infant, echoed through the night.

With heroic defiance, the ninjas attacked, their long blades slicing through the air towards the demon's torso. But as their swords made contact, the creature disintegrated into thin air, enveloping the defenders in a cloud of fine black dust. The tormented, childlike shrieks faded into the depths of the murky forest, leaving the ninjas standing in stunned silence, covered in the remnants of the vanished horror.

"What was that?" One of the warriors commented "I'm sure it was Kane" Miko replied

"How can it be him? The demon just vanished right in front of us"

"I've overheard our superiors talking and they said Kane possesses the devil's abilities and there's a human skinned book compelling him to do its bidding" "Hai, but that doesn't explain the hallucination. Do you think it was Kane or the manifestation of the bewitched book?"

"How would I know? But let's not stand around chatting. Quickly, gather our brother's remains and return to the abbey" Miko instructed with uneasiness in his voice, so with the large hessian bags that they'd brought with them, the men loaded the body parts in them, and flung the packs over their shoulders, then made a swift exit for home.

Dawn was breaking when the group finally returned to the monastery, placing the near-empty body bags at the Abbot's feet while Gideon stood closely behind him. "Is this all that remains of Shusuki and Naoki?" He questioned.

"Hai, there wasn't much left of them. It looks as though carnivores had their fill before we got there" Miko explained

Simultaneously the Abbot and Gideon scrutinized the men, noticing that they looked both confused and threatened, a look that wasn't customary for these savage warriors.

"What's wrong? Something else has happened. What is it?" The Abbot asked intuitively

"Ahh, we encountered an apparition while recovering the bodies" Miko explained as he gave his comrades a quick glance.

"An apparition?" Abbot queried

"What did it look like? Was it a bear?" Gideon interjected
"Hai, sort of a bear"

"Please continue to describe what you saw Miko" Abbot encouraged

"We heard something behind us in the shadows, on the path we had traveled and when we turned around there was this distorted being, half bear half-human.

I mean it had the body of a bear but deformed human hands and feet and it had

these red glowing eyes just staring at us" Miko continued, providing a comprehensive report of the experience and an absolute description of the demon.

"Did it attack?" Gideon asked

"Hai, but when we drew our swords and struck the beast, it just simply dissolved into a cloud of black dust. Also, because of the path we tracked, we believe that Master Kane is heading towards Kyoto"

"Is that the demon's residue you're covered in?" "Hai" Miko responded

"Ok, go and wash the sediment off and return to the altar to pray, but first take the body bags to the attending friars in the crematorium" Abbot instructed

"Hai" The men agreed, bowing to their superiors, then collectively advanced down the corridor.

"Do you believe what they have said is true Gideon?"

"Hai, they have no reason to fabricate and their description of the beast does resemble what I have witnessed, although at the time Kane did not have the ability to completely transform. I believe that the human skinned book is aiding his possession plus it appears to have a power of its own"

"You are right my friend, the sooner he's captured the better for everyone" The Abbot stated

"I want to be included with the succeeding group of warriors you send" Gideon implored again

"You will, but let's focus on your recovery and the burial ceremony for Shusuki and Naoki and then you can depart. I believe that your own experience with the demon will be invaluable to the other warriors once he is detained. Also, I would be very interested to learn about Master Kane's origins before he was adopted into the monastery. When you begin the hunt for Kane, start at the village he was found in, someone there might have information. If you can find anything, it would be most appreciated. I think it will provide us with a clearer insight into what we are actually dealing with"

"Hai and thank you Abbot" Gideon said, then retreated back to the confinement of the library to further study the monastery's journals on demons and exorcism rituals. On his quest for knowledge, Gideon spent weeks in the library, only leaving the treasured publications to pay his respects at the cremation ceremony for their late comrades, to then withdraw back into the library, his driving passion for Kane's destruction, consuming his every waking moment.

The day of his departure had arrived and Gideon was ordered to pick another two ninjas, replacing Shusuki and Naoki, so the old monk chose Miko, who had exceptional tracking skills, and Haruto, a novice ninja that revered the old monk and would do anything he asked.

"Before you start your search, go to the village and gain information about him. When you have learned more, send Haruto straight back here to report" The Abbot requested, addressing Gideons escorting monks.

"Hai" The two ninjas obeyed and the Abbot indicated his blessings over them with his customary prayers and smoking incense before making their way along the dusty road.

The remote pastoral settlement where Kane lived as an orphaned derelict lay two days' journey away. Upon arrival, the brothers wasted no time and immediately began their investigation.

They chose not to wear their traditional ninja uniforms but instead dressed as monks, wearing their usual tunics adorned with scapulars and cowls. This disguise was intended to be less intimidating, allowing the villagers to feel more at ease when conversing with them.

"When you're speaking with the townspeople, describe Kane as a large child, abnormally hairy, its color dark brown and not black like a customary Japanese youngster. I understand that most of them won't recall him because it was many years ago but mention that he ended up being adopted by the monastery. Be gentle with them and don't tell them anything more. Eventually, someone will remember him" Gideon instructed and the three men began knocking on the doors of the elevated houses.

By the afternoon Gideon approached the residence of a very old woman and as she opened the door, she was surprised to see a monk standing on her porch.

"Hai?" She said

"Good afternoon. I'm wondering if you remember a war orphan, it was many years ago, around fifteen as I recall. He was a very large child, heavily covered with brown hair all over his body, he would've been about five years old at the time. The monastery two days ride from here adopted him"

The old woman didn't answer straight away, instead, she just glared at Gideon with a spooked look on her face, dismayed as she ogled his grisly unmasked facial injuries. "Hai, I remember him. How could I forget? They found the child living under my house" She finally expressed

"May I come in to further discuss your experience in private?" Gideon questioned The woman moved to one side, signaling the monk to enter and they both sat down on tatami mats.

"What made you remember this boy?" Gideon prodded

"My memory might be fading a little but I'll never forget him" She said in a modest tone, her eyes downcast, afraid to look at the monk.

"I am sorry that my scars are upsetting you" He said softly "No, it's alright" The woman lied, shaking her head "Would you like some tea?" She continued

"Hai.....Please tell me about the boy"

"I heard a whimpering sound coming from under my house, so I went outside to find out what it was. I could see a huge arm with matted hair, reddish-brown and sticky looking, you know primitive" She said, staring at the ground, nervously wringing her hands together.

"Go on" Gideon encouraged, intrigued with what she was about to say.

"I tempted the boy with food, trying to make him come out of the hiding place but it took three days before he accepted the bread and when he began eating it, he

sounded like a wild dog, growling and snarling at me. He was feral" She took a sip of tea, gaining her composure

"Did he eventually come out?"

"Hai, after throwing chunks of bread and meat under the house, it was like feeding a broody chicken"

"I eventually lured him inside and tried cleaning him up, but all of that hair made it too difficult, so I shaved him all over, except for his head and that's when I saw a large birthmark on his chest"

"What did it look like, this birthmark?" Gideon interrupted "Can you draw it for me?"

So the old lady gathered her ink brush and paper and carefully drew a picture of a sickle.

"That is it.....I'm fairly sure of it. My mind isn't like it used to be" She chuckled Gideon stared at the piece of paper and immediately recognized the symbol..... it matched the same mark on the human-skinned book.

"Are you certain this is what you saw on his body?" "Hai, of course" The old lady answered curiously "Why do you look for him?" She continued

"We just need a bit of background history, nothing to be concerned about" He pacified

"Do you want more information about the boy then?" "Hai, if you know anything else, I'd be most appreciative"

"He didn't stay here long. His untamed behavior was too much for me, so I asked some of the village men to take him away to the monastery.

But I must tell you that gossip began circling around the village once he was gone, you know, about how the *"animal child"* came to be"

Gideon naturally moved closer towards the old lady as she discreetly squirmed backward, putting distance between them.

"A man passed through the village not long after the boy had left. He seemed to be searching for the boy."

"The drifter told the story of a large child covered in hair. It had been captured but eventually escaped the tyranny of the Samurai."

"After some time, the only reason the Samurai set him free was that they thought he was possessed, which scared the superstitious warriors, so no one would touch him or want to be around him"

"The man said that the boy's mother was in labor for many hours one stormy night while her friends gathered around. This baby was going to be her thirteenth child. Unbeknown to the small group, the visiting midwife was a witch and as she began delivering the baby, the malicious old woman, who had different colored eyes, clutched a strange book above the mothers bulging stomach, circling it around, then

released it. The book immediately hovered in mid-air, while the witch chanted a spell and as the child finally emerged, it was so large and hairy, the excruciating pain from its size and the massive blood loss swiftly killed the mother"

The following night, a wet nurse was looking after the baby and all the child did was continually wail an ungodly cry, like it was calling for something, until a giant animal skulked into the house, from the shadows.

It was said that as the creature picked the child out of the bassinet, it stood on its hind legs and the baby stopped screaming, instead it began crooning and effortlessly changed into a deformed creature with wooly paws and lengthy talons.

The traveler claimed the creature was the child's father. He stole the baby that night, it was the Devil himself, very powerful and extremely evil. After the demon and the child vanished, they were never seen again.....until the boy turned up under my house"

"Whatever happened to the strange book?" Gideon asked

"No one knows. It just disappeared with the sorceress... ..anyway that's all there is" The woman sighed and finally looked into Gideon's eyes.

"If you don't mind me asking, did the child cause those injuries to your face?" "Hai.....he is no longer a child though, but a very dangerous man. I fought a fierce battle with him but he wasn't able to defeat me" Gideon divulged modestly but with a tinge of pride in his voice.

"You are very brave" She complimented

"Thank you San (madam). Your story has been enlightening and will help with our quest" He smiled, blessing the woman and proceeded on his way, gathering the other monks.

"I have new information that needs to be communicated to the Abbot. We know more about Kane's origins and I believe his powers are increasing" He warned, so Gideon transferred the details of the old woman's story to Haruto, tacitly whispering in his ear and the young ninja headed back to the convent post haste.

"Master Gideon, please allow me to find a horse for you. It is many days travel to Kyoto and after your convalescence, I think it would be best" Miko advised "Hai.....you're right" Gideon agreed, so that afternoon the two monks were provided a horse, food supplies and given shelter for the night by the villagers, before beginning their arduous hunt at first daylight.

Gideon harbored no apprehensions about catching up with Kane; he placed unwavering trust in Hiro and his accompanying ninjas. His primary concern lay in gathering information and deepening his understanding of the situation at hand.

Years spent poring over literature on demonic possession and grappling with his own struggles against Kane had honed Gideon's insights. With each revelation, he began to speculate that the entity they faced was not merely a human spirit possessed but

something entirely unprecedented—an entity outside the realm of the church's past encounters.

The knowledge he would amass during this expedition was set to become his greatest asset, promising to secure glory and honor for his legacy. Gideon saw this pursuit not just as a mission, but as a defining moment in his ongoing battle against the forces of darkness.

The horse trudged down the frequented road, carrying the monk on its back, with Miko walking in front of it, as he led the way to Kyoto.

"Master Miko" Gideon said breaking the silence between them "Hai" He answered, still moving onwards

"I know that your devotion to our brotherhood is resolute, but are you fully aware of what you're about to undertake when we finally arrest Master Kane?"

"I think so, he is bewitched by a poltergeist and is a dangerous murderer" Miko replied innocently

"He is more than that my son" "What is he then?"

"I believe he's a skin-changer"

"A what? I've never heard of that before Master Gideon. Is it a sickness?"

"No, he was born like that, he's not an authentic Japanese man either, he's a half breed and I'm sure his ancestors originated from another land, or universe. There's black magic involved.

Be very careful when we eventually come into contact with him Miko, I don't want you in harm's way. Be aware of his deceptive tricks" Gideon warned

"Tricks?"

"I'm not sure if Kane has fully evolved yet but I know he is getting stronger by the day and my studies have taught me that he can "steal" the faces of different people and could appear as someone you know"

"Avoid looking directly into his eyes too, as he can absorb himself into your body and take control of your actions and he is able to run incredibly fast over a long distance" "How many of these creatures exist Master Gideon?"

"I don't know, but one thing I'm sure of is there's one in Japan and it must be destroyed as soon as possible"

The duo pressed on with their expedition, their minds heavy with thoughts of the impending confrontation with Kane, weighed down by a deep sense of apprehension.

Since leaving the village, Gideon had been troubled by a pervasive, stifling odor that hung in the air. It was noxious, a sickening blend of stale urine and wet dog, growing more offensive and nauseating with every step along the highway.

"What's that horrible smell? It's all around us," Miko remarked, wrinkling his nose in distaste. His words were punctuated by the sudden appearance of a motionless shape in the middle of the road, about fifty yards ahead.

As soon as it was spotted, the creature darted into the underbrush. It circled back, staying just within sight of the monks, stalking them from behind the tree line. Gideon remained vigilant, covertly observing its every move, keenly aware of its presence.

The greyish-brown animal sported a long, white-tipped tail, with triangular-shaped pupils of different colors. As it approached closer to the men, a dreadful stench emanated from it, becoming increasingly intoxicating and causing them to gag.

Quickly, they grabbed their shawls and pressed them against their faces, desperate to shield themselves from the overpowering odor.

"The smells getting worse and I think it's coming from that wolf over there" Miko said, pointing in its direction

"I know, it's been following us since we left the village. That's a witch dog, could be another skin changer" Gideon declared

"What does it want?"

"Just to spy on us and find out what we know. Don't worry Miko"

Gideon pulled on the reins, his horse coming to a sudden halt and turned his face directly towards the spying creature and with power in his commanding voice, he screamed

"Be gone with you beast.....All the forces of darkness cannot stop what God has ordained for you.....get behind me skin-changer"

The wolf-like dog stared at him for a moment, then howled a long drawn out cry, as in protest at his words and ran off into the murky depths of the forest, disappearing into its darkness and taking the foul stench with it.

"Thank goodness for that. The smell was unbearable, I think it was trying to kill me"

Miko joked

"Don't take these things lightly Miko. You are about to witness some terrifying events. But that was definitely a scout...

..a vessel of treachery and deceit"

"Do you think it's Kane?"

"No, I believe Master Kane is still trying to work out his identity. He hasn't acquired the knowledge or skills to fully mutate or summon a creature for his own bidding yet. This is something else. Let's move on Miko, the sooner we get to Kyoto the better" It took the monks four days to reach their destination. As they approached the impressive city gates, they passed through outlying orchard fields and a bustling street market. Miko was struck with astonishment at the diverse array of people milling around, passionately bargaining over the value of commodities at various stalls.

Next to the entrance, a lively theatrical performance captivated a crowd. Laughter echoed as people enjoyed the slapstick comedy, the unfamiliar joy pulling Miko in closer. He unexpectedly halted just behind a group of amused spectators gathered around the stage.

"Why are you stopping Master Miko?" Gideon asked with displeasure in his voice. "Oh Master Gideon, look at the show, isn't it wonderful? I've never seen anything like it before. Can we just watch for a minute?" Miko pleaded, his lack of experience of the mainstream world adding to the curiosity.

"We must keep moving on" Gideon tried convincing him "We've traveled for days, may I please watch for a little while?"

Still mounted on the horse, Gideon looked down at the fledgling monk and felt leniency entering his heart, so he relented.

"Hai.....alright but just for a short while Miko, we still have to find lodgings before there are no vacancies left. I don't want to spend another night camping" He huffed Observing that the number of people watching his performance was increasing, the enthusiastic showman invigorated his entertainment and began telling jokes while a contortionist twisted her body into unusual shapes and positions on the side of the stage.

"Tell me everyone.....What would bears be without bees?" He shouted "Ears" And the crowd exploded into laughter at the oneliner

.

"How can a bear catch fish without a pole?" "They use their bear hands"

"What happens when a bear is in the rain for too long?" "He becomes a drizzly bear"

After every joke, the crowd roared with laughter and then the presenter recited a short ditty as another performer entered the stage, cloaked in a large bear pelt.

"Fuzzy wuzzy was a bear a bear was fuzzy wuzzy
when fuzzy-wuzzy lost his hair
he wasn't fuzzy wuzzy.....was he?"

Appreciating the clever satire, Gideon chuckled quietly to himself as he merrily watched Miko clapping and cheering when suddenly the entertainer abruptly turned his face directly towards the old monk and spoke with an inhuman voice, the slow deep rumble was a polar opposite to his usual high pitched tone and it said: *"Beware, Gideon—Shadow Bear knows you're coming for him."*

Then, as if nothing had happened, the man turned back to the actors in front of him, his voice slipping seamlessly into an excitable falsetto. He became entirely absorbed in the performance, as though those menacing words had never been spoken. "Miko!! Miko!! Gideon shouted, trying to get the boy's attention.

"Hai Master Gideon" He finally replied still attempting to catch a peek at the show "Did you hear what that man said to me?"

"Hai, his jokes are really funny.....look at him now, he's fighting the bear skinned covered man"

"So you didn't hear him tell me a threatening message?" "No" Miko answered perplexed at his questions

"Are you alright Master Gideon, you look very pale"

"Oh, look—the bear is killing the man, standing over his victim… and now he's flung off the pelt, returning to being just a man. Hmmm, that's a strange performance. It's peculiar how it mirrors what Kane has become."

Miko continued, "Come on, let's book a room so you can get some rest, Master Gideon."

As Miko led the horse into the city, Gideon remained silent, his thoughts lost in the unsettling resemblance of the performance.

After securing their lodgings for the night and drawing Master Gideon a hot soothing bath, Miko asked permission to venture outside and take in the city's vitality before dark and understanding he was once a young man himself, Gideon agreed.

"Don't stay out too late, Miko. It's not safe. Keep your eyes and ears open for any information about Kane. If he's been here in the last few weeks, someone will know something."

"Hai Master Gideon, I will be back soon" And Miko bowed, shutting the partition doors behind him.

As he immersed himself in the soothing water, the old monk closed his eyes and allowed the recent demonic episodes to play out in his mind. He replayed them repeatedly, searching for any hint of vulnerability or weakness.

However, instead of uncovering frailty in Kane, the skin-changer bound to the human-skinned book, he came to a frightening realization. It was the book itself that harbored the true demonic energy. The prospect of finding it and delving into its enigmatic contents thrilled him. He longed to study its mysteries and deepen his knowledge of other spirit worlds.

A shiver ran through him at the thought of Kane's impending transformation and the increasing strength it would bring. In that moment of contemplation, the monk understood the grave threat they faced, not just from Kane's evolving abilities but from the malevolent power embedded within the ancient book.

The bustling crowds seemed to pulsate with a life of their own, overwhelming Miko as he took in the lively spectacle. Everywhere he looked, people clad in vibrant clothes engaged in animated conversations—buyers and sellers, old friends catching up, and new acquaintances forming, each driven by their own goals for the evening. The scene revealed a gradual assimilation of Western influences through the locals' evolving attire, a shift from traditional styles to more contemporary fashion.

Further along their path, Miko found himself drawn into a prestigious tea house. Inside, he was captivated by the sight of Geisha girls, their dramatic appearance enhanced by elaborate hairstyles adorned with cascading floral ornaments. Each movement they made seemed to mesmerize onlookers, especially as they skillfully played traditional Japanese instruments.

Amidst this cultural immersion, a male geisha named Hokan performed elegant tea ceremonies and recounted captivating stories, adding to the enchantment of the tea house experience. Miko couldn't help but be swept up in the allure of this blend of tradition and modernity unfolding before him.

Miko lingered in the tea house, blending seamlessly into the dynamic streetscape, his monk's demeanor granting him the freedom to move about unnoticed. He absorbed the snippets of conversation that floated past, each one a potential clue in their pursuit of Kane.

Deciding to explore further, Miko made his way towards the Izakaya Bar, a place he suspected Kane might have frequented. Stepping inside, he ordered a calming jasmine tea and settled into a quiet corner, his senses attuned to the ebb and flow of the bar's atmosphere.

As he sipped his tea, Miko's observant gaze fell upon a commanding figure at the opposite end of the bar.

The man's authoritative voice cut through the air, commanding those around him with a harsh, unyielding power. To his left sat the second-in-command, equally formidable, exuding an aura of icy indifference that matched his superior's stern attitude.

Miko watched discreetly, his covert mannerisms concealing his scrutiny as he pieced together the dynamics of this intriguing scene. Each sip of tea brought clarity to his thoughts, revealing potential insights into Kane's whereabouts and the shadowy forces at play in this unfamiliar setting.

"What did you think of that strange recruit, Goro?" Miko overheard them discussing loudly, their voices betraying no concern for who might be listening.

"Hai, he's exactly what we've been looking for. He seems strong and intelligent enough although he's very inexperienced but that will come with time. He will be a valuable asset to our comrades in Osaka" Goro replied

"Will they give him safe passage overseas as payment, like he asked?"

"If he succeeds in the missions they give him"

"Have you ever seen such a bulky, hairy man before Goro, he looked like a sideshow freak?" The second in command asked

"He's definitely a half-breed. His complexion wasn't Japanese either and he had these strange black eyes.....I can't explain it but they weren't normal"

"I know it was a while ago, but I can't get the rogue out of my mind. He left an eerie impression on me. Well, he's on his way to Osaka now and I don't think he'll be back here anytime soon....thank God" Goro sniggered,

"Hai, he was in a hurry to leave Kyoto, I wonder what he's running from?"

"Whatever it is, only he knows," Goro concluded. "He struck me as the type who'd be up to no good wherever he goes."

With the new information he'd just overheard, Miko finished his tea and slinked out the back door and headed straight for the lodging house to relay the important message to Gideon and the two monks sat together discussing their next strategy, until the early hours of the morning.

"While the men were talking, did they happen to mention Kane's name?" Gideon queried

"No, they merely described the man as hairy and bulky, like a sideshow animal. I assumed they were talking about Kane because he matches that description. I'm fairly certain Kane is heading to Osaka. The men mentioned that someone there would provide him safe passage overseas if he completes certain jobs."

It's the best lead we have so far Master Gideon. The man's name in the bar is Goro" "Did you hear when Kane left Kyoto?"

"I think it was some time ago, maybe four weeks"

"Of course.....I have spent the past month convalescing, so it's no surprise that he's gone, I didn't expect him to hang around. I'm not concerned that he has escaped, our ninjas will be hot on his trail. We will spend another night here, so I can gain my strength for the trip to Osaka and then be on our way" Gideon instructed

"You've done well my son" He continued, then the two monks parted and retired to their designated rooms.

Chapter 5

Weeks ago, late in the afternoon, Kane strolled through the intricate streets of Kyoto with calculated intent. His plan was shrewd: exchange the witch's gold tooth for essential merchandise. With a keen eye, he targeted a reputable gem dealer, confident that he could negotiate a trade for a horse, new clothes, and some cash to fund his journey to Osaka.

As he passed various shops, Kane observed the Samurai warrior class dominating the city. He noted how the lower classes bowed deeply in respect, aware that any reluctance could result in immediate execution. Kane, ever astute, adopted the persona of a simpleton, masking his true intellect and intentions.

By presenting himself as unassuming and harmless, Kane kept a low profile, deftly avoiding trouble. His strategic mind and relentless drive to fulfill his destiny propelled him forward, navigating the dangers of Kyoto with cunning and precision.

As he entered a gem trader's store, Kane unwittingly wandered up to the adjacent counter, his fingers nervously fumbling with the gold tooth in his pocket. He began admiring the lustrous and enticing jewelry on display, trying to maintain an air of nonchalance.

The shopkeeper glanced up as Kane entered, quickly sizing up his customer with a hint of disdain. Clearly unimpressed with Kane's presence in his prestigious shop, the merchant gave a slight nod.

"Hai... can I help you?" he asked, his tone indicating a begrudging attention toward Kane.

"I have something I'd like to sell" Kane replied

"I'll be with you in a moment" The man instructed in a peevish tone, all the while keeping his eye on the large brute, then quickly finalized the sale with his previous customer and shuffled over to Kane.

"What are you doing here? This isn't a shop for a peasant farmer. Get out! You're driving away my customers. People will see you in here and stop buying from me."

He whinged

"I have something that might take your interest" Kane tried pacifying the shopkeeper and began pulling out the hefty gold tooth.

"What is it?" The man rudely asked his passion for gems and expensive items, overriding his desire for Kane to leave.

Withdrawing his hand from the coat pocket, he casually opened his fist, extending it out to reveal the solid gold tooth, its brilliant yellow hue radiating like the sun and it instantly captured the man's eye, hypnotizing him.

"Awww It is very beautiful. How much do you want for this?"

"Enough money to buy a good horse, some nice respectable clothes and supplies" "That's a lot, but I don't trade in other goods, although I can see why you want some new clothes, you look like a beggar" The man joked

"Here feel its weight" Kane offered and the trader quickly seized the tooth from his hand, then shuffled back over to the counter, placing it on the scales.

The experienced trader assessed the tooth's color with a monocular, noting its rich deep orange-yellow glow, a clear sign of high gold content. Satisfied with his examination, he turned his sharp gaze on Kane.

"Where did you get this from?" he queried, suspicion lacing his tone. "I inherited it," Kane bluffed smoothly, though his heart raced.

"Why, what's wrong with it?" he continued, feeling alarmed. His mind raced with the fear that the trader might alert the Machi-bugyo, the Samurai who served as chief of police, prosecutor, and overseer of both criminal and civil matters.

"There's nothing wrong with it only that it's 985 parts per thousand in gold by

mass and it weighs 4.175 ounces. I've never seen anything so perfect before. It's very heavy, the person who wore it must have suffered from an aching jaw" The man said, diverting his eyes back to the incandescent nugget.

"I will give you two pouches for it each pouch contains one thousand yen, that's

the best I can do" He firmly announced

"Give me three pouches and it's yours" Kane negotiated

"Hmmpf, you drive a hard bargain, Mister" He agreed and before Kane could say another word, the gem dealer sauntered into the rear office and fetched the money. "Here you are" He said, handing over the three sacks.

"Thank you for your fair business" Kane expressed his gratitude and before walking out the door, as an afterthought, he paused and faced the merchant.

"Could you please tell me where I can buy a good horse and some decent clothes?" "Hai just keep going down the street and you will find what you need"

The shopkeeper automatically replied, his gaze still fixed on the gold tooth.

Kane privately smiled to himself as he exited the shop, satisfied with his cunning success. He proceeded down the road, finding the appropriate traders and acquiring everything he needed. After purchasing a sturdy horse, he arranged to leave it with the dealer until the morning of his departure for Osaka.

As night fell, Kane entered the busy Izakayas Bar, blending into the crowd as he ordered a small pitcher of sake. He then found a solitary table, his eyes methodically scanning the room. Some patrons passionately discussed political issues, while others gossiped with friends.

Earlier, Kane had returned to his boarding house and meticulously shaved his exposed body parts, including his head, where the coarse brown hair was always sprouting. Embracing the customary baldness of a monk, he then changed into the

decent clothes he'd purchased, completing his disguise. Now, he sat in the bar, strategically observing and calculating his next moves.

The bar buzzed with lively atmosphere, patrons exuding high spirits, their smiles and laughter filling the establishment. Amidst this cheerful ambiance, Kane's keen eyes picked out a group near the bar. Their faces were somber, with a seriousness that contrasted sharply with the surrounding joy. The men exuded a dark aura, their expressions almost poisonous, revealing their true identities.

"Goro, I need to speak with you privately," one of the patrons declared to the man seated in the center of the group. Soon after, both men left the bar, disappearing into the night. Kane observed their departure with keen interest, recognizing "Goro" as the key figure for his plan.

Despite having only enough funds for his journey to Osaka, Kane sought something far more valuable—a letter guaranteeing legal and safe passage overseas.

He hoped "Goro" could provide this assurance in exchange for a different form of payment.

Once the two men re-entered the bar and sat in their allocated seats, Kane serenely wandered over to the gathering and mutely stood behind Goro, startling the overseer.

"Huh? Who are you and what do you want?" He declared, astounded by the big man's abrupt presence.

"I have no name and I need a job, only for tonight" Kane answered

"Ok? That's strange, no name eh?. Sounds like you don't want to be found. What are you willing to do?"

"Anything"

"I might have something for you" Goro smirked, as he slyly glanced at his second in charge.

"There's just one thing though about payment" Kane warned

"What.....you want to be paid a King's ransom?" Goro dissolved into laughter as the other men chuckled along with him.

"You look like a worldly and connected man, do you have many associates in Osaka?"

"Why? Goro blurted out defensively, wondering why Kane was so interested in his outlying network of allies.

"I don't want your money. If you give me an errand I will make sure that it's carried out with precision but for a specific payment. I need a letter with your mark on it, addressed to one of your partners, who could guarantee me safe travel overseas" Kane explained

"What are you scurrying from boy? Like a rodent"

"I'm not running from anything. Monks do not run away from their aversions.

I am taking a spiritual journey to foreign lands, spreading the word of my faith, which is Buddhism.....it has been ordained by my monastery, that is all"

"Alright, monk, if that's what you claim to be. I suppose you won't do anything illegal, being a Buddhist and all," Goro scoffed, his tone dripping with sarcasm.

"I will do anything you ask of me. All I want in return is a letter with your mark on it" Kane reaffirmed.

"My recommendation carries significant weight in Osaka, but I know my colleagues there will demand more from you before granting your passage overseas," Goro informed, his voice laced with a hint of warning.

"I am telling you, monk, it won't be pretty. Come, and we will discuss the job." With that, he stood up and walked out of the bar into the busy street.

"Hai and thankyou" Kane responded, accompanying Goro outside with the outlaw's second in charge, following close behind.

As the early morning hours unfolded like an invitation, Kane welcomed the realization that he was forging a new path forward. The wintry mist kissed his skin coldly, yet he breathed it in deeply, feeling a surge of elation come over him.

His calculated plans were finally in motion, and satisfaction coursed through his emotions.

Prowling through the labyrinthine alleyways, Kane eventually reached the address Goro had provided. Standing outside the opulent residence, he was struck by its lavish grandeur. The sight of the ornate architecture and pristine grounds vindicated Kane's purpose, convincing him that what lay ahead was fitting for its esteemed occupants.

"Some people have too much wealth," Kane muttered under his breath as he stealthily made his way along the side of the mansion. His keen eyes quickly identified an unsecured window on the ground floor.

With practiced precision, he gently slid the window open, enough to accommodate his sturdy frame. Kane slipped into the house with utmost caution, swiftly surveying his surroundings. He wasted no time in pinpointing the room Goro had directed him to infiltrate.

The mansion was cloaked in an unexpected silence as Kane moved with calculated stealth toward his target. Every step was deliberate, every movement cautious and clandestine. Finally, he reached the secured vault, the very objective of his mission. Weeks earlier, Goro had acquired the safe's combination from a corrupt associate who was a close friend of the homeowner. This moonlighting felon had observed the "lord" entering the sequence of numbers on numerous occasions, and Goro had generously compensated him for this crucial intelligence.

Kyoto buzzed with urban legends, and among them whispered the tale of a necklace rumored to bestow immense wealth and status upon its possessor. Though the treasure could never be sold intact within Japan, its individual gems held substantial value. Goro, with his connections, had already secured a guaranteed buyer eager to acquire the precious stones once the prize rested in his envious grasp.

Kane manipulated the safe's dial, his movements precise and deliberate. He listened intently for the satisfying click as he inputted the sequence of numbers. The heavy bolt lock yielded under his skillful touch, and the vault door swung open, revealing a breathtaking sight—a magnificent necklace adorned with monumental rubies, emeralds, and diamonds. Even in the dimness of the room, its concealed beauty shimmered with allure.

Kane carefully lifted the necklace, feeling its weight and marveling at its opulence. After securing his prize, he gently closed and relocked the vault door, leaving no trace of his intrusion. He swiftly retraced his steps to the open window, silently gliding through and closing it behind him with expert stealth. With the necklace safely in his possession, he melted into the shadows of the night, disappearing into the darkness as if he had never been there.

By the time Kane reached the back alley of the Izakayas Bar, he saw Goro candidly leaning up against the wall, smoking a churchwarden pipe, as he casually waited for his burglar to arrive.

"Did you get it?" Were the first words he spoke

"Hai.....here it is" Kane answered, withdrawing the priceless jewel from his coat, handing it to Goro.

"Well done monk. You're full of surprises, personally I didn't think you had it in you" He demoralized while he fondled the necklace, admiring its beauty.

"Where is my letter?" Kane demanded

"You'll get it tomorrow," Goro dismissed Kane's urgency with a wave of his hand. "It's already tomorrow! Don't you realize the sun will be rising soon? I need it now; I'm leaving in half an hour. You got what you wanted, now be a decent fellow and give me the letter," Kane retorted, his voice edged with growing frustration.

An unsettling transformation stirred within Kane, a primal force eager to burst forth. As Goro finally lifted his gaze from the mesmerizing jewels, he noticed a crimson glint in Kane's eyes. The intensity of his stare surged, the fiery hue flickering like coals in a forge. The once-composed "tough guy" of Kyoto involuntarily recoiled, a shiver coursing through him at the unexpected display of fervor.

"Ok, ok, I've already written the letter, here take it. Ask for Dai, his boatyard is in Dojima, the very last berth from the entrance of the marina" He relented, shoving the piece of paper in Kane's hand

"Get out of here and don't ever come back you freak" Goro yelled, before retreating to his customary seat in the bar

"Oh don't worry I won't" Kane shouted back and as he read the letter and saw who it was addressed to and noticed Goros signature, a big smile appeared on his face, because it was exactly what he needed.

Quickly returning to the boarding house, Kane grabbed his belongings and hurried towards the stables, saddling his horse and before the breaking of dawn, he rode through the city gates and headed down the road, in the direction to Osaka.

The morning burst forth with a vibrant pulse of light, bathing everything in a radiant golden shade as daylight triumphantly broke over the horizon.

The elderly gem trader was up early, his heart racing with anticipation as he cradled the newly acquired witch's tooth in his trembling hand. Today was the day he would transform this precious gold into a magnificent ring.

Excitement propelled him forward as he hurried to the local blacksmith's shop. Upon arrival, he was greeted by the sight of the blacksmith already hard at work, the forge roaring with a blazing fire that cast long shadows across the walls. The air sizzlied with energy as they prepared to melt the gold and forge it into something truly extraordinary.

"Here it is" The gem trader announced to the blacksmith, handing him the tooth. "Ok I'll put it in the liquifying pot and we'll begin reducing it down. You understand that a percentage of its value will be lost during the smelting" The blacksmith educated

"Hai.....but I can't sell it as a tooth, that's why I need it condensed and then we can mold it into a sellable ring" The gem trader advised

"Not a problem, let's start the process," the blacksmith replied, his voice resonating with confidence and expertise. With practiced hands, he carefully placed the witch's tooth into the appropriate container, positioning it within the heart of the blazing forge.

Burning heat engulfed the chamber as both men leaned in, their eyes fixed on the mesmerizing transformation unfolding before them. They watched in awe as the tooth gradually dissolved into a shimmering, bubbling liquid, its essence merging seamlessly with the molten gold in the crucible.

Once the blend had reached its optimal state, the blacksmith swiftly poured the molten gold into a waiting casting dish, where it gleamed molten and radiant before gradually cooling and solidifying into a new form—a symbol of craftsmanship and the magic of creation.

"Ok, it's done, now we have to wait for the solidification process. Come, my friend, let's have some grilled fish and tea at my house. We will return in a few hours" The blacksmith suggested and the men vacated the shop.

As time passed the gold cooled and formed into a perfectly spherical ring, just as the gem dealer had ordered, so when the men returned, they hurried over to the forged metal, admiring the finished product.

"This is perfect" The owner praised and plucked the ring from the template, eagerly thrusting it on one of his fingers.

"What are you doing, I need to refine it?" The blacksmith asked

"Just trying it on to see how it fits, this will fetch a lot of money," the gem dealer boasted proudly. With a gleeful grin, he raised the newly crafted ring high in front of his face, admiring its allure and potential value.

The blacksmith, however, stood frozen in horror as he witnessed his friend's physical body undergo a dark and grotesque alteration.

The dealer's neck elongated unnaturally, stretching into a thin appendage with a pronounced Adam's apple. His fingers twisted and lengthened like deformed tendrils, each knuckle swollen and misshapen.

A disturbing cry of agony erupted from the dealer's distorted form as his body contorted further. Thick, bristly hair sprouted across his skin, resembling that of a wild animal. In a moment of utter dread, the dealer glanced down and saw his feet morphing into abnormally large, beast-like appendages akin to those of a hybrid Sasquatch.

The blacksmith, however, stood frozen in horror as he witnessed his friend's physical body undergo a nightmarish and malformed transformation.

"What is happening to me? The ring is damned!" he screeched in terror, his voice distorted and desperate. But the blacksmith had already bolted, fleeing from the horrifying mutation unfolding before him. He abandoned his friend, now a terrorized, deformed monster, curled in a fetal position and sniveling on the cold ground of the deserted workshop.

Through tears and agonizing screams, the wretched man cried out in torment, cursing the strange farmer who had sold him the wretched object.

"I hope you die a cruel death!" he shrieked, his voice full of bitter hatred. Unbeknownst to the grieving victim, true evil had originally possessed the gold tooth. When the human skin book incinerated the witch, her soul, filled with rage and hatred, clung to the only remaining part of herself—the tooth. Combined with the potent sorcery from the ancient book, the curse manifested violently, infusing the soft metal with depraved power.

The man's transformation into a partially malformed skin-changer was the result—an unnatural blending of human and beast. He would forever wear the scars of the curse, condemned to live out his days as a tragic and disfigured creature.

As the day blossomed into a balmy afternoon, Kane rode leisurely along the trail to Osaka, feeling relaxed and content. He whistled a merry tune, the sound blending harmoniously with the rhythm of his horse's trot. Despite his outward calm, he remained vigilant, knowing that the monastery's ninjas could be pursuing him closely. Anticipating their pursuit, Kane urged his horse onward with a firm kick to its belly.

Instantly, the animal responded, breaking into a swift gallop that devoured the trail beneath them. Determined to cover as much ground as possible before nightfall, Kane pressed forward, his senses sharp and alert, ready to make camp and rest when darkness descended.

* * *

The three remaining ninjas of the original trailing pack—Itsuo, Taichi, and Hikaru—had parted ways with Shusuki and Naoki, opting for a different route through the dense forest. It took them four days to reach Kyoto after Kane's departure. Upon receiving news that the murderer had been spotted in the city and was en route to Osaka, leaving another innocent victim in his wake, they wasted no time and pressed on with renewed will power.

Revitalized by their mission, they pursued Kane with unrelenting vigor, their sense of duty and justice propelling them forward. Every step through the dense forest and each rumor confirmed in Kyoto only fueled their quest to apprehend the elusive culprit before he could inflict further damage.

"We must find him soon" Itsuo remarked

"Hai.....everywhere he goes, he leaves a trail of depravity. Is there no end to his horrors?" Taichi added

"My heart bleeds for that poor gem trader. It's a shame we couldn't speak with him" Itsuo said.

"It was a bit hard when he's paralyzed with fear, plus he's closed the jewelry shop, hiding his unsightly looks from prying eyes" Hikaru remarked

"I heard someone say that he has animalistic goblin features" He continued "Apparently he mutated from placing a cursed ring on his finger that'd been refashioned from a gold tooth. When I spoke to the blacksmith he said his friend bought the tooth from a giant stranger dressed in farmer's clothes. The man used the

money to buy a horse and new clothes. He made me promise to find the scoundrel and punish him" Itsuo announced.

"Can't he remove the ring?" Hikaru asked

"No, the ring has seemingly "married" itself onto his finger" Itsuo informed "Hai.....the poor fellow, he didn't deserve what that wicked Kane did to him" Taichi agreed, feeling empathy for the afflicted gem trader and then the three ninjas briskly resumed their hunt.

Kane discovered a narrow path branching off the main road, leading him deeper into the damp, ancient forest. Towering trees, primitive and majestic, stretched skyward with rough, gnarled bark softened by a delicate coat of moss, giving them a woolly, feather-like appearance.

Dismounting from his horse, Kane secured the reins to a low-hanging branch and carefully retraced his steps along the trail. He methodically obscured the hoof prints left in the moist soil, erasing any trace of his passage. As twilight began to seep through the canopy, he melded into the encroaching darkness like a shadow, disappearing into the depths of the forest.

Since his transformation, Kane's senses had sharpened dramatically, allowing him to perceive even the faintest sounds of forest life—the rustling of foraging animals, the whisper of wind through leaves, and the crackling of twigs underfoot.

As twilight descended, Kane lit a small fire and prepared a simple meal from his supplies. Amidst the quiet of the forest, he heard cautious footsteps approaching his campsite. Instantly alert, he rose to his feet, his eyes scanning the darkness for any sign of danger. It was then that he spotted a wolf-like dog with a distinctive

white-tipped tail, standing about five yards away, observing him without aggression. Sensing no immediate threat, Kane cautiously crouched down and extended a hand in a gesture of trust. The dog, with its strikingly different colored eyes, hesitated briefly before cautiously approaching him.

"You're quite a remarkable-looking dog. Where did you come from?" Kane murmured softly, his hand gently stroking the animal's head. Gradually, a bond of trust formed between them as they nestled beside the small fire, finding solace and warmth in each other's company amidst the cooling forest air. Eventually, exhaustion overtook them, and they drifted off to sleep together under the canopy of trees.

In the early hours of the next morning, the wolf-dog sat attentively, its keen eyes fixed on Kane as he packed his saddlebags. When Kane mounted his horse and set off down the road, the enchanted dog joyfully bounded ahead, as if it had appointed itself his escort and guardian.

"Do you think you belong to me?" Kane joked playfully, addressing the canine. The dog turned its head towards him and emitted a yip that uncannily sounded like "Yep," prompting Kane to burst into laughter.

"You're quite the character. I think I'll call you 'Lady Vixen.' How does that sound?" Kane suggested, half-serious. To his surprise, the dog responded with another "Yep," this time more clearly, almost resembling a woman's voice. The unexpected sound nearly caused Kane to lose his balance on the horse.

"What are you?" Kane asked, his unease growing as the dog turned back towards the road, giving him a mischievous wink that sent a shiver down his spine.

* * *

Meanwhile, Hiro had pushed himself relentlessly, fueled by an unyielding persistence to capture Kane. Days had passed without rest, his single-minded pursuit overriding any need for sleep. Yet, his resilience was waning, and the toll on his mind and body was becoming apparent.

Sleep deprivation gnawed at Hiro's sanity, causing his thoughts to blur and his grasp on reality to falter. The urge to sleep became an unbearable torment, leading to episodes of micro-sleeping where he would drift into brief, involuntary slumbers.

In one disturbing episode, his delusions merged with reality in a tragic twist. Convinced he had finally cornered Kane, Hiro attacked a large, heavy-set man in a state of disoriented frenzy. Mistaken identity led to brutal consequences, leaving the innocent man grievously injured by the roadside, bones broken and wounds bleeding.

Caught in the throes of exhaustion and delusion, Hiro's relentless pursuit had led him to a devastating mistake, amplifying the urgency of his quest while deepening the darkness of his torment.

With exhaustion bordering on madness, Hiro stumbled upon a secluded cavern not far from the main road to Osaka. Collapsing from sheer fatigue, he welcomed the tranquility of the surrounding nature, the quiet peace luring him into a profound sleep.

Without knowing, Hiro had outpaced the remaining ninjas, putting a day's distance between himself and his brothers. When he finally awoke, disoriented and groggy, he was startled to find his three comrades standing dignified before him, their presence unexpected yet somehow comforting in this remote sanctuary.

"Hikaru, Itsuo, Taichi, how did you find me?" Hiro exclaimed, startled by their sudden appearance.

"How could we not? You were snoring like a warthog," Taichi chuckled, unable to suppress a grin.

"Yeah, you pride yourself as a stealthy warrior, but your resting snort could wake the dead," Itsuo added with a playful jab.

"You'll have to work on that if you want to keep sneaking around unnoticed, Hiro." Hiro couldn't help but laugh at himself, realizing his supposed ninja skills didn't extend to his sleeping habits. With his brothers teasing him affectionately, the tension of their tracking momentarily lifted, replaced by solidarity and good-natured banter in the midst of their relentless chase.

"We thought you'd be days behind us Hiro, knowing that you took the main road to Kyoto, instead of cutting through the forest" Itsuo mentioned

"I haven't slept since we left the monastery" Hiro explained

"Did you visit Kyoto?" Hikaru asked

"No, I went straight through the city. Why?" Hiro asked, his voice tinged with confusion.

"Kane left a token in Kyoto" "What do you mean, a token?"

"A gem dealer purchased a gold tooth from Kane and after he melted it down to form a ring, he placed the piece of jewelry on his finger and instantly changed into a goblin or troll, something hideous like that" Hikaru educated his brother.

"We found out that Kane is heading for Osaka" Itsuo briefed

"What? We have to find that chikushou (son of a bitch) before he causes any more harm. Come on, let's get going" Hiro announced and the four ninjas rapidly departed.

Osaka, hailed as Japan's active economic nucleus and a pivotal regional port, played a crucial role in the nation's trade network. Primarily known for its trade in rice, Osaka also exchanged other commodities such as bamboo, pottery, silk, and lamp oil.

The city's residents were famed for their keen business flair, but they also earned a reputation for their lack of civic spirit. They spoke in the boisterous and blunt Osaka dialect, their voices cutting through conversations with a brusque and unmistakable edge.

They were often criticized by outsiders for their perceived gluttony, a habit that sometimes led to extravagant feasting until they were sick. Despite these stereotypes, Osaka thrived as a center of commerce, particularly in Dojima, which boasted Japan's largest seaport.

The robust rice trade in Dojima ensured a stable and flourishing grain market, fueled by long-standing trade relationships that contributed to Osaka's economic vitality and prominence in Japan.

Kane entered Osaka, a bustling metropolis far larger than Kyoto, with a mix of excitement and wonder filling his heart. It was his first encounter with such a sprawling, densely populated urban environment.

The city, however, did not immediately captivate him with its appearance. Instead, it greeted him with a chaotic scene of hundreds of people rushing about, each seemingly absorbed in their own urgent tasks. Merchants crowded the streets, eager to sell their wares, often thrusting products into the faces of the passersby, viewing everyone as a potential customer.

Osaka's spirited but overwhelming atmosphere left Kane intrigued yet slightly taken aback, marking his introduction to the energetic pulse of urban life in one of Japan's most dynamic cities.

"Are you making any money, mister?" One of the traders asked, thrusting a bottle of cologne towards him, as he gingerly rode through the crowd.

The hustling boulevard stalls were teeming with crowds hungrily devouring food, creating a lively spectacle that both amazed and swamped Kane. The vibrant array of colorful garments worn by passersby dazzled his eyes, adding to the sensory overload of the cityscape.

Pausing to take in the scene, Kane instinctively looked down to check on his faithful companion, *"Lady Vixen"* the wolf-dog who had accompanied him thus far. To his disappointment, he realized she had slipped away unnoticed, seeking refuge and independence in the forest long before he had even noticed her absence.

Kane descended slowly towards the harbor, an obvious sense of apprehension mingling with his curiosity. The rhythmic chugging of boat engines filled the air as vessels maneuvered in and out of the busy port. Upon arrival, he found himself captivated by the lively scene—an energetic blend of activity and the distinct aroma of the ocean, which added to the harbor's allure.

Arriving at the final mooring berth, Kane dismounted from his horse with care, unfastening the saddlebags and hoisting them onto his sturdy shoulders. Securing his sword around his waist, he made his way towards a merchant who was engrossed in unloading his catch from a moderately sized fishing trawler. The noisy harbor promised tales of adventure and opportunity, drawing Kane deeper into its intriguing depths.

"Hello sir, I am looking for a man named Dai, can you show me his location?" He queried.

Still bent over his catch as he sorted through the seafood, the fisherman gave Kane a suspicious glimpse and without even uttering a word, raised his arm and pointed towards a shabby building.

"Hai, thankyou" Kane voiced, while he bowed obligingly to the impolite man and subsequently walked to the shanty, knocking on the door

"I've been sent by Goro to meet Dai, is he around?"

"Who are you and why would Goro send our boss a moronic-looking fellow like yourself?" One of the occupants humiliated, as the other men sniggered with contempt.

"I am a monk on a spiritual pilgrimage and I need safe passage overseas" "A spiritual pilgrimage? Now I've heard everything" The group kept chuckling

"Just tell me where he is and I'll be on my way" Kanes patience was beginning to strain.

"The boss is out the back"

"Thank you" And as he entered the rear entrance, he viewed an overweight man with a long spindly beard sitting at a desk

"What do you want, stranger?" He said in a gruff voice

"Safe passage overseas.....I am a....." Kane began to explain but the paunchy bovine cut him off before he could say another word

"Hai, Hai, you're a monk, I heard you earlier. The only foreign ship in port at the moment is heading to America in the morning. Do you have the money to pay for your trip?

"I have a letter from your associate in Kyoto.....Goro" Kane grappled for the note in his knapsack and quickly held it out for the fat man to accept, but he didn't take it straight away, he just looked up and studied the monk with an inhospitable stare. "Goro eh? I haven't seen him for months" He finally said and snatched the letter from Kane's hand.

"I also have a horse, a saddle and a pouch of money, if that would be enough payment?" Kane added with a tone of hope in his voice

"Hmmm... In this letter, Goro mentions I should offer you a job on top of what you're already willing to pay me. Show me the money bag first," the greedy man demanded, his eyes narrowing with suspicion as he scrutinized Kane. Kane obliged, tossing the sack onto the table with a clink of coins.

The merchant's eyes sparkled with gluttony as he greedily counted the silver coins. "What would you do for your fare, monk? Would you kill for it?" he sneered, a smirk spreading across his face.

"Isn't my offer enough for you?" Kane growled, his voice dropping to a deep, menacing tone that sent a shiver down the trader's spine.

"I've read the letter, and it doesn't mention anything about me doing an extra job. My horse, saddle, and money should be sufficient." Kane made it clear that he didn't want to resort to violence unless absolutely necessary.

"Where did that come from? Your voice just changed," Dai challenged, his suspicion growing.

"I caught a cold on my journey here. I've spent many nights camping in the freezing woodland," Kane fabricated, maintaining his facade.

"I think there's more to you than meets the eye, boy," the merchant muttered, casting a distrustful gaze at Kane.

"Well? The horse, the saddle, the silver and Goros letter.....Is it sufficient or not?" "All of that plus one small job will cover it, you must understand that the travel fare and forging your papers are very expensive and restricted. He finally stated at Kanes dismay

"Fine.....What is it you want me to do?"

"There's a man who's swindled me out of a small fortune, and he won't pay me back. I want you to teach him a fatal lesson, and then we'll consider your travel costs settled."

"Where is he?" Kane asked dispiritedly

"You can't do anything now, it's daylight" The fat merchant

laughed "Watch me"

"Ok? valiant monk. He has a stall in the market selling bolts of colored silk and cloth. You can't miss him, he's fat and arrogant like me. It's the third booth along, immediately after turning the right corner off the wharf"

As Kane began walking out the door, Dai shouted "Hey Goliath, you haven't told me your name"

"I have no name, I left my identity behind at the monastery" Kane replied without turning around to face him

"Well that's going to be difficult then" "Why?" Kane sounded agitated

"Because *"no-name"* doesn't cut it, you can't enter another country without your name on the papers and that sword you're carrying won't be allowed in either. I'll tell you what. Give me the sword as well and I'll put together all the documents you'll need"

Kane stood motionless, thinking hard about Dai's increasing need to add more to his payment and after a couple of minutes, he unbuckled his sword, turned and walked towards the desk, slamming it down in front of him.

"There.....it's yours.....my name is Kane?" He could feel the demon's irritation surging through his veins.

"Kane who? What's your clan name?" The opinionated brute persisted

This question baffled the young monk and he had to think quickly before the patronizing pig became suspicious

"My Dharma name is "Shunro" It was given to me when I arrived at the monastery as a child" Kane announced

"Ok Kane Shunro go and do the job and don't forget to come back and get your papers" Dai laughed and dismissed Kane with a flick of his hand.

Walking past his horse, Kane paused to stroke his beloved traveling companion's velvet neck, whispering a heartfelt "thank you" before proceeding towards his assignment. As he turned the corner, Kane spotted the stall keeper he was tasked to confront. Instead of approaching directly, he slipped into an alleyway, observing discreetly from a distance, calculating the perfect moment to execute his plan.

Despite his sinister reputation and the dark deeds he had been compelled to commit, Kane wasn't accustomed to harming innocent people without cause. While stealing jewelry felt justified in his mind, he found the idea of senselessly attacking someone he didn't know morally troubling.

From his vantage point, Kane watched the stout man bicker with potential customers, his voice rising sharply as he defended his merchandise. The swarming crowd provided cover as Kane calmly approached the stall. With practiced ease, he withdrew his Kunai knife, concealing the weapon up his sleeve as he moved closer. In the bustling market, Kane blended among the shoppers, his presence unnoticed until he deliberately picked up a bolt of cloth, drawing the wrath of the merchant. "Hey you, don't touch the silk! You'll leave your grubby finger marks all over it," the trader bellowed.

"What did you say?" Kane leaned in, cupping his ear with a feigned hearing difficulty. "Are you deaf? I said don't touch my wares, boofhead!" The man insulted, leaning forward to confront Kane.

Swift as a shadow, Kane seized his moment. With practiced precision, he withdrew his knife and struck with lethal intent, driving the blade into the merchant's chest in one quick motion.

"Dai sends his regards," Kane whispered coldly before melting back into the crowd. As the injured man slumped over his merchandise, the fabric absorbed the spreading crimson stain, changing from luxurious silk to a haunting, vivid red, a stark reminder of the violence that had just transpired in the heart of Osaka's busy marketplace.

Dai sat behind his desk when Kane returned to the shack and jumped with fright when he noticed him standing mutely in the doorway.

"Geez Kane, you're a sly bastard for a big fellow" He nervously divulged "Where's my papers?" Was the only thing Kane said

"Did you teach my selfish friend a lesson?"

"Hai.....it's done.....now where are my papers?" "What did you do to him?" Dai asked

"I'm sure you'll hear about it" Kane flatly commented as one of Dai's crewmen rushed into the office with beads of sweat forming on his brow.

"Dai" He alerted "Hai, what is it?"

"The fabric trader is dead, someone stabbed him in the chest" The man announced as Dai focused his gaze on Kane, with an immoral grin that betrayed all innocence. "Ok Dai..... where are my papers? I won't ask you again" Kane threatened as he held out his hand.

Feeling intimidated by Kanes change in attitude, Dai quickly gathered the relevant documents and twisted them into a scroll, handing them to him.

"Which boat and when? Kane demanded as he unraveled the papers and regarded them, making sure everything was in order.

"At the other end of the wharf, it's called *"Sea Changer"* and it leaves port at 5 am sharp. Best if you get there half an hour earlier though. The ship is bigger than an oxen's balls, you can't miss it"

"Nice doing business with you Mr Shunro. Enjoy your new life in America, it's going to be a real eye-opener for a fledgling like yourself.....Sayōnara" He said while scribbling in a journal but Kane had already left.

Returning to the market, Kane noticed a cluster of Samurai huddled around the fabric trader's stall, their stern faces questioning the assembly of onlookers. They were asking if anyone had seen anything, their presence intensifying the crowd's nervous energy. With a quick step, Kane slipped away, heart racing, weaving through the maze of stalls and alleyways until he reached the docks.

There, he found a stack of crates covered by a large tarpaulin. Glancing around to ensure he wasn't followed, Kane ducked underneath the cover, his breathing shallow and rapid. He concealed himself in the shade, the scent of saltwater and fish filling the air, and waited for dawn, every creak and footstep passing making his heart pound with apprehension.

The sea air carried a blend of fish, salt, and water, a simple yet monumental scent. As Kane lined up to board the ship, he inhaled deeply, relishing the aroma that encapsulated his freedom. He exhaled slowly, savoring the moment and etching it into his memory—the day he finally escaped Japan once and for all.

"Present your papers please" A crew member shouted in an American accent. "Paper's big fella" The seafarer brusquely demanded as he visually judged Kane and his papers

"What's your business in America?" He quizzed

"I'm a Buddhist monk on a spiritual pilgrimage" Kane

answered politely in flawless English he'd studied at the monastery, desperately trying not to raise any suspicions.

"Ok? Well, good luck with that Mr Shunro.....not sure how you'll be received in the Americas but whatever floats your boat.....sorry for the wordplay. Alright, move forward please" He quipped motioning Kane to board the ship.

"Hai and thankyou" He replied, nodding to the sailor.

Once he'd been allocated a room, Kane placed his belongings on the cheap bed and meandered out to the deck, watching as the ship leisurely withdrew from the port.

His dreams soaring like a bird, exhilarated by the hope of his new life. As the shoreline dwindled in the distance, he glanced to his left and that's when he saw her.

Motionless at the bow of the ship, the elegant lady's sandy-colored dress fluttered in the breeze, flowing like graceful bird wings. Her sculpted figure was twine-thin, her waist resembling a decanter. When she turned her face in his direction, Kane noticed her flawless complexion. The mysterious woman's angelic ears and petite nose were so perfect that an artist couldn't have fashioned her any better. It was a pleasure to watch her long brown hair tumble over her shoulders as she ran burgundy red fingernails through it. When she broke into a smile while chatting with an admirer, her enchanting oyster white teeth jolted Kane like an electric shock.

He wondered if she had noticed him, but that thought quickly evaporated when the beautiful lady turned around, walking off in a nonchalant manner, without showing him an ounce of recognition. Leaning against the rails, he placed his hands over his face and sighed with anguish, realizing there was a cavernous pit in his soul. The craving for physical love left him grappling with mixed feelings of shame and disloyalty towards the Buddhist faith and his promise of abstinence.

He began to believe that a life without physical love was meaningless, yet he also understood that the blessing of a non-judgmental and trusting relationship would never be his. The diabolical creature within him would expel any chance of a devoted and compatible connection. He could never reveal his true self—beast and all.

Loneliness, envy, and the weight of his terrible deeds hardened his heart. A cruel bitterness grew within him, leaving his body feeling abandoned, like an empty temple without a soul.

The canvas sails billowed as they caught the rising wind, propelling the ship deeper into the vast expanse of the ocean. Kane gazed upward at the heavens, where swirling gulls danced in the turbulent air, their white forms contrasting with the grey horizon like scraps of paper spiraling through the sky.

The waves surged like towering peaks of dark animosity, their chaotic motion unforgiving. Kane felt his stomach churn as the ship rode the roller coaster of the squall, the violent motion making him queasy.

Quickly retreating to his quarters, Kane collapsed onto the bed, his body drenched in a cold sweat. A massive headache pounded in his temples, throbbing with an intensity that clouded his thoughts.

The unfamiliar sensation of seasickness gripped him, unsettling his mood. Unconsciously, a chilling, animalistic howl erupted from his throat, reverberating through the ship's corridors and cargo holds.

The unearthly sound made the hairs on everyone's arms stand on end, enveloping them in an inexplicable sense of alarm.

"Did you hear that? What could make such a hellish sound? It sounded abnormal" One of the sailors questioned with superstitious delusions of bad luck in his mind. "Do we have any animals on board?" Another commented

"Not to my knowledge"

"It came from the cabins at the stern"

"We have to let the captain know" So the two seafarers headed for the bridge and when they arrived, the captain was already aware of the satanic yowl because he'd heard it too.

"Cap'n, did you hear that god awful sound?" The men queried "Yes, do you have an idea where it came from?"

"We think it came from the stern"

"Well go and check it out boys" The captain ordered and as the men walked the corridors with dread, the older sailor began voicing his superstitious beliefs. "This voyage is already cursed" He began

"Stop with your bullshit Charlie, it was just a noise" His companion said annoyed at the old matey's irrational insecurity.

"Yeah well there's a woman on board and that means bad luck" Charlie continued

"It could have been a hideous mermaid trying to distract the crew" The old salt added "Shut up Charlie.....do you actually believe in that crap?" The novice sailor snapped "You're a young cynic and have not been at sea as long as I have.....these legends have merit to them. I heard that during this ship's maiden voyage a series of unusual incidents happened resulting in three crew members dying and their spirits are still roaming the deck.....so the ship is cursed" Charlie warned

"Ok? So if the ship is cursed and you're so shit scared of it, then why did you come on this expedition eh? Tell me that Charlie"

"I needed the money.....the money made me do it" And with that last comment the two men burst out laughing.

Kane heard the loud conversation and laughter as the crewmen moved along the hallway, knocking on each passengers' cabin.

"Hello, are you ok?" They asked each person as they opened their prospective doors "Yes, I'm fine. What was that horrible noise earlier?" A man queried

"That's what we're trying to find out, but don't worry everything is under control. Just remain in your cabin for the time being" The younger of the two sailors instructed then progressed onwards until they reached Kane's berth, knocking loudly.

"Hello, is everything alright?"

It took Kane a couple of minutes to answer, as he tried to muster up the strength to budge, eventually opening the door but only enough for his face to appear.

"Whoa, you're a big guy. Is everything alright in there sir?" The junior mariner asked gawking up at him, as Charlie stood closely behind.

"You're looking a bit green there Rabbi" He added

"Hai.....daijoubu (I'm alright)" Kane deliberately answered in his native language, hoping that his confusion of English would send them away.

"Ok then, whatever you just said is ok with me. If you continue to feel sick Rabbi, we have a brew that will fix it"

"Hai" Kane swiftly retaliated and closed the door in the men's faces "He's a weird one" Charlie concluded

"He's a Japanese monk.....what else do you expect"

Kane dropped back onto his bed and buried his head in the pillow, thinking miserably to himself, *"How in God's name am I ever going to survive this trip?"*

Chapter 6

Three days had slipped by since Kane set sail from Japan. Under the cover of nightfall, the group of ninjas crept into Osaka, skilfully seizing clothes left unattended in the locals' yards as they dried. Hiro, Hikaru, Itsuo, and Taichi rendezvoused at a predetermined spot, donned in the attire of ordinary citizens. Their seamless integration went unnoticed amidst the busy streets, evading any suspicion from the vigilant Samurai patrols.

"Spread out into the city and don't engage with anyone, try to gather information about Kane, anything. Just blend in with the streets, I'll scout the pier, and remember.... pay attention to the locals' gossip," Hiro instructed.

Their ninja-yoroi outfits and weapons were stashed in an abandoned shed near the wharf, each planning to pilfer a haversack to carry their outlawed gear. As the morning marketplace filled with customers, Itsuo navigated the stalls, seamlessly merging with the shifting crowds, akin to shoals of fish.

The air was thick with the savory aroma of sizzling food and the lively cacophony of hungry customers, punctuated by the distinct clink of coins changing hands along the boulevard.

Itsuo approached the silk trader's stall, which sat empty with a signboard boldly proclaiming *"Closed until further notice."* He wondered why such a prominent stand would be vacant in the midst of a busy market. Nearby, Itsuo conveniently overheard two women conversing in hushed tones as they stood before the empty booth, discussing the recent events that had unfolded just days before.

"What a dreadful thing to happen last week" One of the lady's commented "Hai, I can't believe he was murdered in plain sight" The other woman added

"I know I shouldn't say this, but I'm not surprised, he was an offensive man, the way he would abuse his customers, still he didn't deserve to die so violently"

"I wonder if anyone saw what happened"

"I heard someone say it was a remarkably large man with a bald head touching the silk because after he left the stall, that's when the owner collapsed, bleeding all over the bolts of material "

"Well, I hope another fabric trader opens up because I make all my own clothes" Then the gossiping ladies moved on.

Itsuo swiftly made his way through the crowded wharf, his mind racing with the urgency of his discovery. Finding Hiro amidst the chaotic backdrop of ships and traders, he delivered the news with a stately expression.

"Kane was here in Osaka last week," Itsuo reported, his voice tinged with concern. "And another crime has been committed by his hands."

Hiro's gaze hardened with resolve as he absorbed the grim tidings.

"His corruption runs deep. Peace cannot prevail while he roams free. Death is his only redemption."

"Do you think he's still in Osaka?" Itsuo asked, his brow furrowed with uncertainty. "We will find him," Hiro affirmed, his voice serious.

"His size will make him conspicuous. Gather the others and retrieve our ninja-yoroi from the abandoned shack. We must prepare."

With a nod, Itsuo disappeared into the crowd, determined to rally their ninja brethren for the impending chase.

* * *

Before leaving Kyoto, Gideon proposed a meeting with the man known as "Goro." The monks were conspicuous as they entered the rowdy Izakaya Bar.

"Which one of you is Goro?" Gideon announced firmly.

"Who wants to know?" one of the gang members retorted, while Goro sat quietly in the background, scrutinizing the monks.

"Gideon and Miko," Gideon declared confidently.

"We are monks from a sacred monastery, and we are on a mission to find a man we believe has contacted Goro."

"He's a large, hairy brute. He might be masquerading as a monk," Miko interjected, much to Gideon's displeasure. The old monk promptly gave Miko a faint elbow to the stomach, signaling him to be quiet.

"I am Goro," the leader declared, standing up and approaching the monks. Gideon glanced at Miko, who gave him an approving nod, confirming that this was indeed "the boss."

"Why are monks searching for a man with such dishonorable intentions?" Goro questioned.

"He's wanted for murder and must be brought to justice," Gideon declared firmly. "His name is Kane.... is that the man you spoke with?" he continued.

"I knew he was running from something. He was in a big hurry to leave Kyoto," Goro admitted.

"He didn't tell me his name."

"What was his purpose for meeting with you?" Gideon pressed. "He wanted a job," Goro replied.

"For money?" Gideon asked, his eyes narrowing.

"No, he wanted a letter signed by me for safe passage overseas."

Gideon became instantly alarmed, realizing that his quest for Kane might be in vain. "And did you provide him with this letter?"

"Hai.... he skillfully accomplished what was expected of him."

"So, has he already departed for Osaka?" Gideon asked urgently.

"Hai."

"Please excuse my ignorance, but it's not logical that he'd be able to board a ship without the appropriate papers. Who did you refer him to?"

"I told him to visit a man called Dai," Goro confessed.

"Thank you, Mr. Goro. You've been most helpful. Also, I've heard talk that a local gem dealer has been possessed by an evil entity," Gideon added.

"Hai, after placing a bewitched ring on his finger, which was fashioned from a gold tooth. But you won't be able to speak with him as he has locked himself away from the world forever."

"That's alright, I have a fair idea who was responsible. Thank you for your time" Gideon said and the monks promptly exited the bar.

"I will need to speak with the blacksmith before we leave. You can ride with me Miko, we will cover more ground that way" So they briefly interviewed the blacksmith, acquiring more information about what had happened to his friend, then they set out for Osaka, once and for all.

Itsuo and his brothers returned to the appointed shack, where they met up with Hiro. As the clan retrieved their kit bags, Itsuo informed Taichi and Hikaru about what he had overheard in the marketplace. Together, they quickly formulated their next plan. "Kane's probably still in the city; we have news that he was definitely here," Hiro asserted.

"But what if he's already left Osaka? Then we'd be wasting our time searching for him here," Taichi countered.

"Do you know where he's gone, Taichi? No, you don't. Going off on a wild goose chase would be squandering valuable time. At least we know his destination was Osaka. He's either been here or is still here," Hiro snapped, frustration evident in his voice as he addressed his brother. The group sensed Hiro's growing impatience with Kane's elusive escapes and the trail of destruction left in his wake.

"What do you want us to do?" Hikaru interjected, breaking the tension.

"Pair up and continue searching the city. Remember, any piece of information is vital, even if you think it's insignificant. Hikaru and Taichi, roam the streets. Be cautious of the Samurai. Itsuo and I will revisit the seaport. Everyone report back here in three hours. We stay in Osaka until we find something. Our hunt doesn't end here," Hiro declared firmly.

The brothers split up and resumed their search through the streets for clues, their presence unnoticed by the local residents, who remained oblivious to the fact that ninjas had infiltrated their city.

Late in the afternoon, a thunderstorm unleashed its fury. Raindrops fell like oversized hailstones, pelting down with the force of rigid bullets. People scattered in all directions, desperately seeking shelter from the deluge.

Hiro and Itsuo found refuge under the awning of a warehouse, huddling together with three wharf clerks. They stared out into the grey expanse of the rippling sea, where quarreling seagulls cried out in the distance, their haunting calls echoing through the empty sky.

Itsuo's stomach rumbled like bottled thunder as the tantalizing aroma of flame-grilled fish and pungent onions drifted towards him, carried on the humid air.

"Are you alright? Your stomach sounds like this storm" One of the clerks remarked "Hai" Itsuo replied meekly, cautiously watching Hiro's reaction to his unmanageable bodily functions.

"If you want something to eat, there's a cafe two doors down" The friendly man suggested

"No, he'll be fine, thank you" Hiro answered on behalf of Itsuo

"He doesn't sound fine.....he sounds hungry. Don't you have any money?" The man continued

"No, we are Buddhist monks and don't carry money with us. We rely on the lay community to provide what we need to survive" Hiro added

"Buddhist monks? You're not wearing monk clothing? Nevertheless, come with me. I know the cafe owner and I'll ask him to give you something to eat" The obliging man offered, so he ushered the monks into the eatery and wandered over to the proprietor, who stood with his back to the servery.

"Hey Yuto, there are Buddhist monks that need something to eat" He notified the cook, and the man promptly dished out a hearty meal of casseroled seafood, handing the bowls over to the wharfie and he carried the dishes to their table. "There you go. That should fill the hole in your gut" He jested

"Thank you" Itsuo answered and subsequently tucked into the marinated stew with enthusiasm, while Hiro just stared at the assortment of submerged fish chunks. "It's my pleasure.... enjoy your meal," he grinned, then swiftly exited the premises.

Before leaving, Hiro requested an additional loaf of bread, explaining it was for their friar brothers. As they waited, he began to ask questions, his voice tinged with an undercurrent of interrogation.

"Do many overseas ships visit this port?"

"Hai, there's a few," the chef replied, turning to face them.

Hiro and Itsuo exchanged uneasy glances, noticing the unsettling demeanor of the cafe owner. His features seemed distorted, his head shaped strangely like a horse's, with a disproportionately large mouth. As he spoke, his jaw moved awkwardly to the side, almost disjointed, and occasional slobber escaped from one corner.

"What vessels dock here then?" Hiro pressed on, his apprehension growing visible. "Korea, China, and over the last twelve months, America," the cook answered, his smile widening to reveal thin lips retracting over large, piano-key teeth.

"Have you seen a big man around here recently? I mean, he's so huge, you couldn't miss him," Hiro inquired, his tone urgent.

"No, I haven't seen anyone like that," the cook replied, his smile remaining unnervingly wide as he turned to fetch the bread.

As he turned, Hiro caught sight of a distinctive strawberry-colored sickle shaped birthmark on the cook's neck. It stood out starkly, almost glaring, like an old dog's balls.

"Thank you then. We appreciate your hospitality," Hiro said gratefully as they departed for the shack, mindful of the approaching time to reunite with their brothers. Hikaru and Taichi eagerly awaited their arrival, noticing the loaf of bread under Hiro's arm as they approached. They jumped to their feet with excitement.

"Where did you get that?" Taichi asked eagerly.

"From a cafe on the wharf," Hiro replied, breaking the loaf into equal portions and offering wedges to the men. But Itsuo quietly refused.

"If he doesn't want to eat, we'll gladly have it," Hikaru chimed in enthusiastically. "He had a big bowl of fish casserole at the cafe, so he's probably not hungry, right, brother?" Hiro informed the others.

"Hai... but I don't feel well," Itsuo complained, clutching his stomach.

"That'll teach you, Itsuo. You shouldn't have scarfed down that casserole so fast," Hiro smirked, his voice lacking sympathy.

"I know, but I think there was something wrong with it. I feel like I've been poisoned," Itsuo replied, his words tumbling out just as a torrent of vomit erupted from him and didn't cease. The sickness intensified, dizziness setting in, and he suddenly felt a wetness at the back of his pants.

"I need to lie down," he groaned, rushing into the abandoned shack and clutching the seat of his soiled trousers.

"Did you eat any of the fish casserole, Hiro?" Taichi asked, concerned. "No, it looked disgusting, so I passed," Hiro answered firmly.

"I wonder if both dishes were poisoned," Taichi speculated.

"I don't know, but we're paying that shady cafe owner another visit," Hiro declared ominously.

Itsuo lay on a bed of moldy straw, wracked with stomach cramps that came in relentless waves of spasms. Each bout of vomiting weakened him further, his body temperature fluctuating wildly. The discomfort of alternating between intense sweats and chills overwhelmed him.

"Help me!" Itsuo screamed at his brothers from inside the shack. They rushed in immediately upon hearing his cries.

"Are you alright, Itsuo?" Hikaru asked with deep concern, while Hiro and Taichi watched anxiously.

"I feel like I'm dying... I'm burning up," Itsuo moaned, his voice strained with pain and fear.

"I can't swallow, and I'm having difficulty breathing," Itsuo gasped, swiftly vomiting once more.

"He should see a doctor," Hikaru urged, looking to Hiro for guidance.

"And what? Who do we say he is.... a ninja on the hunt for a fugitive? The Samurai would be notified, and we'd be in serious trouble. We have no identification on us; that would only raise suspicions. We could end up locked up or worse, beheaded, while Kane gets away scot-free," Hiro retorted sharply, disdain clear in his voice. "What do we do then? He looks awful," Taichi interjected urgently.

"You stay here, Taichi. Hikaru and I will go back to the

cafe," Hiro decided firmly. "Hai," Taichi agreed solemnly. The remaining ninjas left the shack, their steps quickening as they headed back towards the dockyard eatery, anxious and determined to uncover the truth.

Hiro entered the cafe alone, while Hikaru obediently lingered outside at his alpha brother's insistence. As he stepped through the door, his gaze fixated on the cook, who was busy fussing over the stovetop, oblivious to Hiro's presence with his back turned.

Hiro stood there, glaring at the filthy man, his anticipation mingled with simmering anger. The injustice of serving toxic food ignited Hiro's fury. He believed the deformed chef had intentionally tried to poison them both, and his animosity grew as he thought about the blatant disrespect and intimidation they had faced.

His thoughts spiraled into irrationality and exaggerated revenge fantasies. Hiro fixated on the violence he intended to unleash on the inferior imbecile, determined to teach him a severe lesson.

"Hey, cook!" Hiro shouted as he approached the servery, his voice laden with impatience. The man didn't turn around immediately.

"Chef! I'm talking to you!" Hiro shouted again, his tone escalating in pitch as frustration boiled within him.

Slowly, the chef turned to face Hiro, who was stunned to see that it wasn't the same man who had served them the poisoned food earlier.

"Hai.... can I help you?" the chef responded apathetically, clearly unimpressed by Hiro's hostility.

"Where's the other man who served me earlier?" Hiro

demanded, panic creeping into his voice.

"There's no other man. There's just me, and I've been here all day. What do you want?" the chef replied, growing impatient.

"No, no, there was this handicapped man who prepared my friend and me a bowl of fish casserole," Hiro insisted, his heart racing with uncertainty.

"Fish casserole? I did'nt make that dish today. As I've already told you, I'm the only one here and have been all day. I can't afford to employ anyone else," the chef stated firmly, his expression unwavering.

"I'm not delusional.... this can't be right. He had a huge mouth with a dislocated jaw, and on his neck, there was a peculiar birthmark shaped like a scythe," Hiro
insisted desperately.

"Nope, don't know anyone that fits that description," the chef replied indifferently. "What's the problem anyway?" he added, seemingly unaffected.

"My brother is gravely ill after eating the fish casserole from here, and I think he was intentionally poisoned," Hiro accused, his voice tinged with anger.

"Well, you can't blame me because this is the first time I've met you. If you both ate the food, then why aren't you sick?" the chef retorted curtly.

"Because I didn't eat the sloppy crap. It looked disgusting.... that's why," Hiro snapped back, frustration bubbling under the surface.

"There's nothing I can do. I hope your brother gets over his illness," the chef affirmed dismissively, turning back to the stove to continue cooking. Hiro stood there, overwhelmed with an impulse to jump over the counter and exact revenge on the ignorant chef. However, his deep-seated Buddhist faith and rigorous ninja training restrained him. With a heavy heart, he left the cafe and returned to the shack with Hikaru, his mind racing with outrage and doubt

.

The late afternoon sun began to set, casting long skinny shadows on the ground from the masts of docked tall ships. The slanting rays painted the sky with a warm orange colour.

Entering the abandoned cabin, Hiro and Hikaru found Itsuo looking worse than before, while Taichi sat beside him, desperately trying to ease his suffering from the intense stomach pain that seemed to be consuming him.

"He's vomiting and having diarrhea.... he can't keep this up. What are we going to do?" Taichi pleaded, looking up at Hiro. But Hiro stood there silently, trying to grasp the severity of the situation, his mind struggling to process what was unfolding before him.

"HIRO!!!" Taichi screamed, trying to jolt him out of his trance. "What are we going to do??" he pressed urgently.

"I don't know... give him some water," Hiro managed to respond, his voice fringed with helplessness.

"I've tried that already. Every time he sips water, he just vomits," Taichi explained urgently, his worry all over his face.

"That's it.....I'm going to fetch a healer," Hikaru suddenly declared, breaking the tense silence as Hiro snapped back to reality with a start.

"No, you're not! What did I tell you about that? It'll put our mission at risk," Hiro exploded, his temper flaring as the pressure of the situation felt like it was crushing his mind.

"Yes, I am. Screw the mission, Itsuo's health is more important than catching Kane," Hikaru shot back defiantly. Without another word, he turned to leave, but Hiro grabbed his shoulder, spinning him around forcefully. In a split second, Hikaru reacted instinctively, swinging a punch that landed squarely on Hiro's nose.

Stunned by the unexpected blow, Hiro shook his head in disbelief as blood streamed into his mouth. He glared at his brother for a moment, tasting the warm, bitter liquid, before retaliating by hurling a large amount of blood-stained saliva into Hikaru's face. The act ignited their brawl instantly.

Hiro grounded himself, blocking Hikaru's spinning hook kick with his forearm. He swiftly shifted backward, moving fluidly to disrupt his brother's advance and unsettle his balance. Seizing the opportunity, Hiro lunged forward, throwing a curved punch with his right fist, driving his knuckles into Hikaru's temple.

Hikaru staggered back, seeing stars and his vision blurring from the impact. Before he could regain his bearings, Hiro intercepted with swift, precise movements.

Channeling his anger into action, Hiro launched himself with a jump kick, slamming his foot into the side of Hikaru's stomach.

The force of the blow winded him and left him reeling, fracturing two ribs upon impact. Hikaru collapsed to the ground, clutching his side and gasping for breath. "Well, isn't this just great? We've got Itsuo lying here sick as a dog, and now you've injured Hikaru. How are we supposed to apprehend Kane with half of us down and out?" Taichi cursed, frustrated by Hiro's self-centered and confrontational attitude toward his brothers.

Hiro remained silent, glaring down at Hikaru with disdain.

The distant barking of dogs intermittently shattered the silence of the night as the group of ninjas attempted to get some much-needed sleep. However, in the background, Hiro couldn't escape the incessant moaning of Itsuo due to his illness.

"Shut up," Hiro muttered to himself callously, rolling onto his side and glaring at the suffering Itsuo.

"Please help me," Itsuo pleaded, noticing his brother wasn't asleep.

Hiro rose from his bed, his face contorted with contempt, and walked over to Itsuo casually.

"Do you think you'll still be able to continue hunting for Kane?" he asked flatly. "Not the way I'm feeling," Itsuo whispered weakly.

"So what are we going to do with you?" Hiro questioned, crouching down beside his sick brother. He watched disdainfully as Itsuo heaved, attempting to vomit again. "Let me help you," Hiro offered, placing his large hand over Itsuo's mouth and pinching his nose simultaneously. He callously observed Itsuo struggle for breath, the lack of air akin to drowning.

Even though Itsuo felt tired and lethargic, his warrior soul fought desperately to remove Hiro's hand from his airways. Feebly punching and slapping at him, Itsuo struggled against his attacker. But with each futile attempt, Hiro only pressed down tighter, constricting Itsuo's breathing further. The fear mounted as Itsuo realized there was no escape from his brother's suffocating grip, his strength ebbing away until he could no longer resist.

Leisurely withdrawing his hand, Hiro sat, self-gratified,

leering at Itsuo, mesmerized by his victim's petrified death stare as the sense of triumph flooded through him.

Finally able to resume the search for Kane without any more interruptions, he gently closed Itsuo's eyes and silently retired to his bedding. He lay down with his back turned to the lifeless brother, the pang of guilt a sensation far beyond his understanding.

The sun's rays eventually heralded a new day, awakening Taichi. Instantly alert, he hurried towards Itsuo while Hiro remained frozen in his cold-blooded posture, awake and listening intently.

"Itsuo... Itsuo, wake up!" Taichi exclaimed, shaking the lifeless man frantically. "He's dead!" Taichi announced, bewildered by what had occurred, then rushed over to Hiro, trying to rouse the already awake killer.

"Hiro, wake up! Itsuo's dead," Taichi urged urgently. "Huh? What?" Hiro replied, feigning confusion. "Itsuo is dead," Taichi repeated.

"How?" Hiro asked, rising and walking over to the deceased brother.

"I don't know, but he is," Taichi replied, standing just behind Hiro as he watched him pry open Itsuo's mouth.

"He must have choked during the night.... see? There's residual vomit," Hiro concluded, pointing to the congealed mass oozing from Itsuo's mouth.

"Poor Itsuo... what a horrible way to die," Taichi remarked solemnly. "What are we going to do?"

"Stop asking me that, Taichi! I'm not the sorcerer of solutions!" Hiro bellowed loudly, waking Hikaru.

"What's going on?" Hikaru groaned, clutching his painful torso as he focused on the commotion.

"Itsuo died during the night.... looks like he choked," Hiro informed his brother, gently running his fingers through the deceased man's hair.

"Rest in peace," he continued, his manner surprisingly graceful. "I can't believe this," Taichi whined.

"It's early, but once the market opens, go find a large sheet of cloth. We'll wrap Itsuo in it for burial," Hiro finally stated.

"Hai," Taichi complied, yielding to Hiro's directive.

As the day unfolded, Taichi wandered leisurely through the bustling marketplace, immersing himself in its vibrant sights and sounds.

The brilliance of the day bathed everyday life in a kaleidoscope of colors, while the enticing aroma of food wafted through the air, offering a soothing balm to his wounded soul after the loss of Itsuo.

Rather than rushing to find the cloth and return to the shack, Taichi allowed himself the luxury of being engulfed in the positive sensations that surrounded him. He sought a reprieve from the overpowering presence of Hiro, whose dominating opinions had been a source of tension. Instead, Taichi wandered aimlessly, letting the marketplace's energy penetrate him, until he unexpectedly found himself standing before Osaka's magnificent Shinto shrine. The shrine stood proudly in front of the city gates, a serene oasis amidst the busy city life.

Here, surrounded by the sacred atmosphere and the peaceful beauty of the shrine, Taichi found a moment of quiet introspection. The solemnity of the place offered him a refuge from his swirling emotions, allowing him to reflect on Itsuo's passing and find a temporary escape from the pressures of his circumstances.

Feelings of euphoria gently welled up inside Taichi as he stood observing the crowd streaming through the gateway, reminiscent of trails of ants moving in parallel but opposite directions. Finding a grassy hill to settle on, he sat down and let himself be enveloped by the cheerful sounds of the crowd. In that moment, amidst the vibrant energy of the marketplace and the serene beauty of the shrine, Taichi discovered a fragment of joy that still lingered within him.

Immersed in the vigorous atmosphere, Taichi soaked in the midday sun before deciding to leave his perch. As he stood up and brushed off his pants, preparing to

depart, his gaze caught sight of a familiar figure passing through the gates of Osaka: an old man seated atop a horse, guided by a young monk.

"Master Gideon! Master Gideon!" Taichi shouted eagerly, waving his arms with a surge of relief flooding his senses.

"Master Taichi?' Gideon replied, briskly pulling on the reins, startled by the unexpected encounter

"I am so glad to see you.....and of course I'm glad to see you as well, Master Miko"

Taichi panted excitedly

"You seem unsettled, Master Taichi.... I didn't expect to find you here in Osaka," Gideon remarked, his voice sounding disappointed.

"It's reasonable to assume your team would have made more progress. Your group departed weeks ahead of me."

"Hai. I'm glad to see you've recovered from your grievous

injuries, Master Gideon," Taichi interjected quickly, attempting to steer the conversation away from their perceived lack of progress. He sensed Gideon's dissatisfaction with their efforts, and in that moment, Gideon turned to face Taichi fully, revealing deep gashes and a disfigured white eye.

"Where are your brothers?" Gideon asked formally, his gaze probing.

"This way, Master Gideon. Follow me," Taichi responded promptly, leading Gideon through the throng of people with Miko close behind, guiding the horse until they reached the secluded cabin.

As Miko helped Gideon dismount, Taichi entered the shack alone and was immediately met with Hiro's furious attitude.

"Where have you been? Do you think this is a vacation? Where is the cloth I asked you to get? We've been waiting here for hours, staring at our deceased brother.

Have you no consideration for us?" Hiro shouted, his face inches from Taichi's. Before Taichi could respond, Gideon suddenly appeared in the doorway.

"Why are you yelling, Master Hiro?" Gideon's voice was calm but firm.

"Master Gideon!" Hiro exclaimed, astonished at the unexpected arrival of his revered mentor. He quickly bowed in respect.

Gideon and Miko entered the cabin, their eyes scanning the scene silently. Without a word spoken, they immediately noticed Hikaru seated in the corner, grimacing from his injuries, and Itsuo lying lifeless on a straw bed across the room.

Gideon approached Hiro slowly, stopping just inches from his face, locking eyes with him.

"Explain to me what has happened here," Gideon demanded

in a hard tone. “Hai Master Itsuo passed away from food poisoning, and there was a

disagreement between Master Hikaru and me that led to his injury,” Hiro replied, skirting around the details deliberately.

“What was the nature of this disagreement?” Gideon’s voice remained clinical, devoid of emotion, as he pressed for clarity.

“Hikaru wanted to fetch a healer for Itsuo, but I tried to explain that it would alert the Samurai and could lead to imprisonment,” Hiro quickly defended his actions.

“And did your altercation serve your purpose? Did you vindicate your stance through violence? Or did you, in the end, hinder our mission by harming your brother and triumphantly diminishing our ranks?” Gideon’s voice was unwavering, his gaze piercing, colder than ice, causing Hiro to bow his head in shame.

“How did Master Itsuo become so gravely ill that he died?” Gideon pressed on. “He ate a bowl of fish casserole from the eatery on the wharf,” Hiro muttered. “Hmph.... That explanation doesn’t ring true. We’ve had a few cases of food poisoning at the monastery before, and if properly managed, no one has died from it,” Gideon stated, unimpressed by Hiro’s inadequate explanation.

“I have spoken the truth,” Hiro asserted firmly.

“Master Gideon,” Taichi interjected, stepping forward and seeking permission to speak to the elder monk.

“Hai, Master Taichi.... What is it?” Gideon responded.

“Master Hiro is telling the truth. However, while Master Itsuo did not die directly from food poisoning, he choked during the night on his own vomit. That was Master Hiro’s conclusion after examining him this morning," Taichi clarified earnestly.

"So you're only telling me half-truths, Master Hiro. If he was so sick, why was he left unattended overnight? Why did no one stay up with him?" Gideon demanded sharply, shifting his scrutiny to expose the gaps in Hiro's account.

"Master Hikaru, what are your injuries?" he asked, turning to the injured brother. "I think some of my ribs are broken. It hurts to breathe," Hikaru groaned in pain. "Look at what your arrogance has caused, Master Hiro. Your selfishness has endangered us all," Gideon admonished, his voice carrying the weight of disappointment.

"I warn you, Kane poses a real threat. As his supernatural strength grows, so does his power. What sort of team do we have to face such a menace? A selfish and weak one, it seems."

A heavy silence fell upon everyone as Gideon contemplated how to address the dire consequences of their current situation.

"Master Miko and Master Taichi, go into the city and procure a burial cloth for Master Itsuo, a long, thin green stick, and another horse," Gideon finally announced with authority. "Master Hikaru will ride my horse and accompany Itsuo's body back to the monastery."

"With all due respect, Master Gideon, I don't feel well enough to travel that far on my own," Hikaru confessed, his voice strained as he coughed up a small amount of blood.

"In that case, Master Taichi, once you have gathered what I've requested, prepare for the journey. You will escort them to the monastery and inform the Abbot of what has occurred. Request additional skilled ninjas for our mission in Osaka. The pursuit of Kane must continue," Gideon instructed.

"And as for you, Master Hiro," Gideon's gaze turned poker-faced, "you will remain here and face punishment through flagellation. Pray that God will show you mercy for your actions. That is all. Now, go."

The room fell silent as Gideon's orders lingered in the air, each member of the group understanding the gravity of their roles in the unfolding events.

"Master Gideon, may I ask.....have you seen Master Shusuki and Master Naoki during your travels? We haven't come across them and I was wondering if they might be on their way here" Taichi asked

"They are dead.....slaughtered by the demon beast in the alpine region near Kyoto.....This is why Kane is so treacherous. I cannot emphasize this enough. Take Master Miko and do your duty.....I'll wait here with Master Hiro. Ninja's; always remember your disciplines and time is of the essence" Gideon ordered, so the two younger monks hurried out of the cabin.

Searching the streets and fields for Gideon's needed items, they paused at a

post-and-rail fence near the local horse stables, hopping up to survey the available horses.

"Which one do you think, Taichi?" Miko asked.

"Who's going to pay for this? The switch and blanket didn't cost us anything.... but a horse is different," Taichi replied, voicing his concern.

"It's alright, I have the money," Miko whispered with a sly grin. "Where did you get that?" Taichi questioned.

"Master Gideon gave it to me. He is always well provided for wherever he goes," Miko declared proudly. "He's not just wise and respected, but a Master of ninjutsu and a revered High Buddhist Monk."

"Do you think Master Gideon is upset with us?" Taichi inquired.

"Yes, he is," Miko explained sadly. "Remember, Kane murdered Abbot Eshin, who was not only Master Gideon's best friend but also his closest confidant. Now the beast has claimed Shusuki and Naoki, and possibly Itsuo as well."

"But Itsuo didn't die at Kane's hand; he passed due to food poisoning and choking during the night," Taichi argued, countering Miko's assertion.

"One of you should have fetched the doctor regardless, and then you left him alone, unsupervised all night. Taichi, our faith and our brothers must always come first," Miko stated firmly.

"Hai.... but then there's Hiro. He's always so aggressive and defiant. And he's a tough opponent in combat too.... just look at what he did to Hikaru," Taichi replied, expressing his concerns.

"Don't fret over Hiro. Master Gideon will straighten him out soon enough.... it's been a long time coming," Miko reassured, a sense of shared understanding between them evident as they both chuckled lightly.

Gideon moved methodically to Itsuo's body, bending down to examine it closely. Inserting his fingers into the mouth and down the throat, he searched for any obstruction that could have caused his death, but found nothing significant enough to cause asphyxiation.

"Master Hiro, you claim Master Itsuo choked last night.... is that your final conclusion?" Gideon demanded, rising to his full height and locking eyes with Hiro. "Hai, but I'm not a doctor, Master Gideon," Hiro replied, a note of panic creeping into his voice.

"There's no blockage in his airway, anyone can see that" Gideon stated, his voice sharp. "If he did choke as you say, his desperate struggle to breathe, the sharp coughing, the dry heaving, even an attempt to cry out—shouldn't all that have been loud enough to wake you? How could you not have heard it?" Gideon pressed, his intensity cutting through the air, sensing Hiro's deceit.

"Our journey has been long and difficult, Master Gideon, and we were all exhausted. When we finally had the chance to rest, I suppose we just passed out," Hiro explained, his voice betraying his nervousness.

"Your explanation doesn't seem plausible, Master Hiro.... you're lying," Gideon replied, his tone dripping with skepticism as he attempted to unsettle the egotistical ninja.

At that precise moment, Taichi and Miko entered the shack with the gathered items. "Master Gideon, the second horse is tied up outside," Miko announced, bowing respectfully.

"Good.... hand me the branch," the old monk demanded, stripping off the residual leaves and striking the air to test its resilience. Satisfied, he handed the long green stick to Hiro.

"Begin," he commanded. Hiro reluctantly removed his shirt and knelt on the earthen floor, preparing for the self-torture.

"Fifty lashes, Master Hiro, for neglecting your brother and hindering our mission. After each strike, loudly ask God to show you mercy. Master Miko will keep count," Gideon ordered firmly.

"Master Taichi, wrap Itsuo's body in the blanket and start heading back to the monastery with Hikaru. Sling the body over the horse you purchased, and Master Hikaru will ride mine. When you arrive, inform the Abbot of our situation and request additional ninjas to be sent to Osaka. Once they arrive, tell them to find a man named 'Dai' who resides on the wharf. I will visit him soon to address this problem.... and ask the Abbot for more money to support our mission as well," Gideon commanded, his voice stern and unyielding.

"Hai," they answered in unison, beginning their preparations for the long journey back to the monastery, perched high in the mountains and far removed from the grueling hunt for the skin-changer.

Gideon stood motionless to one side, silently overseeing Hiro's punishment. With his hands cupped over one another, he resembled a statue, leaning on a

distinguished-looking staff that served both as a weapon and a symbol of his power and rank.

Miko counted the strikes as Hiro lashed himself, each stroke accompanied by Hiro's loud declarations of faithfulness to God and pleas for forgiveness. When the count reached fifty, Gideon stepped forward, his voice cutting through the air with harsh authority.

"Let this serve as a warning, Master Hiro. Your actions have consequences, and you will be held accountable. Do not forget the gravity of your duty," Gideon admonished sternly, his gaze piercing and relentless.

"Being chased is as potentially lethal as it gets. You try to escape at any cost. You focus. You think. You deal with the trauma later or you don't. Survival comes at a

cost, Master Hiro, a cost you must pay because it is expected of you. Do not deceive yourself into thinking you are the alpha male on this mission. The malignant demon we search for is devious, powerful, and sustained by supernatural abilities,"

Gideon stated, his voice severe.

"He is no ordinary man. He has an unclean spirit dwelling within. Prayer and unity are our only salvation from this devil."

"Your hostility towards your brothers and complete disregard for everything we've taught you is an insult to me and to the monastery. Your bitterness and overinflated ego will be your undoing, Master Hiro. Do not allow your poison to ruin this mission." The old monk didn't move a muscle during the entire chastisement, remaining steadfast in his original position. The only part of him showing the disgust he felt were his eyes, which flared with a burning intensity of frustration.

"Now get up and help Brother Taichi place Master Itsuo on the horse and secure him properly. I am heading for the wharf now to pay Mr. Dai a friendly visit. Master Miko,

you come with me," Gideon commanded. He then exited the shack with calm authority, moving swiftly through the entrance with Miko following closely behind.

In contrast to their bald heads, Gideon and Miko wore traditional simple woolen tunics tied at their waists with leather belts. These outfits were designed to cover as much flesh as possible. As they perused Osaka's exciting shipping port, the most recognizable part of their ensemble was their cowls, completing the monks' habit.

These distinctive characteristics set them apart from the dozens of other people crowding the pier.

"Excuse me, do you know where I could find a man named Dai?" Miko asked persistently, following his superior's directive. As they roamed the wharf, they finally encountered someone who could help.

"I know Dai. He's not a spiritual, so why do monks want to see him?" the man queried with suspicion.

"It's no concern of yours," Gideon intervened firmly, noting Miko's unease in the presence of the gruff individual.

Simultaneously unloading freight from a cargo ship, the ill-mannered dock worker bellowed to another docker,

"Hey Arata, show these monks where Dai lives."

"Sure thing, boss. Follow me, it's at the end of the wharf," Arata replied, flashing a smile that revealed his only two remaining rotten teeth in his rough head.

The trio walked down to the last assigned berth, where Arata knocked forcefully on the door.

"What do you want, Arata?" one of Dai's employees rudely muttered as he confronted them.

"These monks want to see Dai," Arata replied nervously, intimidated by the irritable man's demeanor. Miko watched with unease, while Gideon stood behind him, dedicated in their mission to interrogate the man known as Dai.

"More monks? What is this, Monk Week?" the plain-faced worker grumbled. "The boss is out the back."

"Dai, there are two monks here who want to talk to you," he announced before opening the door wide to let them pass.

"Kuso (shit), more annoying monks," Dai muttered to himself before shouting out, "Hai... send them in."

"A young monk and an old one eh?" Dai mocked, staring at the difference in their age.

"What do you want?" He continued

Gideon stepped forward, his presence commanding as he engaged with the fat man sporting a long, spindly beard.

"Has another monk visited you lately? He's a sizable, robust man with huge arms. Perhaps he has grown out his hair or was bald like us. His name is Kane. I cannot tell you much more, though that ought to be enough," Gideon articulated calmly, devoid of agitation.

"Hai, I remember him... He was still bald, and he boarded the ship *'Sea Changer,'*

which left port a week ago," the man responded.

"What country was the *'Sea Changer'* sailing to?" Gideon pressed on. "America," came the straightforward reply.

"How did Kane acquire the right papers to travel overseas?" Gideon pressed, his tone insistent.

"I put his passport together for him," the man replied. "Can you do the same for us?" Gideon inquired further.

"It depends. I'll need payment first, and I know monks don't usually have a clan name, so you'll need that as well. Are the passports only for the two of you?" Dai asked.

"No, there will be one more joining us. For curiosity's sake, what clan name did Kane use, and what reason did he give for traveling to America?" Gideon questioned.

"He said he was on a spiritual pilgrimage, and his Dharma title was Shunro.... Kane Shunro was his name on the papers," the man responded.

"So he used his Dharma name. When will the *'Sea Changer'* return to Osaka?" Gideon asked, getting to the heart of the matter.

"Well, it's a little over 5,100 nautical miles one way. If the weather holds, another ship from America should arrive back here in three weeks, your trip will take about 26 days," Dai explained, watching Gideon closely to gauge his reaction. But Gideon remained composed, his expression unchanged by the new information.

"I assume you no longer want the passports?" Dai broke the silence, testing the monk's commitment.

"On the contrary, I still need three of them, and I'll have the money for you soon. Prepare the papers, Mr. Dai. We will depart once the *'Sea Changer'* returns. I'll be staying at the Hozenji Temple while we wait, if you need to contact me," Gideon instructed calmly.

"I want to see payment first, Monk," the greedy proprietor insisted. "You will get your money."

"Alright. So, what names shall I put on them?" Dai inquired, eager to proceed with the transaction.

"Gideon Rencho, Miko Daishi, and Hiro Shakku.... Would you like me to write that down for you?" Gideon challenged.

"No need, I'll remember. I'll have the papers ready once I receive the full payment, which will be a total of 3,000 yen," Dai replied confidently, attempting to exploit the monks' perceived naivety and sanctity.

"Come, Miko. Thank you for your assistance," Gideon said calmly. The monks left Dai's office and returned to the shack, where Taichi and Hiro were finishing preparations for Taichi and Hikaru's journey back to the monastery.

"Wait until nightfall before you leave Osaka, Master Taichi. That way, you'll travel in the shadows and avoid raising suspicions among the Samurai," Gideon instructed. "Hai, Master Gideon," Taichi replied respectfully, bowing to his leader.

"Master Gideon, did you find any more information about Kane's whereabouts?" Hiro asked cautiously.

"He boarded an American ship called the 'Sea Changer' a week ago," Gideon informed them solemnly. "The problem is, it won't return to Osaka for three weeks. Then there are the 26 days of our traveling, giving the demon more time to evade us."

"What are we going to do? I heard that America is huge. How will we find him? He could go anywhere," Hiro exclaimed, frustration evident in his voice.

"Quiet, Master Hiro. We will stay at the Hozenji Temple in the meantime. It will give you an opportunity to discipline yourself through meditation and prayer. Safe travels, Master Hikaru and Master Taichi. Remember to request more money and some of our finest warriors. We will await their arrival patiently at the temple," Gideon concluded, bidding them farewell as the group dispersed.

Chapter 7

In the deepest reaches of the ocean, an uncanny grey mist descended upon the *"Sea Changer,"* its wintry presence thicker than pea soup. Lifeless and shadowy, the mist coiled in erratic, ghostly fingers that snaked around, enveloping the tranquil waters and shrouding everything in camouflage.

The gossamer-like vapor ensnared every nook and cranny of the ship, rendering it motionless in the still waters. It draped over the vessel like a spectral veil, casting an unsettling aura over the ocean's depths.

Kane reclined on his cabin bed, clutching the human-skinned book to his broad chest. He savored the tranquility of the calm waters, a rare respite from weeks of relentless seasickness. His body was weary and hollow, drained by violent bouts of illness. Despite craving nourishment, his mind recoiled from the thought of food.

The gnawing pain robbed Kane of his lucidity, plunging him into memories of childhood hunger at the monastery. It clouded his rational thoughts. As he stroked the treasured book, a scratching sound echoed from beneath his bed. Rolling over, he peered into the darkness of the hollow and saw a small rodent staring back at him.

This creature was no ordinary rat. Its body was ordinary, but its face was disturbingly human-like, adorned with long, jagged fangs protruding from its elongated mouth.

Dark bags instantly materialized under Kane's eyes, aging his youthful face into that of a haggard elder. The cabin's noises intensified, distorted shadows whispering and shifting across the walls. Kane felt besieged, as if under assault. Abruptly, the temperature plummeted to an arctic chill.

"He is coming," hissed the disfigured rat, its human-like face contorting unnaturally. Suddenly it propelled itself onto Kane's bed, its presence filling the cabin with a hideous vibe.

Against the backdrop of pitch-black shapes, a white mist emerged from the human-skinned book. It swirled around like a miniature tornado, merging into the tall, featureless white figure that Kane had seen in his dreams.

Hovering in the center of the room, the spectral entity remained silent. This time, however, instead of the apparition speaking directly to Kane, the message came through the ugly rat perched at the foot of his bed. Its appearance was unsettlingly familiar, and it mimicked the ghostly tone and rhythm of the spectral figure. *"Prepare yourself,"* the rodent's voice warned, its words laced with a unsettling resonance that filled Kane with terror.

"My son, you are entwined with life's destiny. You are now part of our universal heritage, and your life's experiences will be inscribed in the book you clutch so tightly. Your totem animal and the book will be your guides. Protect both with your life," the rat hissed, its words punctuated by sharp

gnashing of its teeth.

"I don't have a totem animal," Kane pleaded, addressing the white phantom hovering before him. But as he spoke, the rat let out a piercing scream, its bizzare form contorting in rage. With a sudden burst of ferocity, it lunged at Kane, its repulsive fangs aiming for his arm in a violent protest against his insolence.

"You talk to me, impudent child.....I am him and he is me.....we are one" The diseased looking rat warned

"Ok? So is this rat your totem animal?" He directed his question towards the vile rodent

"Yes, I am the spirit being, a sacred entity of our clan," the rat hissed.

"We have the ability to come in and out of your life to guide you on the tasks that need to be completed along your earthly journey. Your totem animal serves as your primary guardian spirit, offering wisdom. You must remain open to learning its lessons."

"So, where is my totem animal? Have I seen it yet? Kane asked

"Yes you have.....it is the wolf-dog with the white-tipped tail you so fondly named "Lady Vixen"

"But she vanished back into the woods before I entered Osaka" Kane informed the skanky rat creature.

"Did she?" The rat sniggered with a demonic cackle, its voice deep and evocative. Abruptly, it vanished back under the bed, leaving Kane to shudder at the unreal sounds of disembodied voices that filled the air.

Terrifying black shadows whirled frantically around the room, their chaotic movements creating a sense of impending doom before they finally streamed out through the cabin's porthole, disappearing into the thick, billowing fog outside.

Meanwhile, the white, faceless specter melded back into the human-skinned book, leaving behind an unsettling aura of lingering despair that filled the cabin like the predatory fog.

Suddenly there was a loud knock at the door. "Yes, who is it?" Kane answered

"Mr Shunro.....the cap'n wants to know if you're ok in there?" A gruff voice bellowed through the closed entrance.

"Yes I'm alright thank you"

"Well things don't sound alright in there plus we haven't seen you for a while.....not even in the dining room to eat"

Kane rose from the bed, his pulse racing with trepidation, and cautiously unlocked the cabin door. With a creeping sense of unease, he opened it just a crack, allowing only his face to peer out into the dimly lit hallway.

"You don't look so good Mr Shunro" The crewman announced noticing the black bags under Kanes eyes.

"I've been very ill from the rough seas lately, so that's why I haven't ventured out of my room.... satisfied?" Kane blurted out, his frustration evident in the clear English he used.

"Oh, so you do speak English.... interesting," the crewman replied, a hint of skepticism in his voice.

"We've had complaints about some worrying noises coming from your room." "Like I've already said, that was me being intensely ill.... does that pass your interrogation?" Kane shot back, his irritation barely concealed.

"I'm a private man and I spend a lot of time studying the scriptures, meditating and practicing my Buddhist faith" Kane quickly added

"No problem. Sorry to have disturbed you. If there is anything you....." The sailor tried offering his passenger further assistance, but Kane briskly closed the door, shutting it in his face, before he was able to finish the sentence.

As the seafarer shuffled away from Kane's cabin, strolling down the corridor, a neighboring passenger cautiously opened his door and motioned the crewman over. "Yes, Mr. Kent, what can I do for you?"

"What's happening in there with that Japanese monk?"

"I'm not authorized to discuss it, Mr. Kent. What seems to be the problem?" "The creepy noises and that foul stench could wake the dead."

"The monk isn't used to sea travel and has been quite ill from the rough seas. That might explain the strange sounds and odor. Rest assured, everything is under control. Good night, Sir," the sailor reassured before continuing his rounds, eventually making his way to the captain's quarters later that night.

Kane, with his keen sense of hearing, caught every word of Mr. Kent's complaint. A shiver of paranoid dread coursed through his rational Buddhist mind, unsettling his composure.

* * *

"Come in," the Captain directed as the investigating sailor knocked on his door. "Everything seems to be in order, Cap'n. Looks like the fog is finally lifting. With any luck, we'll catch a good breeze tomorrow and head homeward. This past month at sea has been quite strange," the sailor reported.

"Yes I agree but it good to hear that things are in order, Charlie. Did you check on the Japanese monk?" the captain inquired.

"Yes, I did, Cap'n," Charlie replied cautiously.

"And how is he now that the seas have calmed? We haven't seen him for weeks. For all we know, he could be dead," the captain expressed concern.

"He's alive, Cap'n, but he doesn't look well though. There's something off about him," Charlie revealed, hesitating slightly.

"What do you mean, something 'off' about him? And don't start with your superstitious talk, Charlie. I don't want to hear it," the captain responded, his intuition aroused.

"Well, even Mr. Kent in room three is complaining about strange noises and odors coming from the monk's cabin. When I questioned Mr. Shunro, his body language and tone pretty much told me to back off. He didn't want any interaction with me, Cap'n," Charlie reported earnestly.

"Well, he's been suffering from seasickness, and he's an introverted Japanese monk. Who knows what kind of customs and practices these foreigners have? Being reclusive might be one of them.... It's a strange world, Charlie. As long as he's alive, that's all I care about," the captain mused.

"Aye, aye, Cap'n," Charlie replied, turning to leave. "Charlie," the captain called after him.

"Yes, Cap?"

"Keep a close eye on Mr. Shunro. Report back to me if you notice anything out of the ordinary," the captain ordered firmly.

Charlie nodded with compliance and promptly exited the quarters, making a beeline for the crew's mess hall, where he quickly poured himself a cup of coffee and settled at the large dining table.

"Are you alright, Charlie? You look a bit off," one of his seafarer mates remarked, eyeing him curiously.

"Yeah, I'm fine. Just had to check on that Japanese Monk in room two, on the Cap's orders. Something about him doesn't sit right with me," Charlie replied, staring down at his coffee mug thoughtfully.

"What do you know about monks being normal people, Charlie?" another sailor teased, causing a ripple of chuckles to spread through the group.

"Laugh all you want, but I've sailed to Japan and back enough times to know a thing or two. This one's different. He's not like the usual monks I've seen. And have you seen his size? He's not the typical small stature of a Japanese man.... he's a giant," Charlie explained, his voice lowering conspiratorially.

"Maybe he's not entirely Japanese. Could have some Russian or Polish blood in him, for all we know," another crew member chimed in, stirring his own coffee thoughtfully. Charlie took a sip of his beverage, his mind racing with thoughts about Mr. Shunro and the agitated feeling he couldn't shake off.

"Maybe, but I'm on edge about the bloke. The Cap'ns got me watching him, and I'll be damned if I don't," the old sailor concluded, his voice wavering with unease. "Don't let your superstitions cloud your head, Charlie," his friend retorted, eyeing him questionably.

"You know there's a woman aboard, and they say they bring bad luck. Females distract the men from their duties at sea, stirring up the wrath of the unpredictable seas. Heard about those poor souls who met their end on this ship's maiden voyage?" Charlie stroked his long grey beard nervously as he spoke, eyes darting around as if expecting something sinister.

"Hmph.... No response? Nothing to say? Just as I thought. My shift's starting on deck, so I'm off to the helm," the sailor hurriedly excused himself, clearly spooked. "Alright, see ya, Charlie," his friend bid farewell, watching him depart with a troubled expression.

As Charlie emerged from the stuffy confines of the ship's interior, the cool, moist air enveloped his face, mingling with the warmth of his breath. He stepped out into the cold night, pulling up the collar of his weathered brown jacket to shield his neck from the chill. Taking command of the helm from the previous sailor, he cast a glance over the quiet, moonlit expanse of the ocean stretching endlessly around them.

"I'll be bloody glad when we dock in America," he muttered to himself, his voice barely audible over the gentle lapping of the waves against the hull.

Drawing in a deep breath of salty air, Charlie's senses tuned into the sounds of the night. The distinct sequences of groans, roars, and high-pitched squeals echoed through the darkness. It was the eerie melody of a distant whale song, carrying across the water like a haunting serenade. Despite the unease he had been feeling, the familiar and almost sociable nature of the whale's song brought a fleeting smile to his weathered face.

Suddenly, Kane emerged on deck, silently standing just a few feet behind the old sailor.

"Mr. Shunro, for such a big fellow, you're surprisingly light on your feet. I didn't even hear you approach.... so, you've finally left your cabin," Charlie remarked, his voice betraying a slight tremor as he turned around, startled by the unexpected noise. "What's that sound out there in the ocean?" Kane asked.

"It's the whales. They sound unearthly, but they're just gentle giants—a bit like you, eh, Mr. Shunro? Nothing to be scared of, right?" Charlie said, his chuckle coming out forced.

"I'm not scared," Kane replied bluntly, puzzled by the sailor's assumption and oblivious to the implication that he might be frightening.

"Oh? Ok? Yeah, well, I suppose a burly chap like you wouldn't be scared of anything " Charlie cleared his throat, the creeping anxiety twisting his stomach into

knots.

Without uttering a word, Kane walked past Charlie and headed towards the starboard bow.

"Mr. Shunro, passengers aren't allowed on the main deck at night. It's a safety issue," the sailor cautioned, but Kane ignored him and kept walking.

"Defiant Japanese prick" Charlie muttered under his breath.

"I can hear you," Kane said flatly, continuing towards the bow and disappearing behind the forecastle deck, making it difficult for Charlie to keep an eye on him. "Shit," Charlie muttered, feeling alarmed.

Kane leaned against the guardrail, staring vacantly into the abyss of darkness as he contemplated the earlier message from the deformed rat and his future in the foreign world of America. His thoughts kept returning to the terrible circumstances that unfolded at the monastery and the gang of ninjas hot on his trail.

Then he heard the faint sound of approaching footsteps, like the wet crunch of someone walking on a moistened, gritty road. They were neither a threat nor of any interest to Kane, but whoever was coming up the passageway was light and small-boned. Kane turned around to see who was advancing towards him and, as he gazed into the gloomy depth of the fog, a beautiful lady with long brown hair silently emerged from the drifting mist and casually stood beside him.

"Hello" She greeted softly

"Hello" Kane answered restlessly. This was the first time in his entire life that he'd spoken to such an alluring woman.

"You seem nervous" She commented with a diminutive smile.

"Do I?" He answered sharply

"Yes you're not comfortable talking to a woman?"

"Being raised in a remote monastery, it's not traditional for monks to converse with the opposite sex"

"Oh, I see"

Kane observed her with intense scrutiny.

"What do you want?" He openly exclaimed

"I know who you are.....your name is Kane Shunro" She confessed

"How do you know me? I don't know you Miss.....?" And as he earnestly looked at the strange woman, he noticed that her eyes were different colors.

"Your universal father has assigned me to you....."

"Stop beating around the bush lady, who are you?" Kane was becoming irritated with her avoidance of coming to the point.

"I am your totem spirit guide. You fondly named me *"Lady Vixen"* The beautiful lady proudly announced

"What? But you're no animal, you're a person" Kane was astounded at how an unkept dog could morph into such a nice-looking woman.

"I have the ability to transition between animal and human

form at will.....just like you Kane"

"How do you know about my skin changing? They call me a demon, you know?"

"I have always known you, even before you were born. I will guide and protect you as best I can, but your own choices will shape your path.... and you must suffer the consequences. I reveal myself now because you're maturing, realizing your differences and unique abilities. Remember, Kane, I am not here to save you; I am only your spiritual guide."

"Will you always be with me when I'm in America?" "Not always. I am elusive, watching from the shadows." "How did you get a passport for this trip?" Kane probed.

"I have connections. In human form, my appearance opens many doors. Being a sorceress has its advantages."

"When we anchor in America, I will disembark in human guise. After passing through the checkpoints, I'll revert to my natural form as a wild dog. You'll see me again when necessary. This is our last conversation for now. Trust yourself and watch your back. Whats coming is your destiny. Farewell, Kane."

Placing a dainty, gloved hand on his arm in a reassuring gesture, the beautiful *"Lady Vixen"* smiled and gracefully wandered down the passageway. Kane watched after her as she gradually disappeared into the mist, like a grand drape closing.

In the distance, Charlie had observed the entire encounter, silently watching from his post. Though he couldn't hear their conversation, he found the meeting highly suspicious. He wondered why a high-class lady would be associating with someone as unusual as Mr. Shunro, the Japanese monk. Charlie's superstitious mind raced with apprehension.

Kane remained on deck for another ten minutes, deep in

thought, before casually strolling back towards his cabin. He passed by the old sailor at the helm without a word.

"Do you know Lady Vixen, Mr. Shunro?" Charlie boldly asked.

"No, I don't know her," Kane replied evenly.

"Okay? Then what was she doing up here on the deck with you when she should have been in her cabin?" the sailor pressed.

"I don't know. Maybe she was just getting some fresh air.... like me?" Kane replied, his tone nonchalant.

"I saw you talking with her," Charlie pushed rudely for more information.

"Hai, so we were talking. Is that a crime?" Kane's patience wore thin, but he didn't want the annoying old sailor probing into his affairs, so he pacified him with a deceptive answer.

"If you must know, Lady Vixen asked me about my Buddhist faith and life as a monk. She was intrigued. Are you satisfied?"

Charlie didn't reply. Instead, he gave Kane a crafty smile, revealing his chipped and sparsely distributed teeth—a testament to a difficult upbringing in poverty. As Kane stared down at him, Charlie noticed a brief flash of scarlet red gleam in the monk's eyes, a subtle warning that rattled the hardened sailor to his core.

The following morning, gusting winds filled the sails eagerly, propelling the ship onward. Under the rising sun, the shadows of masts stretched and then receded as the day bloomed into brilliant blue skies and a sparkling ocean. The crew rejoiced as the gloomy fog finally lifted.

The old ship had sailed through tranquil seas and storms alike, but despite her many adventures, she still required tender care. Junior sailors worked diligently from early morning, applying layers of pitch to waterproof the vessel and protect it from the salty brine.

Cautiously, Kane entered the dining quarters for breakfast for the first time, choosing a solitary table tucked away in the far corner of the room.

As he surveyed his surroundings, the atmosphere felt dense and peculiar. Purple curtains muted the small windows, and kerosene lamps cast a soft glow over each table, illuminating the diners absorbed in their meals.

The dimness of the room provided Kane with a refuge, a sanctuary where he could recharge and momentarily escape the burdens he carried. It encouraged contemplation, inviting him to examine both his modest existence and the potential for greater fulfillment and happiness ahead.

"Good morning Mr Shunro. There are eggs and smoked ham or stew"

The mere thought of consuming what the cook had prepared, especially after his illness, triggered a deep down revolt in Kane's gut. A heavy, tight sensation surged, compelling him to instinctively cover his mouth.

In human form, he shuddered at the idea of eating anything derived from animals. "Do you have any noodle soup?" Kane asked politely.

"What? No, we don't," the cook snapped back. "Eggs, ham, or stew, that's it?"

"Do you have any tea?" Kane maintained his composure. "Of course we do."

"Can I have a pot of tea and a slice of bread with jam.... if you have bread and jam, that is."

"You're a fussy bugger, Mr. Shunro. Most people jump at the

chance to eat my stew," the cook remarked proudly.

"I am a vegetarian, always have been," Kane explained. "Even as a kid?"

"Hai, growing up in the monastery with the Buddhist faith."

"Well, they must have been some special vegetables because you're the size of a bull," the cook chuckled.

"It runs in my family, from my father's side, I'm told," Kane replied, feeling slightly bewildered.

Even among the diverse crew on this ship, Kane felt the sting of judgment and ridicule for his physical size and monkhood. It reinforced the feeling that he could never escape the prejudices that labeled him an oddity and an outcast.

"Thank goodness nobody knows about my skin changing... they'd all jump overboard," Kane thought wryly, managing a smile to himself.

"Ok.... a pot of tea, bread, and jam then," the cook announced briskly. As Kane watched him disappear through the galley door, a short, fat, balding man entered the dining room. He promptly sat at a vacant table and meticulously arranged the cutlery before him.

"Here's your breakfast," the cook declared returning within minutes, placing two chunky slices of bread with a blob of jam on Kane's table. "Your pot of tea is on the boil," he added.

"Hai, thank you," Kane replied quietly, offering a small smile. Turning his attention from the cook to his meal, he couldn't help but notice the fat, bald man leering at him through thick, bottle-like spectacles.

Abruptly, the man stood up and approached Kane's table while he began to carve his bread. Sensing his presence, Kane lifted his head and locked a cold, dark stare on him.

"You're the monk in room two?" the fat man blurted out forcefully. "Yes, I am. How can I help you, Mr...?" Kane replied calmly.

"Mr. Kent... and you are?" He prodded further.

"Mr. Shunro, pleased to meet you," Kane spoke softly, bringing his palms together in a gesture resembling praying hands, gracefully bowing his head towards Mr. Kent with respect.

"Well, Mr. Shunro, I'm tired of the weird noises coming from your cabin, and then there are the dreadful smells. Don't you monks bathe? You're not in the remote mountains anymore, Mr. Shunro; you're mixing with civilized people here," Mr. Kent complained with disdain.

Kane felt intense annoyance rising within him as he scowled at the ignorant, racist remarks. It took all of his self-control to restrain the anger bubbling up from within.

"I apologize for any inconvenience I have caused you, Mr. Kent... I have been unwell from the rough seas we've experienced... I will keep the noise and the smell to a minimum," Kane replied, his words sounding apologetic, but his demeanor was tinged with contempt. Deliberately avoiding eye contact, he focused on his breakfast in front of him.

Sensing the discomfort between them, Mr. Kent coughed awkwardly, clearing his throat.

"Well... okay then... that's all I wanted to say. Good day, Mr. Shunro," Mr. Kent muttered, feeling the tension.

Kane remained silent, his expression unreadable.

"What was that all about?" the impertinent cook asked as he approached, placing the pot of tea on Kane's table.

"Nothing of importance... thank you for the tea," Kane replied with a faint smile, his manner calm as he continued eating, as if unaffected by the exchange.

* * *

A month had slipped by since the *"Sea Changer"* set sail from Osaka, and Kane welcomed the news that they were just a week away from reaching the shores of America. His grounded nature struggled with the relentless rocking of the ship's undulating waves, which tossed it like a see-saw.

Despite enduring recurring bouts of seasickness, Kane endeavored to mask the sound of his retching, mindful not to disturb his unsympathetic neighbor, Mr. Kent. Lighting four sticks of incense, he let their fragrant smoke permeate his cabin. As the aroma filled the air, he began chanting calmly, each repetition symbolizing the mindfulness of his mantra. His mind transcended into a state of unified emptiness, merging with cosmic truth.

Kneeling before his makeshift altar, Kane took a deep breath, sanctifying the ritual with the practices of his Buddhist faith. His senses awakened to the balance of the six forces: hearing, contemplation, mindfulness, awareness, effort, and presence. Continuing the chant in his native tongue, he intoned, "right speech, right intention, right action, right livelihood," each word resonating with the solemnity of his devotion.

Fully immersed in his practice, Kane concentrated intently on refining his behavior towards himself and others. With each deep, rhythmic breath, he induced a sense of peace and tranquility within himself. Gradually, a feeling of contentment began to stir, easing his mind.

As the steady ebb and flow of his breath moved through his body, Kane became acutely aware of the inner battle raging within him. On one side, the volatile instability of the demon threatened his serenity. On the other, the sanctified teachings of his Buddhist faith offered a path to inner harmony. He grappled with these conflicting forces, striving to find the delicate balance necessary for profound reflection and ultimate control.

Abruptly, a loud banging reverberated on his cabin door again.

"Mr. Shunro... I know you're in there... open the door," the indignant voice commanded.

Kane ended his droning chant and humbly lifted his head, reluctantly standing up as the persistent thumping continued.

"Who is it?" Kane spoke through the door without opening it. "Mr. Kent."

Sighing deeply, Kane opened the door and faced his enraged neighbor directly. "What can I do for you, Mr. Kent?"

"There's a stench coming from your room again, and that droning sound is very annoying. I don't know what voodoo shit you're doing in there, but stop it now. Some people are trying to rest."

"The 'stench' you refer to is incense, which is part of my meditation ritual," Kane tried to explain, his tone edged with frustration.

"I couldn't care less what it is. As I've told you before, you're not in the jungle anymore so stop acting like a wild man," the loud American barked, his irritation palpable.

"I am not a wild man, just a Buddhist monk on a spiritual pilgrimage," Kane replied calmly, trying to radiate a sense of loving-kindness.

"No one in America is going to accept your foreign mumbo jumbo.... certainly not the people I know anyway," Mr. Kent scoffed dismissively.

With patience and reverence for his faith and its teachings, the large monk responded

"Mr. Kent, if you bought a gift for someone but that person did not accept it, to whom does the gift belong to then?"

Mr. Kent remained in the doorway, unimpressed by Kane's philosophical retort.

"I don't know.... the gift would still be mine because I was the one who bought it," Mr. Kent replied with a smirk, feeling satisfied with his answer.

"Exactly," Kane nodded calmly,

"So now that you've been angry with me, if I don't accept your insults and choose not to react with anger, then these negative feelings remain yours alone. It's like the gift returning to its owner."

Mr. Kent stood in the doorway, momentarily taken aback by Kane's insightful analogy.

Almost like a cartoon character caught in the throes of frustration, Mr. Kent began grinding his teeth together. The tension in his facial muscles caused his eyes to bulge and his lips to harden, transforming him from a sensible fellow into a primitive version of himself. The torment in his brain seemed to override his demeanor, leaving him visibly agitated.

"Enough with your mind fucking" He shouted, clenching his fists tightly by his side. "This is your last warning Mr Shunro, stop with the black magic bullshit or suffer the consequences"

Kane sensed wild fury in Mr. Kent's eyes as reason seemed to vanish, replaced by a maniacal intensity reminiscent of a foaming, rabid dog. Suppressing his own rising anger, Kane fought to maintain a sense of calm and compassion, reminding himself to practice love and protectiveness even in the face of provocation. Without another word, he slowly closed the door in Mr. Kent's face, leaving his abusive and ranting neighbor standing in the hallway, looking bewildered and foolish.

Kane struggled to prevent the surges of outrage that triggered feelings of vulnerability, leaving him open to bullying and mockery. This survival mode felt cold and indifferent, yet he understood that to thrive in the upcoming country, he needed to mentally adapt and conquer the repulsive emotions brewing beneath the surface.

Resuming his prayers, Kane dedicated the rest of the afternoon to quiet meditation, focusing on a safe journey to America. He held onto the hope that Mr. Kent would keep his distance, allowing him to find peace and stability for the rest of the trip.

Gently lifting the human-skinned book, Kane contemplated its eerie exterior before delicately opening the cover. His fingertips traced the faint indentations left by previous scribes, now vanished with time. He wondered about the secrets it had once held, the centuries of wisdom nestled within its pages.

Flipping through the book, Kane reached a section where the writing, ancient symbols, and advanced mathematical formulas suddenly became clear and tangible. As he read, he uncovered a detailed account of his life's journey up to the present moment, but found nothing about his future.

"What good are you?" he cried in frustration, hurling the

book across the room before slumping despondently onto his bunk, hands covering his face.

From the shadows in the corner of the room emerged a black creature woven of muscles and spells. It appeared as a pulsating silhouette, hinting at its true form with an aura of cunning intelligence.

"Which is your true nightmare? The hideous dream you have when you sleep or the unfulfilled truth that awaits you? The allure of your skin changing will only tempt the brave. Human words are powerless; believe nothing you hear and only half of what you see."

Suddenly, it dissolved back into the sinister abyss from which it emerged, casting a dense and oppressive darkness in its wake.

After being shut out, Mr. Kent stormed into the dining room, visibly perturbed. He promptly ordered a straight whisky, downing it in one gulp as soon as the cook placed it on the table.

"Give me another one.... No, forget it, just bring me the bottle," he snapped, slamming the empty glass down with a bang.

"Are you alright, Mr. Kent?" the concerned cook asked upon returning with the full bottle of whiskey, noting his customer's obvious agitation.

"That bloody monk Shunro, he's nothing but a self-righteous bastard," Kent blurted out, pouring himself another drink with a brisk hand.

"Why? What happened?" the nosy cook prodded, eager for some juicy gossip.

"I went to his cabin and asked him to stop the disgusting smells and noises, and he started spouting some voodoo mind crap, then slammed the door in my face," Kent grumbled.

"What do you mean, voodoo mind crap?" The cook pulled out a chair and sat opposite Kent, eyes wide with curiosity, eager for more intriguing details.

"I don't know, something about a gift and because he won't accept my grievance, the curse of anger falls back onto me. He's a pain in the arse," Kent grumbled, downing another drink with impatience.

"Yeah, those Japs think they're better than the rest of us, especially the religious ones," the cook asserted, trying to stoke Kent's animosity.

"Probably. I export goods to the Japanese, that's why I'm on this ship... returning from a business trip. I find most of them respectful and pleasant, but Mr. Shunro.... he's completely different," Kent mused with a hint of frustration.

"In my line of work, I meet all sorts, and I pride myself on being a good judge of character, but this bloke, I can't quite figure him out."

"I overheard old Charlie saying he saw Mr. Shunro on the top deck with Lady Vixen the other night. They looked quite familiar with each other, chatting away" the cook added, leaning in eagerly for a reaction.

"Really? That's strange.... monks aren't supposed to have anything to do with women. They're not allowed to touch them, talk to them or vice versa," Kent remarked, his voice thick with skepticism as he poured himself another drink.

"Well, old Charlie swore he saw Lady Vixen affectionately touch the monk's arm before they parted ways," the cook chimed in, barely containing his excitement at the juicy gossip.

"A real monk would have established strong boundaries with

Lady Vixen. Perhaps Shunro is merely pretending to be a Buddhist monk," Kent suggested, his suspicion growing as he topped off his glass.

"The cap'n has Charlie watching him closely. There must be something fishy if he's under scrutiny," the cook added, leaning in purposefully.

"Yeah, that's a good idea.... and I'm going to do the same. We've only got a few days left before we dock in San Francisco, right?" Kent confirmed, his voice determined. "Aye," the cook nodded.

"Over the next few days, I'll keep a journal of everything I've seen and anything else suspicious. If Shunro's up to no good, I'll have evidence to report him as soon as we reach shore," Kent concluded, lifting the empty whiskey bottle and inspecting it closely. With unsteady steps, he rose from his seat, swaying slightly as he made his way out of the dining room, leaving the amused cook chuckling quietly to himself.

Attempting to stagger back to his room, Mr. Kent bumped into the walls from side to side, the ship's rocking accentuating his intoxication. His movements became jerky as he suddenly froze upon seeing Kane standing at the other end of the hallway.

Kane stared back at him with a calm appearance.

"You!! I've got my eye on you, monk.... You better watch yourself because I'm documenting everything," Mr. Kent slurred loudly, waving his finger around in a drunken stupor.

Kane remained silent, his stare fixed on Mr. Kent with unnervingly large, black eyes that seemed to pierce through him. The surrounding sounds seemed to amplify, drowning out everything else, and Mr. Kent's senses heightened. His watch ticked slower and slower, each beat resonating like heavy footsteps echoing in his mind. The silence and Kane's intense gaze created an atmosphere thick with foreboding, unsettling Mr. Kent.

Fumbling nervously in his coat pocket, Kent struggled to find his keys. With a jittery hand, he finally grasped them and swiftly unlocked the cabin door. Slamming it shut behind him, he quickly turned the key in the lock, hoping to keep the creepy monk at bay.

As Mr. Kent stared at the closed door, he sensed a strong, bitter odor wafting through the air, followed by a low growl and the sound of something large and ferocious scraping its razor-edged fingernails against the wooden surface.

"Go away!" Kent shrieked, his voice quivering with terror as he backed away from the door.

An uncanny silence followed, broken only by the sound of an enormous, chilling breath blowing under the door. The stench of decay permeated the air, making Kent gag in revulsion and fear.

"I know it's you, Shunro!" he yelled, his voice trembling. He felt a surge of panic and disgust, compounded by his intoxicated state.

"You've got something inside you, something ugly and evil," he continued to shout, his words booming from the cabin. Suddenly, a human-faced rat darted out from under the bed, its sharp fangs sinking into Kent's ankle through his socks, drawing blood and causing him to scream in terror and pain.

In the suspended moment of disbelief, Kent clutched his hand over the deep wound, but the blood continued to gush between his fingers, staining the floor with a rapid darkening pool. A freakish, inhuman chuckle resonated from beyond the door, sending a cold sensation through his brain like a corrosive acid eating away at his sanity.

Panic seized him, his heart racing, his breath coming in jerky gasps as the walls of his cabin seemed to close in on him.

The sense of impending doom grew more intense, leaving him feeling claustrophobic and trapped. He pressed harder on his chest, feeling the pressure build and the dizziness engulf him, as if a hand were clamped tightly over his mouth.

Floating in and out of consciousness, Mr. Kent found himself enveloped in the deep, velvety darkness of his cabin, except for the soft illumination of moonbeams trickling through the small porthole. The room seemed strangely quiet now, devoid of the earlier drama that had filled it with dread. Gingerly, he inspected the wound inflicted by the rat bite, wrapping his handkerchief tightly around it to stem the slow trickle of blood.

After a moment's hesitation, Kent summoned the courage to rise, his movements tentative and deliberate. He limped out of the cabin, his senses seeking solace in the cool embrace of the night air on deck. Leaning against the weathered wooden guard rail, he stared out into the vast, undulating expanse of the dark ocean. The moonlight danced on the restless waves, casting shifting patterns of light and shadow that mirrored the tumult within him.

Memories of the encounter with Kane flashed vividly in his mind. The creepy monks' revolting presence—it all replayed like an unbelievable melody, each note tinged with uneasiness.

"Good evening Mr Kent" The helmsman greeted when he

noticed Kent standing there.

"What? Oh.....yes Good evening" Kent replied but he didn't feel like chatting so he began walking towards the rear of the ship away from intrusive eyes.

"Nice night, you know that you're not supposed to be up here at night, Capt'n orders, not mine" The sailor continued

"I know but I really need the fresh air right now. I feel quite ill. Would it be alright if I walked down to the afterdeck? I need to clear my head"

"Aww no, Mr Kent, I told you, passengers aren't suppose to be up here in the first place" The sailor drawled in his buccaneer twang

"I'll be fine, you can't stop me anyway. I've been sailing on these ships for years. I've got my sea legs"

Kent farewelled as he dismissed the sailors' warning, giving him a quick cheerio with the tip of his hand.

"Alright, but I've warned you—don't tell anyone I let you go down there. Be careful, Mr. Kent; the sea is a bit rough tonight," the helmsman shouted after him as Kent vanished into the murkiness.

Kent's gaze lifted to the glittering expanse of stars above, their distant twinkling offering a fleeting connection to the familiar warmth of his family. Memories of his wife's tender smile and their young son's infectious laughter flooded his mind, casting a gentle glow amid the darkness of his thoughts.

He reminisced about their last embrace, the way his wife's arms wrapped around him, her comforting presence a soothing balm to his weary soul. Their son, a bundle of energy and joy, always eager for his father's return, brought a smile to Kent's lips even now.

As he stood under the canopy of night, surrounded by the vast ocean and the timeless stars, Kent found comfort in the memory of their love. It was a flame that flickered brightly in his heart, a beacon of hope guiding him through the challenges of the present. With renewed hope, he looked ahead to the day when he would hold them both in his arms again, the anticipation of their reunion like a compass leading him home.

"Not long now.....only two more days," Kent muttered under his breath as he limped to the farthest end of the ship, his hand protecting his injured ankle.

"I've been expecting you," a voice unexpectedly cut through the shadows and substance.

Kent spun around, eyes widening with apprehension as he saw Kane emerge from the darkest corner. "It's you again.....stay away from me," Kent warned, brandishing a pocket knife.

"I don't like monks, never have, and now after meeting you, I definitely hate them. What the hell are you? Some mountain-bred experiment?" Kent spat.

"You're awfully confident, Kent. Watch who you insult. Not every man is what he seems," Kane growled, standing his ground but making no move forward.

"Stay back.....don't think I won't use this blade," Kent threatened, shaking the knife at Kane, only to nervously drop it on the deck.

"Hai, a true master of Tantojutsu I see.....such a fearsome warrior," Kane mocked. "I'm going to report you, Shunro, I'm writing everthing down in this notebook.....tell the world what you really are. Masquerading around as a monk when you're really the devil. You wait, you cunning son of a bitch. As soon as we've docked, the authorities will lock you up," Kent blurted, waving the notebook infront of Kane, his voice thick with rage and accusation.

Swiftly, he bent down to pick up the knife, momentarily breaking eye contact with Kane. But when Kent straightened up again, the huge man was suddenly right in front of him. His eyes burned a fiery red with hostility, wild and disturbing.

As Kent stared in horror, Kane's teeth elongated into jagged fangs resembling broken glass, and coarse bristles sprouted from his face like a boar's hair.

Kent braced himself against the guard rail, arms tense and unyielding as Kane closed in, his words dripping with malice. Thick saliva clumped and splattered on Kent's face as Kane sneered

"You are just a tiny little man, a nobody. Taste the darkness—it's been waiting for you."

With a swift motion, Kane seized Kent by the head and shoulders, effortlessly dodging the feeble stab attempt.

In one brutal, decisive motion, he hurled Kent over the side of the ship. He watched impassively as Kent flailed and thrashed in the water, his desperate movements gradually swallowed by the infinite blackness of the ocean, never to resurface again. As Kane peered over the railing, distant voices drew nearer, prompting him to swiftly leave the scene. He hurried back to his quarters, skillfully evading the approaching sailors. Unbeknownst to him, however, Lady Vixen remained concealed on the after deck, her black hooded coat billowing in the breeze. She had witnessed everything.

Chapter 8

San Francisco was a lawless, untamed city. Prostitution, gambling, and brawling ran rampant as the gold rush surged, catapulting the population of Yerba Buena from a mere four hundred to a staggering twenty-five thousand. It marked the largest peacetime migration in U.S. history, drawing prospectors, trappers, and hunters eager to trade for beaver pelts, tanned buffalo hides, and other goods coveted by both natives and settlers alike.

As the *"Sea Changer"* glided into Yerba Buena cove and dropped anchor, Kane gazed in awe at the bustling bay. The sight stirred his imagination, consumed with thoughts of the dynamic new world he was about to step into.

"Can everyone please make their way to the dining room? The Cap'n would like a word before you disembark" Old Charlie shouted as he rounded up the passengers before disembarking.

"What's this about?" The gentleman escorting Lady Vixen to America queried "Not sure, the Cap'n just wants to see everyone" Charlie said dismissively The eight passengers and crewmen gathered in the dining area, arranging

themselves against the rear wall in an orderly manner, awaiting the Captain's arrival. Kane positioned himself at the end of the line, attempting to blend into the far corner despite being the largest person in the room.

Following Mr. Kent's death, the killer had retreated to his cabin. There, he had cautiously showered and shaved, preparing for his new life in America. Now, he stood fully dressed in his Buddhist habit, every bit the solemn monk with his bald head and serene demeanor.

"Good morning everyone and thank you for meeting with me. After nearly two months at sea, I know you're eager to disembark, so I won't keep you too long. We've discovered that Mr Kent is missing.

His final encounter was with Seaman Murray on the top deck. Does anyone have more information to add to this mystery? What about you Mr Shunro? I heard there were grievances between both of you.....something about odors and noise?" "Hai.....Mr Kent wasn't pleased with my meditation and praying. He didn't like the incense or my related chanting" Kane answered confidently

"So when was the last time you saw Mr Kent?"

"After he came to my door and complained.....around 9.30 pm" "And that was it?.....you didn't leave your cabin after that?"

The Captain pushed earnestly for more facts

"Hai....I never left my quarters.....I was deep in meditation all evening"

"Captain.....may I interject?" A soft female voice resonated "Yes Lady Vixen, you have something to say?"

"I happened to see Mr Kent as he came out of the dining room and he appeared very drunk. He mumbled something about going up to the top deck"

"Who was at the helm that night?" the Captain questioned his crew. "I was, Cap'n," Henry answered sheepishly.

"Why was Mr. Kent on deck that night? You know its against the rules. You must have seen him," the Captain interrogated.

"My focus was on the bow, trying to navigate safely through the night. I didn't see or hear anything," Henry lied like a professional.

"Yeah, Cap'n, he drank a full bottle of whisky," the cook added, taking the heat off his friend Henry.

"Plus I knocked on Mr Shunro's cabin door around 10.30 pm and he was there" Lady Vixen included

"Why did you visit Mr Shunro?" The Captain challenged

"I am intrigued with the Buddhist faith and Mr Shunro had promised to give me a spiritual gift for Enlightenment"

"Do you have the gift with you Lady Vixen?"

Kane's heart began to pound like a tribal drum because he knew that Lady Vixen was lying through her teeth.

"Yes.....I have it in my bag" She said gently, her voice filled with complete innocence and she rummaged through her purse.

"Here it is" She continued, pulling out a Zen Chime and handing it to the Captain. Examining the expertly crafted chime quintet, the Captain admired the beautiful wooden frame and the five silver rods, noting the sturdy mallet accompanying it. "What is it for?" the Captain asked innocently, directing his question towards Kane.

"It brings calming, gentle spiritual vitality and aids in maintaining focused alertness during meditation sessions," Kane replied calmly.

"This all seems a bit unusual to me," the Captain admitted,

turning to the Doctor. "What do you think?"

"Captain, considering Mr. Kent's intoxicated state and his foolish decision to wander alone to the afterdeck in the dark, despite knowing the risks, I believe he has fallen overboard. It appears to be a regrettable accident," the ship's doctor concluded solemnly.

"The seas were rough that night too" Henry added mainly to defend his previous lie "I'll proceed with issuing the death certificate for accidental drowning, lost at sea, and I'll notify his family," the doctor declared, bringing the discussion to a close.

The Captain stood in silence for a few moments, reflecting on the tragic turn of events. Finally, he made his decision.

"Alright, you're all cleared to disembark," the Captain announced, his voice carrying influence and gratitude.

"Your baggage has been unloaded onto the wharf, and the authorities are ready to inspect your passports. Thank you for your patience and for sailing aboard the majestic *'Sea Changer.'"*

With that farewell, the group began to move towards the gangplank, each member disembarking one by one and handing their papers to the waiting customs officials.

"Mr Shunro. What is your reason for entering America?" The customs officer stated, inspecting Kanes papers then visually examining him up and down

"I am on a spiritual pilgrimage"

"You're a big fellow.....not a typical-looking Asian. Ok... ..Good luck with trying to convert these greedy godless bastards. What do you call your God anyway?" "Siddhartha Gautama" Kane informed

"Well, I've just learned something new. I suppose your pilgrimage is warranted considering the thousands of Chinamen that are arriving here these days. Alright, you can proceed Mr Shunro, ...next!!"

After retrieving his luggage, Kane wandered through the swarming streets of San Francisco, his senses overwhelmed by the stark cultural differences around him.

As he neared the city's edge, he spotted a large tent reminiscent of a circus structure, towering impressively on the boundary of a paddock. Intrigued, he followed the sounds of men shouting and the lively cheers emanating from within.

Approaching closer, Kane observed a man energetically calling out to passersby, his voice carrying over the noisy crowd gathered around the tent. He seemed intent on drawing even more spectators into the already substantial throng.

"A round or two for a pound or two.....Who'll take a glove?" The spruiker's voice rang out repeatedly, a blend of invitation and challenge.

Standing just five meters from the tent entrance, Kane caught the spruiker's eye. "You there, Mister.....looking to make a bit of coin? A round or two for a pound or two, you've got the look of a sturdy bloke. Give it a whirl," the spruiker enticed, his grin wide and hopeful.

"No thank you," Kane politely declined, continuing on his quest for a motel.

"Your loss, Mister! A round or two for a pound or two... ..Who'll take a glove?" The spruiker persisted, his call echoing down the street as Kane walked away. With nightfall approaching, he began asking passing strangers for directions to any lodgings.

"Excuse me, could you tell me where I might find....." Kane began, only to be cut off by mocking laughter from a group of young men.

"Piss off, you baldy Jap! We're not interested in anything you're selling," one of them sneered, the others joining in with derisive laughter.

"Look at the fucking size of him.....he's bigger than a Grizzly bear," the jeers continued unabated, slicing through the air. Kane stood there, dumbfounded by their cruelty. He couldn't fathom why they would lash out at him when all he had done was ask a simple question.

Across the road, in the dimly lit alleyway, a solitary woman caught his attention. She stood there, smoking a cigarette, the small glowing ember acting as a beacon amidst the encroaching shadows.

"Excuse me, madam, can you tell me where I can find a room?" Kane asked timidly. He felt uneasy speaking to a woman other than Lady Vixen, his spiritual guide, and was taken aback by the scantily dressed woman before him.

"Hello, handsome. You're a big boy, aren't you?" the woman greeted with a flick of her spent cigarette, crushing it under her high-heeled shoe.

"I can take you to a room, but it'll cost you," she continued, blowing smoke in Kane's face.

Coughing from the smoke, Kane tried to respond.

"Hai, I understand I need to pay for the room. Could you just point me in the right direction of one?" he managed to say.

"So you don't want to have some fun with me? I won't charge you much, and I've got my health certificate," she pleaded.

"You sell yourself for money?" Kane asked, astonished. He felt a mix of disbelief and pity for the heavily made-up woman before him, who seemed to lack self-respect.

"I'm a prostitute, you ignorant fool. I need money just like everyone else," she retorted fiercely, her defiance clear.

"Your reliance on using your youth and beauty to control others will only enslave you," Kane countered calmly.

"I'm not enslaved. This is my choice, I can stop at any time, if I wanted too..... and I don't need your moral judgment. What are you anyway? A strange Catholic priest or some other religious fanatic?" she shot back, continuing her insults.

"I am a Buddhist monk from Japan.... I apologize for disturbing you," Kane replied quietly, ending the conversation and turning to walk away from the woman.

"Hey, wait! If you're looking for a room, there are a couple of boarding houses down the road. Take care of yourself; this is the wickedest town in America," she called after him. Kane kept walking without responding, as if he hadn't heard her at all.

Standing before a run down, frequently visited building with a sign advertising "Rooms for Rent," Kane entered through the creaking doorway and was immediately confronted by the landlord.

"Yes? What do you want?" the large, round woman interrogated brusquely. "A room for the night, please," Kane requested politely.

"We don't rent rooms to Japs.... especially religious ones.... you're a monk, aren't you?" she retorted sharply.

"Hai," Kane replied evenly, meeting the woman's stormy attitude with calm composure.

"Go to Chinatown then, they'll take you," she crudely directed, dismissing him without further consideration.

"Where exactly is Chinatown?" Kane inquired, unfazed by the landlord's rudeness. "On the far edge of town, where you *"Jonnies"* belong. Just keep heading in the same direction, you'll stumble upon it. Now get out of my house," the pudgy woman dismissed him bluntly, her impatience evident.

Bewildered by the unwarranted hostility he encountered due to his appearance and religion, Kane lingered outside the boarding house, contemplating his next move. His attention was drawn to a solitary dog standing at the end of the road. Under the dim glow of street lamps, he recognized the familiar shape of Lady Vixen.

"Lady Vixen?" Kane speculated aloud, starting to walk towards her. As he approached, the wild dog let out a single yelp, confirming his suspicion. It was indeed her.

Kane followed Lady Vixen for a mile until they arrived at Chinatown. The dog stopped in front of a modestly built house, sitting down as if indicating that this was where Kane should stay.

As Kane stepped into the house, a bizarre combination of dampness, cigarette smoke, spices and stale fish assaulted his senses like a pungent perfume. He found himself standing in a dubious foyer surrounded by nostalgic trinkets that adorned the room.

Suddenly, a little old Chinaman shuffled out from behind a closed curtain leading to another room and greeted him.

"Hai, Hai.... What can I do for you, monk?"

"I need a room for a night or two," Kane replied, watching as the innkeeper nodded vigorously in agreement with each word he spoke.

"Hai.... I have a room," the innkeeper responded, still bobbing his head in a rhythmic manner.

While the Chinaman fetched the keys, Kane studied him intently, curious about his origins. The old man had winter-white hair braided into a long queue that hung down his back, giving him an air of yesteryear. He wore a loosely cut robe with wide bell-shaped sleeves, the left front panel lapped over the right one, and fastened with a sash, exuding an old-world elegance.

Kane couldn't help but wonder about the stories behind the man's serene yet weathered face, which hinted at a life steeped in tradition and history. The way he moved with deliberate care and the meticulousness of his attire suggested a deep respect for his heritage.

"Here are your keys... room five. That will be $3 per night... includes one meal a day.... good price, eh?" the old man said, stroking his devil-forked beard with both hands. As Kane studied him, he noticed the man's blood-flecked eyes and a face riddled with time and experience.

"I don't have that amount of money for two nights, and I need a couple of nights' rest before my journey," Kane pleaded.

"Hehehe....Journey? You're on a journey, monk? Let me guess.... a spiritual journey?" The old chinaman giggled

"Hai, how did you know?"

"There have been many like you passing through here on the same voyage.... arriving in the new world to spread your faith. Good luck with that, monk. Nobody gives a damn around here. But one word of advice.... stay away from the Mexicans. They say they'll feed your guts and balls to their dogs," he whispered in a gravelly voice, a smirk playing on his lips.

"About the money, how much do you have now?" the old man continued. Kane rummaged through his pouch and pulled out four coins, each one dollar apiece, and handed them to the innkeeper.

"This is all I have after my journey from Japan"

"Hmpf... is that it? You only have enough for one and a half nights," he chuckled.

"I tell you what to do. Did you see the big tent on the way here? Go inside and make yourself known to the ringmaster.... he will let you fight. If you win, he'll pay you a pound or two. That's what he says.... he screams it out every night.... a pound or two for a round or two. How could I forget.....every night. Come; you can stay tonight. Follow me, and I'll show you the room."

The innkeeper handed Kane the key and shuffled down a dimly lit hallway, his robe swishing with each step. Kane followed, the scent of stale fish, spices and dampness growing stronger as they moved deeper into the house.

Climbing the narrow staircase, the old innkeeper led Kane to the second floor, eventually reaching room five. He unlocked and opened the door, revealing a small, dark space. No light shined within, yet somehow Kane could make out the details of the room as he visually inspected the amenities.

A tiny, corroded kindling heater stood in the far corner, accompanied by a pile of sticks stacked neatly beside it. A single chair with a patched-up leg was neatly tucked under a small, worn table. The air was heavy with the scent of dust and dampness, and the wooden floorboards creaked underfoot. Despite its sparse furnishings, the room had an oddly welcoming feel, a quiet refuge from the hectic streets outside.

After thanking the landlord, Kane ventured into the room and walked over to a damaged wooden bedstead. As he sat his hefty frame upon the bed, it creaked and groaned with every move, the thin mattress doing nothing to shield him from the girthy rusted coils beneath.

"Three dollars a night for this hovel," Kane muttered as he stood up and walked over to the window that overlooked the obscurely lit road.

Scanning the street, he saw Lady Vixen waiting patiently below. When she identified his broad shape standing in the window frame, she barked twice before rapidly taking off, heading towards the outskirts of town and into the treacherous wild frontier of the Nevada territory.

"Goodbye, Lady Vixen.... I will miss you, and thank you," he whispered, watching her disappear into the twilight.

* * *

The crowd had a life of its own as field hands, townies, and well-dressed men rubbed elbows and thronged around the fighting ring, like piranhas after a piece of meat. Kane had never been claustrophobic, but in the almighty swell of people, he felt panic rising in his chest. The horde of men was a mean, filthy lot, their conduct transforming from ordinary civil to deranged as they insulted, cussed, and yelled at the fighters in the ring. Kane felt as though entering the tent was like falling into a snake pit.

The air was thick with sweat and anticipation, the noisy racket of jeers and shouts creating a notable tension. Kane's eyes darted around, taking in the chaotic scene—men waving betting slips, the grimy sawdust floor, the flickering lanterns casting eerie shadows on the tent walls. Every movement seemed amplified, every shout piercing through the noise like a sharp blade.

Kane pushed his way through the crowd, each step feeling like a battle against the tide. His heart quickened, the thrill of the unknown mingling with a sense of misgiving. This was a world far removed from the disciplined calm of the monastery and his ninja training, a world teetering on the edge of maddness and violence.

As he finally reached the edge of the ring, he knew there was no turning back.

Before leaving the boarding house, Kane had changed into civilian clothes he'd bought in Osaka, not wanting to draw attention to himself.

His monk's habit had served its purpose; besides, his size alone was enough to draw attention.

Captivated by the brawl unfolding in the ring, Kane unconsciously edged closer. Despite towering head and shoulders above the other men, he still craned his neck for a better view.

"Hey Mister, do you want to have a go?" The ringmaster asked, grabbing Kane's attention by tapping his shoulder.

"I'm just a spectator" Kane replied

"A strong bloke like yourself could make some real money" The ringmaster enticed "How much money?" Kane retaliated

"Depends on how many rounds you win. Stay in the ring for three rounds and you'll be paid ten dollars"

"The man yelling out the front says it's a pound or two.....but you're telling me payment is in dollars?

"Yeah, that's just our spiel, it's a British saying ..... a pound or two for a round or two is a good pitch because it's brief and it rhymes.....so will you take a glove?"

Kane looked at the smiling man, whose tacky, insincere grin beamed from ear to ear and contemplated how much ten dollars would aid his journey.

"Hai I will fight" Kane decided "Great.....follow me"

Navigating through the tightly packed crowd, Kane felt overwhelmed by the uproar. He wasn't accustomed to such turbulence and loathed the constant brushing touches that made him jump with paranoia and suspicion.

An underlying anxiety began to escalate within him. He feared that his elusive enemy might be lurking within the agitated horde, but he desperately needed the money.

As he prepared to step into the ring and become the center of attention, every glance and movement around him seemed magnified, heightening his sense of vulnerability. "Here, take off your shirt and put these on" The ringmaster instructed, and handed Kane the boxing gloves.

"I can't wear these, I've never fought with gloves before" He grumbled "You'll be right....They'll protect your hands"

Kane stepped into the ring amidst a vigorous roar from the crowd, thrilled that a new competitor was about to challenge the renowned champion. As he stood there, scanning the excited spectators, he noticed fists full of cash waving in the air, while the house bookie moved through the crowd, methodically collecting bets.

The atmosphere crackled with tension as the title-holder leaped forward, briskly shoving Kane in the chest. Despite being the aggressor, Kane's opponent felt unnerved by his size, fearing the giant, muscular brute could crush his head like a pea.

Kane stood inflexible, his gaze fixed on his opponent as the champion advanced for a second time, delivering a fierce blow to Kane's gut that made him gasp audibly.

The crowd erupted into jeers and hisses, their disapproval obvious as they doubted the new challenger's skill and resilience. With each taunt, the champion's confidence swelled, bolstering his belief in superiority.

Sweat beaded on Kane's forehead, trickling down to drop lightly on his eyelid.

While the opponent circled him, weaving and bobbing in anticipation of another strike, Kane seized the moment. In a flash of lightning speed, he launched a spinning hook kick, his massive foot slicing through the air like a whip, connecting with the opponent's head with a resounding crack.

The champion was knocked out cold, crumpling to the ground amidst a stunned silence that quickly erupted into thunderous cheers. The crowd shouted with exhilaration and disbelief at the unexpected turn of events. Kane stood amongst the ovation, his heart pounding with the rush of victory and the realization that he had earned their respect in the most dramatic fashion possible.

The enormous, triumphant cheers threatened to lift the roof off the building, enveloping Kane in a wave of exhilaration he had never experienced before. It was as if the crowd's encouragement sent effervescent bubbles of euphoria coursing through his entire body, akin to the effervescence of champagne.

"Fight again, fight again!" The crowd's chant thundered around him, fists pumping in the air with each fervent shout. For the first time in his life, Kane wasn't subjected to bullying or humiliation; instead, he was embraced and celebrated for his innate skill and effort. Smiling faces greeted him from all sides, their joyous energy thrilling him to the point of ecstasy.

The ringmaster entered the fighting circle, seizing Kane's wrist and hoisting his gloved hand high in a gesture of overwhelming victory. The applause swelled around him, fueling a determination to fulfill the crowd's impassioned plea—to fight again. "Do you want to fight again? You should.... Look at the crowd, they love you," the ringmaster flattered.

"Hai, I will," Kane replied, caught up in the frenzied hype.

"Who will take a glove? Who has the guts to fight the new champion?" The seasoned promoter canvassed as he strode around the ring.

"Who will take a glove? Who has the guts to fight the new champion?" He persistently bellowed, his voice echoing over the excited crowd.

Standing firm in the center of the ring, Kane scanned the enthusiastic crowd, soaking in their cheers and chants. Amidst the sea of animated faces, he caught sight of a

peculiar figure—a cool, emotionless Hispanic man staring back at him. His detached behaviour stood in stark contrast to the fervor of the surrounding spectators.

As Kane locked eyes with the stranger, the ringmaster swiftly ushered in the next contender. This time, his opponent was of Asian descent, adding a new dynamic to the unfolding drama in the ring.

"Ok, quiet down everyone. We have an opponent for the champ, but this guy knows how to fight eastern style, karate is it? He directed the question towards the new challenger.

"Hai.....I'm a black belt in Shotokan" The Asian man stated

"Did you hear that? He's a black belt" The ringmaster shouted as everybody chorused "fight, fight, fight"

Shotokan karate, renowned for its strategic use of body parts as potent weapons, emphasizes powerful straight-line strikes targeting elbows, legs, and knees. Unlike styles centered on circular movements, Shotokan focuses on harmony and speed, blending forcefulness with precision.

Kane sized up his opponent, a new challenger embodying a perfect blend of strength, endurance, and explosive energy. The competitor, lean yet well-toned, warmed up with disciplined strikes, showcasing quick and precise movements that hinted at a formidable skill set.

"Are you ready to begin? The only rule is once your opponent is down, you stop fighting," the ringmaster affirmed.

"Hai," the fighters answered simultaneously, their sheer grit visible as the promoter signaled the start of the first round.

Facing each other in the ring, Kane sensed the intensity in his opponent. This wasn't a novice he faced but someone skilled in hand-to-hand combat.

At the starting bell's resounding clang, Kane stood unshakable, poised for action. Across from him, the agile Asian darted around the arena, showcasing his impressive fighting prowess.

With sudden agility, the Asian burst into action, launching forward like an impala and delivering a double palm heel strike to the side of Kane's head. The impact rang through Kane's ears, and before he could recover, the Asian's elbow shot up, slamming into the underside of his chin, snapping Kane's head backwards.

A bitter taste flooded Kane's mouth as blood seeped from his bitten tongue. Stunned, he staggered back as the assailant followed with a fierce uppercut to his abdomen, knocking him off balance.

Kane closed his eyes, drawing upon his inner chi. He felt the power surge from deep within his soul, rising like a simmering volcano preparing to erupt with its molten lava.

Reasserting his stance, Kane steadied himself as the Asian opponent darted back and forth, anticipating each move. Then, in a moment of clarity, his Asian challenger glimpsed a flicker of horror in his opponent's eyes.

A demonic red flash streaked across Kane's pupils. He grinned stealthily, revealing teeth that morphed into barbed, canine incisors. The frightened competitor, his courage waning, miscalculated his punch and collided with Kane's swift inner block. Bones in his hand shattered against Kane's solid forearm.

The Shotokan black belt recoiled, overwhelmed by the unseen force standing before him. Defeated and subdued, he made no move to launch another attack.

"We have a winner" The ringmaster screeched while he took Kane's arm and raised it in victory.

"Do you want to fight again?" He repeated to Kane

"More money for you my friend, remember three rounds is ten dollars in your pocket" He continued.

"Hai.....I'll fight again but this is the last time. Then you will pay me the money" Kane asked in a stringent tone

"Yes, yes, you'll get your money, hold onto your ha.....oops, I was going to say hold onto your hair, but you don't have any do you?" He mocked and sniggered

"Alright, alright, attention everyone.....who will take the glove, who will fight the champion? A round or two for a pound or two, who will take a glove? Come on, there must be someone in this squalid crowd brave enough to take on the champ? What about you Mister?" The ringmaster directed his curiosity towards a gangling man, standing three people deep within the crowd, but the stranger immediately shook his head with a panicked *"no"* then hurried off through the exit door.

Kane watched the crowd intently, their cheers for another battle surrounding him. Yet, amidst the fervor, a heavy deluge of negativity flooded his thoughts. He couldn't shake the feeling of being conspicuous, vulnerable to Gideon's mob of ninjas who would undoubtedly be hot on his trail. Standing in the center of the ring, every eye upon him, Kane realized it wouldn't be difficult for them to track him down. "Enough," Kane suddenly interjected, his voice low and guttural.

"What? You still have one more fight to earn the full ten dollars," protested the ringmaster.

"I said enough. Pay me what is owed," Kane insisted firmly.

"But can't you see that the crowd wants more, and that wasn't our deal, Mister?" the ringmaster complained.

"Give me my money now, or I'll find out where you live, enter your home, and take it from you," Kane warned, his tone brooking no argument.

"Ok, ok.... there's no need to threaten me.... here's your money," the ringmaster relented, reaching into his pocket and pulling out four dollars, which he handed to Kane.

"What's this? You're only paying me four dollars?" Kane questioned, incredulous. "A pound or two for a round or two. You fought two rounds, so that equals four dollars.... I'm being generous, Mister.... I would normally only pay two dollars, but because you put on a good show, I'm willing to pay you extra. Take it or leave it," the ringmaster explained defensively.

Kane clenched the meager payment in his fist, seething with resentment at the ringmaster's unfairness. He knew arguing further was futile; his priority was evading Gideon's clutches. Storming away from the tent, he marched back towards Chinatown. From across the street, a shady character called out to him.

"Hey Mister, wait up!"

Kane halted abruptly, his irritation mounting as yet another persistent American accosted him. He sighed deeply, refusing to turn around to acknowledge the beckoning man, standing rigid under the dim glow of a street lamp.

"Hey, Mister, thanks for stopping. I've got a proposition that might interest you," the stranger persisted, his strong Mexican accent grating on Kane's nerves.

Kane's memory flashed back to the unkempt Hispanic man in the fighting tent.

He had been a stark figure amidst the raucous crowd, glaring at Kane with a blend of menace and detachment. The man's long, thick pigtails cascaded over his shoulders, twisting with every movement, while shaggy mutton chops framed his face, leading into a disheveled handlebar mustache that he absentmindedly smoothed away from his moist upper lip. His dark skin bore traces of both his heritage and the accumulated grime of his rough existence. Despite his rugged appearance, there was an air of confidence and fearlessness about him as he spoke.

"I watched you in the fighting ring, you have strength, skill and above all.....endurance, just the kind of man we are looking for.....you would be paid well" "My name is Alejandro and I am part of a large family who lives West of Nevada and a strong man like yourself would make a great addition to our group" He continued "I don't need money, Mr Alejandro. I am on a spiritual journey and Monk's needs are always bestowed by the community" Kane stated

"Ok? Then if you don't need money then why were you in the fighting ring?" "Hai, well I needed some money to pay for my room before I head off on my pilgrimage" Kane justified

"I am sorry to shatter your illusion Mister, but you won't find many people willing to support you here. People don't accept your type, most of them are Catholics and don't care about your type of religion.....it's dog-eat-dog in this country"

"I am a Buddhist Monk and who says rejection has to be painful Alejandro? The rejection might not even reflect upon me in the slightest, it's only the other person declining my request" Kane educated

"Sí and you'll get a lot of that.....declining your requests" Alejandro chuckled "Are you a Mexican? The old Chinaman who runs the boarding house said that I should stay away from Mexicans" Kane forewarned

"Ahh those superstitious Chinese.....don't listen to him... ..and no I'm not Mexican.....I am Latin American" Alejandro manipulated

"What would I be doing with your group?" Kane probed, becoming suddenly interested with what Alejandro was offering, after falsely learning that he wasn't a Mexican.

"Errands, you know, running messages to those who live

farther in the wildlands" "That doesn't sound difficult. Why would you want a man with strength, fighting skills and endurance then?"

Alejandro began to laugh at Kane's naive perception. "Why are you laughing, that wasn't a funny remark?"

"Mister, wait until you're out west, it's a ruthless territory... ..what's your name by the way? I can't keep calling you Mister"

"My name is Kane Shunro"

"Well Kane Shunro, are you going to accept my offer for work or not? You will be taken care of, have your own cabana and you'll have money in your pocket to finance your pilgrimage later on. How can you lose with a plan like that?" Alejandro persuaded.

"What's a cabana?" Kane innocently asked "It's a house"

"You will give me a house?" Kane seemed astonished that this stranger was willing to provide him with permanent lodging and payment.

"Sí, it's all part of the agreement that you'll enter into if you take the job" Alejandro replied, identifying Kanes growing interest.

"So? What do you think Amigo? No one else will offer you a fine deal like this" He continued.

Kane scrutinized Alejandro for several moments, his mind racing with considerations. Plunging into an unfamiliar arrangement required careful deliberation, especially given his urgent need to evade Gideon and seize the chance to vanish without a trace.

He weighed the potential repercussions of aligning himself with Alejandro, understanding that such a commitment carried long-term implications.

"This decision holds great weight for me. Can I have the night to consider it?" Kane finally requested, his tone reflecting the gravity of his dilemma.

Kane eyed Alejandro cautiously, his brow furrowed with skepticism. The Mexican's proposal seemed too convenient, too perfect—an opportunity that could either be his salvation or a trap waiting to snap shut. Alejandro's confident attitude and persuasive words didn't immediately reassure Kane; instead, they heightened his wariness.

"I appreciate the offer," Kane replied, his voice tinged with doubt.

"But rushing into this decision isn't wise. How do I know you're not leading me into more trouble? And what guarantee do I have that you'll stick to your word?" Alejandro's gaze hardened slightly, understanding Kane's hesitation.

"You've got until tomorrow morning," he said firmly.

"I'll be here at 7 am, horses and supplies ready. But remember, time's ticking. You've got to decide whether you're in or out."

With that, Alejandro turned and walked back towards the fighting tent, leaving Kane standing alone under the flickering street lamp.

The night enveloped him, leaving him to wrestle with uncertainty and the consequences of his choices. He grappled with his thoughts until dawn broke, bringing either clarity or more questions.

Kane entered the rented room, fatigue and uncertainty nagging his mind.

He approached the window, hoping to catch sight of Lady Vixen, but the street below was deserted, adding to his sense of bewilderment. Unsure of his next move, he retrieved the peculiar human skin book from his luggage, seeking unconventional guidance from its cryptic pages.

"Should I accept the stranger's offer?" he murmured to the ancient book, gently caressing its weathered cover. The book remained silent, offering no discernible answer.

Exhausted by the day's events, Kane stretched out on the bed, his thoughts swirling as he drifted into sleep. In the depths of his subconscious, a profound dream unfolded, shrouded in enigmatic symbolism and profound meaning.

From the depths of darkness, a blue vortex surged forth, engulfing Kane in a surreal nightmare. Within its swirling depths, visions danced with eerie wit, speaking to him in puzzling tales, urging action and demanding revelations in exchange. Demonic entities materialized, their voices resonating with lessons on courage, compelling him to confront the shadowy depths of his own mind. Amongst this infernal congregation, his father emerged through the shimmering blue portal, spectral demons parting reverently as he glided forward. With a featureless face, he began to commune with Kane's innermost instincts, guiding him through the labyrinth of his fears.

"I am your cavalier. Protective chivalry is one of my traits. If anyone causes you trouble, I promise I'll be their nightmare. I will torment them until their minds warp, and they will cry out in hysteria. Trust me, I am very experienced in this. Do not fear the unknown, Kane. You must move forward with your universal destiny. Go into the desert; it is the right path."

The next morning, Kane woke with renewed determination,

simplicity pulsing through him. The psychedelic clarity of his dream had distilled everything into a clear purpose. Swiftly, he packed his belongings into bags, his mind set on finding Alejandro.

His heavy footsteps echoed down the staircase, startling the old Innkeeper who was engrossed in paperwork behind the desk. Hastily, the Innkeeper intercepted Kane at the door, halting his exit.

"Are you leaving? I thought you wanted the room for two nights?" He explored intrusively

"As you said, I only had enough money for one and a half nights. I've paid you all I have.....the four dollars.....remember?"

"Hai I remember.....I might be old, but I'm not stupid. You seem in a big hurry this morning. Meeting up with someone?" A crafty twinkle glittered in the Chinaman's eyes, as though he already knew who Kane was convening with.

"I met someone last night and they are helping me travel through the frontier" Kane blurted out quickly.

"I have to go, he is waiting for me. Thank you for your service" He added "Wait.....Before you leave, I'll refund you some money because you didn't eat the all-inclusive meal" He purposely obstructed Kane's departure as he continued rummaging through stuff on the desk.

"Keep it.....I have to go now"

"Be very careful, Monk," warned the Chinaman as he continued rummaging for the cash tin.

"I heard you fought a couple of rounds in the tent last night. That man you're leaving with isn't all he appears to be. Favors come with obligations."

"I don't have much choice if I want to continue my journey," Kane replied "And in this unfamiliar country, an experienced guide would be invaluable."

"Is that what he told you? That he's a guide?" mocked the Innkeeper, laughing sarcastically.

"You have no idea who I'm meeting," Kane protested, frustration mounting. "I've been here a long time, so I know everyone and everything in this neighborhood," the Innkeeper asserted.

"But if you believe you're making the right choice, then I wish you luck. You're not in Japan anymore, young Monk."

As he finished speaking, the Innkeeper glanced up to gauge Kane's reaction, only to find Kane had vanished.

"Hmph.... foolish man," he muttered softly to himself.

Turning the street corner, Kane saw Alejandro moving between a couple of tethered horses as he organized their saddlebags.

"Ahh.....so you've decided to join me. I was just about to leave you behind" He said when Kane approached

"Hai, It's the only chance I have to proceed with my plans"

"Alright then. Here, change into these clothes and wear the hat too" Alejandro instructed, handing Kane a ranchero outfit.

"Why? I am comfortable with what I'm wearing"

"Yeah you might be, but you stick out like dog balls in that multi-colored foreign garb. You'll draw too much attention unless you're looking for a close encounter with Bandits or worse.....the savage native Indians, they absolutely hate foreigners like you" Alejandro smirked.

"Where will I change?"

"Go down that alleyway, and hurry up, we have a very long trek ahead of us" When Kane returned dressed in his cowboy outfit, Alejandro couldn't contain his laughter as he appraised his companion's new look.

"What's so funny? This is what you said to wear," Kane retorted.

"I should've gotten you bigger pants; those are at least three inches too short. And your hat looks like it's balancing on your head like a bird on a perch. Are the riding boots even fitting you?" Alejandro asked through his laughter.

"Barely," Kane admitted. "I might need to cut the fronts off so my toes can stick out. Right now, they're all scrunched up."

"Ok, ok, we can fix that later on. Come on, mount up Kane. Do you know how to ride a horse?"

"Hai, of course, I do"

"Alright, I was just checking because you're a Chinaman" "'I'm Japanese thank you"

"Whatever.....You all look the same to me.....let's get going" Alejandro judged and kicked his horse in the belly, motivating the animal into a trot as Kane followed close behind and the men headed out of town, launching the tough and uncompromising journey into the untamed Nevada wastelands.

As they rode along, the Innkeeper's parting words rang in Kane's mind, and he found himself hoping that he had made the right choice. He believed in the message from his lucid dream—that joining forces with Alejandro and returning to his property was the correct path.

The journey ahead promised to be a marathon with the enigmatic Mexican, and Kane realized he needed to proceed one step at a time. His primal instincts, always lurking beneath the surface, stood ready to react aggressively to any threat, independent of his rational thoughts. He vowed to remain hyper-vigilant against potential sources of conflict, knowing this would pose a persistent challenge for his extroverted nature as a skin-changer.

Chapter 9

Two months had flown by since Kane departed the shores of Japan. Now, as Gideon, Miko, Hiro, and the newly anointed ninja Juji disembarked from the tall ship onto the bustling wharves of San Francisco Bay, they stood together in awe of the city's enthusiastic diversity.

"Do not become influenced by this country's debauchery, my young brothers. I can see, taste and smell the corruption and sinfulness. It oozes from every nook and cranny. We must be mindful of the reason we're here. Find Kane and take him back to the monastery for his final judgment" Were Gideon's first words and the four monks collected their luggage and made headway towards Chinatown.

"Where are we going, Master Gideon?" Miko asked politely

"While we were staying at the Hozenji Temple in Osaka, I inquired about this American country and asked if there were any Buddhist temples that would allow us to stay and Master Asahi informed me that the only place he'd heard of, was a village called Chinatown.....so that's where we are going"

Miko held a deep admiration for Gideon's pragmatic mindset. Despite the stern message delivered by Juji from the Abbot just before their departure from Japan, following Taichi, Hikaru, and Itsuo's return to the monastery, Gideon's Master maintained an impressive composure and strict focus.

On the night Juji arrived at Hozenji Temple in Osaka, Miko eavesdropped on their conversation while discreetly attending to menial chores. The Abbot's uncompromising message explaining why he couldn't grant Gideon's request for more ninjas weighed heavily in the atmosphere. Miko observed Gideon's reaction upon learning that Juji would be their sole companion on the journey to America. His Master's face drained of color, turning a weird shade of pale ivory as he absorbed Juji's words with intense concentration.

"Master Abbot was deeply distressed when Taichi and Hikaru returned with Itsuo's body. He expressed that three young monks have now perished since the pursuit of Kane began, and he is unwilling to sacrifice any more lives. Sending a large number of ninjas would also attract too much attention also," Juji explained earnestly to Gideon as he handed over a thick bundle of rolled notes.

"He believes in your abilities but urges you to bring this chase to an end swiftly. Use your wisdom and tenacity to capture the unholy demon. Innocent lives must not be endangered any longer," Juji continued, his voice reflecting the significance of the Abbot's instructions.

"The money you requested is here. Spend it wisely, as there will be no more. The Abbot dedicated a prayer vigil before my departure, blessing our uncharted journey."

As Gideon accepted the money, a stately determination settled over him, knowing the gravity of their mission and the expectations resting on his shoulders.

"Thank you, Juji, for your honesty. You've done well, my brother," Gideon acknowledged gratefully.

"Are you prepared for this perilous journey?"

As Gideon spoke, he couldn't shake the realization that tracking down Kane would now be even more challenging. With Kane's significant head start and the vast expanse of the country he had fled to, coupled with their limited numbers of ninjas, it could potentially be years before they could return home to Japan.

Gideon felt exhaustion creeping in on two fronts—physical and mental. It shrouded him like a heavy coat: his body yearning for rest while his mind relentlessly pushed forward in the search for Kane. He squeezed his eyes shut and then widened them in a futile attempt to stay alert, aware that his concentration was starting to wane as he shuffled along the street.

"Master Gideon, are you alright?" Miko asked with growing concern, but Gideon seemed oblivious.

"Master Gideon, are you alright?" His young steward repeated, a touch of urgency in his voice.

"Hai, Master Miko.... I'm just feeling old and tired. I fear this journey may soon take its toll on me," Gideon admitted wearily. He turned to Hiro and Juji, instructing them to scout ahead and find Chinatown.

"Choose a suitable lodging and a Sento (bathhouse), then return to me," he ordered, handing Hiro some money.

"Hai, Master Gideon," Hiro acknowledged, and both ninjas hurried off down the road to secure a place where their respected leader could rejuvenate.

"Here, sit down on this bench," Miko encouraged, supporting

Gideon gently. "You don't look well," he continued, his voice tinged with worry.

"It's very hot here, and I'm not accustomed to it," Gideon admitted. For the first time, Miko glimpsed the vulnerable side of his revered Master, his concern deepening.

* * *

Hiro and Juji strolled down the busy main street of Chinatown, carefully inspecting the boarding houses adorned with "vacancy" signs. They stepped into one establishment and inquired about accommodations for their companions.

"We have one room available," the female proprietor informed them.

"We need three rooms, or at least two," Hiro explained in his Japanese accent.

"If you require more rooms, I suggest the hotel at the end of the street," she replied matter-of-factly.

"Thank you," Hiro nodded politely, and the two monks departed, continuing down the road. Their eyes widened as they observed the animated and distinctly different way of life around them. They passed by scenes where white men draped themselves over Asian women, their behavior suggesting a sense of possession and entitlement, while the women appeared submissive and inexperienced. The men seemed fascinated by the exoticism of the women's tanned, youthful bodies, indulging in their fetishes and curiosities.

"That isn't right" Juji commented, staring at the peculiarity of the interracial couples. "They have a different way of living here in America, Juji. It appears that they openly procreate with one another.....but as long as they are both happy I suppose" Hiro stated.

Dressed in Japanese civilian attire that Gideon had purchased to avoid drawing attention in their ninja-yorois, Hiro and Juji stepped into the same boarding house where Kane had stayed months earlier. They were promptly greeted by the elderly Chinese Innkeeper.

"How can I help you?" he greeted them warmly.

"We need two rooms," Hiro informed him, while Juji quietly surveyed the eccentrically decorated foyer.

"Hai, I have rooms available. It's $3 per night, and that includes one meal a day. Will that be one room each?" the Innkeeper asked.

"No, two more will be joining us. Is there a Sento here as well?" Hiro inquired. The Chinaman chuckled to himself, a smile spreading across his face.

Hiro's tone sharpened as he felt a pang of embarrassment at the Innkeeper's teasing in front of Juji.

"What's so funny?" he demanded, his pride stung by the innuendo. The old Chinaman chuckled knowingly.

"They're called public bathhouses, and they can be a haven for more than just bathing. If you're looking for something steamy in there, it's not just because of the mist," he bantered with a shrewd wink.

Hiro exchanged a glance with Juji, unsure whether to be amused or annoyed by the Innkeeper's cheeky manner.

"We are Japanese monks and have bestowed ourselves to chastity, so that doesn't interest us. We have an elderly high priest traveling with us. Could you please provide him with a washbasin and towels then?"

"Oh, don't tell me.....you are all on a holy pilgrimage? The Innkeeper goaded "No, we're not, why would you say that?" Hiro queried while he handed over the rental money

"No reason, just seen my share of monks traveling through Chinatown"

"Have you ever met a monk who was large and hairy like a bear?" Hiro asked, his eyes spellbound as he waited for the Innkeepers answer.

"No can't say I have" He blatantly lied and even though he had an impish nature, the old Chinaman's instinct warned him that trouble was brewing.

"Are you sure? You couldn't mistake him, he's not an ordinary-sized Japanese man" Hiro prodded.

Juji nudged his arm, subtly directing his gaze toward an item nestled among an assortment of knick-knacks on an overcrowded shelf. Hiro quickly spotted the object Juji had indicated, and a sudden expression of delight spread across his face. It was at that moment the old Chinaman caught on to their interest.

"No, no, no!! None of my ornaments are for sale" He fretted "Where did you get that Ghau?" Hiro asked

"What?" The chinaman queried ignorantly

"That prayer box on the shelf, where did you get it?" Hiro continued

Under the dim, hazy light, the gold Buddhist amulet gleamed like a distant star, capturing everyone's gaze as they focused on the box. Its exterior bore intricate engravings of their monastery's unmistakable insignia, adorned with inlaid pearls and coral. Normally, a small clay Buddha statue would rest atop the silk inlay, serving to ward off evil spirits and bestow blessings, but it was conspicuously absent.

"It's not for sale, I told you. It's mine and has been in my family for generations" The Chinaman defended and quickly grabbed the box, shoving it tightly under his arm.

"But that belongs to....."Juji tried explaining to the old man where it originally came from, but Hiro interjected and de-escalated the suspicion about the Ghau.

"Hai, it is indeed beautiful. We're simply admiring its craftsmanship, and you're fortunate to have such a precious heirloom," Hiro interjected smoothly, taking command of the conversation.

"Now that we've settled payment for the rooms, we'll retrieve our priest and his steward. We'll return shortly.... and please remember the washbasin and towels." He bowed respectfully to the Innkeeper before guiding Juji towards the door.

Outside, Juji couldn't contain his frustration.

"Why did you stop me from telling the Chinaman that the Ghau belongs to our monastery?" he questioned Hiro.

"I don't want anyone here knowing our true purpose. Our mission is to apprehend Kane and bring him back to Japan. In a foreign land with different laws, revealing our intentions could lead to imprisonment," Hiro explained firmly.

"Keep your eyes open and your mouth shut. I'll handle the talking."

"Hai, you're right. Thank you for your wisdom, Hiro," Juji conceded, acknowledging his elder's guidance.

Returning to where Gideon and Miko rested, the scouting

monks informed them that they had located a welcoming boarding house. However, Hiro purposely refrained from mentioning the crested Ghau that Kane had left behind.

"How far is the hostel? Master Gideon isn't feeling well because of the heat" Miko said with worry in his voice.

"I'll be fine Miko, I can walk to the hostel and once there I can regain my strength.

I just have to adjust to the heat" Gideon reassured, so the men headed towards the boarding house.

Gideon gripped his wizard-like staff tightly as he followed the trio of ninjas down the dusty street. Passersby couldn't help but stare, their gazes lingering on the unusual group as if their minds struggled to process the sight of these unconventional travelers. Some onlookers couldn't contain their amusement, their mouths forming amused grins while shaking their heads in disbelief.

Entering the foyer of the boarding house, they were greeted by the old Innkeeper, whose gaze was fixed on Gideon's damaged eye and rugged facial scars. His expression was determined, yet tinged with impudence.

"Well, now, here's something you don't see every day.... a Zen Buddhist priest," the Innkeeper remarked as he handed over the keys.

"What are our room numbers?" Hiro curtly asked, ignoring his wisecrack about Gideon.

"Ah yes..... it's room five and room six. Do you need me to show you the way?" "No, we are not Orokamonos (idiots) We can find it ourselves" Hiro replied, abruptly snatching the keys from the Innkeeper's hand and he sensed Hiro's displeasure.

Standing silently with Miko by his side, Gideon positioned

himself behind Hiro and Juji. Though he remained wordless, an aura of intensity surrounded him, his gaze piercing and cold as he focused sharply on the anxious Chinaman.

"Alright then, enjoy your stay," the Innkeeper finally muttered, visibly unsettled by the presence of the four stern monks. As they began ascending the stairs, his unease evident, he watched them closely.

Opening the door to room five, Hiro and Juji stepped inside first, while Miko and Gideon lingered in the hallway, waiting for their signal. Once Hiro and Juji signaled that it was safe, Miko and Gideon joined them.

The moment Gideon crossed the threshold, a bone-chilling sensation enveloped him, as if he had stepped into a tomb. Whispers echoed in the air, calling his name repeatedly, the eerie voices seeping into his senses like a paranormal mist.

"Kane's been here" He revealed

"How do you know Master Gideon?" Miko asked

"There is an invisible presence in this room and it's a dark and powerful force" He admitted

"Hai, he has.....there's one of our monastery's Ghau's in the foyer" Juji blurted out, relieved that he was finally able to contribute towards the mounting clues.

"Hai, I noticed it when we entered the hotel, but thank you for bringing it to my attention, Juji," Gideon acknowledged graciously.

"Do you want to stay in this room, or would you prefer the other?" Miko asked, concerned as he noticed Gideon's sweat-covered condition.

"We will take the other room. Hiro and Juji can have this one," Gideon decided abruptly, already stepping back from room five.

"After what I just experienced, I believe Kane's demon is evolving. The spiritual attack I felt was a glimpse of what's to come," Gideon confessed as Miko unlocked the door.

"What do you mean?" Miko asked, his worry evident in his voice.

"The fear within me is my greatest adversary. I must overcome this torment and prepare myself for facing Kane once more. To achieve victory over the demon, I must adapt and conquer this fear, which is proving difficult for me right now," Gideon disclosed.

"You have us by your side, Master Gideon. We're here to support you and face Kane together. Here, lie down on the bed. You're weary from the long journey on the ship... Please rest," Miko encouraged, gently assisting Gideon onto the flimsy mattress just as a knock sounded at the door.

"Hai, who is it?" Miko called out.

"It's Hiro.... I have a washbasin and towels for Master Gideon," Hiro replied from outside the door.

Miko opened the door but instead of allowing Hiro to enter, he swiftly passed through and closed it behind him.

"What's going on?" Hiro asked, confused.

"Master Gideon isn't feeling well right now. He needs to rest. He had a difficult experience in your room and with the heat, he's now feeling overwhelmed about facing Kane again," Miko explained with concern in his voice.

"He won't have to fight Kane again.... I will. I eagerly await the day. It's time we bring the mutant to justice and teach him a lesson," Hiro asserted firmly as he handed the washbasin and towels to Miko.

"Hai, but Master Gideon is spiritually attuned. He senses

paranormal phenomena and has faced the demon before, surviving. If he's already overwhelmed with dread, what will we encounter when we confront Kane again? Master Gideon mentioned sensing Kane's demon maturing, and I'm concerned," Miko whispered apprehensively.

"Don't worry, my young brother. I will confront the devil myself. Let Master Gideon know that I'm going to gather information on Kane's movements," Hiro reassured, giving Miko an encouraging pat on the shoulder.

"Good luck," Miko wished him as he watched Hiro descend the staircase.

* * *

The wind whipped fiercely as Hiro strolled along the busy main street of Chinatown, the relentless sun beating down on his bare head, making him struggle against the oppressive heat. Turning a corner, he ventured deeper into the city and immediately sensed a mixture of sounds blending with the charged atmosphere. Crowds of pedestrians moved along the thoroughfare, navigating through a tapestry of deep footprints and wheel tracks molded into the earth.

Clusters of tightly packed houses lined the street, their walls pressing against each other. Ahead, an elderly beggar sat on a stoop, his weathered arms extended, eyes pleading for charity. Bloodshot and trembling, his unkempt silver-grey hair framed a face etched with deep, red-stitched scars creeping along his neck. Persistently, he beseeched passersby for donations, a poignant figure amongst the transient crowd. Disgust welled within Hiro as he caught the overpowering stench of cheap liquor mingled with the sour tang of stale urine, emanating from the unwashed beggar.

"Mister, do you have any money for a hungry old man?" the beggar croaked through a false, perpetual grin. Hiro, consumed by his own arrogance and sense of superiority, continued walking without acknowledging the man's presence.

Quickening his pace, Hiro's mind raced with calculations of where Kane might have visited. He mentally mapped out potential locations based on what he knew of Kane—his tendency towards shyness and unfamiliarity with San Francisco's culture suggested he wouldn't wander far from his boarding house.

At the next street junction, Hiro paused and glanced back over his shoulder, reflecting on the path he had just walked. Across the road, a solitary stray dog stood motionless, its ears flattened against its head. The mongrel's predatory gaze locked onto Hiro's every move, a silent assertion of dominance, marking him as potential prey.

Hiro briskly crossed the road, stealing a glance back at the stray dog to see if it was following him—and without hesitation, it was. He hurriedly slipped through an open door into a nearby saloon, relieved to evade its cold, sinister glare, hoping the dog would lose interest by the time he left.

Entering the shaded bar, the dim interior heightened Hiro's senses. Rows of alcohol bottles stood in muted colors behind the counter, illuminated by dim lights. The air was thick with the clamor of overlapping conversations, each voice competing for dominance in the lively atmosphere.

"What's your poison?" The bartender asked, sharp as a tack. Hiro blinked, wide-eyed and innocent.

"I don't drink poison! That sounds terrible!"

The bartender burst out laughing so hard he nearly fell over.

"I know, buddy, I know. I meant, what drink do you want?" he managed between chuckles.

Hiro nodded, relieved. "Ah, I see. Could I have a jug of sake?" The bartender's laughter returned, louder this time.

"Sake? You're not in Japan anymore, Mister. We've got whiskey and beer, that's it." Hiro sighed, miffed.

"Fine, I'll have a beer then," he grumbled, wishing the bartender would stop laughing at him.

"That'll be 5 cents"

Hiro paid the money and simultaneously grabbed the glass of beer, then casually made his way to a solitary chair, perching himself at the far end of the bar. While he mimicked sipping on the beverage, he visually scanned the celebratory atmosphere. He noticed cheap glassware crammed into dusty cabinets and three spittoons lining the foot rail in front of the bar. A large clock ticked loudly amidst various pictures hanging on tattered, peeling wallpaper. The room was dimly lit by four bare electric light bulbs and two flickering kerosene lamps, casting long silhouettes that moved on the walls.

Saloon girls, with painted smiles, chatted with half-drunk patrons, cozying up to them and pretending to find them irresistible. Their flirtatious banter was calculated to keep the men in the bar, spending money on drinks and engaging in card games. The air was thick with the smell of alcohol, tobacco smoke, and a hint of desperation, blending together in a heady cocktail that spoke of long nights and empty pockets.

Then he heard a brazen, intimidating voice that boomed over everything else without flinching. The weathered cowboy's gravelly words were concealed behind chipped teeth that resembled stained fingernails. He moved awkwardly, continually stooped, like he was imitating a tarantula's scurry. The cowboy's presence seemed to drain the elation from the room, absorbing it for his own selfish satisfaction and leaving those around him deflated and disheartened.

As the toughened, peculiar cowboy moved through the public bar area, his eyes eventually locked onto Hiro, seated alone with his full glass of beer on the counter. Hiro cringed when he noticed the oddball advancing closer, each step bringing with it

an aura of unease and discomfort. The cowboy's shadow loomed larger, casting a cloud over Hiro's quiet corner, and he braced himself for the inevitable encounter. "Hi Mister, what are you doing in this squalid saloon?" The bizarre man queried "I'm having a quiet drink" Hiro said

"There seems to be a lot of "your kind" getting around this town" He blurted out shamelessly

"What do you mean? "My kind?" Hiro questioned with feelings of disgust emerging from within.

"You know, from Japan and sporting a bald head. A monk or something aren't you?" "Hai, a Buddhist monk to be correct"

Despite his disgust for the strange man and his offensive persona, Hiro thought this impudent pawn might know something about Kane's location. Swallowing his disdain, he decided to appease the cowboy's curiosity.

"You seem to know everyone here," Hiro continued, his tone probing for information. "Yep.... this is my local haunt," the cowboy replied, stumbling slightly as he turned to glance at the crowd of patrons behind him.

"So? You've seen others like me?" Hiro prodded, his curiosity growing.

"Sure have.... maybe a dozen, give or take," the cowboy replied nonchalantly. "Have you seen a man like me but with a much bigger physique?" Hiro asked, leaning in slightly.

"I didn't actually see him, but there was talk about a huge Japanese monk who fought in the tent and became the champion," the cowboy said, his voice taking on a secretive tone.

"They said he was so terrifying that nobody wanted to get in the ring with him. And that's really something, because this is a brutal town with all the Mexicans hanging around," he declared.

"What brings you to San Francisco, mister? And if you're a monk, how come you're not wearing one of those religious 'dresses'?" the cowboy asked, eyeing Hiro with a mix of suspicion and curiosity.

"I am here with a high Buddhist priest. My accompanying group just wants to blend into your American culture as much as possible.... so where is this fighting tent?" Hiro diverted the conversation away from himself.

"A few blocks away from here, not far from Chinatown actually. You can't miss it. Just a big arse tent that gets really rowdy at night when the fights are on.... are you going to drink that, Mister?" The stooped cowboy said, his eyes shifting hungrily toward Hiro's untouched beer.

Hiro didn't answer him directly. Instead, he slowly pushed the glass along the countertop, placing it in front of the unusual man.

"Thanks, Mister," the cowboy said, quickly seizing the glass and scuttling back to the lively mob of drinkers like a crab returning to its tidal pool.

Hiro stared after the cowboy for a couple of minutes, his mind churning with thoughts. He finally stood up and walked over to the entrance of the saloon, hesitating briefly before pushing through the door. His senses on high alert, he recalled the lurking presence of the stalking dog and cautiously glanced out the window to ensure it had moved on. Satisfied that the coast was clear, he briskly left the saloon and headed back towards Chinatown.

As he passed through a dirty backstreet, Hiro's keen ears picked up faint sobbing. Someone seemed overcome with emotion, their cries mingling with gasps for air. Curiosity aroused, Hiro moved stealthily down the alleyway to investigate what was going on.

There, frozen against a brick wall, was Miko, his body pressed uncomfortably close, with a menacing stray dog looming in front of him. The dog's lips curled back, revealing razor-edged fangs, as it emitted a deep-throated growl, foam dripping from its mouth like syrup.

Hiro's heart pounded in his chest as he spotted his brother. The sight of Miko, struggling to hold back tears, filled Hiro with a sickening mix of fear and determination. He approached quietly, trying not to startle the dog.

"HHHelp MMMe," Miko whimpered, his voice trembling.

Hiro gestured for silence, raising a finger to his lips. Slowly, he bent down, picking up a nearby rock. With careful aim, he hurled the rock at the dog, striking it hard on the side of its head.

Abruptly, the dog shrieked in a high-pitched, unnatural voice as blood streamed down its face, staining its fur a vivid crimson.

Without warning, it pivoted and bolted toward Hiro with startling speed, faster than a blink.

Instinct and adrenaline kicked in. Hiro reacted swiftly, hurling himself at the charging animal. With a forceful kick to its midsection, he knocked the dog to the ground.

For a moment, the creature lay stunned, blood mixing with dirt, before it regained its bearings.

Staring at Hiro with an unnerving intensity, the dog hesitated, its gaze unbroken as it cautiously skirted past him. As Hiro cautiously watched it retreat, a shock ran through his body when the dog spoke in a woman's voice—clearly and unmistakably uttering his name, "Hiro."

Before he could comprehend what was happening, an unseen force shoved him hard in the chest, sending him stumbling backward. Hiro struggled to regain his balance, as the dog sprinted away, disappearing into the murkiness of the alleyway, leaving him shaken and bewildered.

"Miko, are you alright?"

"Hai, brother and thank you for saving me"

"That dog was possessed. It looked exactly like the one we saw stalking us in Japan.... but that couldn't be right, could it?" Miko continued, a mix of confusion and fear in his voice.

"Let's get you back to Master Gideon. What were you doing out here anyway?" Hiro asked

"Master Gideon told me to go and look for you.....plus he said that I could have a little time to myself. Then that dog found me.....I did not encourage it at all. I noticed it shadowing me for ages, and when I tried to escape, it became aggressive and trapped me here in this dead end backstreet"

"Don't worry about it now. Come on let's go" Hiro encouraged and the two ninjas returned to their lodgings, informing Gideon on what had transpired.

Stepping through the door, Miko felt a wave of terror engulfed him, leaving him pale and trembling like a frightened child. Facing Gideon, his embarrassment at showing his nervousness was overwhelming, and he wanted nothing more than to disappear. But this was his moment to confront his fear, to demonstrate maturity, and to tap into the inner strength instilled in him at the monastery.

"What's happened to Master Miko?" Gideon snapped irritably, his concern for his young steward evident.

"I found Miko cornered in an alleyway by a stray dog it was extremely aggressive.

If I hadn't arrived in time, it would have mauled him," Hiro declared proudly, casting himself as the valiant protector of his defenseless brother.

"What kind of dog?" Gideon's voice quivered with apprehension. "It was a...." Hiro began, but Gideon cut him off sharply.

"I am talking to Master Miko," Gideon interjected firmly.

"At first, I thought it was just a random dog. But when it trapped me and I was face to face with it, I recognized it. It looked exactly like the wolf-dog that stalked us between Kyoto and Osaka. Same greyish brown coat, distinctive white-tipped tail. This time I got to see its eyes.... different colors with triangular-shaped pupils. But what struck me most was that smell. The same the foul odor," Miko explained to his Master, his voice carrying a mixture of relief and lingering fear.

"Kane's bewitched wolf," Gideon admitted under his breath, his voice laden with concern.

"What? Does that dog belong to Kane? How and why?" Hiro blurted out, his surprise evident.

"I have read about these totem animals in various religious doctrines I've studied. Not all are benevolent. There's the sea of white light from our universal divine father, but also the black abyss of demonic evil. The yin and the yang. Light and dark. It's a choice each person makes. Despite his Buddhist teachings, Kane has chosen the dark path. We must be hyper-vigilant from now on, my brothers. we are being

watched," Gideon cautioned, his tone grave.

"Also, Master Gideon.... I've uncovered Kane's movements. I overheard about a large Japanese man who fought in the boxing tent and was hailed as that night's champion. They described him like a monk with a shaven head. I believe it's a promising lead," Hiro revealed, bowing respectfully.

"Thank you, Master Hiro. We will visit the fighting tent tonight," Gideon affirmed decisively.

* * *

The atmosphere buzzed with electrifying energy, spreading through the crowd like a contagious fever as the brutal spectacle unfolded in the center of the ring, akin to vultures circling over a decaying carcass. Gideon and his companions slipped unnoticed into the throng, blending into the chaotic scene.

They bumped into the grizzled promoter as they navigated through the crowd.

"A pound or two for a round or two! Who will step up to the challenge?" he bellowed repeatedly, scanning the audience.

"What about you? Fancy testing your bravery against the

champion?" he prodded, his eyes lingering on Hiro and Juji.

"No, they do not," Gideon replied tersely, his voice showing disdain.

"Well, look at you, the big shot with your fancy cane. Not up for a fight, huh? Shame, you Asians know how to fight," the promoter taunted, undeterred.

"Have you seen others like us fight here?" Hiro inquired, ignoring the jab.

"Yeah, sure have. There was this one guy, massive bloke he was, fought here about four ago. Became the champ after just two rounds. But he seemed scared stiff of his own strength, which was odd, so he took off," the promoter recounted casually.

"You pay to fight?" Hiro questioned.

"Yep, that's the deal. This is a betting joint; folks put down their money on who's gonna win, and the winner takes it all," the promoter explained matter-of-factly. "Hai.... thank you.... we've heard enough," Gideon interjected firmly, signaling an end to the conversation.

"You didn't happen to see where this big guy went after he left, did you?" Hiro persisted, disregarding Gideon's clear desire to move on.

"He just headed outside. No clue what became of him after that. Alright then, have a good night....a pound or two for a round or two who will take the glove?" With that,

the promoter's voice faded into the background as he disappeared into the thronging crowd.

Stepping back into the artificial glow of the street lamps, the four men gathered closely to discuss their next strategic move.

"Hiro, your persistent defiance is trying my patience. I don't appreciate your constant need to stroke your own ego," Gideon seethed, his displeasure palpable.

"What do you mean, Master Gideon? I was only trying to gather more information about Kane. We're at a standstill in finding him. I didn't mean any disrespect," Hiro defended himself.

"Well, you are disrespectful, and this isn't the first time. Persist with your disobedience, and I'll send you back to Japan. Consider this your final warning," Gideon warned sternly.

"Hai.... I apologize for my behavior. It won't happen again," Hiro conceded, bowing respectfully to the high priest. Regardless of his outward compliance, underneath his calm pretence, he seethed with frustration and resentment.

"Master Gideon may I interject? Your dignified presence seems to be drawing attention from the townsfolk, and those suspicious men over there are watching us closely," Miko remarked, his voice sounding concerned.

"It might be wise for Hiro and Juji to scout the area while we retreat to our room—out of sight, out of mind."

"This is the wisdom and respect I want from my ninjas, Master Hiro, not your contempt and recklessness. It's putting everyone at risk," Gideon continued sternly, directing his disappointment at Hiro.

"Take a cue from Master Miko. Now go and don't return until you have new information."

"Hai, Master Gideon," Hiro and Juji acknowledged in unison, bowing before swiftly departing to carry out their mission.

In the dim, pre-dawn light, the gentle cooing of pigeons provided a serene backdrop to the dusky street where Hiro and Juji stood, a cautious twenty yards from the group of Hispanic men. The men, their faces obscured in the shadows as they leaned nonchalantly against a wall, engaged in boisterous insults and taunts while passing around a bottle concealed in a brown paper bag.

While the ninjas huddled together, strategizing their next move, Hiro's attention was drawn to the two large dogs accompanying the Mexicans. Their powerful bodies strained against their leashes, barking wildly with a ferocity that seemed almost tangible. Hiro's outward calm concealed a storm of turmoil within; his mind raced with caution and unease, each fleeting thought sharpening his sense of impending danger.

The dogs possessed muscular jaws and razor-sharp teeth that could pierce metal effortlessly, their pointed ears giving them a predatory appearance as their yellow

eyes locked onto potential prey. It seemed as though they were already savoring the taste of sweat and fear from anyone foolish enough to cross their path.

"Hey, Gringos, looks like my dogs want some Chinese for breakfast!" the man holding tightly onto the chains taunted, his companions laughing loudly. "We're Japanese, not Chinese! Get it right!" Hiro shot back defiantly.

"What did you say, puta?" the man shouted, his face contorting with anger. Suddenly, he bent over and released the snarling dogs, which bolted straight toward Hiro and Juji with alarming speed, their teeth bared and eyes wild.

"Run!" Hiro urgently commanded.

As they sprinted down the nearest alleyway, Hiro and Juji were assaulted by the putrid stench of rotting food spilling out of garbage cans. The odor clawed its way into their nostrils like invasive tentacles, overwhelming their senses in the narrow, dimly lit passage.

As they navigated obstacles with the dogs in hot pursuit, Juji demonstrated swift agility by vaulting halfway up a brick wall. He grabbed a nearby drainpipe and climbed effortlessly, reaching the safety of the roof. Hiro followed suit, but as he grasped the pipe, its rusty hinges buckled under his weight. It partially dislodged from the wall, leaving him dangling ten feet above the snapping jaws of the dogs, who leaped and snarled below, driven by their bloodlust.

Reacting swiftly, Juji hurled his dagger with precise aim, striking one of the dogs squarely in the neck. The blade penetrated deep, severing the spinal cord and killing the animal instantly. With a quick release, Hiro dropped onto the remaining dog, swiftly twisting its head to snap its neck. He then propelled himself upward, grabbing the swaying drainpipe and using it to scale the wall, finally reaching the roof where Juji awaited.

Breathing heavily, the two brothers reunited, their hearts still racing from the adrenaline-fueled escape.

"My dogs! You've killed my fucking dogs!" the Mexican screamed, his voice reverberating through the alleyway as he stood in shock, watching the ninjas murder his animals.

Drawing his pistol in a swift, enraged motion, he aimed at the fleeing ninjas. Four shots rang out, bullets whistling past their heads, but the nimble adversaries were too fast. They leaped from rooftop to rooftop, swiftly disappearing from sight.

As they vanished into the night, the screams of the Mexican's furious threats lingered in the air.

"I will find you and gut you.... you're dead, putas!" His voice faded into the darkness, filled with a chilling promise of revenge.

Finding a secure spot to regroup and strategize their next move, Hiro formulated a cunning plan.

"We need to return to the boarding house and inform Master Gideon about what just happened. Those men won't let this go," Juji whispered urgently.

"Hai, I know exactly what to do. We'll tell Gideon that we've uncovered vital information about Kane's whereabouts. It's urgent, and we must leave town immediately," Hiro schemed.

"What information, Hiro? We don't have any details. What will you tell him?" Juji questioned, concern furrowing his brow.

Sitting thoughtfully on the roof, Hiro pondered for a moment.

"I'll say that Kane is traveling along the coast. We heard it from someone who clearly remembered Kane's fierce fighting," he improvised confidently.

"We could go back and eliminate those Mexicans. That would solve our problem," Juji suggested pragmatically.

"And what then? How do we handle six bodies? American law isn't forgiving, especially for us Asians. Gideon has already warned me — one more mistake, and I'm sent back to Japan. Lying is our only option. Go back to the boarding house, tell Gideon and Miko to pack up, and wait for me out front," Hiro instructed decisively. "Where are you going?" Juji inquired, his voice worrisome.

"I'm going to 'borrow' a horse," Hiro replied quietly, his tone revealing the seriousness of their predicament. With that, the brothers parted ways to execute their respective roles in the deceptive plan.

Miko stood at the front counter of the boarding house, awaiting the return of the old innkeeper with more clean towels for

Master Gideon's midday prayer. As he waited patiently, his eyes wandered over to the Ghau, a prayer box from their monastery, discreetly displayed nearby.

Glancing around cautiously, Miko seized the opportunity. With a quick, stealthy movement, he slipped behind the desk, swiftly pocketing the prayer box. He then returned to his original position at the lobby counter, all without attracting any notice. "Here's your hot water and towels," the innkeeper announced as he finally emerged from behind the curtained door, presenting the requested items.

Miko nodded politely, his heart racing with the hidden Ghau now safely concealed on his person.

"Thank you" Miko said and began climbing the stairs when Juji entered the foyer. "Miko.... where is Master Gideon?" Juji's voice was urgent, cutting through the air as the old innkeeper listened intently nearby.

"He's in his room, of course. What's wrong? You seem worried," Miko replied, trying to maintain composure.

"Come on, we need to speak with him," Juji directed, his urgency not tolerating any delay.

Once inside Gideon's room, Juji conveyed the fabricated details Hiro had instructed him to deliver.

"Why the sudden departure?" Gideon inquired, his brow furrowing with suspicion. "Kane is holed up in a coastal town. He's been there for a while but is planning to leave soon," Juji lied convincingly.

"Who did you hear this from?"

"Oh, we went back to the fighting tent and spoke to more men. They said the large monk headed down the coast," Juji responded, weaving his lie with practiced ease. "How will we get there?" Gideon pressed, his mind already calculating the logistics. "Hiro is outside buying a horse for you as we speak," Juji assured him.

"Where did he get the money?" Gideon probed further.

"We returned to the fighting tent. Hiro fought and won against their champion. The prize money was enough to buy the horse," Juji fabricated again.

"A typical Hiro move.... but well done, I suppose" Gideon acknowledged. "Miko, gather our belongings. We're leaving."

Without hesitation, Juji hurried into the next room to pack his and Hiro's gear, the urgency of their fake mission propelling them into swift action.

As they guided Gideon down the stairwell, the Chinese innkeeper busied himself behind the front counter.

"You're leaving?" he asked, surprised by their sudden departure.

"Yes, we have urgent matters to attend to. Thank you for your hospitality," Miko replied hastily, urging their Grand Master towards the waiting horse outside.

"Why the rush? Everyone is always rushing out of here," the innkeeper persisted, his curiosity getting the better of him.

"We have vital business elsewhere. Have a good day," Juji swiftly concluded, deflecting further inquiries as they hurried Gideon out the door.

While they packed their belongings into the saddlebags, Miko felt a sense of perplexity gnawing at him. Earlier, when he had gone downstairs to fetch the hot water and towels, he had engaged in a casual conversation with the old innkeeper. In passing, the innkeeper had shared a tale about a massive monk who had stayed at the inn many weeks before. According to the innkeeper, the monk had ventured to the fighting tent to earn money for his stay and food. After that fateful night, the monk had departed with a Mexican companion, likely heading towards the Nevada desert, where many of them resided.

"I warned him to stay away from those Mexicans, but he didn't listen to me. He said he was on a spiritual journey," Miko distinctly remembered the innkeeper saying.

Despite hearing this crucial piece of information, Miko trusted his older brothers and believed they wouldn't deceive Master Gideon. Therefore, he kept silent, choosing

not to disclose information that could have saved the group valuable time and trouble.

Fussing around the front counter, the old Chinaman meticulously dusted his array of trinkets on the shelf, each one picked up and polished with loving care. Moving along the mantel, he reached where the Ghau usually rested, only to find it missing. Instant fury surged through him, propelling him towards the open door where he shook his fist wildly and screamed after the departing monks,

"You thieving bastards, bring back my ornament!"

But it was too late. The group was already half a mile away, their distant silhouettes melting into the heat haze as they vanished over the horizon. The old Chinaman stood fuming, his ornament gone, and his curses echoing fruitlessly in the empty street.

Chapter 10

The wind, sharp and cutting, whipped through the desolation, leaving Kane's lips cracked and parched. The torrid heat bore down relentlessly, each breath filling his lungs with gritty dust, triggering bouts of coughing and spluttering. Sweat mingled with the dust on his brow, his body odor intensifying in the dry heat. Dehydration gnawed at him, forcing him to lick his lips repeatedly, aggravating their already raw condition.

"How much further is this ranch of yours?" Kane grumbled to his guide, Alejandro. "It's not my ranch, señor. I'm just the recruiter for the workers.... It's probably another five days' ride," Alejandro replied nonchalantly.

"What?? We've already been out here in this blasted desert for a week. I feel like I'm getting sick from the heat," Kane complained.

"Ahh, that would be sunstroke. Don't worry, Kane, there's an oasis not far from here. We can rest for a couple of days, fill our canteens, and water the horses," Alejandro chuckled, finding humor in Kane's usually unseen frailty.

"Good, because I can't take this anymore," Kane sighed in relief.

They rode on towards the waterhole in a heavy silence, broken only by the distant screeching of eagles and the distant baying of wild dogs. Kane's parched eyes strained against the harsh sunlight until, finally, he spotted a cluster of large trees in the distance, and his heart leapt with relief.

"Thank God," he thought to himself.

"See, señor? Nothing to worry about. Alejandro will take care of you. I've made this trip many times. Back and forth, back and forth that's my job for the boss man and

the cartel. He always needs new workers," the Mexican declared proudly.

Amidst the golden sands, nestled a tranquil pond shaded by happy palm trees. As they entered this oasis of refreshing greenery, Kane felt rejuvenated, despite the relentless assault of the sun's scorching rays. The oasis maintained its cool composure, similar to a serene cucumber in the desert heat.

While the oasis provided a welcome respite for the parched travelers, it also harbored enigmatic secrets that tantalized the curious, drawing them in with its enticing scents and the allure of its seemingly endless, chilled waters.

As Kane dismounted his weary frame from the saddle, his horse audibly sighed with relief. It ambled over to the pond, eagerly dipping its muzzle into the water and drinking deeply.

"I need to wash off this gritty sand," Kane declared, filling his canteen and taking a deep gulp.

"Yeah, I know you're itching to cool off, but this watering hole is bottomless," Alejandro cautioned, his back turned as he unpacked his bedroll and cooking utensils.

"See that sandy bank? It's six inches above the water and made of sugar sand. It's unstable and tricky to climb out of, like quicksand. This oasis has been here for centuries, shrouded in mystery."

The water shimmered with an icy blue hue, casting a spell so irresistible that Kane couldn't resist its allure. Alejandro heard the massive splash and turned abruptly to see Kane floating in the center of the pond, his dusty clothes heaped at the water's edge.

"This is incredible!" Kane laughed, his broad frame buoyant as he swam around, occasionally submerging his scorching head in the cool water.

"You shouldn't have done that. Now you'll need my help to get out. You're such a big guy, I'll need my horse to assist," Alejandro remarked, a touch of exasperation in his voice as he unsaddled his horse.

"No, I'll manage on my own when I'm ready," Kane retorted confidently.

"Alright then. Good luck with that. I offered once, and I won't offer again, sabelotodo (smart arse)," Alejandro muttered under his breath, shaking his head at Kane's stubbornness.

As Alejandro busied himself setting up camp, he couldn't help but notice Kane's vigorous splashing in the pond. Expecting a struggle to get out, he turned his head to witness a startling sight: Kane's arms, thick and robust like twin hydraulic lifters, effortlessly lifted his massive frame out of the water.

"Ay Dios Mio!" Alejandro exclaimed in disbelief.

"I knew you were strong, but that's beyond belief. Who are you?"

Kane stood buck naked before Alejandro, methodically drying his face and hair with his shirt. Alejandro observed in awe as he took in the sight of the muscular figure before him. Kane's legs were sturdy and powerful, each muscle clearly defined as he moved. His buttocks were rounded and robust, reminiscent of basketballs, and his broad penis emerged prominently from a thicket of black pubic hair, extending halfway down his inner thigh.

"Ouchy wow wow, you could seriously hurt someone with that weapon of yours," Alejandro teased.

"What do you mean.... weapon?" Kane asked innocently, pulling on a pair of pants while leaving his chest bare.

"Your pene, your polla, your dick," Alejandro laughed, watching Kane glance down at himself.

"I didn't know it could be used as a weapon," Kane replied, still oblivious to Alejandro's playful innuendo.

"It's pretty clear you've never been with a woman.... you know, had sex with one," Alejandro remarked.

"No, I haven't.... I'm not allowed because I'm a monk, and we take a vow of celibacy," Kane explained.

"Well, that's a shame, because with that size polla (cock) of yours, you'd make a girl very happy," Alejandro concluded, then distracted himself with starting the fire.

While Alejandro got things going, setting up his camp oven over the flames, Kane's stomach rumbled with hunger, the discomfort from prolonged lack of food gnawing at him.

"What do we have to cook?" Kane asked Alejandro, his stomach grumbling audibly. "We've only got tweleve dried figs, eight sweet potatoes and some beef jerky.... that's all," Alejandro replied, scanning their meager supplies.

"And you're telling me we still have five more days before reaching the ranch?" Kane's tone betrayed his growing frustration, hunger beginning to gnaw at him uncomfortably.

"Sí, Senor, that's right. But don't worry, Amigo, I'll go out and try to bag a couple of jackrabbits. They're easy to shoot," Alejandro offered, ready to take action.

"I'll go hunting," Kane declared abruptly, knowing full well that potatoes and beef jerky wouldn't come close to satisfying his appetite. Even though he was a vegetarian, Kane's inner carnivore craved for something more substantial.

"Are you sure? You don't know the desert like I do, and there's only an hour of daylight left," Alejandro cautioned.

"I'll manage," Kane reassured him. After unpacking and unsaddling his horse, he set off into the dusky red hues of the desert.

The sun hung low in the sky, a small-scale orb peeking just above the jagged silhouette of hills as it started its descent behind distant sand dunes. For Kane, it was a realization that very few moments in life were as exquisite as this, embedding themselves into memory like hidden treasures. Here, in the quiet majesty of the desert, he began to reconnect with his truest self.

The air retained a comforting warmth, occasionally stirred by gentle gusts that brought a cool refreshment to his parched lungs. Kane savored each deep breath, revitalized by the crisp, rejuvenated atmosphere around him.

With each passing moment, Kane's transformation accelerated. His strides, once deliberate, now thundered across the terrain in a frenzied gallop. Limbs stretched, his feet and hands ballooned to twelve-inch diameters, adorned with claws that grew to formidable six-inch lengths. His mouth widened into a hairy muzzle, teeth extending into menacing four-inch fangs, powered by newly bulging muscles in his jaw. Dense, wooly fur erupted across his body as he emitted an instinctive, guttural growl that reverberated with pulsating menace. In the distance, a mule deer stirred

beneath a sparse bush, its ears twitching at the ominous sound. In a surge of fear, it bolted from its refuge, racing directly into the path of the rapidly advancing predator. Kane thundered toward the terrified antelope, his canter akin to a runaway horse closing in on its prey. With a swift strike of his forepaw, he brought the animal down, shattering its spine. In a seamless transition to full bear form, he clamped his long fangs onto the deer's neck, delivering a fatal blow, then savagely tore into its snout, ripping away its face. Deep, jagged claw marks marred the mutilated body as Kane slashed open its abdomen, eagerly feasting on the steaming entrails, drenching himself in a shower of flesh and blood that sated his primal hunger.

After devouring his fill, Kane used his razor-sharp claws to sever a hind leg from the carcass, seizing the meaty prize in his massive jaws. With deliberate steps, he retraced his path toward the oasis, all the while focusing on reshaping his bear form back into human. The challenge remained stark and undeniable—the evidence of his grisly feast was unmistakably smeared in blood across his entire body, a macabre testament to his actions.

Adding more sticks to the campfire, Alejandro stirred the burning embers as Kane emerged into the oasis.

"What happened to you?" Alejandro exclaimed, his expression twisted in horror. "Is that your blood? Are you injured?" He rose and moved closer to Kane.

"No, it's not my blood," Kane replied, casually tossing the antelope's hind leg near the firepit.

"Well, then whose blood is it? And where did you get that

meat?" Alejandro fired off questions, concern showing on his face.

"I came across an injured animal under a bush. It couldn't escape, so I took the opportunity to secure some proper food instead of the beef jerky and potatoes," Kane improvised his story on the spot.

"Okay, so you killed a mule deer?" Alejandro confirmed, examining the severed leg. "Yeah, a deer," Kane affirmed, his tone masking a deeper truth.

"How did you get covered in so much blood?" Alejandro's voice held a mix of suspicion and concern.

"When I broke its neck, I must have twisted too hard, and a bone punctured through the skin, severing an artery. The blood just sprayed all over me. And cutting off the hind leg was a messy job," Kane explained, his tone carefully measured.

"What did you use to cut it off? The cut is so clean, like it was done with a very sharp knife. Do you have a knife on you?" Alejandro persisted, scrutinizing Kane closely. "Hai, I have a blade," Kane replied, retrieving the makeshift weapon from his bloodstained pocket and showing it to Alejandro. As Alejandro examined it, his suspicion grew—the knife was conspicuously free of any flesh or blood residue.

"I should have given you my gun, then maybe you wouldn't look like you just walked out of a massacre," Alejandro speculated aloud, masking his relief at not having armed the unsettling stranger.

"Well, I'll start cooking while you clean yourself up. You can wash yourself in the waterhole," he suggested, his tone tinged with distrust. The realization that his companion wasn't being truthful left him unnerved and cautious.

The pale, sickle-shaped moon cast its silvery radiance across the night sky, resembling a celestial talon suspended in the vastness above. Kane stood amongst the swaying palm fronds, their tips reaching towards the heavens where a blanket of stars seemed to stretch into infinity. The haunting cries of distant coyotes intermittently pierced the stillness, echoing through the Mojave Desert's chilly night air.

In the midst of this expansive solitude, Kane felt a profound sense of humility wash over him. The grandeur of the cosmos enveloped him, dwarfing his own problems and insecurities. He found comfort in the warmth of the crackling campfire, a stark contrast to the desert's biting cold. As he gazed up at the glittering expanse above, he was reminded of the vastness of existence and the fleeting nature of his own exsistence.

In that moment, Kane's thoughts turned to living his life to the fullest, embracing the transient beauty of the night and the boundless possibilities that lay ahead.

"It's so beautiful here," Kane sighed, overwhelmed by the stark beauty of the desert. "Yes, it is. But the desert is deceptive, like a sheep dressed as a wolf," Alejandro cautioned.

"What do you mean?" Kane leaned forward, intrigued by Alejandro's mysterious warning.

"It may look peaceful, but beneath its sandy surface lie ancient secrets," Alejandro began dismally.

"Like what?" Kane's curiosity stirred, eager for Alejandro's tales.

"For instance, this watering hole," Alejandro continued, his voice dropping to a conspiratorial whisper.

"There are stories of unexplained whirlpools that have dragged down unfortunate swimmers. Those who survived claim they felt an otherworldly force pulling them into the icy depths.

Then there's the legend of a young Washoe Indian boy who drowned here. His body was discovered a week later, bloated and dressed in a chalk-white frock—a garment unheard of for Washoe males. To add to the mystery, his tribe lived over a thousand miles away.

The supernatural powers of this desert are profound.... and we still have to cross through the Nevada Triangle, where even stranger things have occurred," Alejandro added, relishing Kane's wide-eyed absorption of his tales.

"That's enough....I'm going to sleep now. We'll rest here one more day, then keep heading for the ranch" Alejandro advised and bundled himself into his sleeping bag. The next morning, Alejandro noticed a swarm of vultures in the distance, their dark forms circling high above for what seemed like an eternity.

"That must be from your kill last night.... How did you manage to go so far from camp?" Alejandro questioned Kane, his wariness of the mysterious man still evident. "Well, as I told you before, the deer was badly injured and slow. I simply tracked it until it couldn't go on," Kane explained calmly.

"Uh-huh. Senor, you're one strange Gringo. There's something about you that just doesn't quite add up," Alejandro admitted, casting a sidelong glance from beneath his sombrero.

"I have unique skills, Alejandro.... That's why you're taking me to see your boss, isn't it?" Kane countered, seeking to justify his presence.

"Yes, senor.... That's very true," Alejandro affirmed, though a shadow of doubt lingered in his mind as they continued their journey through the rugged terrain. Half an hour later, the pair rode past the remains of the animal, where vultures had gathered. As they moved along, Kane and Alejandro watched the scavengers tear

strips of flesh from the bones with their sharply hooked beaks. The birds' bald heads bobbed rhythmically, their keen eyes scanning for any sign of danger. To Kane, they resembled hungry pigs, emitting raspy hisses and grunting noises as their large wings thrashed violently in their relentless squabbles over every morsel.

"They are quite ugly birds. Why don't they have feathers on their heads?" Kane queried Alejandro.

"Buzzards always have their heads buried in carcasses, so being featherless keeps them cleaner while they eat," Alejandro explained matter-of-factly.

"It's another day's ride until we enter the Nevada Triangle. Stay alert, Kane," Alejandro cautioned, his anticipation visible as they got closer to the ranch. Spanning over 25,000 square miles, the remote wasteland of desert and mountains possessed a rugged, untamed beauty all its own. Despite the relentless heat, Kane found peace in the isolation, feeling his heart liberated amongst the vast expanse of wilderness.

As they journeyed northwest, the landscape shifted from the sandy dunes and salt flats of the Mojave Desert to a desolate mountain range. The once abundant cacti gradually gave way to sparse Joshua trees, their spiky leaves and white flowers dotting the barren terrain.

"Why doesn't it rain here, Alejandro? I thought mountains bring rain—like in Japan. Why not here?" Kane pondered aloud.

"We're in a rain shadow," Alejandro responded, his voice carrying the weight of local knowledge.

"These mountains block the rainy weather and hinder plant

growth on this side. On the other side, it's a different story—rain and even snow. But here, it's all blocked, creating this desert—the Mojave Desert."

"Why is it called the Mojave Desert?" Kane pressed for more information. "Because of the native Indians that inhabit this land—they're known as the Mojave tribe, a fierce clan with heavily tattooed warriors," Alejandro explained, his voice carrying pride of the local history.

"Does your ranch's leader also live in this desert?" Kane inquired, curious about their destination.

"The ranch is further north, near the Colorado River, where the mountains are transformed into blazing pillars of fire by the stunning sunsets and sunrises," Alejandro replied, a touch of reverence in his voice.

"We are now entering the Nevada Triangle and then futher along, into Death Valley," Alejandro continued, his tone turning somber.

"Death Valley? Why is it called that?" Kane persisted, his curiosity unabated. "Over the years, travelers have perished in Death Valley due to drifting sands that erase tracks and a lack of water," Alejandro explained gravely.

"It's become their grave, earning the valley its terrible name."

A distant, threatening roar echoed through the atmosphere, unsettling in its intensity, as if the very earth itself yearned for confrontation. Alejandro's instincts kicked in swiftly; he shifted in his saddle, turning to witness the unexpected onslaught of dust and debris hurtling toward them. With urgency gripping his heart, Kane maneuvered his horse to face the rapidly approaching sandstorm, a towering wall stretching for miles and rising thousands of feet high.

"Get off your horse and do as I do!" Alejandro's voice cut

through the rising panic. The two men dismounted quickly, following Alejandro's lead. Kane pulled hard on the reins, urging his horse to kneel, its head lowered to the ground.

"Grab your scarf and wet it with your canteen water. Tie it tight over your nose and mouth. Lie down behind your horse and whatever you do, don't stand up—quickly!" Alejandro's instructions were urgent, thick with the seriousness of their peril.

Within moments, the thick wall of swirling dirt, sand, and rocks bore down upon them with relentless force. The storm pelted them mercilessly, a deafening onslaught that showed no signs of relenting.

As Kane lay vunerable behind his horse, his neckerchief shielding his face from the biting sandstorm, he squinted through the blinding haze. Amidst the swirling chaos, he thought he glimpsed a figure moving steadily past—a silhouette upright and seemingly unperturbed by the fury of the storm. The shape appeared slightly stooped but unmistakably human, yet there was an unsettling presence about it.

Suddenly, another figure emerged, trailing closely behind the first, their form not entirely human nor fully animal.

More figures materialized from the dust-laden gloom, some barely discernible in the superstorm. Kane could make out a few who were completely naked, while others wore ragged remnants of clothing. As they drifted aimlessly past, a powerful vibration emanated from Kane's saddlebag. He knew instinctively it was the human skin book, its eerie presence disturbing in the midst of the storm, seemingly agitated and attempting to escape its confines.

Abruptly, Kane's horse began to panic, spurred on by both

the relentless storm and the unsettling vibrations from the saddlebag. It kicked wildly, struggling against the elements and its mounting unease.

"KEEP YOUR HORSE STILL!" Alejandro's voice sliced through the hurricane of sand, his words battling against the storm for clarity. Gasping for clean air, he struggled to be heard over the commotion.

The last creature to pass by was grotesquely deformed, its body a twisted blend of animal and human features. Matted facial hair stiffened with dried blood framed its boar-like mouth, and it halted abruptly in front of Kane. Glaring with fiery orange-red eyes, the beast seemed to recognize him, sending a chilling wave of dread down Kane's spine.

As the hurricane gradually began to dissipate, the horde of specters vanished along with the wall of swirling sand, dispersing as though the typhoon had been their transitory home.

Covered in a blanket of sand and dust, the two men finally stood up from their gravelly caskets, brushing themselves off as their horses shook the sediment from their backs.

"Does that happen often?" Kane broke the silence, his voice still shaky.

"Sí, señor.... and you never know when," Alejandro replied as he mounted his horse. Kane checked the saddlebag cradling the human skin book, ensuring it wasn't damaged.

"Get on your horse, we still have a long way to the ranch," Alejandro ordered.

"You didn't happen to see anything moving in the storm?" Kane asked timidly as he mounted his horse.

"Like what? Nothing can stand upright in a sandstorm; the force of the wind knocks you off your feet in an instant"

"So? Like what? Did you see something?" Alejandro pressed, his curiosity provoked. "Nothing.... I just thought I saw people walking amongst it," Kane admitted, his voice barely a whisper.

"That's the Nevada Triangle playing tricks on you, amigo. Come on, let's go. We're running tarde (late), so darse prisa (hurry up)," Alejandro concluded, then kicked his horse in the underbelly, urging it forward.

In the oppressive heat of the following days, the relentless heatwave made Kane's eyes sting as perspiration trickled down his forehead like condensation on a winter

window. The sun's unyielding rays turned each moment into an ordeal, the air heavy with a suffocating warmth that seemed to wrap around him

Inky sweat stains spread under his armpits, the sun's intensity so fierce it could drop a cow. Alejandro rode ahead with steady pace, while Kane trailed behind, frequently pausing to wipe the sweat from his brow.

"How much further?" Kane complained, his voice dripping with irritation.

"Amigo, be quiet we have company," Alejandro revealed, his tone hushed and

serious.

"Who? I can't see anyone for miles in this dust bowl," Kane grumbled, squinting into the shimmering heat.

"We're being followed have been since the sandstorm," Alejandro explained.

Kane scanned the area in a slow, 360-degree circle. Eventually, he spotted a line of men high up on a mountain ridge, sitting immobile on their horses, watching their every move.

"Keep going, Gringo," Alejandro said, his irritation clear as he noticed Kane staring back at them.

"Who are they?" Kane asked, trotting his horse closer to his partner. "Mojave warriors," Alejandro replied tersely.

"What do they want?" Kane pressed, his anxiety mounting.

"Everything you own," Alejandro said bluntly, spurring his horse forward.

* * *

Living along the banks of the Colorado River, the Mojave tribe skillfully utilized the desert's resources, but it was the river and its floodplains that truly sustained them, providing food and shelter. Fiercely defending their territory, they were known for their bravery in battle, with war parties traveling hundreds of miles, surviving only on chia seeds and water. Their combat was brutal; they wielded clubs, striking down on their enemy's heads, driving them to the ground, then swinging upwards to crush their jaws.

The Mojave took scalps and prisoners, the captives later sacrificed to serve fallen warriors in the afterlife. Before returning to their tribe, the warriors purified themselves by singing cycles of dreamed songs that told stories, ensuring the dark spirits lost their way and did not follow them home. The tall, imposing men wore minimal clothing, just simple loincloths, and caked their hair with mud, twisting it into various shapes. However, it was their boldly tattooed faces, marked with thick, menacing patterns, that truly instilled terror in their suffering victims.

In the early morning of the following day, Kane woke suddenly to the unexpected sound of diverse voices murmuring among themselves.

As he opened his eyes, the first light of dawn illuminated the scene, casting a radiant glow over six Mojave Indians milling around the remnants of the previous night's campfire with Alejandro. The soft, early morning light painted their figures in a warm, golden glow, blending the tranquility of dawn with the quiet activity of the camp.

The sight filled Kane with a sense of ancient spirit and connection to the land. Rubbing the residual sleep from his eyes, Kane stood up and casually walked over to the campfire. He poured himself a cup of coffee, the rich dark brew steaming in the cool morning air. As he sipped the hot beverage, he noticed that despite the impressive height of the Mojave Indians, who ranged from 5'10" to over 6', he still towered over all of them. The men glanced at him with a mix of curiosity and skeptisim, their bold, tattooed faces inscrutable in the morning light.

The scene was charged with a quiet intensity, the air dense with the unspoken understanding of warriors and the importance of ancient traditions.

(Speaking in Yuman, the native language of the Mojave People) "Who is this giant?" One of the Indians bluntly asked Alejandro

"He's a nobody, I'm just transporting another worker back to the ranch. I saw him

lingering around the boxing tent in San Francisco" Alejandro answered, speaking the Yuman language fluently, as he had lived in the area all his life.

"Is he abnormal?" Another Indian asked as he sauntered around Kane, blatantly eyeing him up and down.

"I don't know. He's a foreigner.....comes from Japan I think"

"He must eat plenty of corn and fish to grow to this size, he's bigger than a buffalo" The Indian rudely badgered and his companions laughed.

"What is going on? Why is everyone laughing at me" Kane protested

"It's esta Bien (Mexican)....its ok.....they are only curious about your size. They are saying that you are bigger than a buffalo and must eat lots of corn and fish.....nothing to get upset about Amigo" Alejandro tried appeasing his traveling companion

"He will be a good beast of burden for your boss Alejandro" The Indian continued speaking in his native language

"Si, Si.....he will. I think the boss will be pleased with this one" Alejandro responded in part Mexican and part Yuman

"He doesn't have a scalp.... what happened to his hair?" One of the Indians inquired, his hand rubbing over the back of Kane's head, caressing his baldness.

"He says he's a religious man in his country and they shave their heads," Alejandro explained, attempting to defuse the situation.

"Stop touching me!" Kane exclaimed sharply, his patience worn thin. With a swift pivot, he shoved the inquisitive Indian backward, sending him sprawling to the ground.

The Indian landed flat on his backside, stunned by the sudden forcefulness of Kane's reaction. Alejandro hurriedly intervened, speaking in a stern tone to diffuse the tension and maintain order among the group.

Instantly, the pack of Indians snatched their clubs, raising them threateningly toward Kane's head. Alejandro swiftly positioned himself between them, arms outstretched, desperately trying to prevent an escalation.

"ENOUGH!" Alejandro screamed, his voice a volatile mix of anger and distress. He feared that the longstanding rapport he had built with the Mojave tribe would unravel, all because of some outsider he had picked up.

"I feel sorry for this fool's horse.... just look at it. The poor animal looks ready to drop dead. Maybe you should let him carry the horse the rest of the way, Alejandro," the fallen Indian remarked, brushing sand off his backside. The others chuckled, pulling faces and mocking Kane's weary steed.

Kane, seething with indignation, clenched his fists at his sides, glaring defiantly at the jeering group.

"Are we ready to leave soon?" Kane asked Alejandro, his tone edged with impatience.

"Not until my friends are ready to leave, Gringo," Alejandro retorted coolly, showing little regard for Kane's urgency.

Hours dragged on as Alejandro and his band of Mojave warriors lounged around the fire pit, chatting and laughing casually. Their nonchalant attitude grated on Kane's nerves, wearing down his patience to a breaking point. Frustration simmered within him, threatening to erupt. He felt like shouting or pounding his fists on the ground in a fit of childish frustration.

Sitting beside his horse, removed from the cluster of men, Kane lethargically scrawled pictures in the sand with a twig, periodically glancing over at the jovial gang. Thoughts of unleashing his bear demon to teach these men a brutal lesson crossed his mind, but he quickly dismissed the idea. The irreversible damage and the risk of leaving a trail for Gideon and his pursuing ninjas deterred him, not to mention Alejandro's gun.

Finally, after what seemed like an eternity, the Mojave Indians decided it was time to leave.

(Speaking in Yuman)

"Goodbye, my friend. I hope the rest of your journey isn't too difficult for you" The leader of the Mojave men farewelled Alejandro, shaking his hand.

"It was an honor to have you at my firepit" He replied, then both Kane and Alejandro watched as the Mojave Indians rode north, into the mountain valley.

"Get your things, it's time to go.... and my friends said, try not to kill your horse," Alejandro announced with a chuckle, tossing gravel onto the firepit to extinguish the embers.

As they trudged across the desert plains, the atmosphere between them turned sullen and tense. When Kane attempted to engage Alejandro in conversation, he received only grunts in response.

"Alejandro.....are you upset with me?" Kane queried his companion but he did not answer.

"Alejandro are you upset with me? Tell me.....what's the problem?" Kane persisted for a response

Unexpectedly, Alejandro jerked on the horse's reins and came to a sudden halt. "Don't you ever offend me in front of my friends again. If you do, I'll put a bullet in your brain"

"That "friend" of yours was degrading me. No one has the privilege to touch me without my permission and being a Buddhist Monk it is an offense to touch our heads. It is a sacred part of our bodies" Kane argued

"Shut up Gringo, it's taken many years to build trust and friendship with the Mojave Indians and I don't need some *"Jonnie"* ruining everything"

"What did you just call me?" Kane protested, feeling outraged

"I called you a *"Jonnie"* because that's what you Asians are out here, so get used to it.....polla (you dick)"

"Don't call me names, I will have your....." Kane began to speak until he heard a distinct *CHK-CHK* as Alejandro pulled back the hammer of his revolver, pointing the gun-barrel straight at Kane's head.

"Are you ready to eat a bullet *Jonnie*? No? Then shut the fuck up" Alejandro cooly remarked, as his intended victim just sat there, perfectly astonished.

About half a mile ahead, Alejandro's sharp eyes caught sight of a Conestoga wagon, its distinctive bent wooden bows and heavily draped carriage unmistakable against the desert backdrop. It was trailed by a smaller, more agile prairie schooner. A lone rider on horseback accompanied the wagon, guiding it steadily across the rugged plateau.

Without a word, Alejandro spurred his horse into a gallop, racing ahead towards the sluggish wagon train, leaving Kane trailing behind in the dust.

The relentless barrage of racial insults Kane endured since arriving in the country weighed heavily on him, chipping away at his self-worth. The hurt penetrated deep into his core, leaving him contemplating whether he needed to change something about himself or his behavior to gain acceptance.

The ongoing stress of feeling unwelcome and marginalized fueled his internal struggle, pushing him to reconsider his choice of trudging through the desert with this angry Mexican. Doubts gnawed at his psyche, each step heavy with the uncertaintly of his decision.

As Kane caught up to the wagons, he hung back from the

group, observing Alejandro engage in lively conversation with the convoy's leader—a quirky man in a colorful flannel shirt and a beaver cap, with long dreadlocks cascading down his back and a thin cigar perpetually in hand.

Rambling along, the prairie wagons shook and rattled as their large wheels rolled over old buffalo skeletons, making a loud crunching sound under the weight.

Trailing the last wagon, he noticed a small face occasionally peeking out from behind the overlapping curtain folds at the rear. The next time he spotted the child, he offered a friendly wave. Gradually, the curtains parted, revealing a lovely little girl with wheat-colored hair braided into thick plaits. Kane guessed she was around seven years old.

"Hello" He welcomed her "Hello" She replied softly "What's your name?" He asked "Sarah..... what's yours?" "Kane"

"Where are you going?" He added

"To our new homestead. Daddy says it's going to be a great place to live. Where are you from.....you look different?" Sarah innocently quizzed

"I'm from another country, far away across the sea.....a place called Japan.....you have beautiful hair"

"How come you don't have any hair? Did you get scalped by the Indians?" Kane began to chuckle at the little girl's candid persona.

"No, I haven't been scalped. I'm a Buddhist Monk, and we shave our heads as part of our faith," Kane explained calmly.

"Oh, okay....well it looks silly. Your horse looks really tired. Maybe you should get off and walk for a while to give it a rest.... especially since you're so big and fat," the girl giggled mischievously, then abruptly closed the curtains, retreating into the safety of the wagon.

"The insults never stop. Even the children are rude and lack self-restraint," Kane thought to himself, feeling the frustration.

"I must remember the Buddhist teachings.... My greatest action is not conforming to the ways of this country. With integrity, I WILL survive." He muttered

"Is that your manservant back there?" The wagoner commented to Alejandro "No, he's just another worker for the ranch" He answered

"What's the name of your ranch?"

"Rancho Los Charro" Alejandro announced proudly "Sounds impressive.....is it yours?"

"I wish it was.....I work for the owner Don Morales"

"Is your traveling partner the only Chinese worker you've taken to the ranch?" "Si.....why do you ask?" Alejandro seemed surprised at the question

"Those *"Jonnies"* work for peanuts and they're not well-liked. If your other workers are Mexican or English or whatever... ..they won't take kindly to him"

"Si, Si.....well he's big enough to look after himself. It will definitely make things interesting that's for sure. Ok, we must be getting along, I hope the rest of your journey is a safe one.....Adios Amigo.....come on Kane" Alejandro farewelled and signaled Kane to join him.

The valley hills ascended dramatically, culminating in a striking rock formation. The narrowing gorge stretched ahead, its V-shaped entrance just wide enough for travelers to pass through. Towering walls of the canyon were rough and unyielding, with overhangs and jagged ledges looming overhead. Confined within the tight space, Kane felt a creeping sense of dread. Every movement seemed restricted, his temple scraping against the underside of a ledge as he struggled to maneuver. The imposing presence of the towering rocks and the earthy, damp aroma intensified his irrational fear, strangling him with a sense of claustrophobia.

"What's wrong with you?" Alejandro questioned when he discovered Kane hyperventilating.

"I don't know.....I've never felt this way before, the rock walls are closing in on me.... I have to get out of here" He quickly answered, the sensation of terror expanding within, significant and potent.

"Well, they're not, so just keep moving" Alejandro expressed coldly, his irritation towards Kane mounting to boiling point.

"I can't!" Kane yelled, his eyes squeezed shut against the oppressive walls of the canyon. Alejandro forcefully gripped the reins of Kane's horse, guiding them both through the narrow passage until they emerged into the open clearing on the other side. With a deep exhale, Kane tilted his head toward the sky, soaking in the warmth of the sunshine on his face.

"What the hell was that all about?" Alejandro cursed, his frustration evident.

"I'm sorry, Alejandro.... I don't know what came over me. I felt trapped, and the fear of confinement just took over," Kane admitted, still shaken.

"Listen, Kane.... You're not in Japan anymore. To survive here, you're going to have to change," Alejandro said firmly, his tone tolerating no argument.

"I am a Buddhist monk, that's who I am!" Kane protested angrily. "Well, here's the thing," Alejandro snapped back, his irritation evident.

"Your monk identity might work in Japan, but out here, you're just another clueless outsider. You need to adapt if you want to survive. Grow a damn beard or mustache, stop shaving your head, and let your hair grow out. I'm sick of looking at your bald head. Enough with the smug attitude. When we get to the ranch, you'll get proper ranch clothes, but after that, you're on your own."

Kane clenched his fists, seething at Alejandro's blunt words, but he knew resistance would only complicate things further.

Eventually arriving at the ranch, they found themselves in a meadow so picturesque it seemed plucked from the pages of a fairy tale. Jungle-like grass stretched out like an emerald carpet, contrasting starkly with the rugged peaks of the mountains that jutted skyward like the jagged teeth of an ancient hag. The scenery was nothing short of idyllic, a paradise unto itself.

Yet, it wasn't merely the visual splendor that captivated Kane's senses. The meadow enveloped him in a symphony of natural delights. Overhead, the sky arched in a vast expanse of deep blue, adorned with fluffy clouds that drifted lazily like offerings in a celestial feast. His ears were filled with the harmonious melodies of tweeting swallows darting after elusive dragonflies, their dance a ballet of life and pursuit. The air hummed with the persistent buzz of midges and the gentle murmur of the breeze, carrying with it the sweet perfume of various blossoms and the caramel scent of wildflowers, each fragrance stirring memories of his homeland in Japan.

Pausing at the meadow's edge, Alejandro turned to Kane, perhaps sensing the awe and nostalgia that mingled in the air between them.

"Look down there, Amigo.... that's your new home. You've

met the desert.... now get ready to meet the snakes," Alejandro chuckled darkly, then spurred his horse down the gentle slope of the paddock, riding with pride through the imposing gates of *Rancho Los Charro.*

Chapter 11

Don Morales had forged a fearsome reputation through a life defined by violence, settling disputes with a ruthless efficiency that made other rancheros think twice before crossing him. His ranch, sprawling over 320,000 acres, was fortified not just by its size but by the loyalty of his hardened cowboys, armed to the teeth and ready to enforce his will with brutal efficiency. When debts went unpaid or cattle were stolen, his response was swift and merciless—kidnappings, torture, and bloody reprisals were commonplace, sending a clear message to anyone who dared to defy him.

Despite the weight of his responsibilities, Morales seemed untouched by the stress, maintaining an enigmatic aura that kept unnecessary attention at bay. He was standoffish and aloof, navigating his world with a calm detachment that contradicted the turmoil beneath. Emotional connections were rare for him, reserved only for moments when his leadership and courage were called upon. His weathered face, framed by long gray hair pulled back tightly, bore the scars of past battles proudly, each mark a testament to his resolve. With steely brown eyes and a perpetually rugged appearance, he was far from charming, yet his presence commanded respect and support in times of conflict.

Don Morales' ranch traced its roots back to his wealthy grandfather, a pioneer who had secured a vast land grant in the late 1700s. Passed down through generations, the sprawling estate became not just a livelihood but a way of life for Morales.

The grand hacienda where he resided had witnessed his birth and upbringing, a childhood spent riding horses and herding cattle across the rugged terrain. Days blurred into weeks as he checked fences, maintained water troughs, and vigilantly guarded against threats to their livestock, all while weathering the extremes of nature and enduring solitude.

From a young age, Morales learned to embrace discomfort, finding solace in the solitary rhythms of ranch life. His independence set him apart from the other cowboys, his stoic demeanor shielding a complexity of thoughts and motives. Unlike his peers, he harbored no aspirations for family or fame, preferring the shadows over the spotlight, which only added to his enigmatic allure.

Only one woman lived at the ranch: an enigmatic elderly Indian squaw who had spent most of her life as Don Morales' cook and cleaner. She moved quietly through the days, keeping to herself and rarely seen, her presence almost ghostly. Don Morales ensured she was always occupied, not out of necessity, but to deter any of his wranglers from entertaining thoughts of a sexual nature about her, even though

she was in her 60s. The air of mystery surrounding her added an extra layer of intrigue to her existence.

Alejandro led Kane through the bunkhouse door, the worn wooden floor creaking under their boots. Inside, the air was thick with the smell of leather, sweat, and tobacco smoke. The bunkhouse was compact, with six beds neatly arranged along the walls and personal belongings strewn about. Kane's gaze wandered briefly, taking in the rugged simplicity of his new surroundings, before settling on the corner Alejandro indicated.

"This is your bunk and wardrobe," Alejandro instructed, his voice cutting through the room's quiet.

"Put your bags down here. Then follow me. Don Morales wants to meet you." With a nod from Alejandro, Kane deposited his belongings beside the rough-hewn bunk, its blankets neatly folded. He then followed Alejandro out into the bright sunlight, the anticipation of meeting Don Morales prickling at his skin like cactus spines.

Kane stood before the imposing doors, the wood polished and heavy under his gaze. Alejandro rapped three times, the sound echoing through the silent hallway. After a moment, a voice commanded, "Enter."

Stepping into the office, Kane was met with a sight that mirrored the authority of Don Morales. Alejandro introduced him respectfully, hat in hand, and motioned for Kane to stand beside him. The room was impressive, dominated by a mounted buffalo head with a perpetually startled expression.

Don Morales looked up from his scattered paperwork, his gaze assessing Kane with a steely intensity.

"Where do you come from, Kane.... and why do you have a bald head? Is that a religious statement?" His voice was dry and authoritative, like the parched desert wind.

"I am from Japan," Kane replied evenly. "My shaven head is called tonsure, a symbol of renunciation of worldly ego and fashion."

"Well, you'll definitely need the ego, but you won't need any fashion out here," Don Morales chuckled, his voice roughened by years of command.

"No more shaving your head. To survive on this ranch, you must fit in. A bald head makes you stand out, and I don't appreciate that."

"Hai, Don Morales," Kane responded obediently, feeling Alejandro's firm nudge in his ribs.

"And that's another thing," Don Morales continued, his tone steady.

"I don't want you speaking in your language. Everyone here speaks Spanish. You'll learn Spanish eventually, but for now, speak English or say nothing. Whoever you were in Japan doesn't exist here."

"Yes, Don Morales," Kane affirmed, his mind racing with the gravity of his new reality on the ranch.

Throughout Don Morales' introduction of Kane to the ranch, a formidable figure stood sentinel behind him. This tall man, with a pitiless gaze that seemed to penetrate through Kane, exuded an aura of staunch authority. His piercing blue eyes remained fixed on Kane, unmoving and intense, as if assessing every degree of the newcomer's demeanor and presence.

"Are you familiar with horseback riding?" he inquired. "Yes, Don Morales," Kane corrected himself. "I am." "Good. Have you ever handled longhorn cattle?" "No, I haven't," Kane admitted.

"And are you proficient with a firearm?"

"Buddhist monks don't use guns. Our defense lies in Ninjutsu, which I've dedicated my life to mastering at the monastery,"

Kane replied firmly.

"So you consider yourself skilled in Ninjutsu?" Don Morales pressed on. "Yes, I do. One of the best," Kane asserted confidently.

"Good, good. I'll keep that in mind," Don Morales nodded approvingly. "However, given your lack of experience with guns and cattle, I'll have Alejandro teach you. Is that understood, Alejandro?" Don Morales turned to the attentive Mexican.

"Si, Senor Morales. Whatever you say, Senor Morales," Alejandro responded, his fingers nervously toying with his sombrero's brim.

"And this gentleman behind me," Don Morales gestured, "is Victor—my bodyguard, bounty hunter, and bunkhouse overseer. Cross me, and you'll answer to him.

His name means 'conqueror,' and he excels in all he does."

Kane met Victor's unwavering gaze, finding himself compelled to bow respectfully to the imposing figure. Victor, with his long dark hair braided into pigtails beneath a weathered cowboy hat, and a coarse beard cascading down his chest in braids, returned the stare. His square-cut coat and sweat-stained neckcloth portrayed a rugged resilience, while his piercing blue eyes hinted at untold hardships embedded into his weathered face. As Kane observed this sturdy man, he sensed that Victor's stoic attitude concealed a lifetime of unspoken challenges.

"Take Kane back to the bunkhouse and introduce him to the other workers. Ensure he learns the ropes, Alejandro," Morales commanded firmly.

"I expect everyone to earn their keep here; no exceptions." With a dismissive wave of his hand, he signaled the end of the conversation. Alejandro and Kane turned on their heels, exiting through the doors and making their way towards the bunkhouse.

"That's just great," Alejandro complained bitterly.

"What? What are you talking about?" Kane asked, sensing his friend's frustration. "You.... teaching you 'the ropes.' I hope you're a quick learner because I won't have the time to babysit you forever," Alejandro grumbled, his tone tinged with annoyance. "Don't worry about me, Alejandro. I am disciplined and capable. I can take care of myself. You'll see that I'll earn my keep," Kane asserted confidently.

"And what about having my own house? You promised that back in San Francisco. Now I'm stuck living with the others in one shack. You lied to me, Alejandro."

"Stop whining and suck it up. It was just something I said to get you here," Alejandro retorted dismissively, his frustration boiling.

* * *

Kane's days had become a relentless cycle of hard labor and little rest. He woke before sunrise, wolfed down a meager breakfast of beans, bread, and strong coffee, then geared up for another grueling 18-hour stint on the range.

Most nights, he managed only a few hours of sleep, disturbed by the relentless snoring and mumblings of the other wranglers. The sounds reverberated through the drafty bunkhouse walls, loud enough to rouse the dead.

In no time, Kane discovered the harsh realities of bunkhouse life: the chilling drafts that seeped through its cracks, the leaks that dripped rainwater onto his bed, and the incessant torment of lice. The pervasive stench of sweat, body odor, mingled with the unmistakable tang of cattle and horses, threatened to overwhelm his senses, almost inducing nausea.

Some of the men managed a weekly wash, but many simply didn't bother.

The cowboys hailed from diverse backgrounds, a tough bunch with conflicting personalities and a propensity for discord. One figure stood out among them: Paco, a narcissistic loudmouth who seemed to thrive on provoking fights and stirring up trouble.

Internally, Kane dubbed him *"Paco the Pig"*

Roping and cattle work turned out to be far more challenging than Kane had expected, and he had a knack for unintentionally riling up Alejandro.

"A cowboy's duty is to tend to the land and the animals. If you want to be any good at this, you've got to master calf roping. We've got branding coming up next month, so

you better step up," Alejandro shouted in frustration, yanking off his sombrero and running his fingers through his hair. "Let's do it again," he demanded.

Kane mounted his horse, adrenaline pumping as the frantic calf darted around the corral, stirring up clouds of dust.

He galloped after it, his lasso swinging erratically above his head. With a wide arc, it sailed through the air and settled around the calf's neck. Swiftly dismounting, Kane raced to the calf and expertly hogtied its legs, securing it with practiced precision. He glanced over at Alejandro, searching for a nod of approval.

"Not good enough.... do it again," Alejandro declared sternly.

"But I've hogtied the calf.... what more do you want? This isn't a competition, Alejandro," Kane protested, frustration evident in his voice.

"You're too slow. We've got 800 calves to brand soon, and you need to pick up the pace. Do it again," Alejandro ordered, his tone uncompromising.

The grueling calf roping lessons stretched on until dusk, with Alejandro releasing a fresh calf into the corral after every third effort. As Kane made his final attempt of the day, most of the cowboys gathered on the fence, including the mocking presence of "Paco the Pig," who laughed and taunted Kane louder than the rest.

The ranchero clothes Alejandro had provided for Kane were the largest sizes available, yet they still didn't fit properly. The shirt strained at the buttons, threatening to pop open, while his jeans refused to fasten around his waist, leaving the top button undone. The "chaps" meant to protect his legs barely covered half their width, leading to awkward movements every time he tried to dismount his horse. This often resulted in Kane stumbling off the saddle in a comedic fashion, much to the amusement of his onlookers.

"You're a shithouse cowboy, but you'd make a great rodeo

clown," Paco brazenly taunted.

Kane brushed off Paco's barbed insults, though he felt the demon of anger simmering inside him. The urge to lash out and put Paco in his place clawed at him, but Kane fought to maintain control. He consciously centered himself, growing calmer and more composed, refusing to let Paco's taunts provoke him into revealing his true feelings.

"Go.... unsaddle your horse and feed it," Alejandro finally directed, while Kane brushed the grime from his pants.

Alejandro stayed in the corral, observing as Kane led his horse towards the stables. Paco, casually chewing on a long piece of straw, approached Alejandro from the side.

"Do you think he'll be ready for the branding?" He asked Alejandro "No, I don't. He's too big and not fast enough"

"Don Morales won't keep him here if he can't do what's expected of him.....he looks useless" Paco continued

"When it comes to mustering time, he can drive the horse wagon, help cook, rustle up firewood, or take on any other odd jobs around the camp," Alejandro decided. "In the meantime, he can muck out the stables."

"You rotated the calves but his poor horse needed replacing too. Did you see the way the animal was hanging its head while he was taking it to the stables.....it was dog tired and depressed" Paco chuckled to himself.

"Don't go riling up Kane. During our trip through the desert from San Francisco, I saw something in him that defies all logic," Alejandro confided.

"What do you mean?" Paco leaned in closer, intrigued.

"Let's just say, he's not what he appears to be. How's he getting along with the other wranglers?" Alejandro inquired.

"He keeps to himself. After work, he heads off into the paddocks alone, disappearing into the darkness," Paco declared with a note of suspicion.

"What time does he come back to the bunkhouse?" Alejandro questioned, puzzled by Kane's nocturnal wanderings without a horse.

"Don't really know, amigo. Some say they've seen him lingering in the bunkhouse between 1-2 am, but no one's caught him returning from his 'nightly walks,'" Paco informed.

"I'm surprised he hasn't been attacked by wolves or a bobcat out there. It's risky going alone," Paco added with feigned concern.

"Yeah.... he's quite the misfit. I'll discuss this with Victor," Alejandro concluded, turning towards the hacienda. Paco remained at the corral, watching Alejandro leave, chewing on his straw thoughtfully.

"Don't worry, Alejandro. We'll uncover who Kane really is," he mused quietly to himself.

Over the passing months, Kane's once bald head sprouted a cascade of long, untamed hair that flowed like a dark river down his back. Coupled with his lengthy raven beard, he now bore a distinctly Hispanic appearance, a stark contrast to his former visage as a Japanese monk.

He dutifully followed instructions, diligently picking up Spanish and honing his rifle skills, yet generally kept to himself. Kane refrained from speaking Japanese, abandoned prayer and religious rituals, and gradually felt disconnected from his Buddhist beliefs. His sole fixation became the ancestral human skinned book, a companion he often carried on solitary walks into the wilderness.

On a particular evening, after finishing all the chores, Kane packed his knapsack and headed purposefully into the wilderness, unaware that Alejandro and Paco were covertly watching him from behind the bunkhouse.

"Did you talk to Victor about this?" Paco inquired, his tone edged with urgency regarding Kane's nighttime excursions.

"Yes.... I did," Alejandro confirmed quietly.

"And? What did he say? What's the plan?" Paco pressed, his desire to see the aloof monk expelled from the ranch simmering just beneath the surface.

"He said Don Morales wants me back in San Francisco for an assignment. I'll be gone for months. Victor mentioned that since you brought Kane's wanderings to his attention, you should be the one to follow him and report back," Alejandro instructed. "Mierda (Shit) Should I go now? Should I saddle up? He's getting pretty far ahead," Paco asked eagerly.

"No, go on foot.... you'll make less noise and be less conspicuous. Take your gun and some water, and leave right away," Alejandro directed.

"Si, Alejandro.... have a safe trip through the desert. I'll see you when you return," Paco replied, preparing to depart.

"Gracias, Paco. Stay out of sight and stay sharp," Alejandro cautioned before Paco disappeared into the gathering dusk.

Alejandro stood by the window, watching intently as Paco swung open the creaking boundary gates and dashed across the dusky, shadowy paddocks. The knee-high grass swallowed him up until he appeared no larger than a speck on the horizon.

Sighing heavily, Alejandro turned away and reluctantly began to gather his belongings, preparing for the arduous journey back through the desolate wastelands of Nevada.

* * *

The isolated waterfall exuded a serene aqua hue, casting a magical ambiance over Kane and the surrounding environment. It descended down the mountainside in a graceful cascade, its waters swishing over the rocks like an endless waterspout before flowing into a pristine, clear pool below.

As the water gently journeyed downwards, it created playful bubbles and sprays that sparkled awkwardly in the fading daylight, shimmering like enchanted crystal drops. Nearby, a variety of wildflowers bloomed, their sweet fragrance filling the air.

Their delicate petals nodded gently in the breeze, while the effervescent water foamed and created delicate white swirls around the rocky edges of the pool. Kane found comfort in the sight of abundant water plants swaying gracefully in the pool's depths, their lush green fronds seemingly welcoming him into their tranquil

sanctuary. The scene held an air of harmony and beauty that captivated his senses, offering a moment of peace amidst the rugged wilderness.

Sitting on a large, flat rock beside the waterfall, Kane sighed deeply and entered into meditation. He began by consciously resetting his emotional state, allowing empathy to guide his thoughts. Shifting from reactive to reflective, he embraced a deeper introspection that brought clarity and insight.

The cool, dewy mist from the waterfall enveloped him like a gentle embrace from nature, soothing his senses and bringing a sense of privacy. Kane smiled, grateful for the refreshing purity that washed away any lingering doubts about the ranch and its inhabitants.

Drawing the ancestral human skin book from his knapsack, Kane contemplated its ancient wisdom, feeling its power resonate within him. As he immersed himself in its profound symbols, a crackling noise disrupted the tranquil ambiance. Something stirred within the encircling forest, catching Kane's attention and sparking a cautious curiosity.

Turning towards the disturbance, Kane locked eyes with a pair of intense, piercing orbs glaring at him from the shadows. The gaze felt like hot coals searing through his being, unnerving yet strangely compelling. As he sat transfixed, dozens of large crows gathered in the neighboring trees, their jet-black, iridescent plumage shimmering ominously in the fading sunlight.

The crows assembled with an eerie synchronicity, their thick beaks snapping together in a collective rhythm that persisted through the air. The clicking sound grew into a sinister tone, sending shivers through Kane's body. The atmosphere crackled with an otherworldly energy, as if the birds were conveying a message from the realm beyond, their alarming presence casting a dark veil over the tranquil wilderness.

Their eerie, fragmented caws reached a fever pitch, shattering the serene ambiance of the waterhole. The menacing cries seemed intent on punishing Kane with their relentless cruelty, offering no respite from their unsettling presence and unnerving shrieks.

Suddenly, the swarm of crows descended in unison from the

branches, their wingbeats intensifying into a rushing roar as they bore down directly towards Kane. Instinctively shielding himself from the aerial onslaught, Kane braced as the flock collided with a deafening cacophony, merging into a tall, murky figure that materialized before him.

The embodiment emitted a guttural caw that reverberated with purpose, hovering dangerously in front of Kane. As fear gripped him, the apparition seemed to feed off his heightened emotions, its spectral form pulsating with hunger.

Kane delicately observed the specter before him, instantly noticing its grotesque face composed of five crow heads: four encircling the perimeter with one larger, dominant head in the center. The creature's face was twisted into a depraved form, with a colossal beak jutting menacingly from its hideous features. Exuding a terrifying presence, the birdman's towering, snake-hipped body was sheathed in glossy feathers, its large, elongated wings convulsing sporadically with an agitated thrashing sound.

As Kane continued to study the monstrosity, he noticed unsettling movements beneath its feathered skin. Surging lumps writhed like twisting serpents, creating a nauseating spectacle that drained color from his face. Drawing closer, the birdman arrogantly snapped its large beak, emitting a low, rough voice punctuated with harsh, episodic caws that sent shock waves through Kane's mind.

"Countless years from now, your soul will turn to the dark side, and there will be no hope of recovery for you." (A harsh caw and a sharp snap of the beak) "As your transformation progresses, you will lose harmony with the natural rhythms of life, leading you to commit

terrible deeds." (Another menacing caw and beak snap)

"But why me? I don't want this.....I just want to be a normal man" Kane pleaded "Who are you anyway?" He demanded

"You bear the sickle birthmark on your chest, a symbol of your ancestors. I am one of your forebears, my life inscribed within the human-skinned book, just as yours will be. When you draw from the book for power or guidance, you will summon one of us, as you have already seen. Do not fear the unknown future. Embrace your destiny and move forward. It is the path you are meant to take." (A sharp caw and beak snap)

"Where did all of this come from? How did this skin-changing begin? It's only fair that I know who I really am," Kane reasoned with the unsightly creature, seeking answers amid the creepy surroundings.

"You come from a long line of medicine men, wielders of profound magical knowledge, employing mind-expanding potions and spells in rituals for centuries. One of them opened a portal to another world and passed through the universal gateway multiple times. Each return granted them the power to alter their

appearances, earning them the title of witch doctors among humans—a legacy handed down through generations. We are one." (A sharp caw and beak snap)

Instantly, a jolt of raw, electric energy surged through Kane's body as their eyes locked, an unbreakable magnetic force. The birdman's dark, beady eyes burned with a malevolent gleam, his scowl radiating pure bitterness. Kane stared unflinchingly at the predator, captivated by the harrowing truth and the torrent of shifting faces that flickered across its eyes.

"So my father was a witch doctor? Will I be able to control my skin changing?" Kane shattered the oppressive silence, his voice cutting through the tension like a hot knife on butter.

"Yes, he is. He resides with us in our universal realm. You already possess the power to control your shape-shifting, so it is time for your Heraldry—your crest, which will bind you to our dynasty. Your totem animal is here, and she will bestow your emblem." (A sharp caw and beak snap)

"Lady Vixen is here?" Kane blurted out.

From the shadows, a wild dog emerged, skulking forward with a quiet grace. Kane immediately recognized his totem animal by its different-colored eyes and

white-tipped tail. As she bounded from one rock to another, drawing closer, she made a final leap. Midair, she transformed mystically, shifting into the beautiful lady he had met on the ship.

"Lady Vixen " Kane sighed pleasingly, offering her a smile.

"Kane, you are part of our multiverse, and your destiny is preordained. Lady Vixen, your lifelong companion, exists with you in both the physical and spiritual realms.

She manifests as a dog, symbolizing the healing of your emotional wounds. I am the Crow, the carrier of souls. We inhabit a multiverse of immense diversity. Know that all the powers within this vast expanse are now yours to draw upon." the birdman chanted, his grating voice synchronized with the sharp snapping of his beak and piercing caws.

An inky fog began to swell at the birdman's feet, enveloping the three of them in an abyss of darkness and the foul stench of desiccated meat. Kane heard a jumble of disembodied voices, all murmuring at once, their chaos punctuated by sinister laughter and echoes of madness.

As Kane strained to decipher the whispers, a demonic voice suddenly screamed out like a thunderclap, piercing deep into his psyche and howling,

"We wait for you."

Suddenly, Kane's right shoulder seared with intense pain, the smell of burning flesh mingling with agony that tore from him in a chilling wail. The sound vibrating through the forest, sending a spine-chilling coldness through all who heard it.

Clutching his injured shoulder, Kane watched as the black fog lifted. In its wake, the birdman exploded into a thousand crows, each bird scattering in every direction.

Their raucous cries filled the air as they vanished into the atmosphere and the dense canopy of sickly brown trees encircling the waterhole, closing in oppressively from all sides, intensifying his sense of claustrophobia.

"The crest you bear carries immense power and signifies the legacy of the

skin-changer lords who are your ancestors," Lady Vixen revealed in a soft voice. Kane examined the freshly scorched emblem and noticed it depicted a two-headed creature, standing erect on its hind legs. One head resembled a bear, while the other resembled a wolf, both adorned with menacing fangs seemingly dripping with blood. "Does this creature represent both of us?" Kane asked.

"Yes, it signifies our bond," Lady Vixen confirmed.

Lady Vixen's attention snapped away abruptly, drawn to an unfamiliar rustling in the brushwood about 50 yards from the waterfall.

"What's happening?" Kane asked, alarmed by Lady Vixen's sudden change in demeanor.

"Someone's lurking in the leafy undergrowth.... and I think they've been watching the entire Heraldry ritual.... I have to go," she nervously explained, swiftly transforming back into her wild dog form and darting into the woods.

Kane rose to his feet, cautiously approaching the spot where Lady Vixen had sensed the intruder. As he neared, he spotted Paco huddled against the base of a tree, trembling and weeping in fear.

"What are you doing here?" Kane demanded sternly, but Paco was unusually speechless, his voice caught in his throat.

"WHAT ARE YOU DOING HERE?" Kane snarled, his eyes flashing with intense hostility. Paco's survival instincts kicked in; he leaped up and bolted from Kane, sprinting toward the ranch. Kane stood there, seething, watching Paco escape into the distance.

* * *

In the days that followed, the ranch was thrown into turmoil by Paco's escalating madness. Every moment, waking or in dreams, became a nightmarish ordeal for the once-arrogant wrangler and his comrades. He incessantly complained of the stifling, stale air burning his lungs.

In the murky shadows of the bunkhouse, he envisioned colossal spiders clinging to their glistening silver webs. Their eyes burned with an insatiable hunger as they feasted on bloated insect carcasses, their fangs dripping with the warmth of freshly spilled blood.

His delusions assaulted him relentlessly, violating his senses with imagined waves of putrid stench that seemed to emanate from the very floorboards of the bunkhouse.

In his desperation, Paco could be found on the floor, muttering to himself, futilely attempting to seal nonexistent gaps in the timber planks, only to grow more frustrated.

As his madness deepened, he would suddenly scream in terror, perceiving threats invisible to the other cowboys who couldn't comprehend his hysteria. The ranch, once a place of stability, now echoed with the disturbing rants of Paco's unraveling mind.

On a particular night, as the wranglers gathered around the dining table for their evening meal, Paco lay on his bed, a scarf pressed over his nostrils to ward off the imagined stench. He eyed the men with growing suspicion, when suddenly, he witnessed them devouring meat infested with maggots. Plump, wriggling grubs burrowed into the putrid flesh like woodworms. Shock and horror gripped Paco as he watched the men turn their faces towards him, deliberately salivating over their food, smearing the meat's dripping blood across their faces.

The primal atmosphere seemed to nurture those who embraced darkness over light. After each grotesque mouthful, the men emitted ghostly cries, their feral shrieks chilling enough to freeze one's veins. The scene unfolded like a descent into insanity, a nightmare that blurred the line between reality and Paco's twisted reality.

"STOP IT, GET AWAY FROM ME, STOP IT!" Paco's desperate cries resonated through the room, directed at the cowboys or perhaps at unseen specters, solidifying their belief that their once-arrogant comrade had descended into lunacy.

Kane approached cautiously, kneeling beside Paco's bed with feigned concern. "Are you alright, Paco? I can pray for you," he offered, his words tinged with deceit. "FUCK OFF.... YOU'RE THE DEVIL, THE ONE WHO'S DONE THIS TO ME!" Paco

screamed, his voice raw with fear and accusation. Kane glanced at the other cowboys, shrugging his shoulders in a false display of doubt and confusion. "Everything will be alright, my friend. Just try to relax," Kane said, attempting to soothe Paco.

"I'M NOT YOUR FRIEND! YOU ARE THE SON OF SATAN!" Paco retorted, his

words laced with terror and paranoia.

"We need to inform Don Morales about Paco's condition. I believe he's having a breakdown," Kane stated calmly, rising and walking back to the dining table. "Yeah, right.... Who's brave enough to tell Morales that one of his wranglers has gone nuts? He won't care anyway. He'll probably order a bullet in his brain," one of the cowboys remarked callously.

"Morales doesn't tolerate dead weight. Putting him down might be the only solution," another agreed, their voices cold and calculating in the face of Paco's spiralling hysteria.

"I'll speak to Morales," Kane offered, determined to address Paco's worsening condition.

"NO, NO, NO! YOU WON'T TELL HIM THE TRUTH" Paco

pleaded, his voice filled with desperation.

Without warning, he violently shoved his coworkers aside, sending them sprawling from their chairs. He darted through the door, sprinting across the paddocks and vanishing into the dense, shadowy woods.

"I'll still inform the boss about the situation," Kane declared resolutely, making his way towards Don Morales' hacienda.

* * *

Centuries-old trees, their sprawling limbs cloaked in darkness, blocked out any semblance of sunlight. Clumps of wet moss hung like gnarled fingers from their decaying branches, casting a ghostly shroud over the forest. Paco felt as though the very essence of the woods was infecting him with its malevolent poison.

Desperately scrambling through the dense undergrowth, Paco stumbled repeatedly, his hands and legs pierced by the thorns of wildflowers scattered across the mulchy forest floor.

He was gripped by a profound disorientation as he gazed upon the bleak, godforsaken landscape that sprawled around him. The desolate terrain, shrouded in a foreboding misery, filled him with an overwhelming sense of doom. As the harsh reality of his predicament sank in, tears streamed down his face, mingling with the cold sweat of despair.

Venturing deeper into the labyrinthine forest, Paco caught a glimpse of a distant fire. The flickering glow of its flames danced through the gaps between trees, drawing him irresistibly closer.

Taking refuge in the shadow of a massive, contorted tree, Paco leaned against its mottled bark. To his surprise, he felt a sticky sap oozing from the tree, reminiscent of the toxic skin of a toad. As he touched it, the sap burned his hand, causing him to recoil in pain.

At first, Paco mistook the scene for a gathering of native Indians engaged in a secretive hunting ritual. They danced around the fire, their voices blending in an ancient chant that vibrated through the night. However, as he focused more intently, Paco's heart sank. Instead of warriors, he saw hideous old women. Their wheezing, crackling voices reached a fever pitch of ecstasy as they neared the end of their spectral incantation.

The hairs on the back of Paco's neck stood on end, his fear escalating like wildfire through his veins. He watched in horror as the old hags moved with unnatural speed, their spindly, arthritic legs scuttling across the forest floor like a swarm of insects.

The surreal and sinister sight left Paco paralyzed with dread, unsure of what dark forces he had stumbled upon in the depths of the ancient woods.

Paco stood transfixed in horror as one of the witches bent down and plunged her hand into the roaring fire. She withdrew a blazing ember, holding it in her palm without flinching, her cackles echoing wildly through the night. He watched, both spellbound and repulsed, as the others continued their ghastly ceremony, chanting to the rhythm of a rumbling drum.

Their unnaturally long fingers, tipped with blade-like nails, reached out in frenzied gestures as they dragged their next victim towards a makeshift spit. In the unearthly glow of flame and fire, Paco's realization struck like a blow: they were cannibals.

Mounds of gnawed human bones lay illuminated by the flickering firelight—ribs picked clean, skulls gaping in silent testimony to torturous deaths.

The agonizing screams of the latest victim pierced Paco's soul, draining him of vitality as the lice-infested witches gutted their prey, savagely devouring steaming entrails. Witnessing their sadistic brutality, Paco couldn't contain his horror.

He heaved violently, the guttural retching slicing through the abnormal silence and instantly alerting the coven to his presence.

Suddenly, all eyes shimmered with the hatred of a thousand years as they turned to glare in Paco's direction. He felt their gaze pinning him down within the shadows, a suffocating weight of malevolence bearing down on him.

In terror, Paco watched as the repulsive hags licked their thin, bloodless lips with forked, serpent-like tongues. With eerie synchrony, they began hurtling towards him, their unsighlty forms moving with a freakish speed that closed the distance between them in terrifying bounds.

Aware that he was seen as another potential meal, Paco fled back the way he came, his breath coming in ragged, panicked gasps. He glanced over his shoulder periodically, his fear mounting as he saw the witches closing in on him. They moved with an effortless agility through the dense underbrush that he struggled to navigate.

Paco's mind raced in survival mode, intensely focused on evading the clutches of these savage flesh-eaters. As they drew nearer, he could hear their collective hissing voices, a terrifying manifestation of his impending doom.

Frantically sprinting through the dense forest, Paco's heart hammered with terror as he felt the branches whipping at his body. Suddenly, he sensed one of the witches closing in behind him. He turned just in time to see her scrawny, withered arm reaching out, fingers like talons stretching toward him.

With a sickening lurch of dread, Paco felt her bony hand clamp onto the side of his face. Her long, caustic nails tore into his flesh like the jagged spike of a coat hanger, ripping open his cheek in a vicious slash that left him disfigured and in agonizing pain.

Howling a blood-curdling shriek, Paco collapsed onto the ground, his body trembling with fear. Swiftly rolling onto his back, he clutched a discarded branch, ready to defend himself against the perceived threat. But to his astonishment, there was nothing—no sign of the demonic hags that had been chasing him.

With a sense of utter shock, Paco slowly realized that the entire harrowing experience had been a frenzied delusion. The forest around him was still and quiet. There was no evidence of the terrifying witches. Yet, the blood from his recent injury still cascaded down his face, a painful reminder of the ordeal his mind had conjured. "What the hell just happened? Am I hallucinating?" Paco muttered to himself, his voice trembling with disbelief.

"It's all because I witnessed that ritual with Kane's demons. Now I know what he truly is—they're out to get me, so I don't reveal his true identity to anyone," he reasoned aloud, desperately trying to make sense of the nightmarish encounter.

The fear and confusion swirled around him, mingling with the throbbing pain of his injured cheek, as he grappled with the implications of what he had just experienced.

Kane knocked firmly on Don Morales' office door and cleared his throat as he waited to be invited in.

"Si, come in," Don Morales bellowed from behind his monumental desk. "What do you want?" he continued sternly as he looked up and saw the burly cowhand.

Removing his hat, Kane approached and began speaking with conviction.

"Good evening, Don Morales. I have news about Paco. He's unwell. He seems to be experiencing delusions, day and night. It's very disturbing for the other wranglers in the bunkhouse. He needs to see a doctor."

"What's wrong with him?" Morales asked sharply.

"I don't know, jefe," Kane replied. "But he definitely needs a doctor."

"All of my boys know how to fix themselves if they get sick or hurt. Paco can do the same," Morales stated with a mix of pride and indifference.

"He's beyond helping himself, Don Morales.... He's gone. Ran away into the forest, screaming," Kane delivered solemnly, the weight of Paco's distress evident in his voice.

Morales leaned back in his chair, his gaze fixed on Kane with a mix of suspicion and curiosity.

"That's not like Paco," he asserted firmly, his voice tinged with skepticism.

"I've never known him to scream or show fear. He's a tough one, egotistical and sometimes a bully, but fearless nonetheless.

He's been with us for years." Morales paused, his fingers interlaced thoughtfully across his belly.

"So, what could have possibly frightened him enough to run screaming into the woods? Do you have any idea, Kane?" His tone carried an edge of challenge, hinting at the rumored tension between them.

"I've heard there's a bit of hostility between you two. Now you're here, claiming to be concerned about Paco's well-being."

"I'm not entirely sure what's happened to him, we all watch him head into the forest alone," Kane began earnestly.

"I've witnessed him talking and screaming at things no one else can see. He keeps a scarf over his face constantly, claiming the bunkhouse smells like a sewer. He spends his time sitting on the floor, trying to seal up gaps in the timber, convinced that's where the stench is coming from. His state is distressing the other cowhands, Senor Morales. I don't know what else to say, but it's the truth—I'm genuinely concerned, not just for Paco, but for everyone here."

"I don't think he's fit for work," Victor interjected sharply from the corner of the office where he sat, listening intently.

"Senor Victor, he's useless now. He's fled the ranch, and no one can locate him. The man's gone completely mad," Kane replied, visibly perturbed by Victor's unexpected presence in the conversation.

"That's of no use to me," Morales declared coldly, leaning forward in his chair. "Paco knows well enough that I won't support any man who can't pull his weight. He didn't come to me with his troubles; instead, he ran off into the wilderness, abandoning his responsibilities. If the wolves get to him, so be it."

"With all due respect, Senor Morales," Kane interjected urgently,

"I don't think that's wise. What if the wolves don't get him? What if he returns and causes damage to the ranch or worse, harms the livestock? It would be better if someone could go find him before things escalate." His voice carried a hint of worry, driven by the urgency of preventing Paco from revealing what he had witnessed during the paranormal Heraldry.

"Si.....that makes sense. Go and wait while Victor and I discuss the situation. We will let you know what I decide," Morales dismissed Kane with a curt wave, prompting him to amble outside onto the hacienda's porch, where he waited in tense silence.

An hour crawled by before Victor emerged to fetch him. Morales, seated dominantly behind his imposing desk, gestured for Kane to stand nearer than usual, a clear sign of the gravity of the moment.

"I have made my decision. I'll dispatch two of my men to locate Paco. His fate hinges on their report: if he's fit for service, bring him back. If not.... dispose of him. The finder has my authority to make that descision," Morales pronounced with chilling finality.

"Senor Morales, let me be the one to go into the forest. The monastery where I grew up was surrounded by wilderness for thousands of miles. I know the forests well and it knows me.....plus you're already one man down and sending two more wranglers to search for Paco would put a strain on the workload here," Kane asserted, his voice carrying a blend of confidence and a hint of challenge.

"Alright Amigo, the job is yours. But I want you to report back to me on your return and I want evidence that you have found him.....dead or alive. I've been thinking about your ninjitsu skills and if you can show me I can trust you, you'll be rewarded and I may have other jobs for you," Morales replied, a smirk playing across his features as Kane left the room, mirroring the same smug assurance on his own face.

Chapter 12

In the crisp early morning light, San Francisco's energetic streets flowed with a symphony of sounds—bicycle wheels whirring, lively chatter filling the air, and diligent vendors unlocking their shops. Alejandro, seeking relief from his arduous desert trek, stepped into his favorite pastry shop for a much-needed breakfast.

The journey back through the unforgiving desert had taken its toll, and Alejandro yearned for a day or two to recuperate from the perilous conditions he had just faced. No matter how many times he traversed the wasteland, the challenges seemed to mount with each passing year. As he savored a steaming pie, Alejandro pondered whether to approach Don Morales about delegating the task of recruiting new workers to someone else—a responsibility he had shouldered for years.

However, he hesitated, fearing it could tarnish his hard-earned reputation with the stern and unsympathetic boss.

Alejandro drew in a deep breath, letting the lively scents of San Francisco envelop him—the briny hint of the ocean mingling with the tantalizing aroma of diverse foods sizzling nearby. In this city where every scent seemed to tell a story of its own, each one a unique thread in the tapestry of cultures and cuisines, Alejandro felt his spirits lifted by the activity and welcoming atmosphere that permeated the air.

"Hey there, Mister, you look tired. How about a hot bath and a back rub?" a charming prostitute called out as Alejandro idled past the veranda of a brothel.

"Ok," was his simple reply. He tipped his sombrero and followed the pretty lady inside.

As Alejandro stepped across the threshold, he was met by the brothel's formidable madam, a woman in her sixties exuding a mix of elegance and ruthlessness. She owned numerous prostitutes, but her primary business lay in sex trafficking—the lucrative trade that fueled her empire.

"Good morning, Senor.....?" the madam greeted with a grin, her aged face adorned with bright red lipstick that creased warmly around her mouth.

"Alejandro, Senora," he replied.

"Natasha, take Senor Alejandro upstairs and bathe him. It's 5 cents for the bath, plus 50 cents for a massage....and you'll find it's worth every penny, with a few extra perks," the madam purred, giving Alejandro a suggestive wink.

"Si, Si....I'll take the massage too," Alejandro agreed eagerly, promptly handing over the money to the madam.

"Ah, yes, thank you, Senor," the madam acknowledged graciously, her gaze lingering briefly on Alejandro's payment before she gestured for Natasha to take charge.

Together, they ascended the narrow staircase, entering the intimate ambiance of the brothel.

Inside the bathroom, the air was thick with the soothing

scent of lavender, mingling with the soft flicker of a dozen candles casting a golden hue. Natasha poured hot water into the tub, its steam swirling around Alejandro as he slowly shed his clothes. The flickering candlelight danced over his weary form, highlighting the dust and fatigue of his recent journey.

Observing Alejandro's rugged physique, Natasha's eyes briefly rested on his dirt-covered skin. Amidst the dense tangle of pubic hair, she noticed his modest penis, nestled within its dark thicket like a small acorn.

Gently easing into the steaming water, Alejandro let out a contented sigh, basking in the soothing warmth that swathed him. Natasha's delicate touch as she began to wash his body added to the tranquility, her soft humming providing a gentle melody in the background.

"That's a lovely song. Where did you learn it?" Alejandro asked, genuinely curious. "At school," Natasha replied simply.

"Which school did you attend?" Alejandro probed further, trying to draw her out. "There's not much to tell about my life," Natasha deflected, her tone guarded.

"And what about you? Did you receive an education?" she countered, redirecting the conversation.

"No, I've never had formal schooling. My life has been one lesson after another from the school of hard knocks. I was born on a ranch, raised on a ranch, and now I work on one. Cattle and horses are all I know," Alejandro explained.

"What about your family? Where are your parents, siblings?" Natasha inquired softly. "They're all dead.... murdered on our farm by bandits when I was about 14 years old," Alejandro revealed somberly.

"How come you didn't die with them?" Natasha asked softly,

her curiosity tempered with a delicate touch.

"I wasn't there. My father sent me away to work on a more prosperous ranch, to earn cash for the family.... and I've been there ever since," Alejandro explained, his voice carrying the burden of the years he had spent laboring away from home.

"Do you have a wife and children?" Natasha asked cautiously, aware of the sensitivities surrounding personal lives in her line of work. To her surprise, Alejandro chuckled instead of taking offense.

"Why are you laughing?" Natasha challenged, feeling a bit unsettled by his reaction. "No, I don't have a wife or children. Who would have me anyway? I'm middle-aged, rough around the edges, and let's just say I didn't hit the genetic jackpot down there," Alejandro replied awkwardly, his vulnerability showing through.

"Well.... from where I stand, a slug is a slug, no matter the garden it lives in. And sometimes, a little worm can have just as much fun as a python," Natasha teased playfully, lifting her dress to reveal her shapely legs.

"Go higher," Alejandro said, his voice catching at the sight of her beauty standing before him.

Natasha complied with his request, slowly revealing her golden triangle of pubic hair. Alejandro, captivated, reached out to touch her. She dipped one leg into the water, straddling the edge of the bath, offering herself to Alejandro. With a sense of excitement, he gently inserted two fingers into her, establishing a rhythmic motion.

Natasha arched her back, moaning softly, matching his movements by lifting her hips to meet his fingers. Alejandro leaned in closer, teasing her with his tongue, immersed in her sweetness.

Running her hands through his coarse hair, Natasha motioned for him to lean back as she began to stimulate him, coaxing his arousal.

"Stop," Alejandro murmured quietly, gently removing Natasha's hand from his groin. "Why? What's the matter?" she asked, confused by his refusal of her advances.

"I want to get out of the bath. It's okay, Natasha, you haven't done anything wrong. It's my issue. I won't be able to satisfy you. My pene (dick) doesn't work that way." "Are you impotent?" she asked.

"Sí.... always have been. Not sure why," he replied meekly, feeling unworthy as a "real" man.

"It's alright, Alejandro. Our time together isn't about me. You've paid your money, so whatever you want, I'm happy to please you."

Alejandro stepped out of the bath, and Natasha dried his body with a luxurious, fluffy towel. Moving slowly toward his genitals, she placed her lips over the head of his miniscule penis and lustfully tongued and sucked the insignificant knob. Even though Alejandro enjoyed the sensation, his penis wouldn't grow.

"Come up here," Alejandro motioned, holding her hands as he gently pulled her to him. They passionately kissed as he fondled her underneath.

She began twisting from side to side, her hands tangling in his wet hair as the slippery sounds of her wet clitoris pulsated with each thrust. Her body was turning a rosy pink, and Alejandro noticed her nipples, hard and firm. He playfully nibbled at them before taking them entirely into his mouth, suckling like an infant. Natasha cried out in ecstasy as she climaxed, her cries resonating down the hallway. At that precise moment, Alejandro ejaculated, a small spurt dribbling from his limp penis onto his leg.

"Where have you been all my life?" Natasha exclaimed, panting. "Are you satisfied?" he asked, a shrewd grin on his face.

"Yes... Sí.... I am. Thank you, Señor. Even with your feeble penis, you're still very good."

"Fantástica. I will hold the vision of you in my dreams, Natasha," he said, starting to dress as she tidied up the bathroom for the next client.

"Goodbye, Natasha. I hope to see you again," he remarked, giving her a tender kiss before exiting the room.

Stepping out onto the street, Alejandro decided to visit his friend at the police station, Deputy Harris, whom he had known since becoming Don Morales' recruiter many years ago. Alejandro didn't always obtain his greenhorns for the ranch through the fighting tent; sometimes, he would swing by the local holding cells, pretending he was just there to say hola (hello) to Deputy Harris. In truth, he was scouting the newly detained felons. Some were repeat offenders due to their alcoholism, known to the police and usually apprehended night after night for drunken disorderly conduct or bar fights. Then there were the "strays" who thought they could run amuck on the streets, assaulting local citizens and stealing their valuables. These drifters were the ones Alejandro was interested in because they had nothing to lose. "Deputy Harris, good to see you again," Alejandro greeted joyfully as he walked into the police station.

"Alejandro, it's been a while.... how are you?" Deputy Harris replied.

"Still the same as always.... I've just returned from the ranch to enlist more workers. Do you have any tramps in the lockup that you think would be suitable?"

"Geez, you seem to go through a lot of wranglers.... what is Don Morales doing with you boys out there.... working them to death?"

"Sí, sí.... it appears that way. Some aren't cut out for it. They think they can handle the remoteness at first, but when put to the test, they buckle and sneak away during the night without anyone noticing," Alejandro enlightened him.

"Months ago, I saw you leaving with a huge Japanese man, he looked like a monk.... he'd be out of his comfort zone in the desert. How is he working out?" Alejandro inquired.

"Sí.... that would be Kane. He's a strange one. There's something strange about him, and I can't quite put my finger on it," Alejandro confessed.

"Really? Well, I have one of my own in custody at the moment," Deputy Harris revealed openly.

"Which lockup is he in?"

"Cell 5.... you can go and check him out, if you want," the Deputy enticed his curious friend. Alejandro wandered down the hall, casually scrutinizing each occupant in the other cubicles as he passed, until he finally reached cell number 5. Standing at the gate, Alejandro observed a bald-headed man huddled in the corner, nursing a bandaged left hand.

"Monk.... do you speak English?" Alejandro asked. "Hai, I do," the criminal answered faintly.

"Why are you here?" Alejandro queried.

"Who wants to know?" the convict replied impudently.

"My name is Senor Alejandro.... so? Why are you here in lockup?" "I was in a fight."

"Did you win the fight?" "Hai."

"Are you traveling with anyone.... and what's your name?" "Hai, I am."

"Who?"

"I am not at liberty to say."

"Well, if you don't answer my questions, I will tell Deputy Harris to keep you in here for a week.... if that's how you want it to be," Alejandro warned, glaring at him.

The prisoner hung his head and sighed deeply before answering, giving the impression that he felt defeated by his circumstances.

"I am traveling with a Buddhist high priest and his stewards.... my name is Hiro."

* * *

After returning from the coastal town they had been misled into visiting, Gideon sought solace beneath the broad canopy of a majestic fig tree.

There, beneath its sprawling branches, he sat in serene contemplation, appreciating the cool refuge it provided from the unrelenting blaze of the sun.

As he meditated and prayed, seeking guidance, his emotional turmoil clashed with his profound faith.

He grappled with conflicting desires: the urge to uncover the truth and the growing bitterness that clouded his judgment. The uncertainty of how to navigate his predicament pressed heavily on his mind, leaving him tangled in a web of doubt and frustration.

"Know thyself and the mission. Pledge my mind, body, and soul to what I have committed to. Show me the truth," Gideon repeatedly mumbled, the rhythmic mantras deepening his trance-like state.

Nearby, Miko watched his Master intently from their hotel window, concerned that the mission to find Kane and the accompanying challenges were troubling the elderly monk.

Two days earlier, Miko felt compelled to tell Master Gideon that Juji's information about Kane's whereabouts was a blatant lie. The burden of this secret had burdened his conscience, eventually prompting him to come clean. Miko disclosed the details of his conversation with the elderly Chinese innkeeper in San Francisco.

He recounted how Juji and Hiros lie had been misled them to another coastal town, wasting precious resources and time. According to the innkeeper, Kane had departed with a Mexican man, likely heading towards the Nevada desert where many vagrants sought refuge.

"I remember the Innkeeper saying that he told Kane to stay away from those Mexicans but he didn't listen" Miko concluded

"I am disappointed in you, Miko. Why did you keep this from me? You know how time-sensitive this pursuit is," Gideon reprimanded sternly.

"I am so sorry, Master Gideon. I will never keep secrets from you again," Miko responded apologetically.

"Why did you in the first place?"

"I am not an accomplished ninja like my brothers, so I am

scared of their retribution," Miko confessed.

"There's no need to fear them. Rest assured, I have the resourcefulness to handle those who try to deceive me.... Remember this, Miko: a liar has no shame and is capable of doing many wrongs. Lies harm others and contradict our Buddhist ideals of truth-seeking. Hiro and Juji understand this well.... Now, go and bring them to me."

As Gideon waited for the men to return, he began to harbor doubts about Hiro and Juji's trustworthiness. He understood that self-serving lies are told to protect or advance the liar's own interests, and knowingly stating lies is a deliberate act of deception.

A knock at the door interrupted his thoughts. Gideon verbally summoned them in, and Hiro entered the room first, with Juji and Miko following closely behind. However, Gideon quickly gestured for Miko to leave their company.

"Master Hiro and Master Juji.... what will become of you?" Gideon began with firm intensity.

"What do you mean, Master Gideon? I haven't done anything...." Hiro started to justify himself, but Gideon cut him off, unwilling to hear excuses.

"You are both liars.... you deceived me about Kane's whereabouts, knowing how crucial it is to find him. I want to hear your reasons for this deception."

"I don't have one," Hiro answered, fearful of Gideon's reaction, while Juji remained silent, paralyzed with fear.

"Liar!" Gideon's immediate response blasted through the room.

"I want to hear the reasoning behind your lies," he sternly repeated. "As I've said, I don't have one."

"Liar!" Gideon screamed in frustration, his patience wearing thin.

"I will be gracious enough to give you one more chance to tell me the truth.... What is the reasoning behind your deception?"

A heavy silence enveloped the room as Hiro contemplated his response.

"We got into a fight with some Mexican men. They sicced their dogs on us, and we had no choice but to defend ourselves. Once they realized we'd killed their dogs, they threatened to hunt us down," Hiro finally admitted.

"What was the fight about?" Gideon probed further.

"They said their dogs wanted Chinese for breakfast," Hiro replied. "And what did you choose to do, Master Hiro? Walk away or retaliate?"

"We didn't retaliate, Master Gideon. We didn't say a word. They just set their dogs on us," Hiro continued, sticking to his story.

"Ah, Master Gideon.... that's not entirely true," Juji interjected at last.

"What is the truth, Master Juji, and why should I believe you now that you've broken my trust?" Gideon demanded, his voice tinged with disappointment.

"Believe me, Master Gideon, I will tell you the truth.... Hiro did retaliate. He told the Mexicans we were Japanese, not Chinese," Juji admitted, fear coursing through him, his face flushed red with shame as Hiro grimaced at his compromised sense of brotherhood.

"Whose idea was it to deceive me about Kane's location, knowing how time-sensitive this mission is and the severe consequences for anyone who impedes it?" Gideon demanded, his voice slicing through the tension.

"It was Master Hiro's idea. He asked me to convey that lie because the Mexicans threatened to kill us. We had to make a quick decision to leave San Francisco. Hiro knew that if we told you Kane was elsewhere, you would leave immediately," Juji blurted out, revealing the truth.

"It is said that prolific liars share the personality trait of a psychopath. Their ability to strategically exploit others and manipulate without guilt suggests an insatiable drive to gain power by any means necessary. Is this your intention, Master Juji?" Gideon rose from his chair and approached Juji, his majestic staff gripped firmly in hand. "Answer the question," Gideon's voice was bitter and disapproving.

"No, Master Gideon, it was not my intention," Juji replied respectfully.

"Let this be a lesson to you, Master Juji. If you ever lie to me again, you will suffer the same fate Master Hiro is about to experience. You can leave now." With a bow, Juji swiftly exited the room, closing the door behind him.

With one arm casually behind his back and the other firmly holding his staff, Gideon circled around Hiro, each step punctuated by the deliberate thud of his staff on the floor.

"You continue to defy and disappoint me, Master Hiro," Gideon finally declared after minutes of oppressive silence.

"I apologize for my betrayal, Master Gideon," Hiro replied meekly, head hung low. "It's too late for apologies. Your deception has cost us time and money that cannot be recovered. The last time you lied to me, I threatened to send you back to Japan, but now it's too late for that. We've come too far, and because of your deceitful tricks, I no longer have the money to send you back. For your punishment, you will perform yubitsume on yourself."

Gideon casually walked over to his belongings, rummaging through his kit until he found an elaborate wooden box. He placed it on the table in front of Hiro and opened the lid with careful precision. Inside lay a blood-stained cloth and a razor-sharp tanto blade. Without uttering a word, Gideon turned toward Hiro, his gaze piercing, silently demanding that the ritual be carried out.

"But Master Gideon, I didn't mean to deceive you," Hiro pleaded desperately. "LIAR!" Gideon's scream reverberated through the room, filled with anger and betrayal.

"You brought the tanto box on this trip? Why?" Hiro asked, his surprise evident. He couldn't fathom why Gideon would have thought it necessary to bring it on their mission.

"Because I know you, Master Hiro," Gideon snapped, his voice seething with anger. "I hoped I wouldn't need it, but your persistent arrogance and disobedience have proven my decision was correct."

Hiro approached the table with a slow, hesitant stride. He picked up the knife, his hand trembling slightly as he positioned his left hand on the cloth. After a nervous intake of breath followed by a heavy exhale, Hiro swiftly amputated the topmost portion of his pinkie. He wrapped the severed joint in the cloth and presented it to Gideon, bowing his head in submission.

Gideon accepted the bloody package and placed it carefully on the table.

"If you continue to offend me, Master Hiro, you will be expected to amputate further portions of your finger. Once that finger is completely removed, you will move on to your right pinkie, making it difficult for you to hold a sword and fight. Your egotistical ways never cease. They will be your downfall. Do you understand?" Gideon snapped in a rigid, unforgiving tone.

"Hai.... I understand," Hiro replied solemnly.

"Now go.... get out of my sight. You sicken me," Gideon angrily dismissed the defiant ninja. Hiro left the room silently, passing Juji and Miko in the hallway. They stared after him in shock, seeing Hiro's blood-soaked hand and understanding the severity of Gideon's punishment.

Entering the street with blood oozing from his severed finger, Hiro desperately sought help from passersby, but was met with disdain.

"Do you have a cloth?" he asked each person.

"Eww.... get away from me.... you dirty Jonnie," came their disgusted responses at the sight of blood dripping from his injured hand. Others quickly moved to the far side of the street, avoiding any contact with him altogether.

He now experienced the deep pang of distaste and rejection of aid from others, mirroring the disdain he had once shown to the street beggar just days earlier. Completely dismayed, Hiro's anger began to simmer with each dismissal. His frustration mounted, intensifying into a heightened state of sensitivity.

Like an insatiable hunger, Hiro's desperate need for acceptance became a survival instinct. Constant rejection and snobbery triggered a cascade of emotional turmoil—depression, jealousy, and profound sadness. This internal confusionl fueled his simmering aggression, leading to diminished impulse control.

When a group of three men heckled him about his bloodied hand and Japanese appearance, Hiro's pent-up frustration exploded. He screamed violently and launched himself at the men. With a surge of adrenaline, he delivered a forceful punch to one man's face, simultaneously kicking another in the leg. The sickening snap of a kneecap breaking sent the third man fleeing toward the police station for help.

* * *

Alejandro lingered at the cell gate, studying the disheveled monk, assessing whether he might fit into Don Morales' team of ranchers.

"So, where do I find your High Priest and his stewards?" Alejandro inquired after a moment.

"Why?" Hiro responded sharply, his head bowed and resting on his knees.

"I have a proposition for you, but since you are traveling with others, I want to ensure everyone is agreeable," Alejandro explained.

"I don't think my High Priest would agree to anything that doesn't align with his mission," Hiro replied cautiously.

"What mission?" Alejandro pressed, curious to learn more. Hiro sat silently, realizing he may have revealed too much.

"What mission? If you don't answer me, I will ensure you stay locked up—not for a week as I said earlier, but for a month. I can help you get out of here, but that's your decision. What do you want to do, Hiro?" Alejandro's voice carried a firm threat.

Hiro lifted his gaze steadily, locking eyes with Alejandro in a thousand-mile stare. "We've been sent from Japan to apprehend a renegade murderer from our monastery and bring him back for punishment," Hiro finally confessed.

"Does this monk resemble you?" Alejandro pressed.

"Hai.... but he's much larger, like the size of a bear," Hiro affirmed.

"His name wouldn't happen to be Kane?" Alejandro's expression shifted with recognition.

"Hai, it is."

"Ay Dios Mio! I know this man and I know where you can find him. Tell me where the rest of your clan is staying, and I will bring them here to you," Alejandro declared urgently.

Upon hearing that Alejandro knew Kane's whereabouts, Hiro's demeanor changed instantly. With renewed vigor, he jumped up, eagerly providing Alejandro with the information he needed.

"They're in Chinatown staying at the Orchard Garden"

"Bueno (Good)"

An hour later, Hiro heard the heavy police station door creak open, followed by the unmistakable sound of Gideon's staff resonating closer. Gideon's footsteps echoed purposefully as he approached the jail cell. Though inwardly fuming over Hiro's latest escapade, Gideon maintained his composure, his silence speaking volumes as Deputy Harris unlocked the gate.

"Master Gideon, I am so grateful for your help," Hiro pleaded, hoping to mend the strained atmosphere.

Gideon grunted in response, a terse acknowledgment of

Hiro's gratitude.

"You may disappoint me a million times, Hiro, or test my patience, but my role is guided by a higher purpose. No matter your stunts or tantrums, I am here solely to safeguard your best interests for the sake of our mission—nothing more," Gideon asserted firmly.

"Master Gideon, Alejandro knows where Kane is," Hiro blurted out excitedly, thinking he was sharing new information.

"Hai I already know. Alejandro informed me earlier. It's the only reason we're here,

Master Hiro," Gideon replied calmly, his authoritative manner unyeilding.

Before Deputy Harris released Hiro into the custody of the awaiting monks, he had to ensure they could pay the fine.

"The bail is one hundred dollars for your comrade to go free without a further court hearing. Can you afford this?" he demanded, his gaze fixed on Gideon while Miko and Juji stood silently in the background.

"That is expensive," Gideon objected.

"Your friend broke a civilian's leg, snapped it completely in half. The victim is now in the hospital undergoing surgery. Hiro is charged with grievous bodily harm.

"Should he stand trial, he risks up to 14 years in jail and the obligation to pay the man's medical expenses. In my view, the proposed bail amount is fair," Deputy Harris asserted.

"Miko, bring me the money pouch," Gideon conceded.

"No, it's okay, Amigo. I will pay for Hiro's bail, but only if you all return with me to the ranch," Alejandro interjected.

"We were going to accompany you anyway, Mr. Alejandro, because you said Kane is now residing there. We need to catch this monster and take him back to Japan as soon as possible," Gideon reasoned. Before he could finish, Alejandro had already paid Deputy Harris, and the group left the police station to collect their belongings from the Orchard Garden.

While Alejandro scouted around town gathering necessary supplies for the trip, the monks diligently packed their horses for the anticipated voyage into the forsaken desert.

"This is going to be exciting," Gideon overheard Miko saying to Juji.

"Master Miko, remember why we are undertaking this burden. The desert isn't for the faint-hearted. It will be arduous and time-consuming. Mr. Alejandro has informed me that it will take weeks to reach the ranch. I want all of you to be cautious and resilient," Gideon announced unexpectedly, catching Miko by surprise.

"Of course, Master Gideon. I am sorry for my naivety," Miko responded simply. "Where is Alejandro? It's been two hours since he left to get supplies, and it's already midday," Hiro whined.

"Enough! I don't want to hear another word from you, Master Hiro. After your recent disobedient behavior, the only thing I want to hear from you is when you ask what can be done for myself, Mr. Alejandro, or your brothers. You are now subservient to us," Gideon snapped irritably, his patience wearing thin.

As Gideon turned to continue loading his horse, Hiro glared at the old man with an intense, fiery look. His eyes were slits, harsh and filled with anger. He believed his glare was covert, but Miko had witnessed the death stare.

"Here comes Alejandro," Juji announced as he spotted the Mexican walking towards them, hauling a multitude of bags.

"Go and help him," Gideon instructed. Miko and Juji jumped to attention and accompanied Alejandro to the awaiting entourage.

"I have bought three sombreros!" Alejandro announced proudly. "It is muy hot in the desert, and you don't want your bald heads to burn away and get sunstroke." "Hai.... that is a good idea, Mr. Alejandro. Thank you," Gideon said, pleased with his friend's practical thinking.

"Call me Señor Alejandro. 'Mister' makes me sound high class, and that's something I'm definitely not," Alejandro chuckled.

"Okay, are we ready to venture into the Nevada Desert? Hold on to your hats....

I mean it, gringos, you'll regret it if you lose them," Alejandro laughed, and the monks laughed along with him.... except for Hiro.

As they rode through Chinatown, the old Chinese innkeeper, who had initially greeted them when they disembarked in San Francisco, stood on the verandah of his motel, his eyes narrowing as he scrutinized the group.

"It's you thieving monks again! Where's my ornament? Have you come back to steal more from me?" he shouted, his voice filled with fury. He gingerly stepped off the verandah and onto the street, shaking both fists in the air, his face contorted with rage.

"Who was that?" Alejandro questioned sharply, glancing at Gideon riding beside him. "No one of importance," Gideon replied curtly.

"Did you take something of his?"

"It wasn't his to own in the first place. We retrieved a sacred item that belongs to our monastery. Kane had left it behind," Gideon justified as they hurriedly moved away from the enraged Chinaman.

"You're still consorting with THAT SAME Mexican.... you foolish monks.... you've sealed your own fate, hahahaha.... I hope Karma comes back to bite you all on the backside.... you deserve every misfortune that's headed your way!" The innkeeper continued to howl, leaping up and down like a petulant child in a fit of rage.

"Now it's my turn to ask.... what did he mean by 'THAT SAME Mexican' does he

know you?" Gideon inquired, his voice showing concern.

"As you can see, Amigo, the man is absolutely crazy. He hates all Mexicans thinks

we all look alike. Similar story with you Asians.... everyone else thinks you all look alike too," Alejandro grinned cheekily, trying to diffuse the tension with humor.

The afternoon sky flourished with vivid orange shades as the sun began its descent toward the horizon, casting a natural calling card beckoning them toward the blistering wasteland. The blazing sun seemed to curse all who dared to walk its path into the desert, and those who found comfort in its harshness were few and far between. Alejandro, however, was one of those rare few, though even he felt the weariness beginning to settle in.

"How long have you been traveling back and forth through the desert?" Gideon inquired, his gaze probing.

"Too long, Amigo," Alejandro replied with a weary sigh.

"What is your purpose for making these trips?" Gideon pressed on, intrigued by the enigmatic Mexican they had entrusted with their safety in this unfamiliar world.

"My boss, Don Morales, needs workers for his ranch, so he sends me to San Francisco to recruit them. They're usually aimless bums with no family ties or life ambitions."

"And Master Kane? How did you find him?" Gideon continued to inquire.

"He was in the ring at the fighting tent. Became the champion after just one round, and then no one dared to challenge him. He's an amazing fighter," Alejandro explained.

"He should be.... I taught him," Gideon revealed calmly. Alejandro looked at Gideon in stunned disbelief.

"You? But you're just a frail old monk.... Sorry, I don't mean to be disrespectful," Alejandro stammered.

"Looks can be deceiving, my friend. Don't ever underestimate me.... I am more than I appear," Gideon replied firmly, giving Alejandro a stern glance that hinted at hidden depths.

"We are Buddhist monks, but our tradition encompasses abilities that some might call supernatural. We excel in espionage, deception, surprise attacks, and blending seamlessly into the shadows. Our faith and our ninja skills define our way of life. We are dedicated to both," Gideon explained solemnly.

"No wonder Kane beat the shit out of those guys.... but there's something else about him that I can't put my finger on," Alejandro confessed.

"Yes, there is.... he is a skin-changer, a demon sent from hell," Gideon revealed with a haunted expression. "He murdered my cherished brother and inflicted these horrific scars as I fought him off. He also took my eye. A vortex of anger swirls inside him, and you never know when he will strike. That is why we hunt him.... capturing him and taking him back to Japan is of utmost importance."

"Si.....I wondered what happened to your face. By the way, why do you call Kane Master? He's not much of a Master of anything at the ranch. He can't ride that well, he can't shoot, he can't rope.... he can't do much but fight. He doesn't get along with the other wranglers either; he pretty much keeps to himself. I often see him heading off into the woods alone," Alejandro observed.

"That doesn't surprise me.... he seeks solitude to hone his paranormal abilities, striving to grow stronger each day. But to answer your question, we address each other as Master because we are ordained men of our monastic order," Gideon explained patiently.

"So.... what does Kane turn into when his skin changes?" Alejandro asked quietly, his curiosity tinged with apprehension.

"A giant, savage, predatory bear, and he lets nothing or no one stand in his way... your wrangler friends should be scared.... very, very scared because you don't know the hideous demon within him," Gideon warned gravely.

For days after that conversation with Gideon, Alejandro spoke very few words. Dumbfounded, his mind kept returning to the ranch, worrying about the safety of his boss and friends. This preoccupation consumed him, driving him to push the monks through the desert much harder than he would have with any other recruits. His main objective became getting back home sooner rather than later.

Chapter 13

Standing in front of a mirror, Kane marveled at his new appearance. He casually plaited his long, black hair and brushed the thick beard that extended down his chin. Since arriving at the ranch, Don Morales and Alejandro had instructed him to adopt the look and language of a typical Mexican man. Over the last few months, Kane had gradually assimilated into this character. As he stared at his reflection, a haughty grin spread across his face, imagining Gideon's reaction to his transformed persona and relishing in the thought of being unrecognizable as the orthodox Buddhist monk he once was.

Exiting the bunkhouse, Kane threw the saddlebags over his horse and prepared to venture into the forest in search of his nemesis, Paco the Pig. As he mounted up, he noticed Victor standing determinedly on the verandah, arms folded across his massive chest, staring in Kane's direction. Without hesitation, Kane rode over to him. "I'm heading out to find Paco now. I don't know which path he took, so it could take a few days, maybe a week," Kane informed.

"Just make sure you find him and bring him back here," Victor replied in his low-pitched, gravelly tone.

"Si.... that's the plan," Kane retorted. With a swift nudge to his horse's belly, he trotted off through the paddock and disappeared into the dense, wooded forest.

The sun's scorch barely pierced through the dense foliage, its feeble rays like an extinguishing candle flame casting a dim glow over Kane's head. The forest canopy formed a chaotic veil of darkness, enclosing him within its oppressive embrace.

Between the towering trees, straggling cobwebs stretched like fibrous cords, their sticky strands poised to ensnare any unsuspecting prey. The spiders, their feverish eyes glazed with hunger, waited patiently amidst the perpetual mist, ready to pounce at the slightest movement.

Kane pressed onward, swatting aside the relentless webs as he crossed a trickling creek that wound its way through the mouldy undergrowth of the forest floor. Along its swirling edges, brown leaves were sucked into the inky water, deepening its hue to a dark molasses-like color. On the opposite bank, trees adorned with damp clusters of brown cup-like fungus clung to their bark, oozing a sticky substance that reminded Kane of slimy mollusks.

In the late afternoon, Kane stumbled upon a crude hut, poorly constructed of bulging rocks cemented together with black mud. Its walls were encrusted with lichen, and the decaying roof hinted at neglect. Skirting the glade, he cautiously approached the stone building. Seeing no guards, he advanced closer, circling the small cabin.

It was then he noticed blood-stained clothes and mildewed robes scattered around, along with a gruesome heap of six human skulls.

Shawls of thick fog slithered from the ground, silent and eerie, coiling around the defenseless cabin like a serpent. They formed a screen of milky vapor, seeming to possess a life of their own as they settled in, enveloping the scene in a haunting haze.

Dismounting from his horse, Kane scanned the shadows on the opposite side of the hut. Suddenly, distressing noises erupted from the depths of the forest—a tortured howl mixed with a despairing screech, resonating through the twilight air.

"It's the witches," a voice abruptly stated from behind him.

Quickly turning, Kane saw Lady Vixen standing there in human form, her bright countenance a stark contrast to the surrounding oppressive murkiness.

"Hello, I'm relieved to see you. Where do these witches come from?" Kane queried. "Because you're connected to an alternate universe, you're hypersensitive to other dimensions. They aren't from our world," she explained in a crooning voice.

"You're looking for Paco, yes?" she continued, moving on to the reason for her presence.

"I am.... do you know where he is?" Kane asked urgently.

"He was here earlier, but the witches have taken him deeper into the forest. This is their coven. It will be dark soon, and they'll return, so we must leave immediately," she cautioned.

"They don't bother me," Kane foolishly replied.

"These witches aren't just any sorceresses. They're from a depraved and demonic universe, extremely powerful because they are Satan's very own brides.

"Their only purpose is to collect souls for their Master and to satisfy their insatiable thirst for human flesh.... Hurry, we must go," Lady Vixen whispered urgently.

Kane swiftly mounted his horse and followed Lady Vixen. She effortlessly leaped over a fallen tree, transforming miraculously mid-air into her canine form, and sprinted deeper into the forest, with Kane in hot pursuit.

The forest was primal, exuding an oppressive aura that emanated from every living thing within it. Whether you were its victim or victor, it left a repugnant taste and smell of mold clinging to your very essence—it was a place to be avoided at all costs.

He followed Lady Vixen for miles, but the twisting canopy of silver limbs and leafy bowers made it increasingly difficult for Kane's horse to keep pace. The animal diligently swerved to avoid every obstructive hurdle, yet despite its natural speed and agility, it couldn't match the relentless pace. Eventually, Kane lost sight of the dog as she disappeared into the engulfing blackness.

"Lady Vixen, where are you?" he called out repeatedly, his voice echoing fruitlessly through the dense scrub.

Finally dismounting, Kane retrieved a blanket from his saddlebag and wrapped it tightly around his shoulders. In the crushing blackness, he huddled against a massive tree, reluctantly listening to the distant, continual moans of the witches. Their agonizing cries reverberated with malice, haunting the stillness of the forest. Daylight finally broke through the darkness, a welcome relief after a sleepless night. Weary but determined, Kane mounted his horse and pressed on in the direction he believed Lady Vixen had taken before they became separated.

Before long, Kane's ears caught a distant, agitated sound—the frenzied beating of wings. Intrigued, he followed the vigorous noise until he reached an unusually open space in the forest. In the center stood a large, solitary tree. Looking up, Kane's heart sank as he saw Paco suspended by a rope from a thick branch. Surrounding him were crows and vultures, their sharp beaks tearing at his flesh with savage brutality, a horrifying spectacle of frenzied feeding.

The rancid, decaying hide of the former rancher swung from side to side, manipulated by the movements of the birds clutching onto the carcass. Their flapping wings vibrated Paco's body around, creating a macabre dance in the clearing.

Though Kane typically had a cast-iron stomach, the gruesome sight overwhelmed him, and he instantly vomited.

Regaining his composure, he puzzled over how Paco could have been strung up so high. Mentally calculating the distance between the suspended body and the ground—nearly twelve feet—sent an instant shudder down his spine. Recalling the haunting shrieks of the witches during the night added to the sinister atmosphere, leaving Kane unsettled in the grim aftermath.

"It must have been them," Kane thought to himself, his mind reeling from the grisly sight of Paco's macerated and blood-soaked body.

Despite all he had endured in the past—Abbot Eshin's murder and the merciless executions in Osaka—this scene unsettled him deeply. He could sense the vile depravity of the malevolent force behind such a cold and callous act.

Never before had Kane encountered such emotions. The dark forest seemed to exude a madness unlike any place he had known. The depth of despair and horror hanging before him felt surreal, as if he were trapped in an unholy mockery of life itself.

Descending from his horse with a heavy heart, Kane approached the tree where Paco's lifeless body hung. He gazed up at the gruesome sight, contemplating how to retrieve him from his macabre perch. A sudden impulse seized him, and unconsciously, he began to remove his clothes until he stood naked beneath the dangling corpse.

Closing his eyes, Kane entered a profound state of meditation, his breath slowing as he focused inward. In the stillness of the forest clearing, his mind transcended the present moment, delving into the legible depths of ancient practices he had studied in the human-skinned book.

As he delved deeper into his trance, a subtle transformation rippled across his body—a subtle shift that marked the beginning of his skin-changing ability.

Initially, his bones cracked and shifted, elongating and contorting beneath his skin. He screamed in agony as his entire body expanded, collapsing onto all fours with a harrowing cry. His face contorted, twisting into a snout as his ears stretched sharply upwards. Hands and feet broadened, sprouting talons like six-inch nails, transforming into formidable paws. Thick brown fur erupted from every pore, his size swelling several times over. When the metamorphosis halted, Kane rose on hind legs with a thunderous roar, revealing daunting canine fangs. Towering at fifteen feet, he swiped the air with immense paws, growling ferociously, jaws snapping with unstoppable force. A surge of unparalleled vigor coursed through his muscles, surreal and overwhelming.

He had become the true skin-changer he was destined to be—

the majestic Shadow Bear.

Shadow Bear swiped at the rope with a powerful motion, cleaving it in two. The birds scattered into the sky, leaving Paco to crash heavily to the ground. He sniffed Paco's motionless form, his senses keen, until a distant dog's bark caught his attention from the forest's edge. Lady Vixen observed the scene, wagging her tail in delight at Kane's transformative mastery—it was a culmination of his destiny.

Bounding towards her, Shadow Bear approached with the exuberance of a giant puppy. They touched noses affectionately, nuzzling each other warmly.

"Good work Shadow Bear" She uttered telepathically

With a final yip, Lady Vixen darted back into the woods, as if pulled by an unseen call.

Within half an hour, Kane gradually returned to his human form, his transformation impressive yet controlled. He dressed and carefully wrapped Paco's body in a blanket from his saddlebag. Lifting the bundle onto his horse, he secured it firmly with the remaining rope.

"Is this Paco?" Don Morales queried when Kane returned to the ranch. "Si.... it is," Kane replied, pulling the bandanna from his face.

"Did you kill him?" the boss continued.

"No.... I found him hanging from a tree. It looks like he killed himself. I told you he wasn't right in the head. Whatever madness took hold of him drove him to suicide," Kane fabricated.

"Why is there so much blood if he was hanged?"

"When I found him, buzzards and crows were feasting on his flesh.... dozens of them. He must have been hanging there for a day or so, judging by his condition. Most of his body has been torn apart by the birds."

Don Morales signaled to some of the ranch hands who stood nearby to remove Paco's body from the horse and lay him on the ground for inspection.

"Take off the blanket," he ordered. Reluctantly, one of the cowboys flicked back the cloth, revealing Paco's mangled face to the horror of everyone present.

"Mierda (fuck), you weren't wrong about the birds having a feast on him. Are you sure this is Paco? You can't really tell," Don Morales expressed, visibly shocked. "It's definitely him, Don Morales. Despite his torn and blood-stained clothes, you can still make out the tartan fabric of the shirt he was last seen in, and here's the bandanna he always wore," Kane pointed out, retrieving the neckerchief from his saddlebag and showing it to his boss.

"Si, Si.... that is Paco's. Another good rancher gone," Don Morales admitted with a heavy sigh.

"Take the body to the family cemetery and bury him immediately. His scent will attract unwanted coyotes and vermin that I won't tolerate on my ranch," Don Morales ordered coldly. Three cowboys promptly lifted Paco's body and carried it to the burial ground.

"What about a funeral, jefe (boss)?" another cowboy inquired.

"You can celebrate or mourn his life and remember him however you wish. Kane, come with me," Don Morales said, turning away from the scene.

Don Morales entered his office, and Victor positioned himself in the doorway, blocking Kane's path.

"Let him through, Victor," Don Morales instructed as he

settled behind his desk.

"Senor Kane well, who would've thought you'd prove trustworthy?" Don Morales

remarked, his tone carrying a mix of surprise and approval.

"It seems you've shown yourself capable and reliable in carrying out my orders with precision. Because of this, I've decided to entrust you with another task. If you succeed, I will appoint you as my permanent hired gun. I have enemies that need dealing with. Is this something that interests you?" Don Morales proposed, deliberately flicking two fifty-dollar notes onto the table in front of Kane, hoping the sight would sway him.

"There's more where that came from if you agree," he added, observing Kane closely as the allure of the substantial sum of money sank in.

"A hired gun? I don't use guns, Don Morales. I am a Shinobi warrior. I am expertly trained in espionage, infiltration, deception, and ambush. I fight using only my body," Kane asserted firmly.

"Well, you sound like the right man for the job then. Don't you want to earn substantial amounts of money so that one day you can buy your own ranch?" Don Morales pressed, his persuasive tone laced with temptation.

Kane stood silently, weighing the money on the table against Don Morales' proposition.

"Si.... I would," Kane finally answered, his voice reflecting a mixture of resolve and calculation.

"Then it's settled. Take the money.... you've earned it," Don

Morales declared, sliding the bills closer to Kane. “And I’ll throw in four bottles of Tequila for the men, so they can toast in honor of Paco’s memory. Victor, fetch the Tequila from my cellar,” he ordered briskly.

Victor returned with four bottles, each placed on the table with a heavy thud.

“Take them.... the men will appreciate it,” Don Morales instructed, gesturing for Kane to collect his reward.

“Gracias, Don Morales,” Kane acknowledged gratefully, swiftly stowing the money into his pocket and gathering the bottles of Tequila.

“I need you back here tomorrow morning at 8 am. I’ll give you instructions for the next job.... understood?” Don Morales affirmed.

“Si, Don Morales.... 8 am,” Kane confirmed, his tone resolute as he prepared to embark on his next mission.

Walking back to the bunkhouse, Kane’s eyes narrowed and his brow furrowed as he wrestled with unanswered questions. Why had Don Morales chosen him as his “hired gun” instead of Victor or one of the more experienced men? He acknowledged Don Morales’ approval of how he handled retrieving Paco’s body, but Kane hadn’t been at the ranch long enough to earn such a crucial role. He still felt like an inexperienced outsider in this unforgiving landscape.

As he glanced toward the cemetery, Kane watched two cowboys tossing shovel loads of dirt over their shoulders, continuing to dig Paco’s grave. A wave of guilt and unease swept over him like an unstoppable flood. He knew Paco’s death stemmed from witnessing the secret ritual into Shadow Bear.

Driven by a deep sense of obligation to his fellow ranchers,

Kane diverted from the bunkhouse and made his way towards the graveyard to offer his help.

"Ah, Gringo.... you came at the right time. Give us a hand, it's damn hot out here," one of the cowboys remarked, wiping his brow with a dirty neckerchief.

"Sí, sí I've got something for everyone. After we bury Paco, we'll celebrate his life,"

Kane enticed, holding up the bottles of tequila, feeling accepted and slightly important.

"Here comes Andy and Carlos," another cowboy announced as he spotted their approach.

Kane turned to greet the approaching men and noticed Carlos carrying his guitar. He casually set the Tequila bottles down near the edge of the freshly dug grave.

Instantly, one of the workers inside the pit grabbed a bottle, popped it open, and took a long, satisfying swig. He wiped his mouth on his sleeve with exaggerated satisfaction.

"Ah, that hits the spot," the man declared, taking another gulp. "Chico.... I thought we'd drink after burying Paco," Kane objected.

"Now's as good a time as any. Stop being such a wuss, Kane. Besides, the grave's deep enough now," Chico retorted, climbing out of the grave just as Andy and Carlos entered through the cemetery gate.

"Here boys, wrap your laughing gear around this," Chico continued, tossing a bottle high into the air towards Andy, who caught it effortlessly with one hand.

"Let's put this poor bastard in his eternal resting place," Chico announced solemnly.

As the men prepared to lift Paco's cloth-covered body, Kane stepped forward decisively.

"Move aside, I'll place him in the grave," he declared boldly, crouching down and scooping Paco up in his arms as though he were a small child.

"Gringo.... you're one strong son of a bitch," Andy remarked with admiration as Kane leapt into the grave, gently laying Paco down at his feet.

For a long moment, Kane stared at the blood-stained cloth, vivid memories of the tragic events leading to Paco's death flooding his mind. A deep sense of shame expanded within him, causing him to question his own morality.

The internal conflict between his lifelong Buddhist values and his newfound identity as a skin-changer weighed heavily on him. He felt the onset of regret and inadequacy, as if he were losing touch with who he truly was. Was there something inherently wrong with him? Did he harbor a malevolent sickness that surfaced periodically, leaving behind a bitter taste of wickedness, shame and death?

These troubling thoughts gnawed at Kane's mind as he grappled with his inner confusion, the burden of his actions casting a shadow over his soul.

"What are you doing just standing there? You want to be buried with him?" Chico challenged, snapping Kane out of his deep trance.

Kane blinked, disoriented for a moment, before slowly hoisting himself out of the grave.

"Come on, boys, let's finish this," Andy urged, rallying the cowboys. They took turns shoveling dirt onto Paco, gradually filling the hole until a mound rose above the ground, marking the newly established gravesite.

"Does anyone want to say a few words?" Chico asked, leaning on his shovel while Carlos began to strum a soft, melancholy tune on his guitar.

"I will," Kane volunteered, clearing his throat as he knelt beside the grave.

"May Paco, who endured so much suffering of body and mind, find peace. May he be liberated from his pain and fear, and may his spirit soar free," Kane recited formally, his words carrying a heartfelt sincerity in the quiet of the cemetery.

Even though he died in a trackless, fearful wilderness as he travels towards the light, may he be protected and guarded by beneficent celestials.

Through God's blessings and grace and the power of the light that streams from the Divine, may all of Paco's negative karma, destructive emotions, and blockages be purified and removed from his soul. Amen"

"That was beautiful," Andy remarked, his voice thick with emotion as he wiped away a tear.

"Si.... very fitting, especially considering how things ended for him," Chico added dismally.

"Here, my friends, grab a bottle. Let's drink and sing to Paco's memory," he suggested, wanting to lift the somber mood.

And so, under the cover of night and around a blazing campfire, the men gathered. They drank from the bottles of Tequila, sang heartfelt country ballads, and invented playful songs about Paco's antics. Between verses, they paused to share exaggerated tales of his adventurous life, their laughter mingling with the crackling fire under the starlit sky.

"Carlos, remember that time when you, me, and Paco rode

into San Francisco, and he insisted on stopping at that saloon for a drink?" Chico began, a mischievous grin spreading across his face.

"Si, I remember.... he got into it with some locals," Carlos chimed in, recalling the spirited incident.

"Well.... after we finished our drinks, we discovered Paco's horse had been stolen. So, he marched back into the bar, casually flipped his gun into the air, cocked it above his head without even looking, and fired a shot into the ceiling," Chico continued animatedly. "

"Which one of you bastards stole my horse?' he shouted, with all the force he could muster. But no one answered."

"So Paco says, 'Alright, I'm gonna have another Tequila. If my horse ain't back outside by the time I finish, I'm gonna do what I did in San Diego.... and trust me, you don't want me to do what I did in San Diego.'"

Some of the men shifted nervously in their seats, eyeing Paco with a mixture of respect and amusement. They knew better than to underestimate a spirited Mexican, especially after a few too many Tequila shots. Paco downed another drink and swaggered outside to find his horse miraculously returned. As he clumsily tried to mount up and ride out of town, a curious patron ambled out of the saloon.

"Say, partner.... before you go.... what happened in San Diego?" the man inquired, intrigued by Paco's reputation.

Paco turned back with a grin, his words slurred from the alcohol.

"I had to walk home," he drawled, punctuating the tale with a drunken chuckle.

The men laughed at Chico's embellished tale, enjoying the light-hearted moment amid their reminiscing. Carlos struck up a lonesome cowboy song on his guitar, and soon the others joined in, their voices harmonizing beneath the beautiful night sky.

"Riding on the range I've got my hat on I've got my boots on
I'm in my saddle and on my horse I wanna be a cowboy
And you can be my cowgirl.....ride alongside I don't want to be lonely
I just wanna be a cowboy with you by my side "

As everyone joined in chorus, singing like a seasoned choir, Kane found himself clueless about the lyrics. Undeterred, he enthusiastically babbled along, attempting to follow the melody but failing to hit the right notes. His off-key contribution drew amused glances from the group.

"Give it up, Kane.... you're murdering the song," someone teased, prompting laughter from the others.

Unaccustomed to the effects of alcohol, Kane felt a surge of rejection and embarrassment wash over him. Coupled with the guilt over Paco's death, these emotions overwhelmed him, and tears welled up in his eyes. Slurring his words, he knelt at the gravesite, apologizing profusely, "I'm so sorry, Paco "

"Why the hell are you crying and apologizing to him, Amigo? He can't hear your terrible singing.... he's dead!" Chico's laughter rang out, joined by the others in mocking amusement.

Suddenly, vivid mental images flashed through Kane's mind—Lady Vixen, the Crowman, Gideon, Hiro, and the haunting images from the human skin book. It was as if scenes were unfolding before him in stark clarity.

Kane shuddered, attempting to shake off the intoxication, when abruptly he heard a clear voice in his mind, speaking calmly but firmly.

"Seek out a place that befits your stature and make it your home. The guardian of our ancestors' dwelling will earn great acclaim and fulfill their destiny. Always keep your true identity concealed."

Like a blast going off in his head, Kane suddenly realized what he was about to do, how he could have easily unmasked his true identity with one honest confession about Paco's death. Instead, he rose from his knees and faced the men, who were still laughing. Forcing a smile, he joined in their laughter, masking his uneasiness with a deliberate show of camaraderie.

* * *

Under the rosy fingers of sunlight that painted the sky, a metallic green dung beetle caught Kane's attention. It moved with purpose, steadily pushing a giant dung ball forward using its powerful front legs. As Kane lay face down in the dirt, he slowly opened his eyes, squinting at the insect nearby. His gaze fixated on the hornlike structure jutting from its head and the imposing spurs on its hind legs, marveling at its relentless determination.

Groaning, Kane rolled onto his back and extended his arm to shield his bloodshot eyes from the intensifying sunlight. Just then, he noticed a looming figure standing over him, their face obscured by the shadows cast by the morning sun, blocking his view.

"Get up," Victor's stern voice reverberated through Kane's haze. "Victor, is that you?" Kane responded groggily.

"Get the hell up," Victor retorted sharply, delivering a boot to Kane's ribs.

"Si, Si.... I'm up," Kane muttered, struggling to rise. He stumbled a few times before managing to stand.

"Don Morales wants to see you now. You were supposed to meet him at 8 am this morning, and he's not happy you missed it. Who the hell do you think you are, puta?" Victor snapped irritably, then turned and strode out of the cemetery toward the hacienda, wasting no more time on the hungover cowboy.

Rubbing his hands over his face, Kane struggled to wake up fully, grappling with his throbbing head and painfully dry mouth. Once on his feet, he shuffled toward the bunkhouse, desperate to clean up before meeting with Don Morales. His mouth felt as parched as the floor of a bird's cage, and he urgently needed water.

Pushing open the front door, Kane was greeted by Chico's amused gaze.

Chico paused what he was doing and let out a wolf-whistle at his disheveled drinking buddy. The other cowboys lounged around, wearing knowing smiles on their faces. "Well, look who finally showed up," Chico announced with a smirk.

"How are you feeling this morning, Princess?" he needled further.

Kane glared at him silently for a moment before responding

firmly, "Don't call me Princess."

"Why not.... you were crying like one last night," Chico teased, glancing around at the other cowboys for support in his jest.

"Just because I felt sad for Paco losing his life unnecessarily, and the way he died, the way I found him.... doesn't mean I'm a Princess. It means I have a heart. It was a tough night, and the alcohol brought out my sorrow," Kane defended himself.

"Leave him alone, Chico.... he's right. It was a sad day. I even got teary-eyed when Carlos sang that cowboy song. Come on, Amigo, admit it. There's nothing wrong with showing emotion for a comrade," Andy interjected, supporting Kane.

"Fair enough, peace, gringo. I was just messing with you. Come on in and clean up.... you've got a big meeting with the boss, and you don't want to keep him waiting," Chico conceded, motioning for Kane to enter the bunkhouse.

Kane sauntered over to his corner of the bunkhouse and began stripping off his filthy shirt, his behaviour despondent. He dipped his hands into the washbasin, scrubbing his upper body, face, and hands vigorously.

"What's the meeting with the boss all about?" Chico probed, sidling up to Kane. "He just wants to talk to me about a job," Kane replied flatly.

"What kind of job.... you think it's gonna pay extra?" Chico persisted, leaning casually against the wall.

"I don't know, Chico.... I'll find out when I speak with him. Now let me clean up. Don Morales is waiting," Kane retorted bluntly, brushing off the nosy cowboy.

As Kane crossed the dusty yard towards the hacienda, a whirlwind of emotions—anxiety, dread, and a strange excitement—surged through him.

He nervously fiddled with the buttons on his shirt, wiping

his sweaty palms on his pants.

Approaching Don Morales' office, he found the doors firmly shut. Standing before them, a million thoughts raced through his mind as he pondered what lay ahead. With butterflies fluttering in his stomach, he knocked twice and waited, the sound echoing faintly in the morning stillness.

Abruptly, the massive doors swung open, revealing Victor standing sternly in the doorway, his appearance cold and disapproving.

"Come in," he grumbled in a low, guttural voice. Kane passed by him and entered the room, where Don Morales lounged behind his imposing desk. The boss rolled a fat cigar between his lips, preparing to light it.

"Good afternoon, Senor Kane. Glad you could make it," Don Morales remarked sarcastically.

"It's still morning, Don Morales," Kane replied innocently, unaware of the sarcasm. "No, it's the afternoon, you fucking idiot," Victor interjected sharply.

"Don't you want this unique opportunity to make some real money?" Don Morales continued, his tone now mocking and challenging.

"Si, I do.... I drank too much Tequila last night and I'm not used to drinking, so it knocked me out. I apologize for my late arrival, jefe," Kane admitted, trying to sound contrite.

"Hmmpf.... Well, you're lucky I'm giving you a second chance," Don Morales grunted, his tone stern. "I usually punish disobedient men.... When I say be here at 8 am, I mean it. No exceptions. If you're late again, I WILL have you flogged. Victor would take great pleasure in it.... If you haven't already noticed, he doesn't like you, Senor Kane. He tells me you give him a bad feeling, that I shouldn't trust you.... Is he right?"

"No, Don Morales.... You can trust me. I just got carried away with the drinks last night, that's all," Kane pleaded earnestly to the intimidating crime lord.

Don Morales was a psychopath, notorious for his complete disregard for the law, his inability to feel remorse or guilt, and his penchant for savage behavior.

His name spread across the surrounding territory, becoming synonymous with volatility and brutal violence.

Years devoid of compassion and shame had plunged Don Morales' soul into an abyss from which there seemed no return. His upbringing under his father's merciless hand had shaped him into a cold and brutal leader by the age of 16. Over time, his soul seemed to be held in a dark pact with evil forces, akin to a property mortgaged to Satan—an immoral contract that would define him for life.

"I'll give you $500 now, and the rest when you return. Succeed, and there's more where that came from," Don Morales declared, handing over a substantial sum to Kane.

"Thank you, Don Morales. You can count on me. What's the job?" Kane affirmed eagerly, clutching the money.

"About a week's ride west to the 'Big Sky' ranch. Kevin Fisher and his crew stole fifty head of my cattle. Take him out," Don Morales ordered sternly.

"Si, comprendo," Kane replied, his resolve hardening.

"Do it quietly and without a fuss. Make it look like an accident. Once you're done, return. I'll send my men to retrieve my livestock from the ranch. Leave early tomorrow morning. Now go and soak your head, Senor. You look like something the cat dragged in."

As Kane approached the bunkhouse, he spotted Chico on the front porch, carving a small flute from wood.

"How did your meeting with the boss go?" Chico asked casually, not looking up from his work.

"Did he tear you a new one?" Chico continued, chuckling under his breath. "No, it's all good Chico. I'm leaving for the 'Big Sky' tomorrow morning," Kane affirmed.

"What? To round up stolen cattle by yourself? You, a greenhorn, herding cattle over hundreds of miles?" Chico scoffed.

"No, it's for something else.... I don't want to discuss it, Chico. I need to pack and prepare my horse," Kane brushed off the curious cowboy as he entered the bunkhouse.

"Something else? Do we have secrets now?" Chico's interest was aroused, and he followed Kane inside like an irritating odor.

"Hey, boys.... Kane's off to the 'Big Sky' all on his lonesome tomorrow morning," Chico announced to the other men in a pompous manner.

"And he's hiding a juicy secret," he persisted.

"Why are you heading to the 'Big Sky,' Kane?" Carlos inquired.

"Look, Don Morales has a job for me there, and he's made it clear I shouldn't talk about it, okay? His orders, not mine," Kane replied firmly.

"Oh, come on, Kane.... aren't we your compadres?" Chico persisted slithering up beside Kane, while he packed his things into a knapsack, carefully placing his sparse clothes on top of the discreetly hidden human skin book.

"Come on, Kane.... spill the beans," Chico goaded relentlessly, jabbing Kane in the back with each word.

"Stop it," Kane demanded.

"Why? Am I getting under your skin?" Chico persisted. "Just leave me alone," Kane implored.

"Tell me something, Kane. You've only been here a short while and now you're Don Morales' favorite pet.... off on secret missions. I bet he's paying you extra for that job. What about us? We deserve a piece of that action. I was the one who found out the cattle were stolen in the first place...,. where's my cut, puta?" Chico pressed. "Cabrear (piss off), Chico," Kane snarled, shoving the annoying, greedy man to the side, sending him sprawling on his backside.

"I'll sleep in the barn tonight," Kane muttered, grabbing his knapsack and storming out of the bunkhouse, slamming the door shut behind him.

In a daze, Chico glared at his comrades as they chuckled at his failed attempt to confront Kane, who towered over him and was twice his size. Determined to salvage his pride, Chico picked himself up off the ground and trailed after Kane, while the other wranglers shook their heads in disbelief.

"Don't do it, Chico. He's bigger than you, and it'll only lead to trouble!" Andy called out, but Chico paid no heed.

"We should go after him," Andy suggested urgently.

"No, he'll be fine. Chico can handle himself," Carlos asserted confidently.

Ten minutes passed and by the soft glow of a kerosene lantern Kane stood with his back to the barn door, He meticulously packed his saddle kit, ensuring the human skin book was carefully concealed at the bag's bottom. Draping the saddle rug over his horse, he began saddling up. Suddenly, Chico appeared in the doorway, standing motionless.

Kane sensed Chico's greedy gaze on him, despite not facing

him. Chico's facade exuded a threatening aura, his anger simmering dangerously. Kane focused on buckling the saddle and fitting the bridle onto his loyal steed, unfazed by Chico's presence.

"I thought you to leaving in the morning, puta," Chico yelled harshly from across the barn.

"Running off with all that money you stashed earlier? I want my cut—50/50, fair and square," he insisted, nagging.

"I'm not giving you a dime, Chico," Kane replied flatly.

"You will," Chico demanded, advancing into the barn, slowly drawing his gun and leveling it at Kane.

"Is this what you want, Chico? Bloodshed over a few dollars?" Kane reasoned, approaching his assailant step by deliberate step.

"Back off, you Chinese bastard. It's not just a few dollars. I saw you cram a fistful of money into your precious pack. I could shoot you right now and take it all. That's your choice," Chico threatened, his grip tightening menacingly on the gun.

"Calm down, Chico. Here.... I'll give you some of the money. I just need to get it from my satchel, okay?" Kane said soothingly as he systematically walked back to his horse. He rummaged through his bag and eventually pulled out a fistful of cash.

Raising it up over his head so Chico could see it clearly, Kane motioned for him to come closer to the stable.

"Come and get your money!" Kane beckoned, his voice sharp and commanding. "No tricks, puta," Chico warned, his eyes narrowed with suspicion as he approached the stall cautiously, his gaze locked onto the cash.

Kane felt his inner demon stirring, gradually rising to the surface as his anger simmered just beneath, transforming his natural brown eyes into an onyx black, shiny and impenetrable. With the gun firmly pointed at Kane, Chico walked confidently over, extending his hand to receive the payoff.

"Give it to me," Chico demanded, clicking back the hammer. But as Kane moved closer, Chico caught a glimpse of his cold, subhuman eyes and the heinous demon within. The monster's intense glare burned with a hypnotic fury, freezing Chico in his tracks.

Without realizing what was happening, Kane thrust his massive hand forward with tremendous force, his rage rising like a phoenix. The blow struck Chico square in the throat, squeezing his windpipe, intent on choking him out.

Chico immediately clutched at his neck, desperately wheezing for air, while Kane seized the gun with his other hand, ripping it from Chico's grasp.

Before the gun could fire, Chico collapsed to his knees, gazing up at Kane, who loomed over him with an obscene grin plastered across his face. As Chico tried to curse Kane, the words choked in his mutilated throat, only a feeble whisper escaping his lips.

"Damn you, demonio," Chico faintly whispered. With one last desperate act, he grabbed the kerosene lantern from its hinge and hurled it at Kane, hoping it would burst into flames and burn the son of a bitch.

Kane reacted instantly, deflecting the lantern with a powerful swipe of his arm. The projectile veered off course and smashed into pieces on the ground. Fuel gurgled out onto the hay, and the lantern's minuscule flame erupted into a blazing inferno.

As the inferno raged, enveloping the barn, Kane swung a brutal punch at Chico's face, knocking him out cold. With Chico lying helpless in the growing flames, Kane calmly grabbed the reins of his horse and strode out of the barn without a second thought. Mounting up, he felt a finality settle over him, knowing there was no return once he left the ranch.

A mile to the west, Kane turned his horse to look back. The barn blazed like a beacon in the pitch-black night, its flames illuminating the surroundings. He saw tiny figures scurrying frantically, desperately hauling buckets of water in a futile attempt to douse the fire. Kane sneered at their hopeless efforts, then spurred his horse into the murky wasteland, the distant screams echoing in his ears as he vanished into the night.

Chapter 14

Kane's stomach growled in defiance, protesting the lack of proper food after days of subsisting on dust-covered biscuits and beef jerky. As he began his journey across the winding sand dunes, the restlessness from the chaos he left behind at the ranch spurred him on. The urgency to escape Don Morales's reach drove him to travel swiftly, determined to put as much distance as possible between himself and his past.

Heading north, Kane calculated that the posse sent after him would likely assume he headed west towards the "Big Sky," the more familiar route.

As he studied the crude, hand-drawn map that Don Morales had provided to reach the "Big Sky," he couldn't help but feel that heading north, in the opposite direction, seemed more promising. It offered a glimmer of hope for finding civilization—or at least that was his desperate hope.

A swirling dust devil whipped across the brutal landscape, drawing Kane's gaze skyward. The sun beat down mercilessly, forcing him to squint as he scanned the horizon for any landmark to guide him. In the distance, a faint blue outline of mountains began to materialize, a remote promise of refuge amongst the desolation. Five days had passed without sight of another soul or creature. Kane's water supply dwindled dangerously low, the relentless thirst clawing at him. Earlier, he thought he glimpsed the imposing paw prints of a desert bobcat, or perhaps it was a hallucination—a mirage dancing amidst the hoof prints chiseled in the sand by unseen devils. The parched wasteland seemed to erase all traces of life, leaving only an unforgiving expanse of bone-dry terrain and death. The occasional spiny cactus offered no relief as Kane licked his cracked lips, tasting the faint memory of his last biscuit, a fleeting reminder of the civilization he desperately sought.

Taking notice of his horse's fatigue, Kane dismounted swiftly. He removed the saddle pack from its flank and tossed it over his shoulder, hoping to ease its load. Suddenly, the animal violently reared up, pulling the reins taut in Kane's hands, its behavior unexpected and alarming in the barren wilderness.

"Woah, boy.... what's got you so spooked?" Kane murmured, attempting to soothe the agitated horse. But his efforts were futile—the animal continued to pull backward, its hooves slipping in the unstable sand, desperately seeking solid ground.

After a minute of pointless struggle, Kane reluctantly released the reins. He watched in dismay as the horse bolted off in the direction they had just come from, bridle still attached, disappearing into the hazy, mirage-like distance.

"This is just great," Kane sighed in despair. Lacking a clear plan, he let the saddle fall to the ground where he stood. With a resigned shake of his head, he turned and began the long, arduous hike toward the distant, obscured mountain range ahead.

The elements became Kane's adversaries, each step a grueling marathon in the relentless desert heat. The sun bore down on him, scraping his skin like sandpaper, while the scorching ground seared the soles of his boots. Despite the protection of a large sombrero shielding his sun-beaten head, his eyes stung from the glare and his tongue felt glued to the roof of his mouth, every breath thick with the dry, leathery sensations of dehydration. Each thought was consumed by the constant battle against the elements, every movement a testament to his enduring will to press onward through the punishing landscape.

"What are you doing?" A soft, ethereal voice resonated in Kane's mind.

"Lady Vixen?" Kane shouted out, spinning around frantically to scan the empty surroundings.

"Why aren't you changing? Your powers will get you to the mountains sooner," the voice urged gently.

"I don't have the energy, my Lady.... I feel very weak," Kane confessed aloud, his words tinged with desperation and fatigue.

"Look up.... there is smoke rising in the distance. Go to the signal and you will find what you need," Lady Vixen crooned reassuringly.

"It looks so far away.... I don't know if I'll make it," Kane lamented.

"What is your alternative? Do it or you will die here.... is that your destiny?" Lady Vixen's voice pressed with urgency.

"I just need water," Kane groaned, casting his eyes skyward to see a dozen vultures circling ominously above.

"Well, that's not a good sign. Now I know I AM dying," Kane chuckled ironically, his humor tinged with surrender.

"Follow the insects," Lady Vixen instructed calmly, her guidance a signal of hope in the desolate wilderness.

"What? What insects?" Kane blurted out, incredulous at the seemingly absurd suggestion. But suddenly, a low buzzing sound filled the air, growing louder by the second. Kane's heart pounded with harrowing panic as he realized a large swarm of bees was heading straight towards him.

Instinctively, Kane raised his arms and stretched out his hands, bracing for the stinging onslaught. But to his astonishment, as the swarm approached, it encircled his body twice, buzzing around him in a vortex. Then, just as suddenly as they had appeared, the bees veered off, flying in the direction of the mountains. They whirled periodically in the sky, creating a mesmerizing mini-tornado.

Kane stood dumbfounded, watching the bees swirling into the distance. A mix of awe and confusion washed over him as he pondered the strange encounter and Lady Vixen's cryptic guidance. With renewed determination fueled by this mysterious sign, Kane set his course towards the distant mountains, following the path the bees had shown him.

"Follow the insects.... you will find water," Lady Vixen's command rang in Kane's mind. He closed his eyes and delved deep within, connecting with his inner "Chi." With amplified exhales, he centered himself, drawing strength from within.

Resuming his arduous journey towards the mountains, Kane fixed his gaze on the massive cluster of insects buzzing ahead, as instructed. Each step forward was fueled by his boldness and the belief that following this unusual guidance would lead him to the water he so desperately needed.

* * *

In weary silence, Alejandro, Gideon, Miko, Juji, and Hiro rode through the ranch boundary gates, their eyes drawn to the charred remnants of the once bustling barn, now reduced to smoldering ruins. Each man struggled to comprehend the devastation before them, grappling with the unsettling realization of what had transpired.

As they reached the veranda of the hacienda, Alejandro wasted no time. He dismounted swiftly, his boots hitting the ground with purpose as he raced towards Don Morales' office. With a forceful knock, he demanded entry, leaving the rest of the monks to gather themselves after their arduous journey through the unforgiving desert.

"That looks like it was a big building," Miko murmured quietly as he helped Gideon dismount.

"Hai, and I have a feeling that Kane had something to do with it," Gideon responded, his voice tinged with suspicion.

While the monks began to organize their belongings, Hiro surveyed the immediate surroundings. His keen eyes caught sight of Mexican wranglers standing stoically on the front porch of their bunkhouse, observing the newcomers with guarded expressions.

Turning to face them, Hiro placed his arms by his sides and bowed respectfully—a gesture of courtesy and acknowledgment. The wranglers remained unmoved, except for Andy, who nonchalantly expelled a glob of chewing tobacco juice onto the ground with a look of arrogance.

The tension in the air was obvious, a silent exchange of scrutiny and unspoken challenges amidst the backdrop of the ranch's unsettling aftermath.

Hiro held his gaze on the Mexican wranglers for another tense moment before Gideon's voice broke through, urging him to gather their belongings and join the others inside the hacienda. Gideon's tone carried a clear warning, reminding Hiro of the importance of maintaining respect and avoiding any trouble during their stay.

"Don't cause any problems with the Mexicans or embarrass me while we're here, Master Hiro.... we are guests and must show respect do you understand?"

Gideon's words were firm, reflecting his understanding of Hiro's impulsive and defiant nature.

Reluctantly leaving the confrontation behind, Hiro followed Gideon's instructions, joining the other monks in the hacienda's foyer. They marveled at the intricate Mexican-styled decor around them, from vibrant terracotta pots adorned with geometric patterns to meticulously crafted ceramic figurines and candle holders on wooden shelves.

The foyer led into a long hallway that extended towards a leafy courtyard, described as Don Morales's sanctuary within the house. Here, the wealthy ranchero entertained infrequent guests and found solace amongst the lush greenery, all while maintaining his privacy.

At the end of the hallway loomed a stark contrast: a desolate bear's head mounted above a robust brick fireplace, its presence casting a shadow over the otherwise warm and inviting atmosphere of the hacienda. The monks waited expectantly, their curiosity spiked as they anticipated the grandeur of Don Morales's office doors opening before them.

"Hey, Juji.... I wish that was Kane's head up there with that lifeless gaze," Hiro chuckled, nudging Juji's arm and gesturing towards the bear's head above the fireplace.

"Have you ever seen Kane fully transform into the demon?" Juji whispered, leaning in closer.

"No.... but I've seen the trail of carnage he's left behind," Hiro replied solemnly. "Then how do you know it's true? I mean, we've only heard about his skin changing, but none of us have actually seen it.... How do we know it's real?" Juji asked in a hushed tone, his curiosity tinged with skepticism.

"It is true.... Look at Master Gideon's mutilated face, Hiro snapped, frustration evident in his voice.

"What could do that? He didn't inflict those wounds upon himself. And Gideon wouldn't abandon the monastery and the safety of his homeland for something trivial. The monastery is his sanctuary. Kane murdered the Abbot right in front of him. That's why he's so determined to hunt down the demon and make him pay for his sins....

It's about honor and justice. Master Gideon has witnessed Kane's transformation; he doesn't lie."

Hiro's words carried a weight of conviction, his answer hard as he addressed Juji's doubts.

Overhearing their conversation, Miko turned towards the mounted bear head and walked down the hallway, captivated by its imposing presence. He stood beneath it, spellbound by the creature's fierce appearance. The bear's mouth was frozen in a snarl, its lips curled to reveal menacing fangs, a testament to its eternal anguish.

Gideon appeared silently beside Miko, his gaze fixed on the mummified beast above them.

"Do you think Kane resembles this when he fully transforms into the demon bear?" Miko asked softly, his eyes still locked on the animal's imposing visage.

"No, Master Miko, Kane is far worse. This bear was born of nature, created by the Divine as a creature of this world with the potential for enlightenment. Kane, on the other hand, is not of this earth. His potential lies only in darkness," Gideon responded sternly, his voice tinged with a deep understanding of the situation.

"I remember him from our days at the monastery when we were children. I'm six years younger than Kane, and despite everything, he was always kind to me," Miko reminisced.

"Once, when I was feeling sad and lonely, he cheered me up with a funny story and even gave me a bread roll he had saved for himself. He had a gift for making me feel better. It's hard to believe that we're now hunting down the same boy I once admired and considered my closest friend," Miko said, his voice filled with disillusionment and sorrow.

"You're not boys anymore. Unfortunately, Kane has chosen his path, and he must be held accountable for the destruction and pain he has caused," Gideon questioned sternly, turning to face Miko squarely.

"Look at me and answer me honestly!" Gideon demanded firmly.

"Hai, Master Gideon.... I will do whatever it takes," Miko replied with determination, meeting Gideon's gaze.

"You must remember this, my son," Gideon continued, his voice serious and paternal.

"Kane is no longer your friend. He is an unholy entity capable of great harm. His Buddhist faith is lost, and with each passing day, he grows stronger and more corrupted. Do not let sentimentality cloud your judgment, Master Miko. If you ever face Kane, you must use all your strength to stop him."

"But I'm just a steward, Master Gideon," Miko interjected, his tone tinged with uncertainty.

"How can I confront Kane, a trained ninja and a demonic force? My training in ninjutsu basics is limited. What chance do I have?"

Gideon placed a reassuring hand on Miko's shoulder. "Your commitment to the monastery's teachings has prepared you more than you realize, Miko. Trust in your training and in the principles of justice and protection. You carry the wisdom of our order within you. If and when the time comes, you will find the strength you need. Don't worry.... you'll always have your brothers beside you," Gideon reassured with conviction, his voice steady and reassuring.

But Miko remained unconvinced.

Behind the closed office doors, Don Morales vented his disapproval to Alejandro about the latest recruits brought back to the ranch.

"Why do you keep bringing me more of these 'Jonnies'? The last one burnt down my barn and murdered Chico. They're nothing but bad luck. I've lost two valuable wranglers since you brought that bastardo Kane into my home!" Don Morales hollered, punctuating his frustration with puffs on his thick cigar.

"Por favor, Senor Morales. These monks are hunting Senor Kane too. He murdered one of their priests back in Japan. They have been stalking him since the beginning. They know him better than anyone and they know what he's capable of. Plus, they are proficient in the same martial arts as Kane.... if anyone has the skills to catch him, it's them, Senor Jefe," Alejandro pleaded urgently, his voice betraying his fear of Don Morales' wrath as he almost fell to his knees.

"Their leader is a high priest, Jefe. His name is Gideon. He has battled Kane before and bears deep scars on his face to prove it. They are good, holy men who only want Kane to pay for what he's done.... that's what we want as well, si?" Alejandro continued, hoping to sway Don Morales.

"Don't tell me what I want, puta," Don Morales retorted sharply, his tone softened slightly as he considered Alejandro's words. He turned to Victor, seeking his agreement and nod of acknowledgment.

"Si, si jefe.... it's fate, really. They found me in San Francisco, not the other way around. Hiro was in the sheriff's lockup when I visited, where I often find recruits, and the others just followed. When I mentioned Kane to Gideon, he explained why they're here in America," Alejandro pressed on, his words carrying a sense of reasoning.

Don Morales stared at Alejandro for what felt like an eternity, his gaze cold and penetrating as he silently weighed the situation. Finally, he spoke.

"Esta bien (Alright) you're off the hook this time, Alejandro. Consider yourself lucky.

But if you EVER bring back any more 'Jonnies,' I will string you up in the forest and let the crows eat your eyes, comprendes?" Don Morales's threat was clea.

"Si, comprendo.... gracias, jefe," Alejandro replied meekly, showing extreme compliance.

"Victor, bring in the high priest. I want to speak with him alone. Alejandro, take the rest of the monks to the guest cabin past the courtyard, away from my men's sight. They're angry enough and ready to kill anyone who even vaguely resembles a monk," Don Morales instructed sternly.

Victor moved toward the office doors with Alejandro close behind him, eager to leave the presence of his unpredictable boss.

Bursting open like a volcanic eruption, Victor violently swung the heavy doors wide, only to confront Gideon standing resolutely before him. Both hands gripped his majestic staff, Gideon's presence startled the imposing brute.

"Don Morales will see you now," he declared in his usual deep monotone voice, masking any hint of fear.

Gideon strode through the doors, drifting past Victor as if on a cloud, his team trailing behind. But Victor swiftly intervened, his enormous arm blocking Miko, Hiro, and Juji. "Only the high priest. Alejandro will show the rest of you to your quarters," he droned on, slamming the doors shut in their faces.

"Welcome, high priest. I've been told your name is Gideon?" Don Morales announced, rising to offer his hand to Gideon. However, the monk respectfully declined, bowing instead and keeping a firm grip on his staff.

"What? Aren't you man enough to shake my hand, or do you think you're too high and mighty to bother?" Don Morales complained, feeling insulted by Gideon's apparent lack of respect.

"Your anger is self-indulgent, Don Morales. I take my celibacy seriously and refrain from all physical contact as part of my religious commitment. I understand this may cause discomfort to you, but it is a matter of my faith. I apologize if this offends,"

Gideon explained calmly.

"Lo que sea (whatever). I will never understand you foreigners. You're in our country now and should follow our ways but if you want to act like a puta (bitch) at our first

meeting, then that's your problem," Don Morales seethed, his frustration evident. "There's a certain pleasure in fault-finding. People often defend their anger, justify it, even nurture it. In our Buddhist practice, we cultivate Metta—loving-kindness devoid of selfish attachment. Anger, if allowed to fester, poisons the body. For your own well-being, Don Morales, it's best to let it go."

"Well, you're not extending your Metta to Kane, are you, high priest? I hear you want him destroyed just as much as I do."

"Kane viciously murdered our Abbot taking a life leads to hell and the realm of

hungry shadows. Even the smallest consequence is a shortened lifespan. Ideally, we'd return Kane to Japan alive, but as a powerful and dangerous demon, our only option may be destruction. So yes, Don Morales, we share a common goal."

"I see the scars on your face; he's clearly done damage."

"Yes, he has. But I'm not defeated. We will destroy that foul creature."

"How did this all begin, and what is Kane? From your description, he's clearly not human."

"You have no idea.... May I sit so we can discuss the details?"

"Si, Si.... Take a seat," Don Morales eagerly agreed, curious about Gideon's revelations.

* * *

Alejandro guided the trio of monks down the hallway, passing by the mounted bear head that marked their path toward the rear of the hacienda. Beyond the high walls awaited a secluded oasis, a haven for contemplation or afternoon siestas, and a gathering place for occasional friends to revel and dine. The courtyard, lush with plants, provided a serene slice of nature amidst the surrounding barren landscape, offering cool respite from the scorching mid-day sun. It was an open-air sanctuary, blending the comforts of indoors with the elements: sunlight and moonlight streaming through, the gentle murmur of fountains mingling with distant calls of eagles and coyotes.

Stepping into the cabin, the men took in its simple yet inviting interior. They promptly placed their bags on neatly made beds, eager to sink into the soft pillows and find comfort in much-needed rest.

"This is where you'll be staying.... and don't come out unless requested to. I'll bring you a jug of water," Alejandro affirmed with a stern tone.

"What? Are we prisoners here?" Hiro blurted out, his frustration evident. "No.... it's for your own safety. The ranchers are out for your blood after what's

happened. Just follow the rules, and everything will be fine," Alejandro declared firmly.

"We haven't harmed your ranchers or anyone here. Why are we being treated like criminals?" Hiro continued to protest, his voice rising.

"To my companions, you're one of them.... a *'Jonnie.'* Right now, you're despised. Don Morales has chosen to host you as his guests, a privilege few receive. So, let it be and obey," Alejandro challenged, his hand subtly resting on his gun, sensing Hiro's growing agitation.

"Kore wa detaramedesu (This is bullshit)" Hiro cursed under his breath.

"What did you say to me, *'Jonnie'*? Are you cursing at me?" Alejandro demanded sternly, clicking back the hammer of his gun as a warning.

"My name is not 'Jonnie.' It's—"

"Shut up for once in your life. Just do as the man asks," Miko unexpectedly interjected, frustrated and annoyed at Hiro's defiance and the escalating tension. "Your younger brother is smarter than you, *'Jonnie.'* Pay attention to what he says. I'll leave the water at the door," Alejandro concluded sharply, then turned and walked back through the courtyard.

Juji, Miko, and Hiro stood in tense silence, exchanging looks of suspicion and contempt.

"I am your elder, Master Miko. Do not speak to me with such disrespect ever again," Hiro scorned, but Miko remained silent. Slowly, he removed his bags and placed them on the floor. He lay down on the bed, facing away from the others, staring blankly at the wall until he drifted into a deep sleep.

From the tranquil depths of the dreamscape emerged a majestic owl, its wings adorned in vivid colours of pink and white, shimmering like butterfly wings in motion. As the owl glided past Miko, he was drawn to its large green eyes, and in an instant, he found himself transported into the owl's perspective, gazing down upon a cradle of dark earth below.

There, he witnessed a snake slithering across the blackened ground, leaving behind a trail of crimson liquid that resembled blood. A deep sense of unease gripped Miko's heart as he soared onward through the dreamscape.

Flying further, Miko encountered a small boy who shared his view of the world. The owl, embodying Miko, questioned the boy about his intentions toward animals and humans. Tears welled in the boy's eyes as he fled to the banks of a clear stream, where fish danced joyfully in the water. Observing the boy seated by the riverbank, Miko descended gracefully, landing beside him.

"Why do you cry?" the owl gently inquired.

"There are lives that feel like nightmares, yet they are the only path to a heavenly victory, and it seems your life could be one of those," the boy sobbed.

"What do you mean?"

"We were brothers once.... do you remember? We laughed and sang, sneaking into the monastery kitchen for cake.... we were innocent, unaware of what lay ahead." "Kane? Is that you?" The owl responded, a note of disturbance in its voice.

"You may not realize it, but you are a warrior. Your destiny is to fight the good fight, to bear necessary suffering so others may have secure lives, and be well. You are brave and virtuous and not aware of what's in stall for your future, unlike me....

I have changed into someone else, and I can't stop it," the boy wept, clutching a macabre book as if trying to choke it.

"What are you holding?" the owl asked softly.

"My heritage it's not from this world.... I never wanted this. You're blessed to be

normal," he continued, his voice heavy with sorrow.

"It's alright, Kane.... I'm still your brother," the owl comforted, but suddenly the boy's face contorted, transforming into a bear's head with blood-dripping canine fangs.

It growled fiercely in a deep, guttural voice.

"NOT ANYMORE!" It snapped, narrowly missing the owl's face.

"Miko, Miko wake up!" Juji shouted urgently, shaking his brother's shoulders to

rouse him.

"No, no, no!" Miko cried out, jolting awake with a sense of dread, beads of sweat forming on his brow.

"You were screaming Are you alright? It was just a nightmare," Juji reassured him,

his voice filled with worry.

"What time is it and where is Master Gideon?" Miko asked urgently, still shaken from the vivid nightmare of his head being bitten off.

"You've been asleep for three hours, and Master Gideon is still with Don Morales," Juji replied calmly.

"What? He's been in that office for three hours? Has anyone checked if he's okay?" Miko questioned, concern evident in his voice.

"We're not allowed to leave, and Master Gideon can handle himself, Miko. They have a lot to discuss. Here Alejandro brought us some water. Have a drink; you must be

thirsty after our long trip," Juji said, offering the jug of water to his brother.

* * *

An eagle screeched overhead as Alejandro and his comrades

gathered on the shady porch of their bunkhouse, deep in heated debate over the latest developments.

Like the birds soaring in the endless blue sky, they too were scorched by the relentless sun.

The brutal heat weighed heavily on the men, casting a haunting pall over the forsaken landscape. Everything in this desolate place seemed to be tainted with cruelty, distortion, and a sense of damnation.

Upon Alejandro's return, the men briefed him on recent events. They recounted how Chico had chased Kane for the money owed from a job at the "Big Sky," only to meet a brutal end at Kane's hands.

They recounted how Kane had set fire to the barn, trying to obliterate all traces of his crime. They also described how Kane had discovered Paco's body, desecrated by crows and vultures, and brought it back to the ranch.

"We held a proper funeral for him," Carlos said solemnly.

Alejandro, in turn, revealed that the group of monks he had brought back were on a mission to capture Kane for a gruesome murder he committed in Japan. He made it clear that they all shared a common goal: to apprehend Kane and deliver justice.

However, Alejandro sadly emphasized that they were dealing with more than just an ordinary human being, emphasising the grave warning issued by High Priest Gideon.

Alejandro looked up to see Don Morales and Victor approaching their bunkhouse, an unusual sight since the boss rarely left his hacienda.

"Amigos, I trust you've been briefed on the situation," Don Morales began without preamble.

"I've had extensive discussions with High Priest Gideon, and we've agreed to join forces to hunt down Kane. They have specialized knowledge of this demon-man, and we can leverage that to our advantage. Kane has taken lives, stolen from me, and razed my property. We will collaborate on this." His voice carried a firm resolve. "I do not.... and I repeat.... I do not want any trouble from you with those monks.

They are my guests and will be treated as such. COMPRENDER?" Don Morales's directive was sharp and uncompromising, with Victor standing steadfastly at his side. "Si, jefe no trouble here," Carlos affirmed, raising his hands in a gesture of

compliance, followed by the others nodding in agreement.

"Good. Tonight, you will host a BBQ for the junior monks while I dine with the High Priest in the hacienda. Remember, Amigos.... they are my guests," Don Morales concluded firmly, pointing a finger in the air as a stern reminder. With that, he turned and walked back towards the house, Victor trailing behind him.

It was approaching 9 PM, and the night sky unfolded in picturesque splendor.

A seamless transition from black to navy provided the backdrop for a full moon, its radiant sandy-white surface adorned with a gossamer glow. The moon loomed large, casting its light across the clear heavens, where stars stretched infinitely.

The three monks stood beneath this celestial spectacle, gazing up at the blanket of stars that seemed to go on forever. Nearby, the wranglers tended to the BBQ, flames licking the grills and sending savory aromas wafting across the paddocks. The sizzle of cooking meat and the sharp scent of onions frying teased their senses, causing their stomachs to rumble in anticipation.

They could almost feel their mouths watering at the thought of the salty meats, generously slathered with BBQ sauces, infused with chili and cayenne pepper.

In the midst of this appetizing scene, Miko approached Alejandro, his manner cautious but determined, ready to engage in conversation.

"Mr. Alejandro, we're so grateful for this meal your friends are preparing, but just a small detail—we're actually vegetarians. Meat isn't really our thing," Miko explained politely.

"Okay, we've got plenty of veggies to grill. Will that work for you?" Alejandro responded obligingly. However, nearby, Carlos overheard the conversation and couldn't resist his usual cheeky antics. He swiftly grabbed a homemade sausage, zipped down his fly, and tucked one end into his pants, letting the rest hang out, mimicking his private parts. With a mischievous grin, he approached Miko, the raw meat dangling conspicuously.

"Don't you love meat, young monk? How about my 'piece' of meat? Does this turn you on?" Carlos jeered, his words dripping with contempt as he punctuated them with a mocking laugh. The other wranglers joined in, their sniggers amplifying the ridicule.

Suddenly, Hiro exploded in fury, launching himself at Carlos with lightning speed, closing the distance until he was mere inches away.

"How dare you insult and humiliate my young brother! You have no honor, no

self-restraint! Your mind reeks of depravity and vulgarity, your ego spiraling out of control," Hiro roared, each word punctuated with a spit that peppered Carlos' face. "If you ever degrade or belittle him again, I will end you.... slowly," Hiro screamed, his voice filled with venomous promise.

"Vete a la mierda, puta! (fuck off bitch)" Carlos yelled back, shoving Hiro with such force that it staggered him.

Without a moment's pause, Hiro sprang to his feet, retreating briefly before charging back with breathtaking agility. With a sudden leap, he launched himself into the air, feet aimed unerringly at Carlos' throat and stomach, delivering punishing blows with lethal precision.

The impact was brutal; a sickening crunch vibrated through the air as Carlos was sent hurtling backwards, crashing to the ground like a collapsing building. Gripping his throat, his screams turned to gasps of agony as the excruciating pain seared through him.

"STOP IT.... STOP IT!!" Miko's cry pierced through the chaos, his voice trembling with urgency as he grabbed Hiro's arm while he loomed fiercely over his adversary. Alejandro hurried to Carlos's side, attempting to assist him, but Carlos's pain was too intense. He waved Alejandro off with one hand, clutching his stomach with the other. "What the hell are you doing?" Alejandro exclaimed in frustration.

"Don Morales expressly warned us not to fight amongst ourselves, and now look at this mess. You're a damn fool, Carlos! Don't you get it? These monks don't understand our Mexican humor."

Alejandro's words were as much a defense of his friend as they were a plea to Hiro to reconsider.

"And you don't understand our faith, our values, or our honor because you don't practice any of those righteous things in your life," Hiro seethed at Alejandro, his voice tinged with resentment.

"ENOUGH OF THIS INSANITY!" Miko's voice cut through the tension like a knife. "We have a bigger problem at hand.... Have you forgotten about Kane? We need to work together, not tear each other apart. Do you want him to escape justice? If we destroy ourselves, he wins," Miko pleaded, his distress evident.

"I've lost my appetite, Mr. Alejandro.... I'm going back to the cabin to wait for Master Gideon," Miko declared suddenly, his decision final as he turned away, leaving the arguing men behind.

Meanwhile, Don Morales and Gideon lounged comfortably in the grand dining room, savoring Pulque, a ceremonial drink reserved for esteemed guests, as they discussed various topics over dinner, including their strategy to apprehend Kane.

"He's got a three-day head start on us," Don Morales remarked thoughtfully.

"Do you have any inkling which direction he might have taken? This is your territory, Don Morales; you know these desert lands better than anyone," Gideon inquired.

"I dispatched him to the 'Big Sky' for a task. Given that he knows civilization lies to the west, my suspicion is he's headed in that direction. Come daybreak, I'll send Carlos and Alejandro to track him down tomorrow. I'll need some men to remain here to safeguard the cattle and the ranch," Don Morales explained, outlining his plan. "How long has Kane been here?" Gideon asked, seeking clarity on the timeframe. "Several months.... perhaps four," Don Morales replied, providing insight into Kane's occupancy in the area.

"It's maddening how I was worried that Kane had traveled

too far during our voyage to America, but here we are.... and he's only three days ahead of us after all. We've been blessed. Anyway, Hiro, Juji, Miko, and I will join your posse," Gideon declared. "The desert heat is relentless, Gideon as you already know. It's a bone-dry expanse of death. Are you sure you want to endure it? With all due respect, you're no spring chicken," Don Morales cautioned, his voice heavy with unease.

"I may be old, but I've survived far worse. No one escapes aging and death. We will unite our forces. When one conducts himself by the Dhamma—in body, speech, and mind—a man's life is celebrated for his righteous deeds on earth and rejoiced in heaven after death. Ending Kane's satanic existence is my sacred duty, for Divinity and for my Abbot. I will be fine, Don Morales. Thank you for your concern," Gideon affirmed, a rigig determination in his eyes. He then smiled and excused himself from the table, bowing respectfully to his host.

"Thank you, Don Morales.... this was an exceptionally productive evening. I will see you in the morning," he concluded, his voice steady as he slowly made his way through the doors and toward the cabin.

Opening the door of their designated cabin, Gideon found Miko sitting alone on his bed, his posture heavy with dispirited solitude.

"What's troubling you, my son?" he inquired.

"It's nothing, Master Gideon. I guess I'm tired," Miko replied, his voice heavy with fatigue.

"Hai.... it's been a long journey from our homeland in Japan. Rest now, Master Miko. We still have much to accomplish. Early tomorrow morning, we head west towards a ranch called the 'Big Sky.' That's where Don Morales believes Kane is heading." "Will you be coming with us?" Miko asked, laying his head down on the pillow.

"Of course.... it's my responsibility. Plus, I have you and your brothers to look after me," Gideon smiled, trying to reassure him.

"Where are your brothers now?"

"They are with the Mexicans," Miko answered. "Well, it's time they returned," Gideon said firmly.

"Master Gideon?" Miko continued, a note of concern in his voice.

"Hai… what is it?" Gideon asked, turning from the door. He walked over to Miko, bending down to sit on the edge of his bed, his posture open and attentive, ready to listen.

"Earlier, I fell asleep and had this terrifying nightmare and it was all about Kane.

It has left me feeling empty, cold, and petrified about what's coming," Miko confessed, his voice trembling.

"Master Miko, there's no need to feel scared. Tell me about your dream," Gideon urged, believing that talking about it would help. He placed his hand on Miko's shoulder, trying to offer reassurance.

"Well.... I was this big owl, and I saw a small boy, and it was Kane " Miko began,

his voice trailing off as he recalled the nightmare. Suddenly, Gideon's head jolted backward, his eyes widening in shock. He stared blankly at the ceiling, the intense rush of unholy depictions from Miko's dream flooding his soul.

He could see a deluge of spectres and demons gyrating above him, each decayed and mutilated, their disfigured faces swirling around, then rushing toward him with merciless agility as they entered his head, their endless spine-chilling screams echoing in his brain. The room dimmed, and Gideon saw Kane in human form emerge from the darkest corner, grasping the macabre, skinned book. Perched on his shoulder was a human-faced rat, and beside him stood a beautiful woman on one side and a snake-hipped crowman on the other. The trio of skin-changing evil stared at Gideon with menace, brooding and threatening, their eyes filled with dark

intent. They tried to intimidate him with their presence, and then Kane abruptly spoke.

"You sacrifice your brothers, and for what? I am eternal and unyielding. I have become the very thing you fear. Do not underestimate my power to destroy you, and do not call upon your gods for help, for they fear me as well. Foolish old man, turn back and go home," Kane warned, his voice dropping into a low, menacing growl.

The crowman's razor-sharp beak snapped through the air with a violent snap, amplifying the threat in Kane's words.

Gideon's pulse raced like a speeding train, the pressure of his erratic heart forcing its way to the pit of his throat, where it became lodged. Clutching his chest, he began taking rapid, shallow breaths, as if he couldn't get enough oxygen. His skin turned ghostly pale, resembling a canvas painted with whitewash, and even his lips seemed to disappear.

Suddenly, he tumbled off the side of the bed, landing in a heap on the floor. Miko jumped up, attempting to break his fall, but it was too late. Gideon lay at the foot of his bed, writhing and crying out in pain.

"MASTER GIDEON, WHAT'S WRONG? HELP ME, SOME-ONE HELP, HELP!" Miko

screamed repeatedly, kneeling beside his beloved master,

trying desperately to comfort him.

"Kane...." Gideon muttered with difficulty.

Walking down the hallway toward the cabin, Hiro and Juji heard Miko's desperate cries for help. They rushed to his side, bursting through the door with urgency, and instantly saw Gideon lying on the floor, with Miko cradling his head.

"What happened?" Hiro demanded, his voice edged with anxiety.

"I don't know.... One minute we were talking, and when he touched my shoulder, he went into this trance. Then he collapsed. He kept staring at that corner over there, like he was hypnotized, and then he became sick. We need a doctor immediately," Miko explained urgently.

"Has he spoken since the attack?" Hiro pressed on.

"He just whispered Kane's name when he was on the floor," Miko informed them, his voice filled with distress.

"I'll go see Don Morales and try to get medical help," Juji decided, rushing out the door.

"Is he still breathing?" Hiro asked urgently.

"Hai, but he's struggling. Where will they find a doctor out here? None of these ranch hands are trained for this. Master Gideon might not make it," Miko fretted.

"Calm down Surely Don Morales has a plan for emergencies like this. He's been

here a long time," Hiro attempted to reassure.

"Do you really believe that, Hiro? None of these uncivilized wranglers have the skills of a doctor. We're stranded out here, and my master is dying!" Miko cried, tears welling up in his eyes. Just then, Juji and Victor burst through the door.

"We need a doctor urgently," Miko pleaded.

"Everything will be fine," Victor said soothingly, moving toward Gideon.

"But who's going to help Master Gideon?" Miko continued, his voice trembling.

"I will Move aside.... I'm a doctor," Victor stated calmly, surprising the three monks.

They exchanged bewildered glances, stunned by the unexpected revelation.

Chapter 15

An aged medicine man, adorned in intricate body paint, hopped and danced around a blazing fire. His posture leaned forward as he lifted his knees high and stomped them down, kicking up puffs of dry dust. With a fearful shriek, he pounded a drum strapped to his thigh and rattled the tail of a dead rattlesnake, its scales shaking like a maraca.

Kane lay motionless beside the fire, slowly awakening from his deep trance. As his vision cleared, he fixated on the chanting Indian. He was captivated by the bear skullcap perched on the medicine man's head and the necklace of bear claws adorning his neck.

"Where am I?" Kane groaned, slowly raising himself off the ground.

"You are here with me," the old Indian replied in broken English, abruptly halting his ritual dance as he noticed Kane stirring.

"Where's here'? And who are you?" Kane pressed, still disoriented.

"I am Mata healer and medicine man. That's what my name means in the

Kitanemuk tribe."

"Where did you find me?" Kane inquired, brushing gritty soil from his clothes. "My Peyote trance led me to you. I found you lying in a small gully. It seemed like

you were searching for water, digging a hole but only uncovering wet sand. You must have passed out while digging," the medicine man explained.

"I know what you are," he continued, grinning broadly.

"What? What am I?" Kane challenged, intrigued by the old man's words. "You're a skin changer.... a bear one. In our tribe, you're seen as a being with magical powers. You play a significant role in our ceremonies. Bears symbolize

strength and wisdom, and they're deeply connected to our healing and spells. Your name is Shadow Bear.... your guardians revealed this to me. Look, I even have a carved bear totem in my medicine bag," he chuckled, toddling about and rummaging through his pouch.

"My guardians? Who are my guardians?" Kane probed anxiously, his mind racing with thoughts of his forebears.

"Lady Vixen.... the crowman and your father without a face, always lurking in the

shadows with that ugly human-faced rat on his shoulder," Mata revealed candidly. "I heard their cries and they guided me to where you were dying.... you didn't have much time left, Shadow Bear."

"Here.... drink this," Mata instructed, handing Kane a cup.

Kane studied the beverage doubtfully. He glanced at the pot from which the stew had come and saw a thick, red liquid frothing away. Bubbles formed into shapes resembling human skulls, expanding and bursting with vigor, splattering the contents. "What is this? It looks like clotted blood," Kane protested, a mixture of curiosity and unease in his voice.

"Drink it it will reveal the freedom and wisdom you seek," Mata encouraged, his

eyes gleaming with ancient knowledge.

Kane peered at Mata with skepticism, then steeled himself and took a deep breath before downing the gooey, hot fluid in one gulp. Instantly, he coughed and spluttered, wiping his mouth in revulsion, while Mata clapped his hands and giggled with childlike pleasure.

"What happens now?" Kane demanded, his voice edged with anticipation. "You will see," Mata replied gleefully, his eyes alight with mystery.

Suddenly, Kane felt a surge of excitement coursing through his body, his senses overwhelmed by the vivid colors that flashed before him and the sounds of the desert that seemed to dance in front of his eyes. The hallucinations blurred the line between reality and imagination.

"What.... have.... you... given.... me?" Kane managed to implore, his voice deepening to a guttural growl as he struggled to articulate his words.

With a sense of profound transformation, Kane effortlessly shifted into his

skin-changing bear form. He dropped to all fours, tossing his enormous head and romping in a playful manner, feeling liberated and authentically himself.

"You are welcome and embraced by my people. Your quest for peace and prosperity is fulfilled," Mata exclaimed, dancing and prancing alongside the Shadow Bear.

Kane could only think that he had finally found his true home and freedom.

For two days, Kane remained in his shape-shifting form, immersed in the rituals with Mata. They drank from the sacred cauldron, danced with fervor, and burned crudely made incense, using the ceremony to purify their minds and bodies. Mata, adorned with large flight feathers from a predatory bird, stretched his arms during the dance, the feathers acting as extensions of his hands, symbolizing his connection to the spirit world.

As dawn broke on the third morning, Kane followed Mata for miles, their journey winding through rugged terrain until they reached the crest of a ridge. The old Indian sat purposefully on his horse, and from this vantage point, they both gazed down at an established native village spread out below. Teepees dotted the landscape, livestock roamed freely, and inhabitants moved about like tiny figures in a child's toy box. The scene below captured a sense of timeless serenity, surrounded by the majestic mountains and embraced by the vastness of the land.

"This is my home," Mata proclaimed proudly.

Kane responded with a low growl, his agreement conveyed through powerful snuffling noises. Mata understood and affectionately patted Shadow Bear's large head.

"Come and meet my family," Mata invited warmly, then began descending the steep mountainside with the towering animal following closely behind him.

Life in the valley for the Kitanemuk people unfolded as one continuous religious ceremony, where the entire world was shrouded in mystery. They revered the natural elements of the earth as their "Great Spirit," believing in sacred powers that operated

in recurring patterns akin to the sun and moon, or the wind. Their belief held that as long as their circle of life remained unbroken, their world would thrive.

Communication with the "Great Spirit" came through dreams, visions, and fire rituals, facilitated by the sacred medicine bundle containing claws, mushrooms, medicinal herbs, and a ceremonial pipe.

Emerging from the dense forest, Mata led the bear into a vast clearing that opened onto flowered paddocks, where a crystal-clear river flowed. Here, naked children played joyfully, splashing in the water, their laughter ringing through the air. Kane observed with awe as the sunlight gleamed on their youthful, brown skin glistening with water droplets. The children suddenly halted their play, transfixed by Mata's presence with the majestic Shadow Bear passing by. Their astonishment was evident in the hushed stillness that settled over the riverside scene.

A crowd of men had gathered at the outskirts of the village, their curiosity excited by Mata's return from his solitary quest in search of his guardian spirit. As he approached, a wide grin stretched across his weathered face, an expression of pride and accomplishment.

"Mata, my brother!" greeted one of the elder Indians, warmly patting him on the back. The others respectfully made way for the medicine man and his bear to pass through.

"Mata, Chief Crazy Horse wishes to see you immediately on your return," the elder continued in their native tongue.

"Where did you find this bear?"

"We found each other.... the spirits guided me to where he lay, near death. I saved his life," Mata replied in a dignified manner.

"It's the largest bear I've ever seen.... it's amazing," remarked the elder Indian, marveling at Kane's size. Before entering the Chief's Teepee, Mata flicked back the buckskin hide door.

Instinctively, Kane settled beside the tent, his massive frame hitting the ground with a heavy thud. He waited patiently, observing the crowd of whispering Indians who stood nearby, openly staring at him in wonder and curiosity.

Standing in the doorway, Mata swiftly scanned the Teepee, taking in the sight of the tribe's elders seated around a small fire pit, passing their camulet (smoking pipe) in a noble ritual.

"Sit, Mata.... How was your spiritual journey?" Chief Crazy Horse inquired, his voice carrying a blend of authority and interest.

"Very enlightening. My guardian spirits led me to a man who was dying in the desert, just a day's journey from my camp. His own spirits guided me to him," Mata explained earnestly.

"He was a challenge to bring back, Chief. He's as big as a bear. I had to drag him all the way with my horse to my campsite," Mata added with a hint of humor, prompting a soft chuckle from the group.

"Where is this man. Did you leave him at your camp?" Chief Crazy Horse smoothly quizzed in his native tongue, his eyes probing Mata with curiosity and a touch of concern.

"No....I brought him back here with me, he is outside" Mata confessed, sensing the Chief's potential apprehension.

"What tribe is he from?" Crazy Horse pressed on.

"He isn't Indian or Mexican I think he's from a completely

different place.... but

there's something else about him. He's a skin-changer.... it revealed itself during our Peyote ceremony," Mata revealed, noticing the rapt attention of everyone present hanging on his every word.

"Skin changers can be demons too, Mata," Chief Crazy Horse said, his voice heavy with grim wisdom.

"Most often, they're twisted witch doctors, lost to madness and darkness." He continued

"What is his animal?" One of the elders interjected impatiently, his frustration evident as Mata sat there with a broad, almost mischievous grin.

"A Bear.... he is our sacred totem animal.... a positive sign from the Great Spirit, a promise of strength and abundance for our people," Mata affirmed, his belief unshakable as he shared his profound insight with the council of elders.

Calmly puffing on the long peace pipe, Chief Crazy Horse mulled over Mata's revelation. The mention of a stranger entering his tribe stirred caution within him. Trusting outsiders posed a significant risk to his people, and the Chief had valid reasons for his suspicions—he had trusted eagerly before, only to witness harm befall his village as a consequence.

During a time when encounters with foreigners were rare and meeting a white man was a remarkable oddity, a band of warriors returned from a hunting trip with a stranger in tow. The young, curious Indian Chief saw an opportunity to learn from the outsider about his world and ways.

When the drifter was first brought into the village, he seemed a shadow of his former self. After a few days, his condition worsened dramatically—his breath came in ragged gasps, and his body was covered in oozing sores, leaking a sickly green substance that seemed to seep from his very soul.

The tribespeople, relying on their traditional and holistic medicines, worked tirelessly to nurse him back to health, but their efforts were in vain.

Meanwhile, Chief Crazy Horse began to notice his people falling ill. What started as fevers, headaches, and body pains swiftly escalated. Within days, red rashes broke out on the faces, hands, and feet of the afflicted. The horrific skin disease spared no one, striking indiscriminately across the tribe.

Amid the suffering, only a handful of tribal members survived the ordeal. Many families lost loved ones, and the epidemic decimated the village population by more than half. Chief Crazy Horse could do nothing but wait as the disease ran its devastating course. While those who survived gained lifelong immunity, the tragedy left an indelible mark on the tribe's history, a stark reminder of the dangers that came with encountering the unknown.

"You remember the plague, don't you, Mata?" Chief Crazy Horse remarked, his voice tinged with seriousness

"That was the first and last time we welcomed a stranger into our midst. If what you're telling us is true, then this skin changer is not just an animal you can try to tame and keep as your pet. He is also a man with free will. Why should I place my trust in him?" he continued, his skepticism clear.

"Chief, I understand your concern, but I also believe he is a gift from the Great Spirit. As your medicine man, I can assure you this is true. I saw it in my dream. He will not harm us. He is a symbol of our strength and pride. His presence is a light of inspiration," Mata declared with earnest conviction.

"When the other tribes and the army see that we have such

exceptional brave within our clan, they'll think twice before challenging us."

"You drink too much of that scarlet broth....the mescal is distorting your visions.... Where is he now?" Chief Crazy Horse reprimanded, his gaze static.

"No, Chief. The broth enhances my visions and reveals the truth to me. He is waiting outside. But I must warn you, he remains in bear form until the Peyote broth wears off.... His name is Shadow Bear," Mata informed the group, standing firm in his belief despite the Chief's reservations.

Chief Crazy Horse led the entourage of elders from the Teepee, scanning the dispersing crowd for any sign of the Skin Changer. Kane, however, was nowhere to be seen.

"What happened to the bear?" Mata inquired of one of the lingering Indians outside the Teepee.

"It wandered off into the fields and vanished over the horizon," the man replied, gesturing northward.

Chief Crazy Horse frowned at Mata, disappointment etched on his face.

"So much for your divine Bear. I'm glad it's gone. Another sign for you, Mata.

It wasn't a sacred totem animal after all." he sarcastically concluded before swiftly retreating into the warmth of his Teepee.

Mata felt a pang of embarrassment as Chief Crazy Horse's distrust weighed heavily on him. He knew that his standing as the tribe's medicine man was at stake—if he lost the Chief's confidence, he risked being replaced by a younger successor, fading into obscurity with the passage of time. Determined to prove his sanity and the truth of his visions, Mata swiftly decided to pursue Kane in the direction of his disappearance.

The enormous bear slowed his thunderous gallop, nostrils flaring as he inhaled the intoxicating perfume of the field flowers. The sweet, potent scent worked its magic, soothing his restless spirit until he finally collapsed among the blossoms. Sunlight pierced his thick brown fur, searing it with a comforting warmth, as Kane teetered on the edge of sleep. His mind flickered between the persistent hum of insects darting from flower to flower and the vivid twilight dreams that beckoned him.

Hidden within the tall green grass, Shadow Bear marveled at the stalks swaying in the breeze, feeling a profound sense of awe. Yet, an immense load bore down on him—the monumental choice he had to make. He wrestled with the reasons to stay with the Indian tribe or to leave them and forge his own path. Years of rejection had carved deep scars into his soul, and as time wore on, his hunger for acceptance had become an all-consuming force, as primal as his need for food and water.

His heart ached for a community that would truly see him, honor him, and embrace him with unwavering love. Now, he had found people who recognized his power as a healer and protector. Kane believed he could stand with them, defending their way of life and fighting for justice when the time demanded it. The fire of this conviction burned brightly within him, igniting a fierce determination to find his place among them.

But on the other hand, the looming threat of the pursuing enemy troubled him.

He couldn't stand the thought of putting the innocent Indian tribe at risk by leading those merciless and relentless predators straight to their door.

As he hesitated, torn between choices, his exceptional hearing picked up a distinct rustling in the grass, drawing nearer. Lifting his head to see, he peered above the vegetation, but all he could detect was the flattening of the grass as something moved quickly towards him. A deep growl rumbled in the pit of his throat, and Shadow Bear let out an almighty roar that echoed throughout the valley. The powerful sound reached Mata, who was a mile away.

Suddenly, the tall greenery parted as the secretive stalker finally reached him, and a little foxy face popped out—it was Lady Vixen. With absolute delight, both animals nuzzled each other, and Kane heard her soft voice speaking to him in his head.

"You made it.... I tried guiding you to water in the desert, but the heat was too much for you. I thought you were going to die until Mata came along and gave you some water," she crooned.

"Yes, I was fortunate he found me, and thank you for your guidance. But I don't know what to do," Kane questioned.

"I don't know whether to stay with the Indians and enjoy their inclusion or just leave them in peace," he continued.

"This is where you're meant to be. It's part of your destiny to experience true love and happiness. These people understand you and, more importantly, accept you," Lady Vixen reasoned.

"But what about Gideon and his ninjas? And I'm sure that after the barn fire, the Mexicans would have joined forces with them. I don't want to put anyone in jeopardy, especially innocent people who have nothing to do with my crimes."

"My 'little birds' tell me that Gideon is sick. He's holed up at Don Morales' ranch. They arrived not long after you left.

Alejandro brought them back from San Francisco and yes, you are right. The Mexicans have joined forces with the ninjas."

Kane heaved a deep sigh of despair, the strength of his moan blowing the petals off the neighboring flowers, scattering their pollen into the air like a cloud of yellow soot. "Don't lose hope. You are meant to stay with the Indian tribe. It is your father's wish that you experience every adventure and emotion in life while you're here living on earth as a man. Before you can ascend into our dimension as a spiritual guide for disciples of our kind, you must endure this growth. It will make you stronger and wiser. He believes that after the years of rejection and oppression you suffered growing up at the monastery, it's now time for you to encounter love, acceptance, and true happiness. This has been planned for you, Shadow Bear," Lady Vixen continued speaking to him telepathically.

"So, I stay with the tribespeople? What about my hunters?" Kane questioned.

"I am staying by your side from now on. I will not leave you.... you have the power to mutate fully at will. You have matured and come full circle. When the time comes, Gideon and his men won't stand a chance," she reassured him.

With that comforting thought, both animals snuggled against each other and fell asleep, prudently concealed among the tall grass and scented flowers.

* * *

The following morning, the piercing cries of eagles and the baying of wild dogs roused Kane from his sleep. Sitting upright, he combed his fingers through his hair and realized that sometime during the night, he had effortlessly transformed back into his human form.... and he was stark naked. Lady Vixen stood next to him, her tongue hanging out as she panted eagerly, impatiently waiting for Kane to pull himself together so they could return to the Indian village.

As Kane's large frame stood up, every muscle in his body twitched and expanded, his physique resembling that of a devoted bodybuilder. He glanced down at his lengthy penis, then at Lady Vixen, searching for an answer to his vulnerability.

She simply tilted her head to one side, indicating she didn't have the answer.

Kane shrugged his shoulders playfully, and without further delay, the pair began the long walk across the fields, heading back toward the Indian tribe.

As Kane neared the village, small groups of young Indian squaws halted their morning tasks, giggling and blushing as they whispered to one another. They eyed the robust, handsome stranger passing by, his beefy hands cupped prudently over his genitals.

"I think you've won some hearts," Lady Vixen chuckled inside his head.

"Hmph," Kane grunted in reply, feeling embarrassed by his helpless state. Just as he felt exposed, Mata rushed towards him with a Pendleton blanket, quickly wrapping it around Kane's waist. The fringe of the woven rug dragged behind him in the dirt, providing a modest cover.

"There you are.... I've been searching for you everywhere. Come, we'll get you some clothes, and then you can meet Chief Crazy Horse. I'm so glad you're back," Mata beamed, his voice tinged with relief.

"I need food and drink before I meet the chief," Kane grumbled, realizing his presence had become a momentous occasion, with every tribe member seemingly accompanying him through the village.

"Where did the dog come from?" Mata inquired.

"I don't know.... when I woke up this morning, she was just there," Kane lied.

"Well, it seems like she's taken a liking to you.... the same could be said for all these young squaws hanging around as well," Mata smirked, giving Kane a sly wink. "Maybe so, but the dog stays with me.... always.... and where is my saddle pack?

I have an important book in it."

"Don't worry.... your saddle pack and book are safe in my teepee," Mata reassured, touching Kane's shoulder.

It was midday when Chief Crazy Horse welcomed Kane into his teepee, gesturing for him to sit opposite with a glowing fire between them, purposefully creating a symbolic separation.

"Mata, can you translate what the skinwalker says?" Chief Crazy Horse asked in his native tongue.

"Yes, I understand his English," Mata affirmed.

"Good. Ask him why he is here," the Chief began the conversation. Mata translated the question to Kane, and thus began the exchange.

"I am a Buddhist Monk from Japan, a nation very far from here. I'm on a spiritual journey in your country and I accidentally took a wrong turn and ended up in the desert. Your kind-hearted medicine man found me and took care of me," Kane explained to Mata to translate.

"Mata tells me you're a skin-changer. How can you be both a Buddhist and a skinwalker?" Chief Crazy Horse questioned, his eyes fixed intently on Kane.

"Where I grew up, Buddhism is our religion, but I'm not purely Japanese. My father, who has passed now, was an unconventional medicine man. I've heard he dabbled in witchcraft. They say the more he practiced, the more powerful he became. One day, he invoked a spell that delved into dark magic, granting him mythical powers and the ability to transform into an animal. The shock of his transformation was so intense, it killed him instantly. When they found his body, he had the features of an ugly rat, a look of terror frozen on his face that paralyzed the man who discovered him," Kane described, weaving together truth and fabrication. He had taken fragments of his ancestry from dreams and ancient texts, but the gruesome details were a concoction to satisfy the Chief's curiosity.

After Mata translated Kane's story, Chief Crazy Horse's eyes widened like a stunned owl. He whispered something into the ear of the closest elder, who then passed it down the line. Kane watched closely as all the patriarchs nodded in agreement once they had heard the Chief's opinion.

"Can you change at will? Show me," Chief Crazy Horse demanded.

Kane was taken aback by the sudden request to transform into a bear, but to appease the Chief, he began focusing his concentration. With a deliberate effort, his fingernails rapidly elongated into absurdly sharp claws. Thick brown fur sprouted from his skin, covering his hand, while distinct foot pads formed in his palm.

However, Kane hadn't anticipated one crucial aspect: his human teeth began to morph into saw-toothed fangs, sharper than any sword or spear the Indians had ever seen. As his mouth filled with a multitude of pearl-white canine teeth, they extended three inches from his jaw, protruding fiercely and intimidatingly. The Indian men recoiled in fear, scrambling backward like a swarm of startled beetles at the sight of Kane's transformation.

"Kane, control yourself," Lady Vixen's voice pleaded, but Kane only smiled, a disturbing grin that exposed his razor-sharp fangs. In a growling voice, he addressed the Indian elders directly.

"I am Shadow Bear. You're either with me or against me. If you're against me, you better run. But be warned there's nowhere on earth you can hide." With that

threatening declaration, he chuckled, a throaty growl filling the teepee as he gradually reshaped back into his human form.

The group of Indians sat in stunned silence for a moment, then erupted into ululating yells and shrieks, displaying their approval of Shadow Bear joining the tribe.

"You are now one of us you can live with me," Mata confirmed, smiling warmly at

Kane. But Kane returned his gaze without emotion, standing up to leave.

"Tell the Chief that I hope that satisfied his curiosity, but I'm not a circus trick " Kane

summoned his dog and they exited the teepee.

"What's a circus?" The question lingered in Mata's thoughts, leaving him mystified. Kane wandered through the village, taking in the industrious scene around him.

Every member of the tribe, from the youngest child to the eldest elder, was engaged in tasks vital to the community's survival and comfort through the harsh winter ahead. As he strolled past the rows of teepees, he noticed women skillfully preserving animal hides, their smiles acknowledging his presence. Across the village, men labored over crafting weapons: bows and arrows, spears, clubs, axes, and knives, their focus on protecting the village from wildlife and potential enemy raids.

Chunks of meat and fish hung over smoky fires, slowly curing to ensure they would last throughout the winter. Nearby, older women deftly wove baskets from reeds and molded pots from clay, their hands moving with practiced efficiency.

In the midst of these scenes, Kane's thoughts turned to the news of Gideon's illness. He couldn't deny a sense of relief at the old buzzard's misfortune; perhaps this turn of events would lead Gideon to abandon his pursuit and return home to Japan with his ninjas.

Strolling down to the river, Kane's attention was drawn to a solitary Indian woman. She waved large eagle feathers and a smoking smudge wand in the air, the fragrant fumes swirling around her as she chanted a haunting mantra. Intrigued, Kane halted a short distance away, his gaze fixed on her, captivated by her ethereal beauty. "What are you looking at?" she demanded, her voice assertive in her native tongue. "What do you want?" she pressed further.

Kane remained silent. He knew she wouldn't understand his words, so instead, he offered a gentle smile and bowed in the traditional Japanese manner. With Lady Vixen trotting faithfully behind him, he continued his leisurely stroll along the riverbank.

"Do you know who that was?" Lady Vixen teased, her soft voice murmuring in Kane's mind.

"How would I know?" Kane replied.

"That's Mata's daughter.... she's a Shaman, a faith healer like her father. She has a deep alliance with the spirit world. Her tribal name is Lone Bear."

"She might be beautiful, but she has a fiery nature," Kane remarked. "Maybe so, but she would be perfect for you."

"What? I don't even know her."

"You're staying in Mata's teepee now, so you will meet her soon enough." "How do you know all of this?"

"I might be here with you, but my eyes and ears are everywhere." "Your 'little birds,' I suppose?"

"Yes.... my 'little birds,' my brother the crowman."

Later that night, the entire Indian tribe congregated around a colossal bonfire. The rhythmic beat of drums and piercing shrieks resonated through the darkness of the valley. Kane, seated next to Chief Crazy Horse as the honored guest, watched in awe as they danced around the flames.

Mata sat close to Kane, poised to interpret any conversation between him and the Chief. His attention oscillated between the sacred ceremony unfolding before them and his vigilant monitoring of the interactions between Kane and the tribe's leader. "Do you like our spiritual dance?" Mata asked Kane.

"Yes, it's very colorful and loud," Kane replied. Chief Crazy Horse then spoke up,

"Look at my warriors, they are strong and proud," beaming

with delight. Kane focused intently on the Chief as Mata began translating his words.

"This is our Ceremonial Fire Dance. In our tradition, fire is a living being and a relative of the sun. We call it the Ray of the Sun. My people pray to the one who resides beyond the sun, not to the sun itself. Our strength resides in the fire; our creator's essence lives in the glowing embers. This powerful force must be treated with great respect," Chief Crazy Horse explained, his admiration for their beliefs evident as Mata conveyed his words.

Kane nodded in agreement, deeply contemplating the Chief's words and gaining a newfound appreciation for their spiritual practices.

As Chief Crazy Horse displayed a traditional war bonnet, Kane marveled at the intricate headgear. The long eagle feathers symbolized the Chief's power and authority within the tribe. Each quill had been awarded to the highly respected Chief, acknowledging his significant achievements—honors that had to be earned.

"This is our eternal flame," the Chief continued, his voice filled with delight. "There is an energy in the fire that goes beyond the physical flames. This energy must be kept strong during the ceremony." He passed the camulet, the sacred smoking pipe, to Kane.

Through the haze of smoke and dust, Kane's eyes caught sight of Lone Bear. She danced alone, her movements fluid and powerful as she circled the fire, her feet pounding into the sandy earth with each beat of the forceful drums.

She knew that anyone invited to sit next to Chief Crazy Horse was an honored guest, so within a few minutes, she had made her way over to Kane. Once she was in front of him, she stood perfectly still, stretching out her arms, enticing him to take hold of her hands.

Kane felt his face flush involuntarily, his eyes widening as he smiled, accepting her invitation. As he stood up, Lone Bear's eyes widened in turn, impressed and undeniably intrigued by his towering, muscular stature.

Feeling the intoxicating effects of the smoking pipe's herbs, Kane clumsily attempted to mimic Lone Bear's dance movements. Her wailing and shrieking inspired him to become fully immersed in the riveting, primeval euphoria.

After a while, Chief Crazy Horse stood up and waved his decorated talking stick in the air. The signal was clear: the music stopped abruptly, and every person halted, instantly ceasing their merriment.

"We thank our Gods and sacred totem animals. Hear our prayers and feel our eternal flame of energy. Bless this tribe and give us strength. We have been granted a sign from the heavens, his name is Shadow Bear. He is part of the tribe and will assist us on our buffalo hunts and help protect us from our enemies," Chief Crazy Horse announced with authority. Once he finished his speech, he sat back down, signaling for the ceremony to continue into the early hours of the morning.

Kane and Lone Bear departed from the festivities a few hours before daybreak. As they wandered across the vast fields, the sun's rays softly and diffusing, gave way to the first strong twinkles of the day, bringing warmth and happiness.

Somehow, Kane and Lone Bear communicated without many words. The gentle touch of her hand guided him to the things she wanted him to notice, encouraging him to imitate words in her native tongue.

"Sihu," she said, picking a flower and holding it up to Kane.

"Seeehu," he feebly attempted to say. They instantly burst into laughter at his exotic accent, bashfully smiling and admiring each other.

Lone Bear wasn't beautiful in the classical sense. She was shorter than average, and her figure was fuller than the other girls, but her piercing green eyes and luminous white teeth gleamed as she gently blew on the flower, scattering its petals.

Her long, flowing ebony hair, randomly braided with colorful beads, tumbled over her shoulders as she bent down to pick another blossom. She blew on it with her

heart-shaped lips, setting Kane's heart a-thump.

He noticed her sweeping eyelashes and delicate ears that framed a button nose. Her elegant personality radiated from within, making her irresistible to him. Kane was mesmerized. It was love at first sight.

Stepping closer, Lone Bear nuzzled into his arm with her nose, a custom and sign of affection among her people. She then waved her index finger, beckoning him to bend down. As Kane leaned in, she whispered something in his ear, her honeyed voice as sweet as any songbird's melody.

"I like you very much" She murmured, but Kane didn't understand a word she said Over the next month, Kane integrated fully into the Indian tribe. His relationship with Lone Bear blossomed into a passionate, twin flame coupling, evident to everyone around them who saw them as soul mates, believing their bond was sent from the "Great Spirit."

Each time Kane saw her, his love for Lone Bear deepened further. His feelings multiplied and grew more profound, captivating him more with each passing moment. Their profound spiritual connection transformed both Kane and Lone Bear, altering their perspectives on the world. For Kane, it spurred him to commune with his universal ancestors, spending devoted hours in prayer with the human skin book.

This spiritual engagement shifted his consciousness, enriching him as a more soulful and educated being with the dark side of his personality.

Despite sharing every thought and emotion with Lone Bear, Kane harbored one strict prohibition: he forbade her from ever reading or gaining knowledge from his idolized book. Every moment of his life was meticulously inscribed within its pages, chronicling the dark deeds of his past—the murder of the Abbot, Mr Kent, and the Mexicans, the struggles with his skin-changing powers that sometimes unleashed wild, animalistic behaviors, and the identities of his dimensional guardians and the pack of assassins relentlessly hunting him. Kane feared that if Lone Bear were to uncover these truths, she would be repulsed and frightened, turning away from him and leaving him to live in isolation once more.

"What is that book you keep praying to? Is it your bible?" Lone Bear coyly asked one day, well aware of Kane's careful protection of it.

"Yes," Kane replied in her language, having learned essential words and phrases during his time with the tribe.

"Can I look at it?" she pressed on, surprised by Kane's sudden and firm response. "NO!"

"Why not?" she retorted, her fiery disposition beginning to

emerge.

"It's not for your eyes. It's sacred to my family. It reveals my identity and my destiny. That's all you need to know," Kane explained firmly.

"If we are to be husband and wife, then I should know who I am marrying. You know everything about me," Lone Bear reasoned, a sense of unease creeping into her

voice as she scrutinized Kane with caution, feeling a lack of equality in their relationship.

"You've lived a simple life, my darling. Your tribe and family have been your protectors, the green open fields and rivers your playground, and the animals your companions. My past has been a lot more complicated than that," Kane began, gently stroking Lone Bear's hand.

"And although you want to learn more about me, if you knew about my journey, where I'm from, and what I've done, you'll wish you hadn't. When we are married and living peacefully somewhere in the mountains, I will tell you everything, especially if we start a family," he continued with a reassuring smile, knowing that the mention of children would sweeten and pacify this spirited woman.

"I know you're a skin changer, a totem god to our Kitanemuk people," Lone Bear's voice trembled with intensity as she confronted Kane.

"I love you for who you are and respect your powers. My people accept you with open arms. I am a Sharman too, and I would understand and appreciate what the book contained."

Kane felt a surge of irritation at her persistence, a deep rumbling snarl forming in the pit of his throat. As he opened his mouth to respond, a sinister growl escaped independently, his lips curling back to reveal his altering sharp teeth. Quickly bringing his hand to his mouth, he began to cough, trying to hide his unwanted transformation, but Lone Bear had already witnessed the sudden change, startling her deeply.

"Would you hurt me just because I challenge your opinion!" Lone Bear's voice rang out, furious and direct.

"No, no, no.... I would never do that. I need more practice with controlling my emotions because they can easily manifest into my bear form. I'm sorry I scared you. Please believe me when I say that I would never hurt you because I love you," Kane replied calmly, his gaze locked onto Lone Bear's determined green eyes.

Cautiously taking a step forward, Kane saw her immediately shrink back from his attempt to hug her. His heart sank, realizing the depth of her fear and the challenge of maintaining his dual nature.

"I can't lose you, Lone Bear," Kane pleaded urgently, his voice thick with emotion. "You're the anchor that keeps me grounded, the light that guides me through the darkness. Without you, I'd be lost."

Lone Bear looked into Kane's eyes, seeing the raw vulnerability that he seldom showed.

"I know you're scared, Kane," she responded, her voice steady despite the turmoil in her heart.

"And I'm scared too. But I've also seen your strength and your compassion. I've felt your love, and it's stronger than any darkness you fear."

He reached out, clasping her hands firmly. "Promise me, Lone

Bear. Promise me that we'll face everything together. That you'll let me into your world, your past, and your struggles. Our love can conquer all if we trust in each other."

Lone Bear nodded, her throat tight with unspoken emotions.

"I pledge to you Lone Bear. From this day forward, my heart belongs to you. I'll share everything with you, because our bond is sacred, and it gives me strength."

With a deep breath, Lone Bear leaned in, resting her forehead against his chest. "Then let us embrace a future of peace together," she whispered, her voice carrying the hope of assured commitment.

"No more secrets, no more fears. Just us, against the world." Kane whispered in her ear.

And in that moment, beneath the blue sky and the watchful eyes of their ancestors, Kane and Lone Bear embraced, their love a powerful force that bound them together against whatever challenges lay ahead.

Lone Bear stared deeply into his eyes, witnessing a sincerity and truth that seemed to emanate from the depths of his soul. As he returned her gaze, he couldn't ignore the extreme beauty and comforting warmth that radiated from within her. It felt as though the very universe had conspired to forge this connection, for in that moment, Kane knew without a doubt that he had found his sanctuary.

"I believe you," she whispered softly, enveloping his broad frame in her embrace. With a delicate tilt of her head, she gazed up at him, her eyes shimmering with unspoken promises. Overcome by a flood of emotions, Kane bent down to kiss her. Their lips met in a tender embrace, a kiss that conveyed a profound love—one that bridged the chasm of longing and united their hearts in a timeless, transcendent bond.

* * *

Crouched low in the swaying grass, Kane draped in a bison hide crept forward toward the colossal herd of buffalo. The 800-pound beasts grazed lazily, oblivious to the imminent threat posed by the approaching Indian tribe. Suddenly, a young brave let out a cry mimicking a distressed calf, hoping to lure the herd towards him.

Several buffalo raised their heads in response to the familiar call. In that fleeting moment, another warrior stood tall, drawing his bow with precision and releasing an arrow that flew true, piercing the closest animal squarely in the throat.

The buffalo held essential significance for the tribe, providing sustenance, materials, and crucial resources. With the aid of their agile horses, they trailed the herds across the expansive plains, utilizing strategic horseback maneuvers to corral the buffalo towards the steep cliffs of the mountains. From meat and clothing to teepees, tools, and even rope, every part of the buffalo was utilized, ensuring the tribe's survival and prosperity.

Kane understood the critical importance of securing enough buffalo for his people. When he witnessed the wounded animal bolt with an arrow jutting from its neck, triggering a frenzied stampede among the herd, he swiftly joined the hunters. Racing alongside their thundering horses on foot, Kane gradually dropped to all fours, transforming into the formidable and agile Shadow Bear. With calculated grace, he surged ahead, eventually outpacing the galloping warriors on horseback.

The thundering buffalo stampede surged across the expansive plains, their movements guided by a steadfast pathfinder leading the way. Kane, swept up in the exhilaration of the chase, felt an unparalleled sense of freedom and joy. Running alongside these majestic creatures, he experienced a deep connection and purpose.

With a swift and powerful motion, Shadow Bear brought down a large male buffalo, effortlessly opening its throat with a single swipe of his paw. The rush of adrenaline as he claimed this kill filled him with an electrifying sense of being truly alive.

Amidst the heavy breaths and thunderous snorts echoing around him, Shadow Bear swiftly dispatched another buffalo, replicating his earlier feat. Meanwhile, the band of Indian braves dismounted from their horses, swiftly moving to dispatch and harvest the fallen beasts. As Shadow Bear continued to bring down several more buffalo, he found himself traversing alongside the herd for miles, their path winding through valleys and narrowing towards a gully ahead.

Sensing the impending trap, the panicked herd abruptly doubled back on itself, creating a racket of desperate bellows that reverberated deep into the canyon. Satisfied that he had secured enough buffalo to sustain and provide for the entire tribe, Kane eased his pace and followed the herd with a newfound sense of calm. His towering figure, larger than even the biggest buffalo, made him unmistakably conspicuous, standing out like a mountain amid the plains.

As Shadow Bear basked in the pride of his considerable accomplishments, a surge of joy coursed through him. With a deep inhalation, he let out a resounding roar that sounded across the land, inadvertently attracting attention that he hadn't anticipated or desired.

From the hillside, a pair of binoculars surreptitiously tracked the unusually massive bear. As the observer continued their vigil, following the bear's movements alongside the herd, the sight of this colossal creature eventually integrating itself among the Indians with an air of camaraderie and warmth deeply unsettled the onlooker.

"What is it, Sarge?" the Corporal asked urgently.

"Here, take a look," the army sergeant replied, swiftly passing the binoculars to his subordinate.

"Is that real? It's the biggest bear I've ever seen. Must be a mutant or something. How did they tame such a monstrous bear?" The Corporal's voice trembled with shock.

"It's real, and that monster seems to be a pet of the Kitanemuk tribe," the sergeant affirmed.

"Wow," the Corporal said, his voice tinged with wonder and apprehension.

"The bear is actually helping them butcher the buffalo carcasses. It's not just enormous—it's displaying a remarkable intelligence. This is incredibly dangerous, Sarge. It looks like the Indians have a secret weapon." He lifted the binoculars once more, peering intently for a closer view.

"Yes, and they'll use that weapon against anyone who crosses their path. They could invade our settlements, pillage, and threaten travelers. It's our duty to protect the innocent and civilize this land. Come, we must inform the Commander," the Sergeant declared sternly, swiftly directing the soldiers to mount up and ride northwest towards their military base, Fort Harper.

Chapter 16

Gideon closed his eyes, basking in the comforting warmth of the morning sun. Wrapped in a vintage Mexican blanket, he reclined on a weathered Spanish chair nestled in the verdant courtyard. His thoughts drifted fondly to his homeland and the serene monastery where he once found solace.

In his mind's eye, Japan's rolling hills and snow-capped peaks stretched majestically before him, each farm plot a unique patchwork quilt of agriculture, scattered and isolated yet harmonious in their diversity. Memories then led him to the monastery's cherished library, where he would immerse himself for hours, engrossed in ancient scriptures and painstakingly transcribing manuscripts—a ritual he dearly missed.

A vivid image of his beloved cat emerged, the feline affectionately rubbing against a table leg with soft meows, drawing closer to him. Overwhelmed with love for his companion, Gideon's heart swelled—until a sudden, chilling terror pierced his thoughts. The haunting image of his cat's mutilated head, placed meticulously on a silver tray and served to him as a macabre meal, shook him to his core.

"Kane.... hell is empty because the demon is here with us," Gideon murmured to himself, his words carrying the weight of a troubled mind. When he finally opened his eyes, he found Victor standing silently before him, holding a glass of orange-tinted water.

"Are you alright, Priest?" Victor's voice cut through the lingering haze of Gideon's thoughts.

"Hai, Hai.... I am sorry.... I was having a nightmare," Gideon responded dismissively, feeling somewhat embarrassed by his aging vulnerability.

"Here.... I have your herbal medication.... Don Morales wishes to speak with you later. He'll come to you, considering you're recuperating," Victor informed him calmly. "That will be fine.... and thank you for taking care of me, Victor. If it weren't for you,

I wouldn't be here to fulfill the mission of finding Kane and bringing him to justice in Japan," Gideon said, his voice slow and strained with gratitude.

"I believe that's something Don Morales wants to discuss with you. He'll explain," Victor replied in his usual detached manner, then turned and headed back into the hacienda upon hearing Don Morales calling for him.

"Victor, Victor, where are you?" Don Morales's voice boomed from his office and down the hallway.

"I'm here, jefe. What's the matter?" Victor asserted as he entered the office.

"I need to speak with Senor Gideon. Is he well enough?" Don Morales inquired. "Yes, he's in the courtyard. I just gave him his medicine. That's where I was when you started hollering for me. I'm not just standing around," Victor replied boldly, and both men shared a chuckle at the straightforwardness of

Victor's response.

Wandering out into the courtyard, Don Morales noticed Gideon nodding off intermittently. He stood back, silently observing the old monk for a while, pondering whether the Master ninja still possessed the fortitude to continue pursuing Kane.

"Senor Gideon, wake up," he said, gently shaking the old man's shoulders to rouse him from his brief slumber.

"Oh, Don Morales, my apologies. I didn't realize you were there. I've been feeling my age since the attack a few weeks ago. That dreadful incident has taken its toll on me this time. I find myself increasingly attuned to Kane's dark presence, whether he's near or far. It's a troubling sign of his growing strength," Gideon admitted, his voice wavering.

"Si.... that's precisely what I wanted to discuss with you. Since your seizure and the subsequent recovery period, Kane has gained a significant advantage over us.

"A day ago, while you were recovering, I had Carlos and Alejandro begin tracking Kane's trail," Don Morales said, his voice steady and calculated.

"It's a daunting task, given the shifting sands of the desert and the time that's passed since his cowardly departure. They're making their way toward the 'Big Sky,' but the fierce rivalry between the ranches means they'll need to proceed with utmost caution."

"It could be weeks before they return. I need to be part of this pursuit. I've come too far to sit on the sidelines. I want to confront Kane myself, to witness his downfall with my own eyes. He needs to understand that despite his power, our ninja skills and Buddhist faith will triumph over him," Gideon declared resolutely.

"I understand how much you have invested in this hunt," Don Morales said, his voice firm and earnest.

"But I strongly advise against tempting the desert again. Unless you want to face an early death and miss your chance at justice"

Gideon sighed deeply, his gaze fixed on the ground with a distant look in his eyes as he responded.

"Don Morales, you speak wisely. Perhaps you're right. My eagerness blinds me sometimes. The desert is unforgiving, and my strength is not what it once was," Gideon admitted sadly.

"I will trust in your judgment. Carlos and Alejandro will always have the support of my ninjas. I will remain here with you and Victor, and share what I can about Japan and our Buddhist beliefs."

"I've already sent your ninjas along with Carlos and Alejandro," Don Morales admitted, his tone carrying a hint of apology.

"I hope you don't mind me making that decision on your behalf."

Gideon paused, reflecting on what Don Morales just said, then he began explaining where he believed Kane's origins came from before continuing.

"That's alright," he said softly, his undamaged eye reflecting the gravity of his words. "Kane.... he hails from a realm of darkness. His past is enshrouded in shadows and deceit, and his very presence jeopardizes everything we hold dear."

"Kane is a skin-changer, hailing from a different dimension of the universe," Gideon explained with a serious intensity.

"It's a realm teeming with skin-changers, witches, and other demonic entities—a paranormal stew where our reality overlaps with the next.

"Imagine a realm poised between shadow and substance, a fragile veil where universal gateways bleed into one another, revealing the darkest, most concealed terrors."

"He enters through these gateways, accompanied by something else—a totem animal, usually. But beware: hunt them, and they'll hunt you back. I suspect Kane's mother was human, but his father—a demon deeply entrenched in satanic witchcraft—shaped his dark lineage."

"How do you know all of this, Senor Gideon?" Don Morales questioned, his curiosity stirred

"At the monastery, my days were devoted to transcribing ancient texts. When I began to suspect that Kane was possessed and saw his shape-shifting abilities firsthand, I immersed myself in the study of evil spirits. Kane possesses a human-skinned book that I am desperate to examine.

"Once Kane is captured," Gideon explained, his voice saturated with resolute determination.

"I plan to take possession of the book and explore the dark universe from which he comes from. I want to deepen our understanding, preparing our monastery from any future encounters with skin changers or similar threats."

"I understand your eagerness to join the hunt," Don Morales acknowledged with a nod.

"Your knowledge and wisdom are invaluable to us. However, I still believe it's wise for you to regain your strength before you accompany any hunting party."

"This decision conflicts with my loyalty and duty to my brothers and our mission, but your points are fair and solid," Gideon acknowledged, his tone reflecting his reluctant acceptance.

"Where's Miko? Did he go with them?" he asked, shifting his focus to the practicalities of the expedition.

"Si.... he insisted," Don Morales replied, his tone revealing both respect and slight amusement.

"Miko claimed to be a skilled tracker," Don Morales said. "We'll need every ounce of expertise we can muster to ensure a swift and successful conclusion. You were ill, so there was no opportunity for farewells," he added.

Gideon cast a knowing glance at Don Morales, silently acknowledging his friend's clever use of persuasion.

* * *

The parched wilderness stretched endlessly, its monotony unbearable. Each stride of their horses felt like a marathon, every moment an agonizing crawl under the relentless sun as the band of hunters pressed onward towards the "Big Sky." Surrounded by withered, contorted plant life, Miko began to hallucinate, envisioning the landscape as a vast, surreal sunflower meadow distorted by the shimmering heat waves. Heartless plants, bearing spiky chain fruits and prickly surfaces, watched silently as the riders passed by. Above, a flock of vultures circled incessantly, the ominous sign hovering close, waiting patiently for their next opportunity.

Nightfall brought no relief; temperatures plummeted to freezing, chilling them to the bone under a sky as cold and unforgiving as the depths of hell. Dive-bombing vampire bats swooped down, their relentless attacks disrupting any chance of rest or peace.

Every sound reeked with menace—howls, moans, wails, and slithering noises filled the air, unsettling Miko to his core. Amidst the desert madness, he struggled for moments of clarity, focusing on the discord of sounds, discerning which horrific creature might invade their camp next—there to inject them with venom or devour them whole.

"How much further to the 'Big Sky'?" Miko sighed wearily, his fatigue notable. "It's just on the other side of that mountain. Maybe half a day's ride," Alejandro replied, his tone lacking concern for Miko's growing exhaustion.

"We're almost there, Miko," Juji reassured his brother, offering a glimmer of encouragement.

"Why aren't you out front tracking Señor Miko?" Alejandro teased with a smirk. "You claimed to be the expert."

"I can't track shifting sands," came the response, tinged with frustration.

"We don't have this kind of terrain where I come from. I've been trained to track in snow or soft earth, not sand that shifts with every breeze."

"We need a plan before we arrive at the 'Big Sky'," Hiro interjected, his voice steady and commanding.

"Si we'll ride in guns blazing, demand answers about Kane," Carlos suggested

eagerly, his readiness for confrontation evident.

"No, that's not our approach. We're trained in espionage and stealth. When night falls, Juji and I will infiltrate the ranch. Our presence must be invisible and silent. The fewer who know, the better," Hiro instructed firmly, his words carrying influence.

"Si, that's the best strategy," Alejandro agreed, acknowledging the wisdom in Hiro's methodical approach.

"Aww, Alejandro, you're taking all the fun out of this trip. What happened to you, Amigo? You used to be up for a fight. Getting soft in your old age, eh?" Carlos teased, attempting to lighten the tension.

"Shut up, Carlos.... you've never been very bright. Your mind's always been on two things fighting and fucking," Alejandro retorted sharply, his patience wearing thin.

"Enough of this bickering," Miko interjected firmly.

"When we face Kane, remember Master Gideon's words. We can't challenge his supernatural powers. Instead, appeal to his humanity and honor as a skilled ninja and a brother of our faith. If there's any decency left in him, he'll want to face us with principled honor."

"Hai.... Miko is right," Hiro affirmed with admiration in his voice, casting a disapproving glance at Carlos and Alejandro.

"You're showing maturity beyond your years. Thank you for your wisdom and clear thinking, young brother"

"It must have been hard leaving Master Gideon," Juji added softly, his tone reflecting empathy.

"I saw you wipe tears away from your eyes when you were saying your goodbyes as he slept."

The group fell silent, the pressure of their mission and the absence of their insightful mentor hanging heavy in the desert air.

"Master Gideon has been like a father to me for as long as I can remember," Miko admitted, his voice tinged with emotion.

"But I remind myself that it's alright.... we won't be gone for too long. We'll capture Kane soon, bring him to justice, and the honor and pride Master Gideon will feel for us will make all the hardships we endure now worthwhile." He innocently continued

As evening descended, the lights of the "Big Sky" ranch flickered to life one by one, casting a revealing glow on the surroundings for the gang of hunters. Hiro and Juji moved with fluid grace, their steps silent and deliberate as they stealthily approached the main house. Their ninja training guided them, each movement calculated to minimize noise and maximize concealment.

On the outer edges of their feet, they glided forward, their senses keenly attuned to every sound and movement around them. With precise skill, they ascended onto the rooftop of the homestead, blending into the shadows as they waited patiently, their breathing controlled to near silence.

Below, two ranch hands wandered aimlessly, blocking their direct path to the house. Hiro grabbed a pebble, tossing it with expert aim to create a diversion in the opposite direction. The distraction drew the ranch hands away momentarily, allowing Hiro and Juji a fleeting opportunity to advance towards their target unseen.

"What was that?" one of the ranch hands muttered.

"I dunno, let's go find out," the other replied. Both men walked off into the darkness, hands on their guns, ready to draw at a moment's notice.

Hiro and Juji seized the opportunity, quickly identifying a weak point in the house's defenses. They meticulously assessed the number of guards, the distribution of light, and any potential traps. Slipping inside, they maneuvered with expert precision, always keeping a light source between themselves and anyone who might spot them, using the glare to remain invisible. The steady drip of a tap in the kitchen masked their footsteps, allowing them to move silently through the expansive rooms.

"Greta! Bring me my decanter" a male voice shouted impatiently, pinpointing his location within the house.

"Yes, Daddy," a young girl's voice answered as she hurried to bring him a tumbler of whiskey.

"Daddy, it's been weeks since anyone has visited the ranch. Can you ask David to ride out and pick up some things for me from Fort Harper?" she asked sweetly, handing her father a list of necessities.

Juji briefly glanced at Hiro, his eyes conveying a mix of urgency and disappointment as he processed the information that no one had visited or passed through the ranch for weeks. They remained silent, their presence hidden in the shadows, as the conversation between the father and daughter continued.

"Why hasn't anyone visited, Daddy? Not even the occasional stranger who sometimes stops by?" Greta asked, a touch of disappointment in her voice.

"I don't know, Greta. Maybe there haven't been any travelers. It's been unusually hot lately," her father replied, his tone rough but dismissive.

"But it doesn't matter. We have everything we need right here."

Juji and Hiro exchanged another glance, realizing that their lead on Kane might be colder than they had hoped. However, they couldn't afford to lose hope. They needed to gather any information they could, even if it seemed insignificant.

Silently, they repositioned themselves, inching nearer to the conversation, their senses heightened, ready to seize any clue that might bring them closer to their target.

"I will send David tomorrow. We're fortunate the army has an outpost that sells these essentials, especially your girly things," he chuckled, scanning the list.

"Why can't I go with David to Fort Harper, Daddy? I haven't left the ranch in ages," Greta whined.

"I send David alone because of the dangerous vagabonds there. They're transient and only care about their own savage needs. The men at the Fort are colder than the devil's teat, and they would take you in a flash. You know this, Greta," he said sternly.

"Okay, Daddy.... is that all?" she replied, her voice heavy with sorrow. She turned and walked out of the room, her shoulders slumping as her father took a large slurp of whiskey

Juji and Hiro, hidden in the shadows, absorbed every word. The mention of Fort Harper aroused their interest. It might not have been the lead they hoped for, but it was something. Silently, they communicated with a glance, agreeing to follow this new thread.

They slipped back into the night, their mission now clearer: head to Fort Harper and see what they could uncover about Kane's location.

Hiro and Juji slipped out of the house with the grace of shadows, their every movement marked by stealth and precision. They maneuvered back to the posse, skillfully evading the casual guards who patrolled the area.

Not a single soul on the ranch had any clue they'd ever been there.

"So? What did you find out?" Alejandro demanded urgently as the ninjas approached.

"Kane didn't come this way," Juji reported. "We overheard the ranch owner's daughter complaining that no one has visited or passed through here in weeks. But she did mention a place called Fort Harper. Her father said many people go there. Maybe that's where Kane has gone."

"Sí, that makes sense. He could blend into the crowd while gathering more supplies," Carlos chimed in.

"He has money. Don Morales paid him for the 'Big Sky' job. Chico was making a big deal about it."

"I know Fort Harper," Alejandro said with a sense of purpose.

"Don Morales has traded with them before. Their leader is Colonel Fitzpatrick. It won't be difficult to secure a meeting with him."

"How far away is this Fort Harper?" Miko asked, his voice tinged with concern. He dreaded the vast, lethal wasteland and didn't know how much longer he could endure its torment.

"Two days' ride, Amigo, north towards the mountains," Alejandro replied.

"Don't worry, Señor Miko. The landscape becomes a little kinder the closer we get, and there's a better chance of finding water, too."

With that reassurance, the gang immediately mounted their horses and slipped into the mouth of darkness, the pitch-black void swallowing them like a ravenous mountain lion.

* * *

Kane's daily life had transformed into a simple, focused existence. He quickly adapted to the expectations placed upon him, joining the men in their relentless search for buffalo herds. They would report back to Chief Crazy Horse, and only when necessary, return to hunt. These animals were sacred, and only the buffalo needed for sustenance were slain.

The boys immersed themselves in mastering combat and horsemanship, leaving little room for thoughts of girls. Toughness and bravery were the cornerstones of their existence. From a young age, they joined battles that consumed their lives, and by seventeen, they were expected to leave the tribe in search of the "Great Spirit."

The women, however, held pivotal roles in their society. They pitched and moved tipis whenever the tribe relocated. Their tasks included tanning hides, skinning buffalo, and gathering berries, nuts, and other bush foods while the men hunted. The men deeply valued their women, recognizing their crucial contributions.

Without them, the tribe would cease to exist.

Children had distinct roles too. They were lovingly cared for by their parents and never beaten. Strength was paramount, and crying was unacceptable. Babies who cried excessively were moved to another location to prevent their cries from betraying the tribe's position to the enemy, who could then plan an attack.

Even the children participated in the sacred rituals, which were a foundation of life in the tribe. Honoring their ancestors was paramount, and they often held grand ceremonies when the entire tribe could gather together.

Despite Kane's days being filled with brave and daring activities, he always sought out moments to be with Lone Bear.

Every time he saw her, a wave of giddiness and happiness washed over him. He longed to hold her tight and never let go, likening the feeling to the relief and joy of finally receiving a meal after a long, hungry day.

Her smile ignited a warmth deep within his heart, making him smile too. He was ravenous for her company and craved her loving touch.

One day, while the men were out scouting for buffalo, one of the braves approached Kane, wanting to have a chat.

"Shadow Bear you are fond of Lone Bear?" he queried in their indigenous tongue,

a language Kane mostly understood.

"Yes, I am.... more than fond of her, though, Black Bird," Kane replied.

"You know that Snow Goose had his eye on her before you came along. He's not happy about you taking his girl."

"Why? Were they promised to each other?" Kane reasoned.

"No, but he had plans to marry her. He had already asked Chief Crazy Horse's permission and received his blessings.... then suddenly you came along."

"Well, maybe he should've acted quicker. I'm not giving her up now. I love her, and she will be MY wife soon. Mata and Chief Crazy Horse have agreed on this." "Maybe so, but remember this, Shadow Bear Just because the Chief and Mata

admire you as some kind of Great Totem Spirit for your ability to skin-change, doesn't mean you're the perfect match for Lone Bear. Snow Goose has grown up with her, knows her well. Unlike you," Black Bird voiced with a touch of aggression

"You've only been with us half a summer.... and you think you love her? Do you truly know her? Love takes many moons to blossom into a dependable, lasting bond."

"Why has Snow Goose sent you to tell me of his disapproval? Is he a coward? One thing I know.... Lone Bear doesn't admire cowards."

"He doesn't trust you, so he doesn't respect you. All I can say is, Lone Bear is a cherished Shaman of our people. Ensure you protect her always and let nothing harm her. Once you're married, she'll be your responsibility always remember

that," Black Bird warned sharply. With a piercing shriek and a forceful kick to his horse's belly, he swiftly rode off into the distance toward his waiting brothers.

Every single day, Kane made a point of taking solitary walks into the valley, seeking moments of reflection and meditation. He sought out open fields or secluded rocks by the creek, where he would spend hours in prayer or practicing his martial arts katas.

These solitary moments were crucial for building his mental fortitude, boosting his happiness, and alleviating the stress that came with the impending hunting party.

Amidst the quiet of nature, he found clarity and purpose, contemplating his feelings for Lone Bear, his personal goals, and the positive changes he aimed to bring into his life.

By his side, Lady Vixen, his loyal companion, savored the respite from the Indian children who teased her incessantly by pulling her tail. She resented eating with the local dogs, often being shooed out of Kane's Tipi whenever Lone Bear prepared meals.

"Out you go, you're a dog, stay outside," Lone Bear would insist, her words sharp and rehearsed, as Lady Vixen obediently scampered out through the tent flap.

A powerful gust of wind suddenly swept around them, swirling and lifting Kane's long black hair into a graceful dance, stirring his emotions. He took a deep breath, allowing the warm breeze to ground him in the present moment, urging him to cherish those he loved and appreciate their time together.

As the wind rustled through the trees and gently swayed the grassy field, memories flooded Kane's mind, awakening a deep sense of righteousness within him. He felt called to embrace the path of the hero he aspired to be—strong for others, ready to confront the uncertainties of the future.

With closed eyes, Kane made a silent wish: to embody the qualities of the wind—confident, adaptable, ever-changing, and completely free.

With her ears perked and head lifted, Lady Vixen growled softly, her gaze fixed and determined as she surveyed a hillside about five hundred meters away.

"What is it?" Kane asked, abruptly pulled from his pleasant daydream. "They are close," Lady Vixen spoke telepathically.

"Who?"

"Your predators I sense them.... They're not far away," she remarked, her

alertness palpable.

Suddenly, out of nowhere, a murder of crows materialized, darkening the lanky, dead branches of a bleached tree. The tree's gnarled trunk twisted over a small stretch of a creek, now overshadowed by the multitude of birds that crowded every inch of its branches. The crows, like dark, menacing leaves, brought the tree to life with their constant flapping, casting a foreboding shadow over the scene.

"Go.... you must go," they all screeched in unison, their voices blending into a chaotic symphony of rattles and clicks.

"Crowman says we have to go," Lady Vixen warned urgently.

"But why? I am Shadow Bear. I can defeat Gideon and his posse of hunters," Kane argued, his resolve firm.

"They are growing in numbers.... It's not just you in danger. What about the Indian tribe and Lone Bear? Your presence could lead them straight to their camp," Lady Vixen countered, her worry evident.

"They don't know I'm living with the Kitanemuk people. As far as they're concerned, I could be anywhere even dead."

"I've discovered that they're unaware of your life with the Indians, and that's precisely why you must leave the tribe immediately and travel alone," Lady Vixen urged with intense conviction.

"If they can't link you to the Indians, the hunters will turn their attention elsewhere; they only seek you."

"I can't just leave.... they're my family. They rely on me. I am their protector and favored totem animal of the Great Spirit. What if I stayed and we fought the enemy together? I am strong and could take out many hostiles. Besides isn't experiencing

joyous things in life part of my destiny? Isn't that what you said my father wanted me to experience? Love and belonging somewhere?" Kane reasoned, torn between duty and destiny.

"We didn't anticipate they would track you this deep into the badlands," Lady Vixen said with a note of urgency.

"We believed the desert heat would deter their pursuit. But, as I've said before, I can only offer my advice—the choice is ultimately yours."

"Make sure it's a fair choice, one that comes from your logic and not just your heart." Kane lowered his head, frowning at the human skin book nestled in his lap. As he focused on the indented belly button, a strange vibration began to pulse through it, intensifying until it reached a frenzied pitch. Suddenly, the book burst open, its pages flipping wildly until they settled in the middle. There, vivid drawings depicted a fierce and harrowing battle scene—a field strewn with the moldering corpses of fallen warriors, their forms abandoned in a sea of blood.

"What is this?" Kane questioned, his voice tinged with disbelief.

"Your father is showing you the future of the Kitanemuk people if you don't leave as soon as possible," Lady Vixen informed solemnly.

"This can't be true. I'll be there fighting alongside them," Kane protested defiantly. "Your power has its limits when faced with a relentless barrage of gunfire," Lady Vixen insisted, her voice stern

"Yes, you are formidable, Shadow Bear, but you are still flesh and blood. What you see before you is the stark truth—if you don't act now, the consequences will be dire. The reality has been laid bare before you."

"A barrage of gunfire? The monks don't carry guns, and the only ones who would are those feral Mexicans," Kane argued.

"My 'little birds' visited me this morning and saw your hunters heading towards the Army Fort," Lady Vixen explained.

"There's an Army Fort out here?" Kane asked, genuinely surprised.

"Yes, they're here to occupy and develop the land, making it safer for new settlers to live and farm," Lady Vixen replied.

"And what about the native Indians where would they live?"

"They wouldn't live anywhere.... like the picture in front of you reveals," Lady Vixen concluded gravely.

Kane gently stroked Lady Vixen's head as he processed the new information and contemplated his decision. As he spoke, he watched the murder of crows disperse into the dark blue sky, their fading calls echoing the urgent warning.... go.... go.... go.

"Thank you, Lady Vixen. I don't know what I'd do without you. I want you to stay close from now on. I've made my choice," he said with strong conviction.

"We're leaving now? Let's go!" Lady Vixen yapped eagerly, wagging her tail with enthusiasm.

Kane paused, deep in thought, before responding.

"No I have another plan. I can't leave things unexplained."

* * *

Walking through the village with his faithful dog trotting beside him, Kane navigated past the clustered tents. He recognized Lone Bear standing at the doorway of their Tipi, her presence drawing his attention like a magnet. As he passed neighboring tents, he courteously waved to a woman carrying a baby on her back, engrossed in daily chores. Groups of young girls trailed behind older women, absorbing the intricacies of traditional tasks like basket-weaving and cooking.

From a young age, these girls were taught resilience, instructed to embody strength and suppress emotions, conforming steadfastly to tribal customs.

Approaching his Tipi, Kane saw Lone Bear rushing towards him. Her face lit up with joy, arms outstretched in eager anticipation. When they finally met, she enveloped him in a warm, adoring embrace, her arms wrapping around his waist tightly. "Where did you go? You've been gone much longer than usual," Lone Bear asked, stepping back and searching his face.

"I had a lot of thinking to do, my love.... I need to meet with Chief Crazy Horse and your father immediately," Kane replied, his tone serious.

"Why? What's wrong?" Lone Bear pressed, her voice tinged with a mix of frustration and fear.

"Something's come to light, and I need to discuss it with the Chief," Kane explained, sensing her growing concern.

"Tell me what's going on " she pleaded, her eyes searching his face for answers.

"I can't tell you at the moment after I've spoken with the elders, I will explain

everything," Kane replied calmly, trying to diffuse the tension.

"You've said that before, like with that creepy book you always carry around!" Lone Bear shouted, her frustration boiling over as she attempted to snatch the book from Kane's grip.

"Stop it, Lone Bear everyone is watching. I don't need this unwanted attention,"

Kane scolded, his voice firm.

"Why? Because all your secrets will be revealed?" she taunted, her tone argumentative.

"Stop it.... I won't ask you again.... and let go of my book," Kane warned, trying to pry her fingers from the journal. In the struggle, Lone Bear's sharp nails inadvertently scratched the human skin covering, drawing blood.

"What is that?" she screamed in disgust, but Kane ignored her, striding past and pushing through the buckskin door of his Tipi with frustration. A crowd of onlookers stared at Lone Bear, whispering amongst themselves, curiosity and gossip spreading like wildfire.

As the final rays of sunlight kissed the heathland, casting a golden glow over the village, Kane entered Chief Crazy Horse's Tipi alongside his friend Mata. He settled among the elders, feeling the scrutiny of their gaze as they regarded him with suspicion and apprehension. Time seemed to stretch on as they sat in silence, the air thick with anticipation.

Finally, Chief Crazy Horse spoke, his voice a low, measured rumble as he casually dragged on the peace pipe, the smoke curling around him like ancient wisdom. "You requested this meeting, Shadow Bear. What is it you wish to discuss?"

"You and your people have shown me great kindness. You accepted me for who I am, welcomed me into your tribe, and gave me a home, and for that, I am eternally grateful. But there's something you don't know about me," Kane admitted earnestly, meeting Chief Crazy Horse's cold gaze as the old man continued puffing on his pipe with stoic calm.

Clearing his throat nervously, Kane continued, his voice carrying the heaviness of his confession.

"While I was living at the monastery in Japan, a fight broke out between myself and our high priest. Unaware of my full strength and abilities at the time, I was unexpectedly stabbed. In that moment, my skin-changing powers manifested uncontrollably, and I accidentally killed the priest by slashing his throat open. There was another monk involved in the altercation, and I believed I had also killed him, but later learned he survived. Now, he's hunting me, leading a group of ninjas who have tracked me here to America. They aim to capture me and return me to Japan for punishment," Kane confessed, his voice tinged with urgency and remorse.

"What does this have to do with us?" Chief Crazy Horse queried calmly, his expression unreadable

"I've learned that they aren't far from this camp, and if they find me here living with you, they could slaughter your people for helping me," Kane explained urgently, his voice betraying his concern for the tribe's safety.

"Is this the only crime you've committed out in the world or do you have more you

want to tell us?" Chief Crazy Horse asked, his demeanor cool and calculating. "Before I met Mata, I was staying with Mexicans at a ranch far from here. Some of the men there challenged me, and unfortunately, they met their death," Kane admitted reluctantly.

"Was this ranch owned by a man called Don Morales?" the Chief inquired.

"Yes, it was," Kane confirmed.

"You've taken on a dangerous enemy, Shadow Bear. He won't rest until he has your head served to him on a plate," Chief Crazy Horse warned.

"You know Don Morales?" Kane asked, surprised.

"This is our heritage land.... we know every part of its beautiful yet savage landscape. We know who lives here and who passes through. I'm already aware of your enemies. Earlier, my scouts told me they are currently staying at Fort Harper," Chief Crazy Horse revealed knowingly.

"How can you be certain it's them?" Kane asked, his voice edged with uncertainty.

"Your adversaries stand out from the usual visitors to the Army Fort. There are three men with shaved heads and two rough-looking Mexicans who arrived together.

It's an unusual mix of companions, wouldn't you agree? They seem to match the description of the men you've angered," Chief Crazy Horse explained calmly, his eyes unwavering.

Kane was at a loss for words, sitting silently until Lady Vixen nudged her snout gently under his arm, urging him to hold her close, a reminder of her steadfast loyalty.

"What do you want me to do, Chief Crazy Horse? I've grown to love this home and don't wish to leave, but if that's what you deem necessary, I will," Kane said earnestly.

"My primary concern is the safety of my people. I cannot risk needless danger for them. This is your burden, not ours. It would be best for you to leave the tribe. You are the target of these men, and we have no stake in the trouble you've brought upon yourself," Chief Crazy Horse replied firmly, his decision clear and resolute.

"Alright it's the best and fairest solution. No one knows I'm here, so I'll leave

tomorrow morning," Kane affirmed, his tone resigned.

"What about Lone Bear? She loves you deeply. She believes you two will be married. You can't just leave her," Mata interjected, his voice tinged with disappointment.

"I love her with all my heart, but it's too dangerous for anyone to come with me. Besides, she won't be abandoned she has her family and the support of the tribe.

I will come back for her one day, I promise" Kane replied bitterly, his spirits dampened.

A heavy silence settled over the Tipi, broken only by the sound of Chief Crazy Horse puffing on his pipe, all eyes fixed on Kane.

"Alright then.... I guess I better start packing," Kane finally said with a hint of sarcasm, breaking the tense silence that hung in the air.

As Kane walked to his Tipi, his movements were deliberate as he gathered the essentials needed for his departure. Inside, Lone Bear lay on a bedroll, her back turned towards him, her attention fixed on the sounds of his hurried packing.

She listened intently as he shoved items into his knapsack, the atmosphere heavy with unspoken emotions that hung between them like a curtain.

"You're a murderer," Lone Bear muttered under her breath, her words carrying a mix of disbelief and anger.

"What did you just say?" Kane responded, his alarm evident in his voice. "You're a murderer," she repeated louder, sitting up abruptly to confront him.

"Who told you that? Were you spying on my meeting with Chief Crazy Horse?" Kane demanded, feeling defensive.

"Yes, I was. When were you planning to tell me the truth? I had no idea that my lover was a murderer, and to think that I was about to marry you. Isn't that something I should know?" Lone Bear accused, her voice trembling with hurt and betrayal.

"I'm leaving tomorrow anyway, to protect you and your

people," Kane tried to justify, his tone strained.

"Don't pretend you're a hero. We wouldn't be in this danger if you hadn't come here," Lone Bear admonished, tears streaming down her face.

"It was never my intention to hurt anyone, especially you, Lone Bear. I truly believed I would spend the rest of my life with you and your people," Kane pleaded, his own emotions raw.

"How many people have you killed?" Lone Bear asked through her tears. "Does it matter?" Kane protested defensively.

"It matters to me," she replied firmly, her gaze searching his face for answers. "Why? So you can condemn me some more? One, two, three, four.... What does it matter?" Kane yelled, his voice escalating into a pulsating growl, his emotions swirling into an animalistic manifestation. Fearing he might involuntarily skin-change in front of Lone Bear, Kane stormed out of the Tipi, grabbing his knapsack and throwing it over his shoulder as he went.

"KANE!!" Lone Bear cried out desperately, her voice screaming with anguish, but Kane pressed on, his heart burdened by internal strife. With Lady Vixen steadfastly at his side, he rushed out of the village, each heavy step reverberating with the weight of his decision.

* * *

The arrival of Europeans in the great frontier had a profound impact on the Midwest long before permanent settlers arrived. French and English colonies along the Atlantic coast displaced

Native American tribes, pushing them westward into territories where they competed with existing clans.

While Europeans brought manufactured goods like blankets, cookware, knives, and guns, which were traded for valuable beaver, deer, and buffalo skins, the economic benefits came at a cost. Fort Harper became a hub for both traditional and exotic trades, attracting a diverse array of cultures. However, this transient population also brought with it a persistent threat of criminal activity, leading to violence that posed an ongoing danger to all Native American tribes in the region.

The local Indians primarily traded furs with Fort Harper, but this was just one facet of the fort's bustling activities. Trade in Chinese goods such as tea, silk, and porcelain also thrived, proving highly profitable. However, a significant challenge arose: the Chinese would only accept silver in exchange for their goods, leading to a drain of silver from Britain and damaging its economy.

To counteract this, East Indian companies and British merchants resorted to smuggling Indian opium into China. Initially valued for its medicinal properties—relieving pain, aiding sleep, and reducing stress—opium soon became a scourge. Within five years, countless visitors to the fort unwittingly fell into addiction. The widespread use of illegal opium not only debilitated individuals but also disrupted the once-favorable balance of trade within the Fort, involving other goods and services.

The military soldiers at Fort Harper made desperate attempts to stem the influx of opium. However, the sheer volume of travelers passing through the fort placed a severe strain on their resources and made it challenging to effectively control the spread of the drug.

Chief Crazy Horse was keenly aware of Fort Harper's perilous reputation and understood the risks associated with his enemies residing there. He was adamant about avoiding any conflict that could draw unwanted attention or unnecessary battles with the well-armed soldiers stationed at the fort. Chief Crazy Horse recognized the overwhelming firepower of the army and sought to navigate the situation with caution to protect his people from potential massacres.

"The end of summer draws near. In seven moons, the season will change," Chief Crazy Horse announced to the assembled elders.

"Given this, and the issue of Shadow Bear and his hunters at Fort Harper, I propose we begin our migration earlier than usual. It's safer to move in advance than to wait for trouble to find us," he continued, met with courtly nods and murmurs of agreement from the council.

"It's settled then. Inform the tribe that we depart tomorrow morning. Start preparations immediately," the Chief ordered decisively, prompting one of the men to swiftly exit the teepee and spread the announcement throughout the camp.

Their conical tents, crafted from sturdy buffalo skin and supported by stout wooden poles, provided resilient shelter for the nomadic tribe. These dwellings were not just temporary abodes but symbols of their adaptable lifestyle, quick to erect and dismantle as they journeyed through shifting landscapes.

Every aspect of their migration bespoke a life in constant motion. Belongings were meticulously piled on horses, and even their loyal dogs carried baggage, a caravan in perpetual readiness. By midday, the tribe was already in motion, a winding procession of people threading through valleys towards the looming mountains, seeking refuge from the turmoil brought by Kane's looming threat.

Amidst the orchestrated flurry, Lone Bear made a deliberate show of her presence. She methodically disassembled her teepee, her movements precise and purposeful, yet her eyes and attitude revealed a mind deeply preoccupied with more than just the practicalities of travel.

With her father's assistance, she packed their horses, each gesture a careful step towards her clandestine plan. Though outwardly focused on the immediate task, her thoughts raced ahead, quickly strategizing her departure from the tribe to pursue the trail of her beloved.

Meanwhile, Kane had spent the night nestled within the dense undergrowth of the forest. He had chosen his position with meticulous care—hidden just beyond the fringe of visibility yet close enough to scrutinize every subtle shift and flicker of movement within the tribe.

As dawn's first light pierced the forest canopy, Kane observed with a calculating gaze as the tribe swiftly packed their belongings and began their westward migration. For Kane, this was the signal to set his own departure plans into motion.

Throughout the night, Lady Vixen had been a silent companion by his side, a presence that provided a fleeting comfort in the wilderness. However, upon awakening in the dim hours of morning, Kane found himself alone. Her absence struck him with a profound sense of abandonment, a potent mix of uncertainty and longing. He grappled with unanswered questions—where she had gone and why she had left him behind.

As the tribe's journey unfolded before him, Kane felt an acute sense of isolation. Their lives separating from his own stirred a tightening ache in his chest, a relentless grip that gnawed at him with unyielding persistence.

On the saddest, loneliest day of his life, Kane felt the weight of Lady Vixen's desertion like a crushing darkness that consumed every moment. Her absence had extinguished the inner light he once held dear, leaving behind a bitter residue of resentment. The ongoing nightmare of isolation and rejection fed his growing bitterness, casting shadows over his thoughts.

He envied those surrounded by love from family and friends, their warmth a stark contrast to his own solitary existence. The shock of Lady Vixen forsaking him gripped him with suffocating intensity, making each breath a struggle against the despair that threatened to overwhelm him.

"Where is the limit? When will the wolves be called off, and salvation begin?" Kane wondered, his voice tinged with despair as he searched for a glimmer of hope amidst the exclusion that enveloped him.

Like an abandoned runt puppy, Kane clandestinely shadowed the tribe's journey for miles until they reached the canyon—a narrow passage hemmed in by towering cliffs, the sole route forward. Despite his deep affection for Lone Bear and her people, Kane realized it was time to part ways and forge his own path.

As he stood there, watching from a vantage point, Kane felt the pain of his lost love and the disappointment of his relationship. Each connection, like fragile paper in a storm, dissolved into nothingness, leaving him yearning for a touch, a comforting embrace that never came. In moments like these, the world seemed cold and indifferent, a vast expanse of abandonment that threatened to swallow him.

He longed to disappear, to dissolve into the rain like melting snow, anything to escape the relentless agony that poisoned his spirit. From his perch, Kane observed the last of the Indians and their horses vanish into the canyon, disappearing between the unforgiving walls of rock.

"Goodbye, my darling Lone Bear. I wish things could've been different," Kane murmured earnestly to himself, his words barely audible over the rustle of the wind. With a heavy heart, he retraced his steps down the ridge, veering northward into the wooded hills, hoping to lead his pursuers away from the innocent Kitanemuk people.

Meanwhile, deliberately falling behind the rest of the tribe, Lone Bear meticulously scanned the surrounding landscape. Then, by chance, her keen eyes caught a figure in the distance, navigating cautiously along a rocky ridge.

"It's Kane, he's still here!" she exclaimed with a surge of excitement. Determined to seize the opportunity, she lagged further behind until the tribe was safely ahead, giving her the chance to change direction and follow her beloved.

However, Lone Bear wasn't the only one who spotted Kane moving along the ridge. Unfortunately, vigilant eyes also noticed her departure from the group, viewing her solitary pursuit as a reckless desertion of the tribe's protection and their attentive braves.

Chapter 17

A few days earlier, Miko stood before the mirror, meticulously shaving his head, a ritual that defined his Buddhist monk identity.

"Why bother with all that?" Carlos jeered from the table nearby, picking at his teeth with a toothpick, his grin revealing decayed, crooked teeth.

"It's my religion and my identity," Miko replied calmly, wiping away the last traces of shaving soap.

"All three of you should look like us," Carlos insisted.

"No, thank you. I take pride in being a Japanese Buddhist Monk. How would you feel if I asked you to stop being a grubby, heathen Mexican man? Could you do that, Carlos?" Miko retorted, a smirk playing on his lips.

"No.... I like being a grubby, heathen Mexican man.... and wildly promiscuous," Carlos shot back, casually spitting a piece of food onto the floor.

"You disgust me," Miko responded, his disdain evident.

Carlos chuckled, a wicked satisfaction in his eyes as he savored the discomfort he had stirred in the young, self-righteous monk.

"I bet you don't even have any balls. Monks don't have sex, so yours are probably shriveled up with cobwebs over them."

"Shut up, Carlos.... Hiro, why do we have to share a room with these vulgar Mexicans?" Miko complained, his frustration obvious.

"Because this is the only room available at the Fort. Carlos, I've warned you before, keep insulting my brother and I will break your neck.... easily," Hiro warned sternly, his voice carrying a hint of steel.

"Not when I've got this, Amigo," Carlos boasted, drawing his gun from its holster and twirling it around his finger with practiced ease.

"You sleep, don't you?" Hiro retorted with a mocking tone, glancing over at Miko who chuckled softly at his brother's jab.

"I'm out of here you monks are too creepy for me," Carlos declared abruptly,

grabbing his sombrero and throwing it on his head.

"Where are you going?" Alejandro asked, his brow furrowed.

"Anywhere but here. There's a tavern at the back end of the Fort called *'Last Chance"* I'll see you tomorrow, Amigo," Carlos replied, his mood defiant as he stormed out of the room, slamming the door behind him in frustration.

"Don't forget we have a meeting with Colonel Fitzpatrick in the morning!" Alejandro called after him, but Carlos was already gone.

Fort Harper was an imposing structure, stretching 500 yards in width and 800 in length, with many of its buildings rising to two stories. Life within its walls was a relentless and monotonous routine for both the soldiers and their families, marked by the harsh realities of military existence.

Many recruits rarely encountered combat, instead spending their days toiling through manual labor in the isolated outpost. Situated far from any town, single enlisted men had no outlet for their boredom or opportunities to socialize with women.

With meager wages, substandard accommodations, a transient population, and formidable Indigenous adversaries who inspired a mix of fear, admiration, and animosity, life on the frontier was a relentless struggle. The soldiers found themselves in a perpetual battle against both the elusive enemy and the unforgiving environment.

Yet amidst this hardship, the isolation fostered a profound camaraderie and solidarity within Fort Harper. Shared difficulties forged bonds akin to those of an extended family, where mutual suffering bred a unique strength. They relied on customs, and a code of honor that set them apart from the distant big cities "back east," finding comfort and identity in their collective resilience.

Life for women at Fort Harper was fraught with challenges and loneliness. Far from their families and friends, they endured an isolated existence punctuated by the harsh realities of frontier life.

The community included a diverse array of social classes, each facing distinct strains. For many women, the isolation meant confronting the prospect of childbirth without the support network they would have had back home. The risk of mortality during childbirth loomed as a constant concern.

Social divisions among women further complicated their lives. Officers' wives often maintained a distance from other women, particularly those married to enlisted men. The latter often found themselves employed as servants for officers or working as laundresses for the army, roles that perpetuated social hierarchies within the fort.

Among these challenges, the women of Fort Harper navigated a complex social landscape, seeking companionship and help with the demands of their daily life.

Perched high on the gables of the buildings, a multitude of ravens screeched discordantly as Carlos made his way slowly towards the tavern, a strange shiver coursing down his spine. Sensing unseen eyes upon him, he adjusted his sombrero slightly, shadowing his eyes, an ever-watchful stance as he navigated through the busy crowd.

Each person moved with purpose, seemingly pulled by invisible forces in different directions, each harboring their own objectives for the day. Amidst the throng, Carlos caught sight of a group of women, their laughter ringing like echoes of youth as they ogled a young soldier, muscles gleaming as he stripped down to bathe in a communal wash barrel.

Slipping through the crowd with practiced stealth, Carlos found himself surrounded in a chaotic blend of perfumes, body odors, and overpowering cologne. Enjoying this sensory overload, he found solace in his anonymity, a sheild behind which he could be anyone, or perhaps no one at all.

In this place, teeming with life and intrigue, Carlos embraced the freedom of being an unknown figure, a solitary soul mixed in a sea of transient faces and secret desires.

The doors of the *"Last Chance"* Tavern swung rhythmically as a steady stream of patrons flowed in and out, Carlos seamlessly blending into their company. If he could just dissolve into the lively atmosphere of the saloon, he thought, he would embody its essence—a spirit as fluid as the wafting smoke that hung lazily in the dimly lit air. He yearned to immerse himself in the infectious laughter and warm smiles that illuminated the shadowed corners of the room, his eyes widening at the muted hues of liquor bottles and their twinkling glints of reflected light.

As the evening progressed, Carlos found himself relaxing into the company of soldiers and barmaids alike, sustained by rounds of spirits and the fellowship that comes with shared indulgence. Surrounded by the boisterous exchanges and fleeting moments of bravado, he settled at a table facing the tavern's entrance.

From his vantage point, he discreetly observed each newcomer, meticulously dissecting their appearance and contemplating their roles within the Fort's complex web of functions and alliances. Every detail was scrutinized, as he pondered how each individual might fit into the larger tapestry of life at the fort.

Suddenly, his scrutiny was interrupted by the appearance of a striking woman in the doorway. Her presence exuded an air of refinement that sharply contrasted with the rugged appearance of the tavern's regulars, captivating Carlos's attention and sparking a newfound curiosity in the midst of the tavern's lively disarray.

She appeared slightly bewildered, her gaze scanning the noisy tavern with a hint of anxiety. Carlos, captivated by her beauty, felt an inexplicable pull and rose from his seat, approaching her with a respectful gesture of removing his sombrero.

"Hello, my name is Carlos. You look lost. Can I help you?" he asked courteously, his tone warm and inviting.

"Oh.... I'm looking for my husband. He told me to meet him here," she replied, her voice tinged with urgency as she continued to search the crowd.

"I have an empty seat at my table. Would you like to sit with me while you wait for your husband? It would be better than standing in the doorway," Carlos offered persuasively, sensing her need for comfort in the chaotic tavern.

The woman hesitated, her gaze assessing Carlos with a mix of curiosity and caution. After a moment, she nodded slightly, acknowledging his kindness.

"Alright.... but I do have a husband, so please don't try anything creepy," she cautioned, following Carlos to his table.

"Of course not. I promise," he assured her sincerely, a flicker of intrigue dancing in his eyes as he settled back into his seat, eager to learn more about the mysterious woman who had unexpectedly entered his world that night.

Carlos demonstrated his respect and manners by pulling out a chair for the lady, ensuring she was seated comfortably before taking his own seat.

"Would you like something to drink?" he offered politely.

"Yes, that would be nice I'll have a brandy, thank you," she replied graciously.

"Brandy it is," Carlos affirmed with a smile. He rose from his seat again and made his way to the bar, swiftly returning with a shot of brandy and a large glass of beer with a tequila chaser in hand.

"Here we go," Carlos exclaimed eagerly, his voice brimming with excitement at the rare opportunity to converse with such an elegant woman. In typical circumstances, it would be unacceptable for a white woman to entertain the company of a Mexican man, as social norms often deemed them beneath her.

"You seem to have had quite a bit to drink already. Do you really need more?" the lady asked firmly, noting the somewhat cheesy grin on Carlos's rugged face.

"I'm fine. I've been drunk plenty of times before, and I'm too old to be scolded, thank you," Carlos replied, his speech slightly slurred as he stumbled over some words. "Alright, let's have another drink then," the lady encouraged, swiftly downing her brandy in a single gulp.

As the night progressed, Carlos made several more trips to the bar, clumsily returning to their table each time with a new assortment of drinks, often spilling some in his inebriated state.

"Oooh.... I think I'm reaching my limit," Carlos chuckled nervously, wiping the spilled beer from his hands.

"Yes, I can see that," the lady replied curtly, her disapproval evident as she observed Carlos's increasingly intoxicated behavior.

"I need to use the restroom, to.... drain the snake, as they say," he continued laughing, his words slurring.

"Oh, and by the way, your husband still hasn't shown up. You've been waiting for hours. What's going on with that?" Carlos questioned suspiciously, struggling to maintain his balance as he stood up.

"Yes, I know. I'm leaving after this drink to wait for him in my room," she informed him coolly, her patience wearing thin.

"Well, don't leave until I get back from the bathroom, okay?" Carlos instructed with a sly wink, trying to maintain a sense of charm despite his obvious state of intoxication. While Carlos was away, the woman skilfully retrieved a pouch from her purse containing a brownish powder. With practiced precision, she poured its entire contents into Carlos's beer, using a spoon from the table to dissolve the potent substance. Sitting poised like a serene figure, she waited patiently until she saw Carlos stumbling back towards her.

"You waited.... Gracias. I better finish this beer. My comrades and I have a meeting with the Lieutenant Colonel in the morning. Gotta look my best," Carlos chuckled, effortlessly downing his beer in one swift motion.

Curious, the lady inquired, "What's the meeting about?"

"We're hunting a man who can change into a bear. Can you believe it? Who'd have thought a man could transform into an animal? He's already killed people. We need the army's help because they know the terrain," Carlos revealed, oblivious in his intoxicated state.

"That sounds dangerous. Do you know where he is? Have you found him yet?" she probed further, keeping him engaged while watching the effects of the administered poison take hold.

"No, but the army has scouts. If he's around, the outriders will spot him," Carlos replied, his focus wavering.

"What will you do once he's caught?" she continued to distract him, buying time as the drug began to work its magic.

"We'll kill him, of course. The monks traveling with us want him sent back to Japan to face justice there. It's too risky to transport a man who can turn into a demon. For everyone's sake, it's better if he's dead. You know, we've been sitting here for hours, and you haven't told me your name," Carlos suddenly realized, the haze of his drunkenness lifting slightly.

It was a surreal moment for Carlos as he stared at the woman's face, waiting for her response. Reality twisted and warped before his eyes, transforming her delicate features into a malformed visage. Her face shifted uncontrollably between human and the snarling, ferocious head of a wolf, her smile turning from gentle to menacing with dripping fangs.

"My name is Lady Vixen, and for my Master's sake, you're the one who's better off dead," she snarled, her voice dripping with malice.

Carlos froze in shock, feeling a dryness in his mouth and an overwhelming urge to vomit. His heartbeat slowed, his breathing became shallow, until finally, everything ceased abruptly. His head dropped heavily onto the table, lifeless.

Lady Vixen stood over him, a satisfied smile on her lips. The lethal dose of opium had achieved its purpose.

"One arch-enemy down, four more to go," she thought to herself, her eyes cold and calculating. With a final, indifferent glance at the lifeless Carlos, she slipped out of the rowdy *"Last Chance"* tavern, her departure unnoticed amidst the mayhem and revelry. Carlos lay still, discarded among the once-lively surroundings he had briefly occupied, a silent casualty in Lady Vixen's covert quest for vengeance.

The wild and extroverted Mexican, met his end in a manner as dramatic as his life had been. His larger-than-life presence, known for its zest and audacity, faded into a stillness that contrasted sharply with the raucous energy of the frontier.

***

Before the crack of dawn, the piercing crow of a bantam rooster shattered the silence of the preceding night, signaling the start of a new day at the isolated fort. Alejandro and his fellow monks rose, dressed, and sat down to a sparse breakfast of hard pilot bread and coffee. Miko wrinkled his nose at the sight of the coffee, which looked like the murky brown water left over after washing dirty clothes. Despite its unappetizing appearance, it was the only comfort available.

"This tastes as bad as it looks," Miko grumbled, taking a reluctant sip. Alejandro was about to respond to the "delicate" monk when a loud knock interrupted him. He casually wandered over to the door and opened it. "Hola.... are you here to escort us to our meeting with the Colonel?" he asked, seeing two military police officers standing in the hallway.

"Is there another Mexican traveling with you?" one of the officers inquired. "Sí, but he's not here with us, Señor," Alejandro answered, a tinge of concern creeping into his voice.

"Oh Dios, what has Carlos done now?" Alejandro muttered, a sense of dread creeping into his mind as he considered Carlos's history of mischievous pranks.

"So, Carlos is his name? Well, he was found dead in the tavern last night," the officer informed him, simultaneously pushing the door open wider. Inside, three monks dressed in cowboy gear stood staring, their eyes wide with shock.

"Dead? How? What happened?" Alejandro blurted out, his questions tumbling over each other in a rush of alarm.

"Who are these three *'Jonnies'*?" the second officer asked, his tone sharp with suspicion.

"We're all traveling together. We have an urgent mission. When we arrived here, we booked a meeting with your Colonel

Fitzpatrick for sometime this morning," Alejandro explained, his voice steady despite the growing tension.

"All of you, pack your things and hurry up. We're taking you to the Colonel," the first officer commanded, his attitude leaving no room for argument. The urgency in his voice underscored the gravity of the situation, and the monks quickly gathered their belongings, their minds reeling from the sudden and grim news.

Standing in front of the closed office door, the more domineering officer began instructing Alejandro and the monks on proper protocol for their meeting with the Colonel.

"Take your hats off before entering the office and don't speak unless he addresses you. Understood?" the officer dictated, his order standing no dispute.

"Respect the rights and dignities of the other officers in the room as well," he added, while the men stood in tense silence, anticipating the moment the doors would swing open to summon them inside. The severity of the situation infiltrated the air, each second stretching out as they prepared for the impending encounter.

Miko felt the pressure of waiting increasing, his legs trembling slightly with apprehension as he contemplated the significance and consequences of Carlos' antics and untimely death.

Eventually, the doors swung open, and the two military police officers marched into the room. Alejandro and the monks hesitated, gingerly inching their way in as they watched the officers briskly stand at attention and salute the Colonel.

The atmosphere was thick with tension, each step they took

weighed down by the uncertainty of what lay ahead.

"Are these men related to the dead Mexican we found?" the Colonel asked, his long, drawling Texan accent adding intensity to each word.

"Sir, yes sir," the dominant officer answered, both men standing at attention and snapping back their salutes.

"At ease," the Colonel directed, and the officers instantly relaxed into a more casual stance. "Bring them here to me."

Alejandro and the monks were ushered forward. The Colonel's gaze fixed on Alejandro as he asked bluntly, "I am assuming that you were a friend of the dead Mexican?"

"Sí.... I'm his comrade. We worked together at Rancho Los Charros. It is owned by Don Morales, Señor Colonel," Alejandro stated, his thick Mexican accent coloring his words.

"I am aware of who owns the Rancho Los Charros, but who are these other three men with you?"

"They are Buddhist monks from Japan. We had a meeting with you today to discuss a proposal," Alejandro replied.

"Yes, that can come later. We have the issue of your dead friend to deal with first. When was the last time you saw him? What was his name again?"

"Carlos, Señor Colonel.... Carlos was his name," Alejandro answered solemnly, a brief flicker of nostalgia crossing his face as he remembered the good times they shared together.

"The last time we saw him was in our room. He said he was going to the tavern. Carlos doesn't.... I mean, didn't get along with the monks, so he left," Alejandro explained, his voice tinged with sorrow.

The Colonel redirected his attention toward Hiro and Juji. "Do any of you monks speak English?" he asked.

"Hai, yes, we speak English," Hiro replied.

"Why are you here with these Mexicans? Aren't you out of your comfort zone?" the Colonel continued, his tone dripping with sarcasm.

"I've heard that Japan has quite a cold climate, and now here you are, trekking through the Nevada Desert with Mexicans. Seems a bit odd to me." He chuckled derisively and began pacing around the room, his hands firmly gripping the lapel of his army jacket, a clear display of his command and influence.

The tension in the room was obvious as the Colonel's mocking words hung in the air, his authoritative presence dominating the space.

"Hai.... I know it seems strange, Shuryo (commander), but we are here to—"

"What did you just call me?" the Colonel interrupted rudely, more interested in Hiro's native language.

"Shuryo means 'commander,'" Miko suddenly piped up, stepping forward from behind Alejandro, Juji, and Hiro.

"And you are?" The Colonel appeared amused by the bizarre spectacle of this diverse ethnic group traveling together.

"My name is Miko."

"You're a bit young to be with these men."

"I travel with my brothers. I am a steward for my Master Gideon, who was brutally attacked by the man we are hunting. That is why we are here. We need one of your army men as a scout to help us track the monster down," Miko explained clearly and calmly.

"So who is this Master Gideon, and where is he now?" the

Colonel inquired, his curiosity stimulated.

"Master Gideon is a high priest from our monastery, and he's resting at Rancho Los Charros with Don Morales," Miko responded.

The room fell silent as the Colonel processed this information, his expression a mix of skepticism and intrigue.

"Ahh yes, I know the ranch and its owner.... we have been well acquainted in the past," the Colonel affirmed.

"Por Favor, Señor Colonel.... before we go any further.... could you please tell me how Carlos died? He was my friend, Señor," Alejandro quickly interjected, his voice pleading.

"It looks as though he drank himself to death. They said he'd been there all afternoon and into the evening, drinking shots of tequila and pots of beer. Apparently, at one point, he was sitting with a lady who looked way out of his class, but they shared a couple of hours together. He was very generous in buying her drinks," the Colonel smoothly illustrated.

"Where is the Chica now? Did she come forward with any information? I will have to explain this to Don Morales, why another one of his wranglers is dead and.... aye, aye, aye.... that means more trips to San Francisco to find recruits," Alejandro whined, dramatically clasping his hands on top of his head and rocking from side to side.

"Get a hold on yourself.... you Mexicans are all the same.... over-emotional. The lady seems to have vanished into thin air, but we will find her," the Colonel snapped abruptly.

His expression softened slightly, a trace of sympathy mingling with his usual stern demeanor.

"She left long before Carlos was discovered. Everyone believed he was merely asleep, not dead. We have no leads on her whereabouts. We'll continue the investigation, but for now, your priority should be to focus on why you're here at my Fort and take measures to ensure you don't meet a similar fate."

"He just lost his friend," Miko commented sharply, but Hiro silenced him with a stern "ssshhh."

The Colonel coughed nervously and cleared his throat, seeming slightly embarrassed, but he composed himself and continued the conversation as he sat down behind his desk.

"So what you're telling me is that you've traveled all the way from Japan in search of a man who attacked your high priest? Seems a bit overzealous, don't you think?

What aren't you telling me?" the Colonel questioned, his tone probing. "What does overzealous mean?" Miko whispered to Juji.

"It means over-passionate," Juji whispered back.

"Shhh," Hiro quickly muttered, signaling for them to focus on the conversation. Ignoring the muted voices of the three monks, the Colonel busied himself with documents he pulled from his desk drawer.

"I'm still waiting for an answer to my question," he blurted out unexpectedly. "Hai.... the man we hunt, Kane, murdered our Abbot and has since killed more innocents here in America," Hiro declared.

"And he murdered my friend, Chico, at Don Morales' ranch too and burnt down jeffe's barn," Alejandro added swiftly.

"I suppose Don Morales didn't take that lightly," the Colonel remarked.

"This is why we are here with these monks. They seek justice as much as Don Morales does, so we're bound together in this mission.... to find Kane and bring him to justice, before he does any more damage Senor Colonel," Alejandro explained. "Ah.... Colonel, there's one more thing about Kane that's not obvious to the bystander," Miko boldly announced.

"What?"

"Kane is a skin-changer, a demon who morphs into a colossal bear to kill his enemies," Miko divulged urgently.

"He has immense power, a threat to all who dare cross his path. Finding him is crucial; he will strike again, and we need your army's help."

"A what? A skin-changer? A man transforming into a giant bear?" the Colonel scoffed, his laughter laced with a hint of unease. The attending officers exchanged amused smirks, their skepticism barely concealed.

"Colonel, may I speak?" interjected a guarding officer. "Yes, Sergeant, what is it?"

"While scouting the western plains, my team witnessed an unusually large bear slaughtering buffalo alongside the Kitanemuk tribe. Strangely, it seemed tame, even affectionately embraced by the braves. I reported it promptly, sir, but no action has been taken as yet," the Sergeant reported grimly.

A heavy silence settled over the room, each person holding their breath, awaiting the Colonel's response.

"I see.... could this be the skin-changing monk you're hunting? Kane, was it?" the Colonel drawled, his voice carrying a note of skepticism.

"Kane.... yes, that sounds like him. How many giant bears do you stumble upon around here?" Hiro responded, his companions nodding in agreement.

"What about Carlos? Where is he now? Am I permitted to see him, Colonel?" Alejandro interjected, distress carved deeply on his face. The thought of his friend's body being discarded troubled his mind greatly.

"He's been taken to the infirmary. You have a choice: either return him to Don Morales for a proper burial or leave him here to be incinerated with the others," the Colonel replied matter-of-factly.

"I will take him back to Rancho Los Charro," Alejandro asserted firmly, his voice laced with determination.

"He lived there most of his life; it's only right he rests there. And what about the chica he was drinking with? Is anyone searching for her?"

"We have her description, and my soldiers have been searching all night," the Colonel said, his tone carrying a hint of frustration.

"Aside from a few tavern patrons who recall seeing them together, no one else seems to remember her. Most of the people there are either drunk or high on opium—an issue we struggle to manage due to its role in the local trade system—so details go unnoticed. Now, let's shift focus. What's our strategy for dealing with this gigantic bear character?" He turned his attention to his two attending officers, his question sharp and commanding.

"Sir, may I speak?" the Sergeant interjected.

"You have permission to speak freely," the Colonel granted.

"Planning is crucial. As you mentioned, Colonel, the Kitanemuk tribe is formidable.

I suggest we survey the tribe first. If the beast is indeed with them, we intervene and capture it. Chief Crazy Horse values his people, so he may be open to negotiation. We either arrest their demon or threaten the destruction of his tribe," the Sergeant proposed with rigid determination.

"Yes, that's a solid plan. Keep the scouting party small to avoid detection by the tribe. Take two other officers with you, observe for a day, then report back to me," the Colonel ordered.

"Colonel, may I join them? I know Kane well—I grew up with him. I understand his thinking and his abilities. I could be an asset to your men," Hiro declared earnestly, bowing respectfully to the Colonel.

"Very well. Leave at once. We need this resolved quickly; we have larger issues to deal with," the Colonel agreed, his tone decisive. Miko and Juji exchanged looks of dismay, surprised by Hiro's sudden request to separate himself and pursue Kane alone.

After leaving the Colonel's office, the four men gathered in front of the building, their faces reflecting the gravity of their conversation.

"Kane is with the Indian tribe.... we've finally caught up with him," Juji began with a hint of excitement in his voice.

"We haven't caught anything yet. He's still free, and we can't be certain he's with the tribe." Hiro countered, his voice tinged with mistrust.

"I doubt the Indians would welcome a demon man among them."

"Senor Hiro, you underestimate these Indians. They have deep beliefs in totem animals. Perhaps they worship bears, and Kane is seen as a spiritual guide. Their medicine men practice dark arts; they would revere a man who can transform into their totem spirit," Alejandro explained, his voice sincere and instructive.

"Anyway, I'm going to fetch Carlos' body and prepare him for the journey home," Alejandro asserted.

"You can't leave us now, Alejandro.... we need your sharp-shooting skills. We struggle to handle a gun, our aim is lacking without your expertise," Hiro insisted. "Well, my friend Carlos deserves to be returned by someone who knew him," Alejandro replied firmly.

"I'll take Carlos back to the ranch. I miss Master Gideon and I'm worried about him. He needs my care," Miko volunteered earnestly.

"Miko, you won't survive the desert alone. Besides, transporting a body through the heat will attract predators like vultures, coyotes, bears, and bobcats. They'll follow the scent of death and hunt you down for an easy meal. I'm sorry, young Amigo, but you're not strong enough for this," Alejandro explained, his voice filled with concern and practicality.

"Hai.... Alejandro is right," Juji affirmed, his voice steady as he scanned his companions' faces, which remained silent and expectant.

"You've been quite vocal about the harsh conditions of the desert throughout our journey." He continued

"What? Why are you all looking at me like that?" Juji suddenly asked nervously. "Ah, I see.... you want ME to take Carlos back to the ranch," he added, realizing he had unwittingly been nominated.

"Juji, you have the wisdom, strength, and determination needed to ensure Carlos is safely returned to the ranch," Hiro said, his tone spiked with flattery.

"Once you arrive, let Master Gideon know that we've located Kane and that his capture is imminent. Our mission will be complete, and we can finally head back home to Japan. There, you can rest at the ranch with Master Gideon." Hiro's words were carefully chosen to persuade Juji, highlighting his qualities to secure his acceptance of the responsibility.

"Come on, let's go to the infirmary," Alejandro instructed wearily, his exhaustion from the relentless desert journey compounded by grief over his friend's death.

"I'll have a horse ready to carry Carlos," Miko suggested, offering a practical solution. "Actually, staying here might be a better plan. It'll give me a chance to track down that chica from the tavern. She can't hide forever. I want to uncover what happened to Carlos and seek justice for his death," Alejandro declared firmly, his determination clear.

"You can't assume the woman had anything to do with Carlos' death, Alejandro. She might have just been a woman enjoying drinks with him," Hiro reasoned with empathy.

"Si, si.... the Colonel did say Carlos was buying her drinks all night," Alejandro acknowledged reluctantly.

"That's likely why she stayed with him.... free drinks," Hiro affirmed gently. "I still want to find her," Alejandro insisted, his frustration evident.

"Carlos knew better than to associate with white women. She must know something crucial. Why haven't they found her yet? This fort isn't that large—it's too suspicious. Something doesn't add up," he pressed, seeking answers for his friend's untimely demise.

"Don't worry about her now. We have more pressing tasks.

Come on, let's retrieve Carlos Miko, meet us at the front of the infirmary with the horses," Hiro directed

decisively. With that, the men set off, shifting their focus to bringing Carlos home and continuing their hunt for Kane across the prairie.

As they entered the hospital and identified themselves to the morgue attendant, Alejandro, Hiro, and Juji were led down to the basement of the building. Despite the attendant's white apron, his haunted eyes, weathered face, and tightly pursed lips betrayed years of witnessing sorrow in that room. The atmosphere seemed designed to confront visitors with the stark reality of death: a cold, rough concrete floor, a low, oppressive ceiling looming overhead, and walls painted in ghostly dark grey.

A solitary fan hummed softly, as if in quiet mourning, and the room was dimly lit by two struggling candles, barely countering the pervasive gloom.

Alejandro felt a cold sweat break out in his hands, overwhelmed by the surroundings. He instinctively moved behind Hiro and Juji, the feeling of despair, fear, and grief obvious in his eyes. He needed to see his friend, to confront the fragility and mortality of life firsthand.

The corpse lay on a rugged table next to a long, narrow workbench. As Alejandro, Hiro, and Juji gazed upon Carlos, they were struck by a morbid fascination mingled with dread.

His face was swollen, his mouth gaping wide, revealing discolored teeth. Remnants of spittle encircled his lips. His eyes, sunken and wet, seemed frozen in a perpetual scream of agony. It was as if his final breath had been a desperate, futile cry against the inevitable. Years of immorality, heavy drinking, and the relentless desert sun had etched themselves mercilessly across his face.

"What is that around his mouth?" Hiro questioned, his voice tense with curiosity. "It's a common sign of an opium overdose. Mixed with alcohol, it's a deadly combination. His heart would have slowed, causing fluid to accumulate in his lungs, which then came out as foam," the morgue attendant explained clinically.

"Are you kidding me? Opium? Carlos never used opium. He drank heavily, yes, but he wouldn't touch that stuff. He wouldn't even know where to find it," Alejandro protested, his shock and anger apparent.

"It had to be that chica he was with. She poisoned him! It's not normal for a white high class chica to sit and drink with a Mexican man for hours? Something's not right here." Alejandro reiterated

"Opium from the Asians is commonly traded around here. It's used as currency, highly valued. Maybe the woman paid for things with opium. It's plausible. Carlos might have wanted to try it, not realizing how potent it could be, especially mixed with the amount of alcohol he had consumed" the attendant responded calmly, trying to infuse reason into the heated conversation.

"Don't rush to conclusions. There are many possible scenarios." he added

"So what's the plan for your friend? Taking him with you or opting for incineration?" the attendant pressed bluntly, sensing Alejandro's growing impatience.

"If we could purchase some cloth and rope from you, we'll

wrap him up and transport him home. Our horses are waiting outside," Hiro replied calmly.

"Return in thirty minutes, and your friend will be prepared. It'll be five dollars for the materials and my services," the attendant informed them briskly.

"Hai, we'll do that. Thank you for your assistance," Hiro acknowledged respectfully, bowing before leading his comrades up the stairs.

Out front, Miko waited impatiently with their horses, his mind racing with worry over the consequences of this latest catastrophe.

"Stupid Carlos," he muttered bitterly to himself as his brothers and Alejandro finally exited the building.

"So, what's the plan?" Miko asked anxiously as they approached.

"The doctor is preparing Carlos for the journey home. Juji will escort him back. Alejandro and I are joining the army officers on their scout for the tribe and Kane," Hiro outlined decisively.

"I thought Alejandro was going to stay here and search for that woman," Miko inquired, a trace of concern in his voice, hoping he wouldn't be left alone.

"He was, but the coroner suggested it was likely a tragic accident," Hiro explained.

"I need Alejandro with us to help scout the western plains; his knowledge of the area is crucial."

"And me? Where do I fit in?" Miko pleaded, his voice tinged with alarm.

"We've already paid for two more nights in the room. It's safer for you to stay here until we return," Hiro stated firmly.

"You always treat me like a child Why can't I come on the scout with you? Juji will

be gone, and I'll be alone here," Miko protested pathetically.

"Exactly. You're proving my point by acting like a spoilt child" Hiro scolded sharply. "Stay here."

Miko looked down at the ground, feeling uncomfortable under the scrutiny of the others. His brow furrowed as he considered his next words carefully.

"Can I do an incense blessing over you then? It seems that it's the only thing I know how to do best around here," Miko retorted sharply, his voice tinged with mockery and irritation.

"Hai, that would be appropriate," Hiro replied nonchalantly, noting Miko's brazen attitude.

"You're not doing any hocus pocus on me. I'm not one of your *'Jonnies'* and I don't believe in that stuff," Alejandro interjected abruptly. Without another word, he swiftly retreated back to the mortuary, focusing on the task of loading and securing the body.

After heaving Carlos' hefty frame over the horse, Alejandro turned to Juji and gestured for him to hold out his hands.

"What are you giving me, Mexican?" Juji asked sceptically.

"Here, take my compass along with this Mojave turquoise necklace. Wear it for protection on your journey," Alejandro offered earnestly.

"I don't need this necklace. I have my Buddhist faith, and whatever Buddha has planned for me is my destiny," Juji replied firmly, a hint of annoyance in his voice after Alejandro's earlier dismissal of his beliefs as "hocus pocus."

"Take it anyway, Amigo. You've got a long ride through the

desert to find the ranch, and this necklace has been quarried from that very desert, so it holds spiritual connection and protection.... Besides, it's quite a lovely necklace, don't you think?" Alejandro joked sarcastically, giving Juji one of his sly winks.

"Keep heading east towards the setting sun. Just point the compass and it will guide you," Alejandro instructed as he placed the compass and necklace into Juji's hand, closing his fingers around it. The monk opened his palm and examined the compass, casually flipping it over. He noticed a crude engraving of a capital "A" scratched on the back, realizing that Alejandro had personalized the instrument, infusing it with his own value and significance.

The three monks returned to their room, where Miko immediately began chanting sacred mantras while burning incense, the ritual aimed at purifying their minds, speech, and deeds. Candles flickered in reverence to the Buddha, and all bowed their heads slightly as they all commenced their rhythmic chanting, seeking wisdom, protection, and blessings for the journey ahead.

"Well, this is it I wish you safe and swift travels, Juji," Miko said solemnly once

their prayers were concluded.

"Please tell Master Gideon that I am well and send him my love. Let him know I hope for his full recovery and regret that I cannot be there to care for him," he continued. "Hai, safe travels, my brother. We will reunite after this mission. Stay vigilant with your cargo—the sooner you reach the ranch, the better. Inform Master Gideon that Kane has been located and we are closing in. This arduous journey will soon come to an end, and we can return to Japan and our beloved monastery soon," Hiro added, his voice filled with hope.

With those parting words, Juji gathered his belongings and departed. Hiro and Miko watched silently through the window as he rode past the fort gates and disappeared into the heartless badlands. As they stared after him, they noticed half a dozen crows take flight, trailing Juji and his grim cargo by about 400 meters, as if sensing a meal awaiting them.

"He will be alright, won't he, Hiro?" Miko pressed, seeking reassurance.

"Hai, Juji is a fierce and wise warrior. He'll take Carlos back to the ranch and, more importantly, inform Master Gideon of our progress in locating and moving closer towards capturing Kane," Hiro affirmed.

"We haven't caught him yet, Hiro You shouldn't make false claims like that," Miko

retorted.

"Enough with your negativity! We WILL find Kane, and we WILL capture him!" Hiro shouted, frustration clear in his voice at Miko's defeatist attitude.

"I'm going to meet with Alejandro and the army scouts now. Stay here. We'll be back in a few days," Hiro instructed, a hint of regret creeping into his voice after his outburst.

"Can I come with you?" Miko persisted.

"No, you're too young. Scouting is dangerous work. Do as you're told. Master Gideon would agree with me—he'd want you to stay here," Hiro said sternly.

"I'll be 17 next year. That's not a child," Miko argued.

"SILENCE!! I'm leaving now. Make sure you're here when I get back. Sayonara, Miko," Hiro concluded abruptly, shutting down Miko's continued resistance and dissatisfaction with his decisions.

Miko stood listlessly at the window, his mind fixed on the soul-stirring caws of tenacious ravens settling on the eaves of the adjacent building. Contempt showing clearly on his face as he watched the army scouts order the gates open. With the only familiar faces left in this wretched fort—Alejandro and Hiro—they all galloped away, swiftly disappearing into the desert's hazy skyline.

Chapter 18

Victor sat on the hacienda's front porch, idly sipping at the fresh lemonade he had squeezed from the ranch's own lemon tree.

The relentless heat of the day, a blistering 45 degrees Celsius, twisted the horizon into a shimmering mirage. It undulated and warped, as if the very earth were melting away into the sky, creating a surreal, liquid dance that grew more mesmerizing the longer he gazed.

Suddenly, a tiny black speck caught his attention, slowly materializing from the oppressive blur of the distance. Intrigued, he rose from his seat and stepped to the porch's edge, squinting to discern what approached the ranch.

For what felt like an eternity, the figure remained distant, maintaining its size until gradually growing larger—a dark silhouette mounted on a horse. Victor hurried inside, grabbing his binoculars. Returning to the porch, he adjusted the lenses to his eyes, stunned by what he saw. Lowering the binoculars briefly in disbelief, he quickly raised them again, attempting to comprehend the sight before him.

Perched atop the weary horse was a tall, slender figure,

cloaked in black, hunched over and obscured from view. When it raised its head, as if sensing Victor's gaze, a large crow's head emerged, sending an ominous chill down his spine. The creature looked to the sky, its grotesque head swaying with an unsettling joy, its colossal beak snapping violently in the air like a menacing warning. Victor kept the spyglass fixed to his eyes, transfixed by the disfigured entity until, inexplicably, it burst into six massive crows, each flying off in different directions.

Driven by impulse, Victor leaped off the veranda, sprinting toward the approaching horse until he caught and secured its reins. But what he saw and smelled made him immediately retch—something so vile that even Victor, who never vomited, could not contain it.

The once naturally white horse now bore a scarlet hue, its hide caked with dried blood that flaked off in crusty patches. Chunks of flesh clung to the saddle, some still identifiable as appendages. The overpowering scent of coppery blood filled the air around Victor, thick and suffocating. Hanging from the saddle horn was a necklace, which he carefully removed.

Rubbing the ornament between his fingers, Victor intermittently blew away the dried blood until the stone beneath revealed its turquoise color.

"This looks like a Mojave tribal necklace," he thought aloud, his voice sounding bewildered

Rummaging through the rest of the saddle in a desperate search for any clue about the mutilated rider, Victor's hands stumbled upon a hidden compass tucked securely under the skirt. As he turned it over, the roughly gouged "A" on the back instantly sparked recognition, and his mind raced with thoughts about what could have happened to his long-time friend, Alejandro.

Shoving the compass into his pocket, Victor approached the second horse tethered behind the first. A lifeless body, wrapped like a mummy in tattered cloth, hung over its back. With a mix of dread and determination, he lifted the head covering, revealing the face of the deceased—another dear Amigo, Carlos.

"FUCK, FUCK, FUCK!" Victor screamed to the heavens, his voice filled with uncontrolled emotion and despair.

"Don Morales needs to know about this," he muttered to himself, grabbing the reins of the horses. Without hesitation, he turned and raced back to the hacienda, the exhausted horses struggling to keep up with his frantic pace.

* * *

Juji sat close to the firepit, prodding at the burning embers with a twig in a futile attempt to coax larger flames.

"Those damn vampire bats," he muttered bitterly, unconcerned about his choice of words.

The high-pitched squeaks of the approaching bats echoed dismally through the pitch-black wilderness, signaling their imminent attack on him and the horses with their tiny, sharp fangs.

"If it's not the bats, it's those disgusting vultures and crows constantly following me," Juji complained, frustration clear in his voice.

"Carlos, I always knew you were a stinker of a man, but the rancid stench you're giving off now is on another level. Everything for miles around can smell you.... Amigo," he spoke angrily to the deceased man, as if expecting him to respond.

"This whole journey, hunting down Kane, tracking him into this godforsaken country, is wearing me down. I just want to return home to Japan, where the monastery is adorned with snow.... cool and tranquil. I miss that deeply," Juji declared with a hint of longing in his voice.

"But here? No, it's always scorching hot. What's the forecast for tomorrow, Juji? Hot.... and the day after? Oh, right.... something different.... Hot," he scoffed sarcastically.

"I truly can't endure it. And then you had to go and die on this crucial mission. You couldn't control your addiction to alcohol and who knows what else you indulged in. You didn't think of anyone else but yourself" Juji sighed heavily, poking at the dying embers of the fire with his stick, lost in thought about the future.

"Once I'm back at the ranch, I'm going to ask Master Gideon if he can send me home straight away. I'll suggest it's a good idea for me to return to Japan, to update the Abbot of our progress and our nearing capture of Kane," he grumbled, as if seeking validation from someone beyond the dead man and the horses.

As Juji laid his head down on the lumpy knapsack serving as a pillow, the amplified screams, howls, and the soft patter of sandy footsteps vibrated through the night—a chorus that would unsettle even the most seasoned desert traveler. Pulling a thin blanket tightly around himself, Juji curled into a ball, adopting a fetal position as he braced himself for the long, lonely night ahead. Hyper-vigilant and filled with fear, he waited, every sense attuned to the desert's nocturnal symphony.

As the morning sun burned off lingering mist, its heat quickly penetrated Juji's blanket, rousing him from sleep. He tossed the covering aside and lay there, staring up at the sky, marveling at the fading stars giving way to the brilliant shine of the sun.

Preparing to rise, he suddenly felt a sharp sting on the back of his leg, causing him to jolt upright. Looking down, he saw two bleeding puncture wounds. The stinging pain shot through his body, and at that moment, he heard an eerie rattling sound. His gaze darted to the ground, where a snake lay coiled between the fireplace and his sleeping spot.

Reacting swiftly, the snake coiled and resumed its defensive stance. Its head reared up, jaws gaping wide to reveal needle-sharp, curved fangs dripping with venom.

Before Juji could fully register the danger, the rattlesnake lunged again, striking his leg with a sudden, searing pain.

Juji's scream resonated across the desert as agony surged through his body. Instinctively, he seized a nearby stick, adrenaline fueling his frantic attempts to fend off the reptile. With desperate swipes, he battled to keep the venomous serpent at bay, his mind racing with the urgency of survival.

Juji's leg throbbed with extreme pain and swelling from the snake bite, intensifying his panic as he struggled to think clearly. His gaze flickered past the second horse, where the ominous gathering of crows and vultures lingered, perpetually shadowing him and his deceased companion.

"I'M NOT GOING TO BE YOUR NEXT MEAL!" Juji yelled fiercely at the sinister birds, his voice strained with fear and will power.

With a sense of urgency gripping him, Juji mounted his horse, his hands tightening around the reins. He drove the steed eastward, urging it to a breakneck gallop. The rhythmic pounding of hooves against the parched earth mimicked his desperate intention, each second of speed a race against time itself.

The wound on his leg bled profusely, leaving a vivid crimson trail on the ground and staining the horse's right side like a coat of red varnish. His breath grew labored, throat and mouth swelling, while lightheadedness gripped him. Drool hung from his mouth, and nausea gnawed at his gut as his heartbeat thundered in his chest.

Sensing a malevolent presence watching him, Juji summoned the strength to glance behind. What he saw froze him with terror—a horrific sight unfolding before his eyes. Six large crows perched on the trailing horse began to merge, combining into one colossal crow-like figure, resembling a monstrous man-bird hybrid.

Juji cried out in disbelief as the monstrous bird's enormous beak opened wide, hurtling towards him with menacing intent. The flapping of its wings echoed in Juji's mind as everything went dark, the last sound lingering in his ears.

* * *

"JEFFE.... JEFFE JEFFE!" Victor's urgent shouts repeating through the hacienda

as he swiftly tethered the horses to the veranda. He bounded up the stairs and burst through the front door, his distress noticeable as he sought out Don Morales and Gideon in the courtyard.

Don Morales, alerted by Victor's first call, rose immediately to meet him at the doorway. "Victor, what's wrong? I've never seen you so shaken. It must be serious," he inquired, concern showing on his face.

"Come with me, Jefe. I can't explain it. You have to see it," Victor urged, leading Don Morales out onto the front porch.

Meanwhile, Gideon stood silently, clutching his staff with white-knuckled intensity, his mind racing with dread over the terrible threat that had befallen them.

Shoulder to shoulder, the horses hung their heads low, visibly drained and likely in shock from the horrors of their journey.

Don Morales approached the horse carrying the wrapped cadaver, his heart heavy with anticipation. With a solemn breath, he lifted the cloth shielding the dead man's face, revealing the grim truth beneath.

"It's Carlos," Victor confirmed, echoing Don Morales's unspoken thoughts.

"And who was on this bloodied horse? Was there any evidence of the other rider?" Don Morales inquired, his finger tracing along the horse's blood-stained hide, examining the dried flakes and rubbing them between his fingers.

"I found this tucked under the saddle of the first horse," Victor replied, handing his boss the compass and necklace.

Don Morales studied the items and immediately recognized their owner. "Alejandro," he murmured, turning over the compass to reveal the crudely scratched "A" on the other side. His suspicion confirmed, his expression hardened.

"This was a massacre, not a murder," Gideon's voice rang out suddenly, startling the two Mexicans who hadn't noticed him approach. They wondered how they hadn't heard his footsteps on the porch.

"These belong to Alejandro," Don Morales affirmed, holding

up the trinkets for Gideon to see

"Do not be deceived by appearances, Don Morales," Gideon warned, his voice carrying an undertone of gravity. His eyes, intense and unwavering, remained locked on the unfolding scene.

"Evil thrives in the shadows of the obvious, and there's no greater transgression than the darkness of hatred."

"Who could have such hatred against Alejandro to do this?" Victor questioned, his voice edged with disbelief and concern.

Ignoring Victor's inquiry, Gideon pointed to something on the hind leg of the first horse. "What's that on the horse's hide?" he asked sharply, his eyes narrowing in scrutiny.

Victor moved around to inspect the horse's hind legs and plucked a large black feather, partially encased in dried blood and stuck near the hoof.

"It's an enormous crow feather," Victor stated, holding it up for everyone to see. As he examined further, he noticed something else lodged there.

Encouraging the horse to lift its leg, Victor carefully scraped off a piece of red and yellow hessian cloth, two sections hand-sewn together. He held the cloth fragments up, revealing them to the others in silence, the implications of these findings hanging heavy in the air.

"What have you found?" Gideon asked, his eyes fixed intently on Victor.

"Just a piece of material, nothing more," Victor replied, handing the cloth over to Gideon.

"Bring it to me," Gideon instructed with a tremor in his voice, a sense of apprehension washing over him.

Taking the cloth, Gideon recognized it instantly as a fragment of a monk's robe, specifically the belt part. Its reddish-yellow saffron colour was unmistakably dyed with roots found only in Japanese forests. He noted the jagged edges, torn and shredded, reminiscent of the violent manner in which the crowman had attacked Juji. "This is from a monk's robe, torn apart," Gideon stated gravely.

"I don't believe it was Alejandro riding this horse. It must have been one of my brothers. Though I can't say which one of course." The thought of Miko suffering such a fate weighed heavily on Gideon's heart.

"It could be any of them," Don Morales agreed, joining Gideon and examining the piece of cloth closely.

"And what about this enormous crow feather? What should we do with it?" Victor interjected, holding up the feather for their inspection, seeking guidance amidst the grim discoveries.

"I'll take that as well," Gideon directed firmly, extending his hand for the crow feather. "Why?" Don Morales questioned sceptically, eyeing the feather in Gideon's grasp.

"I believe a demon crow murdered the rider, and this evil is being conjured by Kane and his human skinned book," Gideon asserted, his voice unwavering despite the incredulity in Don Morales's eyes.

"And how do you know this?" Don Morales scoffed, crossing his arms.

"Does this look normal to you?" Gideon retorted sharply, holding up the feather. "Whether you believe it or not, there are forces beyond our understanding—angels and demons. We're up against a man with powers that span realms you can only imagine. You haven't seen the demon bear. I have. I've fought it and lived to tell the tale. Why? So I can warn others of its existence and hopefully stop Kane before he wreaks more havoc."

Don Morales fell silent, absorbing Gideon's words with a newfound gravity.

"Take these horses to the makeshift barn, wash them down, and make sure they have water and food. Then gather the ranch hands to bury Carlos in the cemetery," he instructed Victor, breaking the tense moment.

Victor nodded silently, untying the horses and leading them towards the back yard of the hacienda, his mind swirling with the worry of the day's revelations and the looming threat of Kane's dark influence.

Gideon quietly departed, drifting down the lengthy hallway until he reached the courtyard where he settled into a seated position to meditate. Holding the large crow feather in one hand and the torn cloth from his brother's habit in the other, he ran his fingers over them, feeling their textures deeply ingrained in his memory.

Studying the cloth, Gideon confirmed it belonged to one of his brothers. Even when they wore Mexican clothes to blend in, they always kept their habit belts, a testament to their heritage and vows. Closing his eyes, the old monk cleared his mind, letting go of the past and the future, focusing only on the present moment.

He began chanting a low, rhythmic hum, raising the items towards the heavens as he engaged in metta meditation—a practice of loving-kindness. Gideon believed that by evoking positive energy and cultivating compassion for all beings, even Kane, he could undermine the darkness that threatened their lives. It was easy to hate the demon bear and its malevolence, but Gideon knew that extending kindness towards it could disrupt its wicked intentions and ultimately lead to its downfall. This, he believed, was the path to restoring balance and peace.

It was a clear vision that unfolded before Gideon's mind's eye. He saw Kane scrambling desperately along a rugged mountainside, pursued relentlessly by a dog. Kane wore Native Indian attire, his arms scratched and bleeding from the thorny bushes that obstructed his path. As he struggled to escape, a massive, dark shadow, shaped like a bird, eclipsed the sunlight that bathed him, casting a sinister gloom over his figure.

In the vision, Kane looked up at the looming bird form with a creepy sense of welcome. Gideon sensed a sickening aura of malevolence wash over him as he witnessed the bird's pitch-black, glossy plumage and heard its frightening, incessant croaking. The bird seemed to communicate with Kane, evoking a deep connection between the material world and his ancestral spirit realm.

Gideon shuddered at the foreboding implications of this encounter. He understood that Kane was not merely a man driven by earthly desires but was entwined with forces that transcended mortal understanding—forces that threatened to unleash untold chaos and suffering upon the world.

"Our lineage flows through you," the voice intoned, a spectral resonance vibrating through the air, punctuated by sporadic, high-pitched knocks and deep, guttural rattles.

"You must master your lessons before you can transcend to our realm and claim your rightful place at the Altar beside your father. Your destiny awaits."

Gideon's voice was hushed, muttered to himself with a mix of awe and trepidation. "Witches.... they are all witches, taking the form of a raven and a dog.

"Shape-shifters.... just like those I studied at the monastery. They are real, and there is more than one. Their menace is spreading. I must delve deeper into their secrets and uncover the full extent of their threat."

As he spoke, Gideon's eyes narrowed with determination, knowing that the ancient forces Kane had tapped into were far more sinister and powerful than he had ever imagined. The revelation vibrated through his thoughts like a grievous warning, urging him to prepare for a battle against adversaries whose true nature defied mortal comprehension.

Don Morales remained seated on the front porch, the woven cane chair creaking softly beneath his weight as he contemplated the dire situation. The loss of his comrades haunted him, their names imprinted in his mind like a inventory of sacrifices to Kane's brutality.

"How many men have I lost because of this puta Kane? Paco, Chico, Carlos, Alejandro.... four good men, and now only three remain, including Victor," he muttered bitterly to himself, counting the dwindling numbers of his loyal hands. He sighed heavily, the responsibility bearing down on his shoulders.

"I still need at least two men to manage the ranch and oversee the cattle. Alejandro's gone; I can't recruit new blood from San Francisco anymore. I need able-bodied men here, ready to defend against the cattle thieves who stalk our lands like vultures."

Glancing out over the expansive desert that stretched before him, Don Morales felt a profound liability.

"I'll send Victor to Fort Harper," he decided aloud, his voice carrying a staunch resignation.

"He'll alert the commander to the murderer lurking in these desolate lands, the one who took my men.

"I'll ask for some soldiers for protection. With the Big Sky ranchers to consider, Kane's demonic presence, and the ever-present threat of Indian attacks, we are left dangerously exposed."

With a heavy heart, Don Morales rose from his chair, his mind set on the grim tasks ahead. Each step felt like an effort as he prepared to navigate the treacherous path that lay before him, ready to safeguard his ranch and honor the memory of those who had fallen.

"Hai, you are defenseless, Don Morales," Gideon's voice resonated sternly across the porch as he materialized at the front door, once again catching Don Morales off guard.

"Stop doing that, Gideon," Don Morales scolded, half-amused and half-exasperated. "Sneaking up on people. How do you do it? How do you float around with that heavy staff of yours, you're like a ghost. You're one spooky gringo."

Gideon smirked cheekily, his eyes gleaming with a deep wisdom.

"I am a High Master of Ninjutsu, trained to move with the grace of a feather. Silence is my ally, a subtle force that touches souls and reveals nothing. Both darkness and silence present their own challenges, yet in every state, I find a profound contentment."

Don Morales nodded, absorbing Gideon's words.

"So, how do we catch or kill Kane? Appeal to his Buddhist

faith?" Gideon's gaze turned somber.

"Kane is inherently evil, a product of ancestors from another dimensions. Yet, he has also known years of Buddhist teachings. His soul is a divided circle, yin and yang.

Nature versus nurture. We must understand both halves to confront him."

As the two men stood on the porch, the meaning of their words hung in the air like a premonition.

"Excuse me? What are you talking about, old man? What dimensions? Have you been indulging in that Indian brew, Peyote? Don Morales had grown weary of this spiritual nonsense, evident in his tone.

"Your lack of understanding does not justify your irritation, Don Morales. I speak only truth. The ancient principles of yin-yang are meticulously documented in the Zhouyi, also known as the I Ching or Book of Changes, penned by King Wen in the 9th century BCE during the Western Zhou dynasty. This is well-established fact, rigorously researched in my esteemed library, where I immerse myself in ancient texts and unravel the mysteries of the universe and divine knowledge. Knowledge, indeed, is power."

"There is no divine entity. Look around, old man. Look at what has just wandered onto my ranch. A bloodied horse with pieces of human flesh stuck all over it, and another one carrying a dead body—both Amigos—and you still speak of a God. What kind of God would allow such horrors?" Don Morales scoffed.

"No one is immune to the presence of evil and suffering in this world. God comprehends this intimately. He often refrains from intervening in the consequences of our choices, for if He were to compel us to always choose correctly, we would be deprived of the chance to learn, grow, and fulfill our divine potential. Without the freedom to choose, we would be unable to exercise faith in Him and His plan for our happiness," Gideon explained with a serene conviction.

"I have no interest in achieving any divine potential. I am Don Morales, the owner and boss of this ranch, and I will do whatever is necessary to defend it—even if it means taking lives. Your God wouldn't approve of that, would he, Senor Gideon?" Don Morales chuckled sarcastically.

"So, what you're suggesting is that you are inherently wicked and take pleasure in causing harm to others? Do you consider yourself immoral?" Gideon inquired, his voice steady and probing.

"What's deemed immoral by one may be considered normal by another. But rest assured, any fragment of goodness in me will vanish when I confront anyone who threatens what belongs to me,"

Don Morales warned before striding into his office and firmly closing the imposing doors behind him.

* * *

The soothing water trickled down the horse's back, washing away the remnants of blood that still clung to its hide. The crimson water pooled on the ground as Victor poured bucket after bucket over the weary animal. Earlier, he had carried Carlos' lifeless body to the cemetery, placing it solemnly in front of the gates before instructing the ranch hands to dig a grave. As Victor carefully bathed the lead horse, he noticed that a significant amount of blood didn't just come from the rider but also from the horse itself. With each gentle stroke of the sponge, deep gashes in the animal's flesh were revealed, a stark reminder that the horse had endured as much terror as its fallen rider.

"What happened to you?" he whispered in the horse's ear.

"This cannot go unanswered. We must strike back with force. I'll request permission from jeffe to ride out to Fort Harper and uncover the truth behind this. Whoever or whatever is responsible will answer for their actions," Victor declared, his voice brimming with resolve as he spoke to the horse.

Victor was loyal to a fault. Don Morales and Rancho Los Charro came before anything else. The ranch had been his home for decades, and his faithfulness remained steadfast, impervious to any urge to renounce, desert, or betray his valued jeffe and friends.

Three hours had passed, and Victor headed to the bunkhouse, where his Amigos sat on the verandah, mopping their brows with neck scarves as they recovered from the grueling task of burying Carlos' body.

"What happened, Señor Victor? How did Carlos die, and who was the rider on the other horse? Where did these Gringos come from—was it from the 'Big Sky' where they were sent? Is this ranch cursed? And besides Carlos, do you think the other dead man could be Alejandro?" they asked in a flurry, their voices a blend of fear and urgent curiosity.

"We don't yet know what happened," Victor declared, his voice heavy with will power. "But whoever is responsible for killing our Amigos will pay with their lives. That is a promise. Whether it was the Gringos from the 'Big Sky' or not, the soldiers at Fort Harper must be informed of this brutality." His words carried unbridled confidence, a vow of retribution.

"But who will go? There are only three of us left to look after the ranch, and of course, there's jeffe, but he'll never leave here.... and we don't have Alejandro anymore to recruit new men either," Andy said, concern sprawled all over his face. "We don't know if it's Alejandro or not, but I do know that we can't expect Don Morales to leave.... I will go. You all will have to keep things going until I get back,"

Victor decided firmly. He then entered the bunkhouse to shower, desperate to wash away the horrors of the preceding hours as he examined his blood-stained hands.

Standing at the office doors, Victor knocked with his huge fist, the sound resonating with three loud bangs that resonated through the building. Don Morales's voice promptly beckoned him in.

"Jeffe (boss).... before you say anything, I just want to—" Victor hurried in, starting to speak, but was immediately cut off by Don Morales.

"I want you to ride to Fort Harper and demand to see the Colonel. Give him this letter; it explains everything," Don Morales instructed, handing Victor a sealed envelope.

"Am I going alone, jeffe?" Victor asked, his voice laced with concern.

"Of course, you're going alone," Don Morales said with a stern expression. "If you haven't noticed, we're short on ranch hands, and I need to stay here to manage everything. The last thing we need is for those thieving putas from 'Big Sky' to return. And frankly, I wouldn't put it past those bastardas at the 'Big Sky' to have a hand in all of this."

Unbeknownst to them, Victor had left one of the office doors ajar. Suddenly, Gideon stepped through, his large staff the first thing the men saw.

"Señor Gideon, adelante, adelante.... I'm glad you're here. I am sending Victor to the Fort to ask the Colonel if he could send a few of his men back here, just for a short while, until we find out who is behind these murders," Don Morales addressed Gideon, his tone resolute.

"I already know who is behind this atrocity, and it's not the ranchers at 'Big Sky.' But given what has happened, this time I will be going," Gideon stated purposefully. "What? No, old man.... it's hard enough traveling days through the desert without having to look after you as well. It wasn't long ago that you were ill. You won't make it, Señor Gideon. That's just the obvious truth," Victor protested, his voice rising with concern.

"I need to find my brothers, especially Miko. He isn't as proficient in martial arts as the others, and he's only sixteen years old. I have a responsibility to find the boy and make sure he is safe," Gideon informed them, his eyes burning with stubborness. "Señor Gideon, we talked about this. You're not strong enough to travel through the desert," Don Morales reminded the old man rigidly.

"Hai, we did, but under the current circumstances, I must be with my brothers. I am their guide and the original pursuer of this mission. It all began in Japan, and what has transpired since is merely an added burden. Even if you leave me behind, I will follow," Gideon declared, his voice solid and unwavering, leaving no room for further argument.

"Si, alright then. Get the ranch hands to saddle the horses

while you put together the necessary supplies you'll need for the trip. Once you've secured the soldiers, come straight back here. I wish you all the luck," Don Morales agreed gruffly.

"Ah, by the way, Señor Gideon.... if you're not going to listen to reason, then your health and safety are your responsibility.... not Victor's. If you end up dying out there, that's on you, Amigo. Remember that," he added as a final warning.

The old monk, in complete silence, just turned around and casually glided back out the doorway.

His purpose was unmistakable, unrelenting in the face of Don Morales's cautionary words.

Within the hour, the ranch hands had brought the horses around to the front verandah and tied them to the post, while Victor packed essentials into the saddle packs and secured his shotgun to the horse, with a revolver holstered at his hip. "You're not bringing those guns with us? Hasn't there been enough bloodshed?" Gideon criticized, his tone filled with disapproval.

"You're not bringing that ridiculous stick with you, Señor Gideon? What good is it other than to announce that you're a foreigner?" Victor retorted bluntly, his frustration evident.

"It is more than just a staff.... I can use it as a weapon. It is one of the oldest and most universal weapons known to man. In prehistory, before metal or even stone spearheads were attached to the ends of sticks, the staff was used quite effectively for self-defense," Gideon replied calmly, his voice carrying a depth of wisdom. "Enough with the history lessons, priest.... I just don't care," Victor dismissed sharply. "Well, you're the one who is uneducated," Gideon shot back quickly.

"This is great.... traveling for days with this old monk is going to

take a lot of my patience, and he's already driving me crazy," Victor thought with exasperation.

"Hey, priest.... you don't like my guns? Then take a look at this little querida (darling) I have here," Victor boasted, sliding his tongue along the flat side of an enormous hunting knife. To tease Gideon further, he let out an arrogant laugh.

"You're in for a real treat, old man," Victor added with a taunting smirk.

"You do not scare me, Victor," Gideon responded calmly, his gaze steady and persistent.

* * *

The jagged mountains loomed in the distance as Hiro rode behind the army sergeant, Alejandro and the other two soldiers following closely. The air was filled with a mysterious and tomb-like silence, broken only by the occasional crunch of hooves on gravel. Hiro absorbed the sight of the thin shafts of light piercing the snowy peaks like moving ribbons, reminiscent of the beloved Japanese Alps back home. His heart swelled with a mixture of awe and apprehension.

Ahead, the mountain range's jagged tips rose like a row of menacing thorns piercing the sky. Thick clouds of mist coiled around their base, evoking the image of shackles

binding the rugged peaks to the earth. Silent and steadfast, the mountains stood as timeless statues, bearing witness to the endless passage of ages.

"How much further?" Hiro asked the sergeant, his voice tense with anticipation. "Not long now. Just past this ridge, and we should have a bird's eye view of where

we last saw the Kitanemuk tribe," the sergeant replied, his tone serious and focused. The group moved silently along the trail until they reached their vantage point.

Peering down into the valley, the officer took out his binoculars and observed the remnants of the once-safe and orderly campsite below. He noted the trampled grasses leading westward, flattened like a compressed arrow pointing straight toward them.

"They're heading further into the badlands. There's a canyon ahead. That's where I spotted a large Indian man climbing the north ridge, completely opposite to the direction of the Kitanemuk tribe. It struck me as strange," the sergeant continued, his brow furrowed in thought.

"A brave like that would be a tremendous asset to the tribe, wouldn't he? They'd certainly want him to stay. But then, I noticed an Indian squaw trailing behind him. He seemed unaware of her presence. She appeared desperate to catch up—perhaps his lover? Beyond that, there are other savage tribes roaming the wastelands. It's a harsh, untamed land, and anyone unfamiliar with it risks a brutal fate alone," he cautioned.

"May I have a turn with your binoculars?" Hiro asked the sergeant, gesturing towards the lenses.

"Oh? Okay? You're a bit pushy for such a skinny *'Jonnie'*," the sergeant remarked, reluctantly handing Hiro the binoculars.

"I may be skinny, but I am lightning fast," Hiro replied with a friendly smile. "Careful, puta," Alejandro warned.

Hiro peered down into the valley. He traced the flattened trail, slowly following it from the field and up the rocky elbow of a ridge. The sergeant, growing impatient, tapped his fingers on the saddle, eventually deciding he had enough of Hiro monopolizing the binoculars. As he reached out to take them back, Hiro instinctively knocked his hand away, preventing him from grabbing them. The sergeant swiftly drew his pistol and aimed it at Hiro's head.

"Do that again, *'Jonnie,'* and I'll blow a fucking hole right through your brain and leave you here for the vultures and wolves to pick over your skinny carcass. How would you like that?" the sergeant threatened harshly.

"Now give them to me"

"Hai.... my apologies. I did not mean to be so rude.... but look over there.... something is moving near that pocket of trees...." Hiro responded calmly.

Relenting, the sergeant lifted the binoculars to his eyes and instantly recognized the large man walking along the trail.

"That's the man I saw break away from the tribe.... there should be a woman close by," he confirmed, lowering the glasses.

Immediately, Hiro yanked the binoculars from the Sergeant and locked onto the cluster of trees. There, his vision zeroed in on Kane. As if on cue, Kane, sensing the scrutiny, spun around. His limbs twisted and stretched, his head contorted, and his mouth grotesquely expanded. His body swelled and grew, a horrific transformation. Snarling and snapping, his enormous, razor-sharp fangs caught the sunlight, glinting like shards of glass, as he morphed into Shadow Bear. Hiro had a front-row seat to the entire horrifying spectacle. He couldn't believe his eyes. With his mouth hanging slightly open, Hiro slowly lowered the binoculars. When he turned to the soldiers, they were staring at him, eyes wide with concern.

"You just had to go and do it again—you've got a death wish," the Sergeant exclaimed, his frustration obvious. His hand hovered over his pistol, ready to draw it once more as he glared at the Asian's arrogant behaviour.

Panic clawed at Hiro's heart from what he had just witnessed and the threat of Kane's close proximity. Yet, months of exposure to the demon's murderous vengeance and destruction had forged a hard tolerance within him. Instead, a seething rage and hatred took root, evident in his expression.

"There you are, you evil Kuso," he mummbled to himself.

"Again, I apologize, but this is the first sighting of Kane since we arrived. I can't afford to miss this chance. If he vanishes once more, it will be over. We can't keep chasing him through this desolate land forever. I intend to end this hunt once and for all," he declared with grim determination.

Without another word, Hiro spurred his horse and charged down the trail, heading straight for Kane. Behind him, the Sergeant's voice faded into the distance, yelling, "Come back, you stupid *"Jonnie!"*

"Let him go, Sergeant," one of the soldiers said. "We've got bigger problems with those savage Indians. Do we track them down or head back to the fort and brief the Colonel?"

"We know what direction they're going. We'll report back as directed," the Sergeant concluded. The posse turned around and made their way back to the Army Fort, leaving behind the perversely strong-willed and egotistical Hiro.

Hiro's horse thundered through the valley, panting and snorting in its struggle to maintain the grueling pace. As soon as they reached the base of the ridge, Hiro leaped from the saddle and sprinted up the mountain, knowing Kane awaited him at the top.

Reaching the trail, Hiro moved swiftly, entering the pocket of trees. There stood Kane, fully transformed into the monstrous Shadow Bear. The beast roared a deafening growl, the sound reverberating through the forest, as it recognized its long-time nemesis.

"Well, look at you. You think you're all-powerful in that demon disguise. Be a man and fight me the traditional way, the ninja way. I always knew you had no honor, hiding behind your ancestral evil," Hiro taunted, cautiously approaching the enormous animal.

"Kane, Kane, Kane.... are you in there?" he continued mocking.

Before his very eyes, Kane effortlessly mutated back to his human form.

"Is this what you want? You've always been an angry smartass, Hiro. Constantly trying to prove yourself. Well, this encounter should put you in the history books," Kane replied.

"This is what I want.... I hate you and want you dead," Hiro seethed.

"Well, that's not very brotherly of you," Kane provoked with a smirk, then suddenly launched himself at Hiro. Both of them collided in the middle, their bodies crashing together with incredible force.

Hiro instantly jumped back, regained his footing, and quickly sprung into a spinning hook kick, hammering Kane square in the jaw. Kane's head flung violently sideways, saliva spurting from his mouth on impact.

The time Kane had spent with the Kitanemuk tribe had its disadvantages. The comfortable lifestyle had caused him to gain a lot of weight, making him an even bigger target and slowing him down tremendously. In contrast, Hiro was lean and agile, every muscle honed for combat.

Both men were intimately familiar with each other's moves and tactics, each trying to anticipate the other's next strike. Their eyes locked, a silent battle of wits and reflexes playing out as they circled one another, every muscle in their bodies tensed for action.

Kane stood back, waiting for Hiro to advance. He knew the little man's ego was too big for him to just walk away.

"Brother, we've known each other since we were kids. We've grown up and trained together. This fight is unnecessary," Kane tried reasoning, his voice tinged with nostalgia.

Hiro didn't answer. Instead, he let out a long, primal scream and charged at the mountain of a man. His foot connected with Kane's stomach in a powerful kick, but Kane quickly grabbed Hiro's neck, holding him at arm's length.

With a swift, brutal punch to Hiro's face, Kane sent blood splattering from his nose and mouth. Hiro's eyes closed, and he made a gurgling sound as he hung there, suspended by Kane's iron grip.

Just as he was about to pass out from being choked, Hiro reached into his pocket and pulled out a small, concealed knife. With a swift, desperate motion, he slashed across Kane's face, once across the forehead and then down the left side of his cheek. Each gash was wide enough to fit a penny, and blood flowed like a torrential waterfall, painting Kane's once-handsome face in a stark crimson mask.

His agonized scream pierced the air, the pain obvious in its intensity.

Hiro fell to the ground abruptly while Kane shrieked a mixture of cries and growls, his hands clutching his wounded face.

"What have you done, you sly, sneaky snake? You're the one with no honor. What happened to fighting the traditional way? LIAR!" Kane bellowed.

As he finished speaking, Kane's hand transformed into a massive bear claw. Blinded by the blood streaming into his eyes, he instinctively swiped at Hiro, the long talons catching the upper part of Hiro's arm. Gnarled crevasses with dark walls and

bone-white depths, where the beast's claws had scraped the flesh away, immediately opened up.

Hiro clutched at his arm and moved backward, watching Kane struggle with his injuries, the air thick with the scent of blood and the sound of their labored breaths. Quickly examining his arm, Hiro saw the deep, bleeding slash and knew he couldn't continue fighting Kane. Blood poured down his arm, and he realized that if he didn't stop the bleeding soon, he might not survive.

"This isn't over, demon! There's a mob of bounty hunters on their way right now to cut your head off and take it back to Japan. Justice for all the people you've murdered. You'll see karma will get you in the end!" Hiro yelled defiantly.

With that, he turned and bolted down the trail, his sole focus finding his horse and getting to safety. The adrenaline masked the pain, but each step throbbed with the urgency of escape, leaving behind a scene of blood and vengeance in the wilderness.

Kane stumbled through the dense forest, his mind swirling with bewilderment and fear about his uncertain future.

"I can't believe they've come all this way and finally found me," he muttered to himself, the gravity of his situation pressing heavily on his conscience.

"This won't end until I'm dead."

While he acknowledged the lives he had taken, he rationalized each death, absolving himself of some blame.

Mr. Kent aboard the "Sea Changer" and The Abbot—they were mere provocations, crafted from a deep-seated hatred of him, he reasoned.

If only they hadn't pushed him, perhaps those lives could have been spared. And then there was the silk merchant in Osaka, along with Paco and Chico—oh, God. The weight of their fates pressed heavily on his soul, each name a haunting pout of regret.

The more Kane dwelled on the death and destruction that seemed to follow in his wake, the more despondent he became. This internal struggle between good and evil wore on him relentlessly. Deep-seated Buddhist beliefs and values, ingrained since childhood, clashed violently with his darker impulses. Two conflicting souls battled for dominance within him, and Kane feared that the evil one was gaining ground.

As he trudged deeper into the forest, shadows lengthening

around him, Kane grappled with the harsh reality of his existence—a life tortured by his past and overshadowed by an uncertain future.

As he sat there, stemming the never-ending stream of blood from his eyes and face, Kane removed his shirt and tore it into makeshift bandages. He wrapped one piece around his forehead and used the rest to cover his face like a makeshift burka.

Focusing intently on his task, Kane heard a rustling sound nearby. He wiped his eyes and strained to see in its direction, and that's when he spotted Lady Vixen.

"Where have you been?" Kane blurted out, relief flooding his voice at the sight of his beloved friend.

"I had a job to do. Your father sent me to the Fort. The number of bounty hunters after you is growing. The Army soldiers now know of your existence and what you are, though they're struggling to believe it. He tasked me with thinning their numbers, one at a time," she spoke directly into Kane's mind, her voice calm and resolute.

"Why couldn't you tell me? Don't you have the power to communicate with me through mind reading all the time, even when you're far away?" Kane's voice was strained, his face obscured by the makeshift bandages that barely contained the flow of blood.

"No, my ability to reach you telepathically only works when we're close. When I'm on a task for your father, I must focus completely. I can't afford distractions," Lady Vixen explained calmly, her eyes reflecting concern.

"Hiro was here, and look what he did to me. My face may never heal from these deep gashes. I needed your help," Kane grumbled bitterly, his pain evident despite his efforts to appear composed.

"I know he was here I saw him ride off. You've hurt him deeply as well; he won't be

back soon. And there's someone else who witnessed your battle," Lady Vixen said, casting a glance toward a nearby tree. With a bark-like call, she summoned the figure into view.

To Kane's astonishment, Lone Bear emerged from the shadows. She hurried to his side, her urgency evident as she sought to aid him. The sight of her triggered a tumultuous mix of emotions in Kane—love, relief, and panic swirled within him, overwhelming his senses. A dizzying rush swept over him, and then darkness claimed him as he collapsed unconscious.

Three days passed before Kane stirred from his ordeal. Lone Bear tended to a small fire, stirring a brew over it. Nearby, Lady Vixen lay curled next to the fire, fast asleep, her form soaking in its warmth. As Kane touched his face, he discovered that his deep gashes were now covered with poultices made from the soothing evening primrose plant, crafted by Lone Bear's skilled hands.

When Lone Bear noticed Kane arousing, she moved swiftly to his side, holding out a cup of the herbal brew she had been preparing.

"What is it?" Kane groaned, his voice raspy from days of rest.

"Willow Bark. It will help ease your pain. Here, drink," Lone Bear offered gently, holding out a cup of the herbal tea.

Kane took the cup, grateful for the relief it promised. As he sipped, he asked, "How long have we been here?"

"Three days. You needed the rest. Besides, you're too big for a small girl like me to move anyway," Lone Bear replied with a hint of amusement, watching Kane drink eagerly.

"Why are you here, Lone Bear? Where are your people? I thought they were moving west, away from the settlers, Mexicans, and the Army.... and me. I'm the threat to your people. If the hunting party doesn't find me with the tribe, they'll leave them alone. They'll be safe. You should have stayed with them, Lone Bear. It was foolish to follow me. I don't even know where I'm going," Kane pleaded, his voice filled with self-doubt and concern.

"I am here because I love you and want to spend the rest of my life with you. I've seen you transform into Shadow Bear, and I think you are magnificent. You are my spiritual sign. My dreams have told me that I must stay with you.... and that's that," Lone Bear declared firmly, her eyes firm.

Suddenly, realization struck Kane. "Where's my Bible?" he asked urgently, his mind racing through the recent events, trying to recall where he had last seen the grisly, human-skinned book.

"It's safe in your bag. You placed it over there near that tree," Lone Bear reassured Kane, pointing towards a large, ancient conifer.

Kane and Lone Bear embraced tightly, their connection obvious. He whispered softly into her ear, "I love you too.... thank you for loving me. No one has before."

Lady Vixen approached them, nudging her snout under Kane's arm, seeking affection. The three of them huddled together, finding solace in each other's presence, praying silently for strength and unity in the face of uncertain times ahead. Suddenly, a remote crack shattered the calm of the forest, followed swiftly by the mournful wails of Native Americans and the thunderous echoes of gunfire.

"What is that?" Kane exclaimed, his heart racing, while Lady Vixen's ears perked up in alarm.

"It's the Army attacking the Kitanemuk tribe," Lady Vixen conveyed directly to Kane's mind.

"Why? The army shouldn't be attacking them. I'm not with the tribe. I have to help," Kane declared aloud, his voice filled with urgency as he processed the gravity of the situation.

"What are you saying? Are my people being attacked by the army?" Lone Bear screamed, her voice thick with fear and disbelief, struggling to comprehend the sudden turn of events.

"You're not going to leave me here alone. How can you help them, Kane? Look at you, you're injured and need more rest. You're in no condition for another fight.

Please don't leave me," Lone Bear pleaded desperately, her eyes wide with concern, gripping Kane's arm tightly.

"I'll just go and see what's happening. I won't engage," Kane reassured, though obstinacy burned fiercely in his eyes.

"They have many guns. You can't fight against guns, even with your supernatural powers," Lone Bear reasoned urgently, trying to dissuade him from risking his life. "Let's go, Lady Vixen We'll be back.... I promise," Kane said resolutely, then

embraced Lone Bear tightly before kissing her passionately goodbye, the burden of uncertainty heavy in his heart as he prepared to confront the unfolding chaos.

Not far away, on the other side of a small gully, another small regiment of soldiers rode toward the already hectic battlefield. The main group moved with purpose, their horses' hooves kicking up dust, while some of the younger men at the back of the line lingered behind, their rifles lazily aimed at rabbits and birds startled into flight as they passed. The distant echoes of gunfire filled the air, intermingling with the frenzied shouts and cries from the ongoing conflict ahead.

"Look, over there! Can you see that man running along the trail, with a dog.... over there, see?" one of the young soldiers exclaimed, pointing eagerly towards where Kane and Lady Vixen were darting through the terrain.

"Go on, Jacky.... you're a good shot. I'll give you $5 if you hit one of them," another young man challenged, a hint of excitement in his voice.

"Alright you're on," Jacky replied confidently, adjusting his rifle and taking careful

aim, his eyes fixed on the fleeing figures in the distance.

With a tense pause, Jacky lined up his shot, waiting for the perfect moment to strike. BANG! The rifle cracked loudly, echoing through the forest.

"Got him!" Jacky exclaimed triumphantly.

Kane heard the sudden explosion, the lethal projectile slicing through the air with deadly intent. In an instant, a surge of agony tore through him, and an excruciating shriek reverberated inside his head, causing him to stagger with the impact.

Kane frantically checked himself for any wounds, relieved to find none, before his gaze darted towards Lady Vixen. The sight of her lying motionless in the dirt, her tongue hanging out and eyes wide open, pierced his heart like a dagger. Emotions surged within him, a torrent of grief and helplessness that gripped his chest and twisted his gut. His hands trembled uncontrollably, his entire body going numb as the world around him blurred into a haze of anguish.

She was gone. He hadn't even had a chance to say goodbye.

Facing the direction of the gunshot, a primal roar of agony erupted from Kane's throat, a sound so raw and devastating that it startled birds into flight from nearby trees. His torment resonated across the valley, booming back towards the soldiers and Lone Bear, carrying with it the gravity of unbearable loss and fury.

"Did you hear that, Jacky? Now that's some eerie shit. Probably just that wild Indian crying over his mongrel dog. You killed his pet, Jacky boohoo," they chuckled

callously.

"Yeah, sounded pretty feral," Jacky replied nonchalantly.

"Come on, let's catch up to the rest of the platoon," the soldiers urged each other, persuading their horses into a quicker pace.

Meanwhile, tears streamed down Kane's face as he knelt amidst the repeated sounds of distant gunfire and battle cries. Ignoring the turmoil around him, he gently lifted Lady Vixen's lifeless body, cradling her close to his chest.

With a heavy heart, Kane carried Lady Vixen back to their camp. The moment Lone Bear caught sight of them, Kane sank to his knees, a gut-wrenching wail escaping his lips. His sorrow echoed through the forest, a raw and primal lamentation.

The loss of Lady Vixen shattered a piece of Kane's soul, leaving him weakened and devastated. She was more than just a friend; she was his spirit bride, a deep and irreplaceable connection that now felt irrevocably broken. Kane feared he might not survive the gaping emptiness left by her absence, a profound pain that tortured his heart and spirit.

Chapter 19

"Open the gates!" The sentinel's urgent cry shouted down from the Army watchtower to the guards below.

Responding swiftly, the guards began to open the gates, their movements methodical yet hastened by the sense of urgency in the air. Through the widening gap, a frightened horse bolted into the compound, its sides heaving with exertion and fear. Slumped over its shoulder, Hiro clung desperately to the saddle, struggling to maintain his balance amid the havoc.

An experienced horseman dashed forward, expertly seizing the reins to bring the agitated animal to a sudden halt. In an instant, Hiro lost his grip and tumbled heavily to the ground, landing with a thud at the horse's feet.

"Someone help me get this man to the infirmary!" the soldier shouted, importance infused in his voice as he scooped up the injured Hiro. With the aid of another soldier, they carefully lifted Hiro's limp form and hurried him toward the medical facility, intent on getting him the help he desperately needed.

Upon hearing that a Japanese monk had returned severely injured, Miko's heart sank. He rushed to the hospital, pushing his way through a crowd of curious onlookers gathered outside.

"Hiro! Hiro!" Miko called out desperately, his voice trembling with worry.

"Your friend is unconscious, young monk. He has to go into surgery immediately. Everyone, please leave," the doctor's authoritative voice cut through the murmurs of the crowd.

"Can I stay?" Miko pleaded, his eyes filled with anxiety.

"No, wait outside," the doctor replied firmly, focused on the urgency of the situation. "But he's the only person I have left at this Fort. There's no one else," Miko implored, his voice cracking with emotion.

"That's regulations, and your loneliness has nothing to do with me," the doctor said curtly, his tone leaving no room for debate. "

You'll be notified when the operation is over."

Reluctantly, Miko stepped back, his heart heavy with worry as he was compelled to wait outside, silently praying for his friend's recovery.

Despondent, Miko slowly exited the infirmary and sank onto a bench outside, burying his face in his hands. He stared blankly at the small stones scattered in the dirt, his thoughts consumed by worry for Hiro.

"I wonder if Hiro will be okay. What will I do if he dies? I'll be left here with these soldiers and Mexicans, with no way back to Master Gideon. I wish he was here now," Miko moaned silently to himself.

Just as Miko finished his melancholy musings, a familiar voice pierced through his thoughts.

"Miko "

Looking up casually, Miko saw Alejandro standing nearby, gesturing for him to follow. "What happened to Hiro?" Miko asked frantically as he stood up to join Alejandro. "Senor Hiro chased after your demon and this is the result. Follow me to your

room, and I will tell you everything," Alejandro persuaded gently, guiding Miko away from the public eye.

"He found Kane? I can't believe we're so close to putting this madness behind us. Then we can finally return home to Japan," Miko exclaimed with a hint of excitement in his voice.

"I wouldn't be so sure, Senor.... Look at your brother.... He may seem like a fierce and experienced warrior, but look at what's happened to him. Don't count your chickens before they hatch, Amigo," Alejandro cautioned wisely.

"What's that supposed to mean?" Miko asked naively, confusion creasing his brow. "You'll figure it out," Alejandro replied cryptically, his expression solemn as he led Miko away to hear the troubling news about Hiro's condition.

* * *

Meanwhile, Lone Bear soberly prepared a funeral ceremony for Kane's dog. She understood the profound attachment Kane had for Lady Vixen, but she couldn't grasp the depth of his sorrow. Unaware of Lady Vixen's true nature—how she transformed into a beautiful woman who cared deeply for Kane—Lone Bear only saw her as a loyal animal who followed Kane wherever he went.

"Kane.... please give me Lady Vixen's body. I must prepare

her for burial," Lone Bear requested gently, reaching out to take the dog from Kane's trembling grasp. Earlier, she had ventured down to the gully, where the creek murmured softly below, fetching water that gleamed like liquid silver. With gentle reverence, she bathed Lady Vixen's still form, cleansing away the dust of the journey, and then anointed her face with a vivid red pigment, symbolizing vitality and the warmth of life. Beside the crackling fire pit, Lone Bear knelt, recited ancient prayers, while skillfully weaving a garland of wildflowers and securing it around the head of their departed companion.

As it rested against the ancient oak, Kane's cherished book, its cover bound in weathered human skin, lay nestled within his knapsack. Without warning, a faint tremor rippled through its yellowed pages, gradually intensifying until the knapsack spasmed violently, ejecting the book onto the mossy forest floor.

Unbeknownst to Kane, this unsettling disturbance served as an inadvertent signal, awakening dormant supernatural entities and malevolent spirits from their slumber in the shadowy recesses of their otherworldly realm.

The book's pages whipped and fluttered with a weird agitation, releasing a swirling white vapor that spiraled upward and coalesced into the form of Kane's father,

his visage a blank void where a face should have been. Perched on his shoulder, the hideous rat snarled incessantly, its voice a sinister chant of *"revenge, revenge."* Lone Bear stood transfixed, her face a mask of disbelief as the mysterious book slowly revealed its hidden secrets.

A bone-chilling gust of wind emanated from the ghostly

apparition, carrying with it the burden of ancient incantations. In a deep, raspy voice, the spectral figure uttered a spell of instant death, its words resonating through the clearing with dark finality.

""Behold the anguish wrought! I curse you, soldier Jacky,
As daylight wanes and dusk unfurls,
May the agony you've sown return in whirls. I summon the direst death possible,
To stain your blood with shadows, your skin with hues morose. A fate more grim, a retribution due,
Let it descend upon a soul as spiteful as you."

"Father.... where is she? Has Lady Vixen returned to you?" Kane pleaded.

"She exists no longer as you once knew her. She is now conscious energy. Her purpose ended," the Father's rasping voice sent a shiver down Lone Bear's spine. "I'll march to the Fort and slay every man there!" Kane screamed.

"Yes, yes, yes.... revenge. Slay them all," hissed the ugly human-faced rat, elongating each 'S' with a sinister hiss, then chuckling with wicked encouragement. *"Do not confront the soldiers.... you are no match for their guns. Your ordained destiny on this Earth must be fulfilled if you are to ascend to our universe,"* Kane's Father growled, his voice heavy with authority.

"We have all endured the same trials as you. If you die here, you will never pass through our gateway to your true home. You are my son, and I want you by my side."

"But I must avenge Lady Vixen!" Kane argued, his fist pounding the ground with raw emotion.

"Look at the death that surrounds you already. Did you not feel your vitality wane when Lady Vixen died? You have lost a significant portion of your paranormal power," the Father reasoned, his voice heavy with formality.

"You're so wise, and your spell is absolutely delicious.... But let him go, give him the satisfaction he desires. Yes, yes, you must kill them all....that would be better.... hehehe," the ugly rat tempted.

"Shut up, Ratigan. You have no say in this," The spectre retorted firmly at his pet rat. "Listen to your father, Kane. He is right. You're injured and lack the strength for a fight. Be sensible. Think about it. We can leave this place, start anew," Lone Bear reasoned, her voice calm yet insistent.

"If you disobey me, there will be severe consequences, Shadow Bear," warned the faceless ghost with a chilling tone.

Adrenaline surged through Kane's body, his anger tightening like a hangman's knot. Sweat broke out on his brow.

"Hmph.... alright. I won't do anything," Kane conceded reluctantly.

"The one who killed Lady Vixen will get his justice," the ghost declared grimly. Without another word, the mystical Father dissipated, returning into the folds of the ancient brown pages of the book, twisting and absorbing back into its depths.

"I'm glad you made the right choice.... so that's what your precious book can do? No wonder you guard it with your life. But what about the ugly rat? What purpose does it serve other than being argumentative and hostile?" Lone Bear inquired, her curiosity stirred.

"The book is a summons a portal to my world, another

universe," Kane explained through clenched teeth, his anger still simmering from his father's ultimatum.

"The rat is actually the other half of my father," he explained. "He was once a man deeply immersed in black magic, but during a potent spell, he was overtaken by a rat demon. Now, he exists as a rodent fiend, a mere minion to more powerful entities.

That loathsome creature is Ratigan. It constantly flatters its stronger master, hoping to earn special favors."

"How do you know this?" Lone Bear asked, her curiosity piqued.

"It's written in my bible," Kane explained. "I've studied those cryptic passages countless times during my solitary meditation sessions. Only I can decipher the indentations on the pages; the astrological symbols and mathematical formulas remain invisible to everyone else."

He sat there deep in thought before saying curiously, "Besides, there's no point in going to the Army Fort I don't even know which direction it is," he admitted, looking

up at her sheepishly.

"It's not far from here. That way, I'm sure," she said innocently, pointing East.

"Come on, we still need to bury Lady Vixen. Help me with her, and then tomorrow we can leave and head further up the mountains," Lone Bear encouraged, her voice steady and reassuring.

Later that night, as Kane embraced Lone Bear, his feelings of love for her grew stronger. She lay in his arms, beside the slow-burning embers of the dying fire. Despite her comforting presence, his face reflected utter hopelessness, grief, and loss. The emotions pressed on his heart so intensely that he began to sob. Salty tears ran down his face, seeping into his knife wounds and causing them to sting,

a painful reminder of the imminent threat of capture and death that still haunted him. A mixture of anger, frustration, and fear of the unknown overwhelmed him. Lone Bear's love and loyalty were admirable, but it didn't feel right to involve her any further in his escape. The only way to end this insanity was to face it head-on.

Gently lifting Lone Bear's arm from around his waist, Kane slid himself from under her. Cloaked in the darkness, he carefully crept down the mountainside and took off across the gully, making a determined beeline toward Fort Harper.

* * *

Days earlier, Colonel Fitzpatrick had communicated to headquarters that the Kitanemuk tribe was harboring a fugitive responsible for a series of brutal murders. He underscored the fact that the Indians had been seen scouting around the Fort, heightening the unease among the inhabitants. Crucially, he withheld the information that the fugitive was a skin changer, choosing instead to stress that the man and the Indians were a significant threat to their mission of securing safe passage for the incoming farming settlers eager to claim the land. Fitzpatrick proposed a preemptive strike on the native tribe, advocating it as a necessary measure to ensure peace and stability within the volatile badlands.

"We will capture the criminal, hopefully with as little collateral damage as possible," the Colonel assured his Commander, though his words were misleading.

"Alright, give the order. Track and seize the fugitive. If the Indians won't surrender him without a fight, then that's their fate" the Commander dictated with finality.

In the Fort's courtyard, three rows of soldiers stood in formation before the Colonel, who was poised to address them. His pep talk was meticulously crafted to depersonalize the enemy, knowing that soldiers found it easier to kill monsters than fellow human beings. He understood that it was more acceptable to take the life of a man deemed a threat to family and freedom than to confront one who shared their values.

Clearing his throat, the Colonel began to speak, his voice slicing through the crisp morning air as his men remained firmly at attention.

"At ease, men," the Colonel began, his tone resolute. "Noble thoughts and ideals have no place in this battle. A soldier who clings to high ideals will not survive. If you wish to demonstrate your heroism, do so after the fighting is done.

We march to liberate and purify our new land. If they resist, eradicate them. Fight with unwavering confidence and strength in your hearts. We will defend the new America at any cost. Join the few men I've dispatched earlier. When you encounter the tribe's murdering man-bear.... kill it.

And, if time permits after the battle, provide a decent burial for the fallen enemies and ensure that captives receive medical care and food. Go forth, and may God guide you."

"ATTENTION!" the Sergeant barked as the Colonel stepped down from the wooden stage.

The soldiers mounted their horses, forming two lines as they exited the Fort and rode with purpose in the direction of the fleeing Kitanemuk tribe.

A slight breeze whirled through the bottom of the treacherous canyon, creating a fast little "dust devil" that only accentuated the oppressive heat and the smell of dead animals, scorching the inside of Private Jacky's nose. The canyon walls loomed overhead, jagged razor-blade ridges jutting out dangerously. At the far end of the narrowing ravine, the walls rose considerably higher, stretching skyward until the canyon eventually opened into a wide, desolate field. Their Indian scout observed that a mob of travelers had recently passed through this way.

Past battles between the Indians and the new settlers had proven to be barbaric. The settlers, bolstered by the militias, sought to eliminate the tribes from the lands they coveted. The result was always devastating for the Native peoples, who lacked the weapons to fight back against such well-armed forces. The memory of these brutal conflicts lingered in the air, a haunting reminder of the bloodshed that had tainted these lands.

This was Private Jacky's first battle with the Natives, and he anticipated it would be swift; their bows and arrows were no match for the Army's firepower. His anticipation was tinged with a mix of fear and grim determination. Aware of the brutal history of such conflicts and their inevitable outcomes, he couldn't shake the feeling that something was different this time. The silence of the clearing was unsettling, as if the land itself held its breath, anticipating the inevitable clash.

"I should be home by dinner time," he thought, trying to steady his nerves. Despite his skill as a marksman, Jacky felt a rising nervousness. He saw it as an invitation to center himself, to grasp a moment of clarity. His heart pounded faster, and he unconsciously rubbed his hands on his thighs to dry his sweaty palms as the large clearing loomed ahead. The only sounds were the horses' hooves and the occasional gust of wind sweeping through the canyon, until the troops abruptly halted at the clearing's edge.

Approximately 100 feet into the clearing, the Sergeant could discern remnants of the Indian tribe's previous camp. The distinct black outlines of their firepits stood stark against the desert's yellow-colored ground. Jacky's eyes swept across the area, his mind racing with the anticipation of what might unfold next. The stillness of the scene contradicted the tension that saturated the air.

The Indian scout awaited the Sergeant's next order, while the troop assembled behind them, standing in patient silence.

"Do you think it's a trap?" the Scout asked cautiously.

"I'm not sure. It's a risky situation. It's clear that our previous men didn't come this way," the Sergeant replied, his voice tinged with concern.

"Corporal, what are your thoughts?" he continued, turning to the next in command. "Send the scout first. They know he works for us, so they won't hesitate to attack if they're lying in wait," the Corporal suggested confidently.

The Indian scout shot a quick, disdainful glance at the Corporal, his scowl unmistakably expressing his objection to the idea of being used as a decoy.

"Go on, Scout. Start walking toward the firepits. We've got your back," the Sergeant ordered, his tone firm and reassuring.

Obediently but with great apprehension, the scout cautiously ventured into the clearing. He moved stealthily toward the extinguished firepits, his senses on high alert, half-expecting a Kitanemuk brave to come charging at him, yelling at the top of his lungs. As he reached the perimeter of the camp, he pivoted and signaled to the Sergeant that the coast was clear.

Two by two, the soldiers rode into the expanse, purposefully trampling their horses through the ashes, disturbing the fire pits and knocking over rocks as they advanced. The Sergeant halted the procession, turning in his saddle to inspect his trailing men. Suddenly, a rushing sound sliced through the air, followed by a heavy "thud."

Panic surged through him as he looked down to see a thick arrow embedded straight through his leg, pinning it securely to the horse. His face twisted in agony and disbelief, the stark realization sinking in that they had stumbled into an ambush. "We're under attack! Take cover!" he bellowed, his voice slicing through the chaos.

The men scrambled in all directions, scattering like startled insects. Amidst the frantic movement, his Indian scout fell, an arrow piercing his back as he desperately tried to flee.

The Sergeant struggled to dismount as his horse collapsed to the ground, moaning and panting from its wounds, but he was trapped beneath the animal. Vulnerable and in excruciating pain from his crushed leg, he lay helpless beneath the weight of the horse.

Bullets zipped and violent screams pierced the air, drenching the atmosphere with a discord of horror that reverberated through the canyon.

Private Jacky could see the Sergeant was in dire straits, so he stealthily maneuvered from one boulder to the next until he reached the injured man.

"I'll get you out!" Jacky shouted, positioning himself to lift the horse enough to free the Sergeant's trapped leg. Just as he began his attempt, an Indian brave charged towards him, tomahawk raised menacingly. In a split-second twist of fate, a stray bullet struck the Indian, who collapsed beside Jacky.

Jacky glanced at the fallen man briefly, noting the bullet's exit wound at the back of his head, blood slowly seeping out, staining the ground crimson. He felt no revulsion or remorse for the fallen brave. To him, the Indian was less than human—an ignorant, wild creature of the badlands, uneducated and uncivilized.

"Hurry," the Sergeant groaned urgently, pulling Jacky's attention back to the task at hand.

With all his strength, the young private managed to lift the horse once more, successfully freeing the Sergeant's trapped leg.

"Thank you but go," the Sergeant grimaced through clenched teeth.

"The arrow has broken off, but a large piece is still lodged in my leg. I'm in no shape to walk, let alone run. Leave me here. I'll be okay that's an order."

Before Jacky could respond, a high-flying arrow struck the Sergeant squarely in the back, burying itself so deeply that only the feathered tail was visible.

Heart pounding in his throat, Jacky squirmed through the dirt on his stomach, backtracking to the nearest boulder, then scurrying urgently to rejoin his comrades clustered together.

"I saw you try and save the Sergeant," one of them said,

admiration evident in his voice.

"You'll get a medal for that," another added, a hint of stateliness underscoring his words.

Jacky's thoughts turned to his other friend, Tommy, who had goaded him into taking a shot at the rogue dog, Lady Vixen.

"Where's Tommy?" he asked, scanning the lawless scene.

"Over there," the young soldier replied, pointing towards a fallen comrade whose body was pierced with arrows.

"Damn.... how many Indians have you killed?" Jacky inquired, his voice tense as he loaded his rifle, preparing for whatever came next.

"Approximately four"

Every time Jacky dared to peer over the boulder sheltering them, a speeding arrow would slice through the air, narrowly missing his face by a hair's breadth.

"One of those damned Indians has me pinned down. Can't risk taking a shot," Jacky grumbled.

"Your head's as big as a melon, that's why!" they chuckled.

His comrade rose to fire, when suddenly Private Jacky heard a sickening "thud." Glancing up, he saw an arrow embedded in his friend's eye socket, dropping him instantly, dead.

"Jesus!" Jacky cried, scrambling away from the fallen body.

"Yeah, they're damn good with those bows," another friend remarked coolly.

The battle raged for hours, Indians suffering heavy losses alongside the soldiers. Jacky couldn't see the other end of the field, but a dozen bodies lay nearby, maimed by bullets, arrows, or blades.

"I'm sick of this crap!" he screamed, loading his gun. Leaping to his feet, he roared like a madman, charging into the open, sighting an Indian sprinting towards him, mirroring his reckless bravery.

There wasn't a moment to spare as their bodies smashed together. Jacky swung the butt of his rifle, driving it mercilessly into the Indian's nose. The brave's head snapped back, eyes fixating skyward as blood gushed into his mouth from the shattered bone. His left foot slipped in the dirt, struggling to find a foothold on the rugged ground, while he instinctively clutched his nose in agony.

In retaliation, the Indian drove his instep into Jacky's shin with a sickening crunch, eliciting a sharp cry as Jacky's right leg lifted involuntarily, his head dropping from the pain. Acting on pure instinct, Jacky seized the back of the Indian's head, fingers digging into flesh, and thrust his knee upward into the man's face.

Suddenly, a searing pain shot through Jacky's left forearm as a long knife slashed across it. He roared in agony, a solitary tear tracing a path down his cheek.

Enduring the agonizing pain, Jacky felt an unleashed primal fury surge within him. He seized the Indian's arm forcefully and sank his teeth deep into the man's hand, compelling him to release the blade. As soon as the knife clattered to the ground, Jacky lunged for it, driving it viciously into the Indian's chest.

The brave's eyes widened in shock as his final breath hissed from his lungs, life slipping away. Jacky stood over him, screaming in primal triumph at the fallen foe. Scanning the battlefield, Jacky's eyes fixed on the surviving Natives making a desperate retreat toward the safety of the distant mountains. Two soldiers thundered after them, riding hard and unleashing sporadic shots to deter any thoughts of turning back. Their shouts sounding across the battlefield, a stern warning that they would not allow the enemy to regroup.

Limping towards the boulder where his comrades still sought shelter, Jacky couldn't ignore the rising stench of death in the sweltering heat. Each step he took made a sickening slapping sound as his boots navigated through pools of blood, scattered organs, and other bodily fluids.

The battle had ended, leaving behind a gruesome aftermath. Soon, the desert's scavengers—vultures, crows, bobcats, and wolves—would descend to feast upon the corpses. Among them would be humans too, likely the victorious soldiers, scavenging usable weapons and collecting macabre trophies of their conquest.

The once sandy-colored field was now a grim tableau of blood, gore, and severed limbs, the air thick with an overpowering depravity.

"Soon enough, these bodies will be swarming with flies, then maggots," Jacky thought grimly.

"Let's get out of here," He suggested to his remaining comrades. "How many of us are left?" one of them asked.

"Not sure.... but by the looks of things, I'd say eight out of the thirty soldiers we started with," Jacky replied, eyes scanning the somber battlefield.

"We need to regroup before heading back," he continued.

"But we can't leave without burying the dead, like the Colonel said.... it's the right thing to do," another friend added solemnly.

"Leave them for the desert. They won't be lying there for long," Jacky reacted callously.

"Hey Jacky, I saw you take on that Indian. You were a force to be reckoned with, and you tried to save our Sergeant. I said it before, you're sure to get a medal or a promotion for your bravery," a buddy praised warmly.

"Yeah, no doubt about it," the others chimed in, each offering Jacky a reassuring pat on the back, acknowledging his valor in the face of relentless combat.

As the sun began its descent, painting the battlefield's horizon a bloody red, the weary soldiers rode back to the Fort. Jacky lagged behind the group as usual, lost in his thoughts. Every moment of the brutal fight replayed in his mind, scrutinizing his

actions and questioning if he could have done more, especially for the Sergeant. Despite these doubts, he couldn't help but anticipate the hero's welcome awaiting him at the Fort.

With his deliberate pace, Jacky gradually lost sight of the other soldiers as they disappeared around a bend, obscured by thickets of bushes along the path's edge. As he neared the dense shrubbery, a murder of crows erupted suddenly, flapping wildly toward his horse. The startled animal reared violently, its sudden movement throwing Jacky off balance and hurling him into the thick underbrush.

Sitting amongst the branches, dazed and bewildered, Jacky quickly noticed a large wasp nest suspended a mere five inches from his face.

The enraged insects surged from the nest like a relentless torrent, hundreds of them descending upon Jacky with vicious intent. Their barbed stingers pierced his exposed flesh repeatedly, injecting venom with frenzied determination. Jacky's screams pierced through the scrub as pain and fury consumed him.

Swiftly, his face, arms, and any exposed skin swelled grotesquely. The venom's effects were swift and cruel, constricting his throat and lips. Breathing became a desperate struggle, each gasp a wheezing battle for air. In his panic, fluid streamed from his nose, thick and black like ink. He wiped it away instinctively, only to see it wasn't blood but some strange secretion, adding to his mounting terror.

Caught in a nightmare of pain and suffocation, Jacky fought against the relentless assault of the vengeful insects, trapped in a battle he couldn't win.

Completely distraught, Jacky frantically tried to dislodge the relentless insects from his flesh, but their persistent grip held firm like a vice, refusing to let go. Attempting to stand, dizziness overcame him, and he collapsed back onto the wasp nest, where the brutal attack restarted with renewed ferocity. He screamed "NO!" but his plea was muffled, drowned out by the overwhelming agony.

In his harrowing final moments, as the venom coursed through his veins, Jacky heard haunting echoes of Kane's father's voice. *"I curse you, soldier Jacky,"* the words swirling furiously, followed by a chilling, demonic laugh that seemed to surround him.

Lady Vixen's death, it seemed, was avenged in the cruelest of ways as Jacky succumbed to an agonizing fate amidst the relentless swarm of vengeful insects.

***

Hiding near the Fort, Kane bided his time until a wagon

approached and requested entry through the gates. Using his ninja skills, he swiftly maneuvered under the carriage, hanging himself from the wheel shaft unnoticed. As the gates opened, the aroma of curry and onions drifted through the courtyard, briefly evoking memories of his childhood.

Dusk was settling in, casting a shadow over the busy Fort where soldiers, recently returned from battle, were being tended to by lively attendants. Kane remained hidden under the wagon, his arms straining under the weight, until it was finally housed in the barn. Taking advantage of the driver's distraction while he tended to the horses, Kane lowered himself to the ground and stealthily slipped out.

Remaining hypervigilant, he surveyed his surroundings keenly. Spotting medics ferrying injured soldiers into a specific building, Kane concluded it must be the hospital where Hiro, his target for revenge, was likely recuperating. With a sense of purpose, he moved swiftly towards his objective.

Practicing deliberate grace, he glided into the courtyard, moving with a silent, purposeful intent. Along the hospital's outer wall, he crept stealthily, his eyes scanning intently through each windowpane.

The first revealed a soldier, vunerable on his bed, head swathed in white bandages. The second framed another, leg elevated and encased in layers of cloth.

Yet, as he reached the third window, set apart from the others, a different sight met his eyes. There, Hiro lay in peaceful slumber, his injured arm securely bound.

"I've found you.... you bastard," he seethed inwardly, before delicately prying open the window and slipping inside.

Standing like a statue beside his brother's bed, Kane's imposing figure cast a shadow over the man he once knew. Memories flickered: the fleeting joys of their childhood at the monastery. But these thoughts soon gave way to a deeper reflection on Hiro's unyielding animosity and his insatiable thirst for supremacy in all endeavors.

Hiro's arrogance and conceit were among his most repugnant traits, exacerbated by his unrelenting grudges—tighter than a fish's arse—never yielding, never humble, perpetually self-righteous and embittered. Sensing a presence beside his bed, Hiro slowly opened his eyes. Upon seeing Kane standing there, his colossal form looming over him, Hiro's eyes widened to the size of saucers, a gasp of horror escaping his lips at the sight of his nemesis so near.

Kane began to growl in his deep, primal Shadow Bear voice, feeling the demon within stir, desperate to emerge fully. His teeth gnashed together violently, transforming sporadically into jagged, serrated fangs, drool dripping from their pointed tips. Ragged breaths escaped him, each exhalation tinged with a menacing growl, as the primal force strained against his restraint, eager to break free and unleash its fury upon the terrified man before him.

"It's you.... Oh, look what I did. Cut up your pretty face," Hiro laughed, his gaze fixed on Kane's wounds. "Now you have the chance, finish this, kill me.... I don't care.... but that's your style, isn't it, demon? Murdering innocent, unarmed people?" His voice carried determination, tinged with unease.

"Shut up.... you're not innocent," Kane growled in response. "Go on what are you waiting for?" Hiro persisted.

Gathering his composure, Kane opted for reason instead of succumbing to the urge to strike down his brother then and there, despite Hiro's reckless provocation.

Drawing in a steadying breath, Kane wrestled the demon within him back under control, the sharp fangs receding as he fought for self control. His voice, though bearing a lingering growl, softened as he began to speak.

"Hiro," Kane began, his voice calm yet firm,

"We need to talk. This hatred between us—it has to end. We were brothers once, and there's too much at stake now to let our past destroy us both." His eyes, still carrying a glint of the beast within, locked onto Hiro's wide, fearful gaze, searching for a flicker of the brother he once knew.

"After you've healed, leave this land and return home to Japan with the others. Tell them you found me dead, or lost in the harsh Americas. Start anew, Hiro, and leave me be," Kane urged, attempting to reason with the stubborn monk.

"Master Gideon won't allow it. You forget, demon," Hiro retorted sharply, his voice tinged with appeal to Kane's memories.

"You brutally took his beloved friend's life. Your very existence threatens the monastery and everyone in it. You're unnatural, Kane, and you don't belong here. You could come back one day, and we can't risk that. There are innocent boys living there."

"I NEVER WANTED ANY OF THIS. LEAVE ME ALONE. I WON'T HARM ANYONE,

BUT IF YOU COME FOR ME, I WILL KILL YOU," Kane growled with such intensity that Hiro's bed vibrated with the deep, guttural sound of his voice.

"You're uncontrollable. For the sake of innocent lives you might endanger in the future, surrender yourself. If you refuse.... I will honor my Japanese heritage and pursue you until you are dead," Hiro threatened, his voice steady and deliberate. A surge of heat coursed through Kane's body, frustration mounting at Hiro's unyielding stance. His mind shifted into fight-mode in response.

"You leave me no option but to end you now," Kane countered, his large hands closing around Hiro's neck, thumbs pressing firmly into his throat.

Hiro's eyes bulged with terror as he thrashed wildly, striking Kane's shoulder with his good arm, gasping and gurgling for air. Saliva sprayed in all directions, his face contorting into a sickening shade of blue. With each passing second, his struggles grew weaker, his frantic attempts to break free becoming feeble against Kane's tightening grip. The primal urge to end it all gnawed at the edges of Kane's fleeting logic.

"STOP!" A voice suddenly yelled from behind him, causing Kane to whirl around in fright. There stood Miko in the doorway, his eyes wide with horror as he witnessed Kane's transformation after all this time.

Kane's fangs still protruded from an elongated snout as he growled fiercely, his demeanor now primal and defiant. "Miko my young brother," Kane snarled, his

voice laced with pain and defiance.

"Please, Kane, stop this maddness and come home with us. Look at what you've become," Miko implored, his voice tinged with sadness and disbelief.

"You've turned into a monster, and you're hurting people, the opposite of everything our Buddhist upbringing taught us. What has happened to you, Kane? We were once best friends. I don't recognize you anymore, and it breaks my heart. I know you're frightened, and yes, there will be consequences. But you can be forgiven. You must honor your Buddhist and Japanese heritage.... please, Kane.... I don't want to see you like this.... I don't want to see you dead."

"I love you, my brother.... you've been there for me when I needed you," Miko continued earnestly.

"There is still good in you, Kane."

Never before had Kane felt so vulnerable, facing the earnest plea of this trusting and virtuous young monk standing before him. Despite his inner turmoil, Kane remained steadfast, though his courage wavered. He glanced back at Hiro, who held his hand up in a defensive gesture, bracing for another potential attack.

Kane spotted a forsaken army hat and jacket hanging on a nearby hook and swiftly snatched them up before slipping out through the open window. Pausing briefly, he turned to Miko and snarled, deliberately baring his knife-like teeth.

"STAY AWAY FROM ME!"

Quickly donning the army clothes, Kane pulled the hat down low over his face, concealing his identity as he merged into the bustling crowd. Luck favored him as the fort gates began to open, allowing people to move freely in and out.

He seamlessly joined a group of travelers departing from the fort, merging into the flow of pilgrims ending their visit. An unsettling feeling gripped his heart, a chill running through his veins as he scanned ahead. About fifty feet away, his breath caught as he recognized Master Gideon and Victor, both riding stoically on horseback.

At the first opportunity, Kane broke away from the travelers, darting around a corner of the fort and breaking into a run.

His large frame swiftly disappeared into the distance, heading towards the distant mountains, leaving behind the echoes of his escape and the weight of his troubled past.

Gideon jerked sharply on the reins of his horse, halting abruptly in his tracks.

A noticeable aura of menace held him rooted in place, a cold wave washing over him as the hairs on his neck stood on end and his mouth went dry. He fought to crush the rising panic threatening to overwhelm him.

Victor, puzzled by Gideon's sudden stillness, pulled up beside him.

"Amigo, the gates won't stay open forever. What are you doing?" he demanded gruffly, eyeing the old monk intently.

After a moment of grappling with the shocking revelation, Gideon urged his horse forward. As he passed Victor, he spoke in a low, grim voice.

"Kane is here."

Chapter 20

Lone Bear sat perched alone on a high rock ledge, overlooking the battlefield strewn with exhaustion and loss. Her cry of anguish carrying through the air, a lament for her fallen people. Peering down at the graveyard below, she was engulfed by a whirlwind of intense emotions—sadness, shock, numbness, denial, and anger—that twisted through her entire being.

"Why? Why? Why? This is Kane's fault," she screamed in her native tongue, her eyes swollen and red from tears streaming down her face. The density of remorse bore down on her, overwhelming in its intensity. She longed for a different outcome, wishing desperately that she could have changed the course of events.

Absently picking up small rocks, she hurled them over the ledge, watching as they tumbled down the cliff, finding their final resting place at the base. Sniffling softly to herself, Lone Bear began to pray, her plaintive words drifting towards their camp. The haunting mantra caught the attention of Kane, who had just returned from Fort Harper, his presence unnoticed as he listened, drawn by the sorrowful wailing of a woman devastated by conflict.

As Lone Bear scanned the grim aftermath below, her keen eyes caught a flicker of movement among the fallen. Down near where her tossed rocks had settled, she noticed a figure stirring. Instinctively, she descended the rugged cliffside with careful steps, driven by an urgent sense of concern.

Drawing closer, her heart sank—a wave of dread washing over her—as she recognized the figure struggling to crawl. It was her father, wounded and clearly in distress.

"Pappa," Lone Bear cried, her voice trembling as she knelt beside him. Tenderly, she cradled his head in her lap, her touch gentle despite the importance of the moment. With eyes that seemed distant and unfocused, she hummed the melody of a familiar song, one Mata had sung to her in childhood, a bittersweet reminder of happier days they had shared together.

The severity of his injury wasn't immediately lethal, but the blood pooling around him painted a grim picture for Lone Bear. She knew his life was slipping away with each passing moment.

Pain shot through his arm like wildfire, causing Mata to wince in agony. It surged into his head like a blinding white explosion, leaving him dizzy and disoriented. Spasms wracked his body, each sensation like needles dipped in acidic cactus juice being jabbed into his skin. The pain ebbed and flowed unpredictably, sometimes overwhelming and debilitating, then strangely bearable the next.

"Why, father? You're our healer, our guide why did you enter the fight?"

"I searched everywhere for you, Lone Bear. Everywhere. Then I saw a soldier chasing Snake Flower. She's just 9 years old. I stopped him before he could harm her, but he got me too," Mata groaned, coughing, blood staining his chin.

"This is Kane's fault. Those men hunting him, backed by the army. If he hadn't come to our tribe, if he hadn't lived with us, none of this would've happened," she seethed. "No.... it's not his fault. He has no control over the white men. Their purpose is to kill every Indian in this land. Go with him, start anew. He loves you, he'll protect you," Mata smiled weakly. As he slipped towards unconsciousness, he glimpsed Kane standing behind Lone Bear. With a fleeting smile, he exhaled his last breath.

"After we bury him, we have to leave immediately," Kane said gently, placing his hand on her shoulder and helping her up.

"Take your hands off me.... I hate you! All this death, it's because of you and you alone!" She screamed, staggering in shock as she rose, then collapsing into Kane's strong embrace.

"I'm sorry, Lone Bear. I never wanted any of this. I tried to divert the soldiers away from your tribe, but something went wrong. The white men attacked anyway. And I don't know why?" he pleaded, trying to comfort her.

"No amount of justification will change what you've done, Kane. Because of you, I've lost everything I've ever known. No family, no clan, nothing. You've ruined my life," she accused bitterly.

* * *

Previously, Lone Bear woke two hours after Kane defiantly left for the army settlement.

"KANE, KANE, KANE.... WHERE ARE YOU?" She called

out, her voice echoing through the densely wooded forest.

"He's always doing this.... takes off without telling me.... leaving me alone," she thought angrily, stirring the fire coals to coax them back to life. As she circled around the pit, her gaze fell upon a disturbing sight—the human-skinned book discarded in the dirt.

With great apprehension, uncertain of the dangers it might hold, she hesitated briefly before picking it up. Blowing gritty dust off the front cover, she inspected it closely.

She noticed a human belly button used as a clasp, though it wasn't fastened.

The ancient skin beneath her fingertips felt weathered, as though it had endured the passage of eons, as she steeled herself and opened the book. Its brittle pages whispered secrets as she traced the hastily scrawled symbols, each revealing a fragment of Kane's lineage intertwined with the ominous depths of the tenth dimension, where malevolent entities lurked.

This time, the book intentionally unveiled its astrological secrets, igniting the Sharman within Lone Bear with deep curiosity.

Amid the faded and sometimes illegible text, revelations of alternate realms and cosmic laws emerged, depicting Kane not merely as a mortal or shape-shifter but as a Prince bound by ancestral duty. Earth, it seemed, was merely a stepping stone—a realm where he must endure mortal trials to ascend to his rightful throne.

With each turn of the page, the weight of his destiny pressed upon her, a burden now shared as the guardian of his secrets and the gateway to his world.

Lone Bear's fragile grasp on the paranormal unraveling before her was tenuous at best. As she delved deeper into the arcane book, a malevolent puff of dirty green smoke billowed forth, engulfing her in its noxious embrace. Coughing and wheezing, she inadvertently inhaled the foul fumes, causing her senses to reel and her stomach to revolt in protest.

Recoiling from the putrid book, she hurled it to the ground in a desperate attempt to rid herself of its spitefulness. Yet, its odious stench clung to her like a curse, stubbornly refusing to vanish despite her frantic efforts to cleanse herself of its vile touch.

Breathless and driven by pure instinct, she sprinted down the mountain, leaping into the cool embrace of the creek. Lone Bear scrubbed furiously at her skin, trying to rid herself of the lingering touch of the noxious green smoke. Each splash sent cascades of water flying, a frantic attempt to cleanse her body of the sinister residue. Fifteen agonizing minutes passed as she submerged herself, the creek swirling around her in a soothing yet desperate attempt to wash away the foul taste of decay that clung stubbornly to her lips. Surfacing from the water, gasping for air, she felt the desperation of unanswered questions pressing upon her. What malevolent forces lay behind the toxic gas that had nearly consumed her?

Exhausted and wary, she retreated to her camp. Dragging her bedroll to a safe distance from the accursed book, Lone Bear sat down and scrutinised its cover fashioned from human skin, sending chills down her spine. It stood as a frightening reminder of the encroaching darkness now casting its shadow over her once peaceful world.

Two hours crept by, and the book remained eerily still, untouched by any supernatural influence. Relieved yet cautious,

Lone Bear decided to return it to Kane's knapsack. The barrier of fabric between herself and the sinister book offered a semblance of protection, however illusory it may have been.

As if snapping out of a trance, Lone Bear suddenly realized that the gunfire and screams from the distant fighting had ceased. A heavy silence hung in the air, thick with unspoken horrors. Reluctantly, she decided to venture toward the battlefield, her heart pounding with a mix of anxiety and anticipation. Every step was fraught with the fear of what she might discover, the haunting possibility of witnessing unspeakable devastation.

* * *

Kane carried Mata's body to their campsite, the same place where Lady Vixen had been buried just days before. Lone Bear dawdled behind him, each step a monumental effort as she physically and mentally dragged herself forward. Her body ached with exhaustion, and her mind swirled with the heavy burden of grief and fatigue, making every movement an act of sheer willpower.

"Where would you like your father's resting place to be?" Kane asked the despondent woman.

"Somewhere isolated," Lone Bear replied in a hopeless tone.

"Off the track so no one will disturb him.... and deep in the ground so the wolves won't smell him and dig him up."

Kane wandered further into the forest, venturing into a deep and mystical part of the woodland where ancient trees stood like silent protectors. The air was thick with the scent of moss and earth, and an bizzare stillness hung around him. With a heavy heart, he began digging with his bare hands, each scoop of dirt a painful reminder of the loss he was about to lay to rest. Regret filled his thoughts as he prepared a grave for his once kind and welcoming friend, his fingers growing raw against the unyielding soil.

Lone Bear ceremoniously prepared Mata's body while Kane continued to dig the grave. Amidst her solemn chants of tribal prayers, intermittent murmurs of obscenities and blame toward Kane escaped her lips. Sometimes, these mumbled accusations grew louder, and Kane couldn't help but catch her insults. Yet, rather than confront Lone Bear, he chose to silently endure her rants. Each word pierced his heart, slowly numbing another part of his emotional psyche with every bitter accusation that permeated the air between them.

Once Mata's body was completely buried, Kane felt it appropriate to honor his friend with a prayer from his Buddhist faith.

"What are you doing?" Lone Bear shouted, her voice cutting through the solemnity. "I'm honoring your father in the way I've been taught as a Buddhist monk," Kane replied, taken aback by Lone Bear's sudden objection.

"You're not a Buddhist monk anymore, Kane. Haven't you noticed that monks don't leave a trail of carnage behind them everywhere they go? But you do, Shadow Bear. Tragedy follows you wherever you go and I don't want to be a part of it. Ultimately,

it will lead to my destruction as well. I want to live my life in peace, not in this chaos you've created," Lone Bear churned, her green eyes flashing with a mix of hatred and vulnerability

Turning on her heels in a huff, Lone Bear stomped back to their campsite. She flopped down onto her bedroll, pulling the bear skin blanket over her head, seeking comfort in its familiar warmth. Despite the turmoil in her heart, exhaustion soon claimed her, and she gradually drifted into a restless sleep.

Kane, on the other hand, trudged back to the campsite, his heart swamped with sorrow, wondering how everything had turned so tragic. Sitting beside his knapsack,

he absentmindedly pulled out the human skin book, flipping through its pages aimlessly, seeking distraction.

Suddenly, an drawing caught his eye—an old woman's face, her skeletal features contorted in agony, her skin papery and fragile with large patches of missing long black hair. Kane winced involuntarily at the sight of the picture. Despite his confusion over why this particular image had mysteriously appeared in the book, it felt strangely familiar, sending a shiver through his body.

* * *

Gideon and Victor dismounted from their horses, drawing unwanted stares and whispers from the curious inhabitants of the Fort. As Victor strode past the gawking crowd, he suddenly lunged towards them in a threatening manner, effectively scattering the onlookers.

"What's so interesting, you busybodies? Haven't you seen a high priest monk before?" he blurted out, attempting to assert his authority and emphasize his role as Gideon's protector.

"Where's the Colonel's office?" he demanded in his thundering voice, addressing anyone brave enough to still be hanging around.

"Up the road and turn left. You'll see Colonel Fitzpatrick's headquarters," a young soldier spoke up, pointing in the direction indicated. Victor marched ahead, with Gideon floating close behind, his majestic staff acting as an anchor to his effortless strides.

Entering the building, Victor marched up to the soldiers standing guard at the door, his presence commanding immediate attention.

"We need to see the Colonel immediately," he demanded, his voice booming through the corridor.

"We have urgent information and have been sent by Don Morales from Rancho Los Charro."

The soldiers' eyes widened in alarm, not just at Victor's towering and intimidating figure, but also at the sight of Gideon standing resolutely behind him. Gideon's majestic staff gleamed with supremacy, adding to the gravity of their arrival and casting an aura of authority that was impossible to ignore.

The soldier knocked three times before hearing the Colonel shout, "Come in," in his Texan drawl. Immediately, the soldier opened the door and announced that Gideon and Victor were outside, requesting an urgent meeting.

"Let them in," Colonel Fitzpatrick entertained the request.

"Yes, what can I help you with?" the Colonel began as Victor stood with his sombrero hat in hand, and Gideon poised next to him, clutching his staff.

"We are here to inform you, Señor Colonel, that a murderous act has been committed against Don Morales' men, specifically

Carlos. I have a letter from Don

Morales" Victor informed the Colonel stepping forward, placing the folded piece of paper on the table.

"I know about the Mexican Carlos. One of your monks, Juji I believe his name was, escorted him back to your ranch. I assume he made it," the Colonel said, his curiosity beginning to stir.

"Hai.... they did make it back, but not alive. You said the lead rider was a monk?" Gideon interjected.

"Yes, the men he traveled with nominated him for the task. I'm sorry to hear that he didn't make it back alive," the Colonel continued with sincere condolences.

"The reason for our visit," Gideon said, stepping forward with confidence to gain more of the Colonel's attention

"We hunt a demon called Kane. He is a skin changer. He transforms into a gigantic bear and has killed numerous people during his pilgrimage here, and those are only the ones we know of. I know that he was responsible for the murder of my brother and the workers from Don Morales' ranch. He must be stopped. All we ask for is the information you've gathered on his whereabouts and safe passage to his location." The Colonel leaned back in silence, his weathered face shadowed by the dim light of the room, as he preferred to read the letter before responding. As he unfolded Don Morales's note, his expression hardened with each line he absorbed. The letter recounted Gideon's explanation and conveyed a desperate plea for the Colonel to dispatch his remaining men to Rancho Los Charro. The request was daunting, bordering on the impossible, as the battle had decimated his forces, leaving only a handful of weary soldiers. His eyes narrowed, a flicker of intensity sparking within them, as he fully comprehended the dire gravity of the situation.

"Look, I've heard the gigantic bear skin-changing story from your other monks. Personally, I think it's a load of hogwash, but my men have reported sightings of a very large bear mingling with the local natives further north from here," Colonel Fitzpatrick said, his tone skeptical yet informative.

"Is Kane still residing with them?" Gideon asked anxiously, leaning forward.

"No," the Colonel replied. "My Sergeant reported that a large Indian man separated from his tribe and was spotted climbing into the mountains, towards the snow peaks. It's uncharted territory up there. I have heard of a small settlement mainly full of fur traders, but that's seasonal," the Colonel explained, enlightening Gideon with the limited information he had.

"You have an injured monk in the infirmary, if you're interested," the Colonel continued, his voice steady yet tinged with a hint of annoyance.

"His name is Hiro. He confronted your monster, fought him, and now I think he regrets his decision. His injuries are severe, but he'll survive. I'm not sure how good his arm will be, considering the deep gashes he received." His words were penetrating, each syllable laden with the brutal truth of the encounter and the grim reality of the monk's condition.

"And the other young monk, Miko? Where is he?" Gideon asked eagerly, his eyes wide with concern.

"There's another Mexican with him, Alejandro?" Victor added, his voice rising with urgency.

"Yes, they're here. Sergeant, go and fetch the young monk and the Mexican, and bring them to my office," the Colonel ordered, his voice firm and commanding. "Sir, yes Sir," the Sergeant replied, snapping to attention before quickly exiting the office.

Miko sat by the window, staring out into the wastelands, his mind adrift with boredom and worry. He blew on the glass, misting it up and drawing simple pictures on the window. He wondered if Juji had made it back safely to Rancho Los Charro. Nearby, Alejandro slept soundly, his soft snores filling the quiet room. Suddenly, a determined knock sounded on the door, jolting Alejandro awake.

Miko instantly jumped to his feet, glad that there was finally some action. He flung open the door before Alejandro could even say "tequila."

"Hai?" Miko answered, his voice eager.

"The Colonel wants to see both of you now. Get yourselves together and come with me," the Sergeant demanded.

Quickly, Miko and Alejandro grabbed their jackets, exchanging curious glances as they followed the soldier back to headquarters, wondering what was going on.

Upon entering the Colonel's office, Miko instantly recognized Gideon standing there, majestic and authoritative. His eyes widened in disbelief and joy at the sight of his beloved mentor.

"Master Gideon, you're here! I can't believe it. I'm so happy to see you," Miko blurted out, rushing forward to embrace Gideon with overflowing adoration and relief.

"Miko, thank Buddha you're safe," the old monk said, a tear glistening in his eye as he returned the heartfelt embrace.

"Victor.... It's good to see you too, Amigo. Can't believe that jeffe let you off the ranch," Alejandro joked, giving the towering man a light friendly slap on the back. “Enough of that,” Victor said bluntly, cutting off Alejandro’s playful gestures.

“We will stay here for two nights before venturing out to find Kane. That gives me enough time to recuperate from our journey here and organize supplies for the trip,” Gideon interjected, steering the conversation back to the matter at hand.

“Also, I need to see Hiro and find out exactly what happened with his fight with Kane,” Gideon added firmly, his tone tolerating no argument.

“Take the priest to the infirmary. We’ll make sure that you have all the materials you need for your journey,” the Colonel accommodated, his voice practical and reassuring.

“Oh, and there’s one more thing, Colonel. If you could be kind enough to loan us an Indian tracker. It will make our trip easier and hopefully quicker,” Victor asked politely, a surprising display of courtesy that left Alejandro and Gideon momentarily taken aback.

“I’m a good tracker, Master Gideon. We don’t need another man on our trip, I can do the job,” Miko pleaded earnestly, eager to prove himself as more than just a caretaker for the old man. He believed his skills were valuable and necessary.

“Hai, Miko.... I know you are good at tracking, but you don’t know these lands. Having someone who can safely guide us through this unfamiliar territory will be crucial. You’ll still be able to assist him,” Gideon encouraged, recognizing Miko’s enthusiasm while emphasizing the importance of local knowledge for their journey. Entering the infirmary, Gideon, Miko, Victor, and Alejandro were escorted to Hiro’s room.

There, Hiro lay with his arm heavily bandaged, his expression a blend of reassurance and nervousness upon spotting Gideon.

"Master Gideon, you made the journey through the desert to be here with us. Thank you," Hiro acknowledged gratefully, recognizing the effort the old man had undertaken to join them.

"Juji didn't make it to the ranch alive. The carnage that Victor and I witnessed distressed us greatly. Kane and his demons are responsible. No man could've mutilated Juji's body like that. It demonstrated the pure evil we're dealing with. It must stop now. That's why we're here, Master Hiro," Gideon stated flatly, his voice devoid of emotion as he addressed Hiro.

"Tell me about the fight you had with Kane. Did he fight as a man or a beast? He did some damage to your arm. You won't be able to join us any further on this mission. You are now disabled and would only be a hindrance," Gideon continued, his tone cold and matter-of-fact, laying out the harsh reality without any sentiment.

"Juji is dead??" Miko shouted, his voice cracking as tears welled up, unable to bear the brutal reality of his brother's demise.

Hiro, upon hearing about Juji's death, showed no emotion. Instead, he glared at Gideon with resentment, feeling a flood of loathing towards the old monk. The initial elation of sighting his mentor evaporated faster than steam in the desert heat.

Alejandro stood there, stroking his long mustache, shaking his head in disbelief.

"If his body was so badly mutilated as you say, Senor, then how did you know it was Juji?" Alejandro suddenly questioned, his brow furrowing with skepticism.

"I knew it was one of my brothers because of this," Gideon stated firmly, pulling out a dirty piece of habit belt that had been found stuck to a horse's hoof.

"Plus, the Colonel told us it was Juji who rode with Carlos," Victor added sternly, reinforcing the grim truth.

Hiro recounted the harrowing details of his encounter with Kane, vividly describing how the battle began with Kane appearing human but escalated when Hiro's blade slashed across his face, triggering a horrifying transformation into a demonic form. He conveyed the immense struggle of facing such overwhelming power with bravery. "Master Gideon, I managed to maim the demon and delay his escape. It's been more than a week recovering in this bed, and I can feel my arm healing swiftly. I know I'll be strong enough to join you in hunting for Kane. Please, Master Gideon, allow me

to accompany you," Hiro implored, his voice carrying a tinge of desperation unwilling to be left behind despite his injuries.

"I will consult the doctor, but just looking at you, my answer is still no. Stay here, and once we have captured Kane, we'll return for you and make our way back home to Japan," Gideon affirmed firmly, unmoved by Hiro's plea.

"Is Miko going with you?" Hiro shouted, frustration boiling over at Gideon's stubbornness.

"Hai, he is," Gideon replied calmly.

"But he's only a child and not trained in ninjitsu like me. He's just a steward!" Hiro continued, disregarding Miko's feelings as he aired his grievances about his brother's perceived lesser role in the mission.

"Miko will assist the Indian tracker the army is providing us," Gideon reiterated sternly.

"But I can—" Hiro persisted.

"SILENCE!" Gideon's voice thundered, cutting off Hiro's protest.

"Your obstinacy infuriates me and jeopardizes the success of this mission. This is what I don't need while battling the demon. Do as you're told," Gideon concluded sharply, before turning abruptly and leaving the room. Hiro seethed with frustration and rage, feeling dismissed and powerless in the face of Gideon's unwavering decision.

Two days later, Gideon, Victor, Alejandro, Miko, and the Indian scout departed from the fort, their horses laden with the essential supplies for their journey. Hiro stood at the window, watching the group leave, his heart heavy with the sting of Gideon's rejection. The old monk's decision had hardened Hiro's willpower, interpreting it as an indictment of his strength and honor. He yearned for a chance to confront Kane once more, confident that this time he would prevail.

Waiting until dusk, Hiro gathered his belongings, swapping his torn shirt for a fresh one, and stealthily slipped through the window, escaping the confines of the infirmary. He made his way to the barn, where he quietly appropriated a horse. With determination chiseled on his face, Hiro boldly rode through the gates of the fort, secretly tailing Kane's hunting party, his mind set on confronting the demon and proving his worth, despite Gideon's judgment.

* * *

Kane and Lone Bear had departed their campsite a day before Gideon's hunting party, giving them a three-day head start. This accounted for the time it took the group to reach the base of the mountains from the fort, as well as the additional two days needed for their preparations for the search.

Kane strode ahead, with Lone Bear trailing behind in a sullen silence. Occasionally, he glanced back at her, worry furrowing lines on his face.

"Are you alright?" Kane asked, but Lone Bear remained unresponsive. "Is this it? Are you never going to talk to me again?" Kane pressed on.

"We have a grueling climb ahead of us. If we don't want to fall prey to those relentless hunters, we have to move faster. I didn't tell you, but I spotted my High Priest Gideon and Don Morales' henchman when I left the Fort. They're closing in."

"Why did you go to the Fort when your creepy father told you not to?" Lone Bear finally spoke, her voice barely audible.

"I returned to finish off my brother Hiro once and for all," Kane explained, his voice tinged with bitterness. "He's the one you saw me fight, the one who scarred my face. He won't rest until he sees me dead. I want to put an end to this pointless chase."

"And did you kill him?" Lone Bear whispered.

"No.... I was about to, but my youngest brother intervened. He begged me to surrender and return to Japan, but I know I'd be condemned to a lifetime of solitary confinement at the monastery. I'm tired of living by their rules, of being told what to do," Kane insisted, his frustration evident.

"So, how's running your own life going for you?" Lone Bear retorted sarcastically. "Death and fleeing from it? Your brother Miko was right. Perhaps you should have surrendered and returned to Japan. Isn't that the honorable path in your culture?" Her words were laced with biting criticism, challenging Kane's choices and stirring the turmoil within him.

"Just hurry up," Kane replied tersely, fully aware of the selfishness in his decision to continue fleeing, especially when it seemed to come at the expense of others.

His words carried a tinge of compliance, acknowledging the consequences of his actions as they pressed onward into the unforgiving mountains range.

The night draped the campsite in an queer silence, broken only by the soft crackle of the campfire—a natural melody in the velvety darkness. Flames flickered, casting a warm glow that painted Kanes face with toasted hues. He sat close to the fire on a moss-covered log, captivated and tranquil, lost in the hypnotic dance of red sparks that twirled gently in the evening breeze.

Lone Bear lay on her bedroll, wrapped in her favorite bear skin, the flickering light of the fire casting shadows across her tired face. She had been awake for hours, too exhausted to tend the fire or prepare dinner. Finally, she sat up and glanced over at Kane, who sat on a nearby log.

"There's a settlement further up the mountains, about two days' walk from here. We could go there to buy supplies," she suggested quietly.

"I still have money from the 'Big Sky' job Don Morales paid me for. It's a good idea, but we'll need to be cautious. We can't afford to tip off our pursuers about our direction," Kane replied, his tone showing a hint of relief that Lone Bear was speaking to him again.

As Kane studied her intently, he noticed the weariness etched on Lone Bear's face, her usually smooth skin now showing deep lines and a parched appearance.

"Lone Bear, are you feeling alright? You look dehydrated and exhausted," he asked with concern.

"What do you think, Kane? I feel terrible. The stress of everything we've been through, running and climbing higher into these mountain forests where only wolves and bears roam.... That's why there's a settlement up ahead, for the fur traders," she responded wearily, her voice tinged with resentful submission.

The following day, Kane and Lone Bear ventured higher into the high country, but her steps grew labored, struggling to match Kane's brisk pace. With each passing day, her condition deteriorated. Energy ebbed away, and she instinctively concealed her hands beneath the pelts she wore for warmth, trying to mask their shriveled appearance.

While pausing to wash her face in a nearby puddle, Lone Bear was struck by a profound shock as she beheld her reflection. Heavy bags hung beneath her eyes, dark and sunken, and strands of hair fell out with each touch. Her once radiant, tanned skin appeared dry and withered, resembling that of a woman in her late nineties rather than the vibrant twenty-year-old she once was. The stark realization of her physical decline mirrored the gravity of their desperate flight through the unforgiving wilderness.

"Kane.... look at me," she murmured quietly, her voice tinged with grief.

Kane paused in his search for dry kindling, turning to face

Lone Bear. As she slowly pulled back her hooded pelt, revealing her face, a profound sense of shock gripped him. Before him stood an elderly woman, her gaze reflecting back at him through tired eyes and weathered skin.

"Oh my God. What's happening to you?" Kane gasped, his voice filled with disbelief as he instinctively dropped the bundle of sticks he had gathered.

Her face appeared weather-beaten and deeply wrinkled, the once-smooth skin now embedded with lines so pronounced that it was difficult to recall her appearance as a young woman. Her once-strong posture now began to stoop, as if bearing an invisible burden that weighed heavily on her shoulders, giving her a semblance of a hunched back.

"How did this happen? My love, what's going on?" Kane screamed in distress, rushing toward her and pulling her into his arms.

"It's the green smoke," she finally confessed, her voice trembling. "What do you mean, the green smoke?"

"While you were away at the Fort, I picked up your bible to put it back into your knapsack. It compelled me to open it, and as I started reading, a large cloud of sickening green smoke exploded in my face. Even after washing myself for ages in the creek, I couldn't get rid of the rancid taste and smell," she explained, her words laden with anguish and confusion.

Kane could feel panic and fear rising up in him. His demeanor shifted abruptly from profound sadness to intense anger. As a tumult of emotions surged through his body, he began twisting and partially shifting into his bear form. Filled with rage, Kane screamed, the sound escalating into a roar of absolute fury as he thundered out the words "FATHER WHAT HAVE YOU DONE?"

Without hesitation, Kane scooped Lone Bear into his arms and sprinted toward the fur traders' settlement. Desperation fueled his speed as he hoped to find a doctor who could save his beloved Lone Bear. As he entered the outskirts of the small town, mostly men stood to one side, watching in silent curiosity and suspicion. Kane trudged down the muddy street, Lone Bear unconscious and limp as a rag doll in his arms.

"Help me.... is there a doctor here.... or a nurse?" he pleaded frantically with every passerby. They stared at him with wide, unblinking eyes, taken aback by the sight of the strange man carrying the collapsed Indian woman.

"They don't like your kind around here, Mister," an old man said from the porch of a shanty house, stuffing tobacco into his pipe. His tone was indifferent, almost amused, as he watched Kane with a mix of disdain and curiosity.

A crowd began to gather around the huge, desperate stranger, their whispers buzzing like a swarm of angry bees. Kane could feel a thousand eyes burning into his skin with judgment and criticism. Each gaze was a dagger of suspicion and prejudice, piercing his resolve. His breath quickened, and his heart pounded with a mix of fear and determination. The weight of Lone Bear in his arms felt heavier with every passing second as the oppressive silence of the onlookers suffocated him. "Help her.... I have money to pay anyone willing to help!" Kane begged, his voice trembling with desperation, rising and falling with the intense emotions that raged within him. The demon bear within stirred, fueled by a powerful urge to break free.

"She's a squaw," another man interrupted, his voice dripping with disdain.

"The only good squaw is a dead one," he continued cruelly, chuckling at his own vile remark.

"She looks like she already is," someone else from the crowd blurted out, their words void of any empathy for Kane's overwhelming grief.

Kane hesitated, his heart aching as he looked down at Lone Bear, still cradled in his arms. As soon as he saw her withered face and sunken eyes staring into nothingness, he knew she had passed away in his embrace.

Suddenly, the monster within him began its full manifestation, to the horror of all who witnessed Kane's body twisting and contorting. Fully aware of what was happening, Kane quickly placed Lone Bear's body down on the porch. He pulled out all the money he had and dumped it next to her, his last desperate attempt to honor her memory before the beast within took over.

"What the hell are you?" a man screamed, his voice cracking with terror.

"You're a skin changer! The Indians around here believe in that voodoo shit.... and now it's true!" Another scruffy, unkempt man yelled, his finger trembling as he pointed directly at Kane.

A rapid sense of impending danger coursed through Kane, hot flushes followed by chills flooding his body. The intensity of his panic attack made him feel as though he was dying, losing control of himself. Spinning around, all Kane could see were more than a dozen men, their faces twisted in disbelief and horror as they stared at him. "BURY HER," he demanded in a low, guttural voice that was noticeably different from his original tone.

Dense fog drifted into the village, shrouding it in a ghostly haze. Then the rain began, at first a gentle drizzle, typical for the altitude, but soon it turned into a torrential sleet, mirroring the despondent mood that hung over the scene.

The crowd of astonished men, sensing imminent danger, began reeling backward, their faces pale with fear as they watched the demon within Kane transmute. With their senses on high alert, some panicked and ran, locking themselves behind the doors of nearby shacks. Others stood frozen, mouths agape, as time seemed to slow down around them. A few grabbed their guns, firing bullets at the intimidatingly muscular creature with piercing blue eyes.

One man shot at point-blank range, but the bullet had little effect on the beast. Kane didn't merely withstand it; he seemed unconcerned by it altogether. The terrified man shot again, twice more, the sound of bullets striking the bear echoing through the air, but again, they had no effect.

Kane stood there, his gaze fixed and perisistent, showing no signs of harm.

Then, without a sound, he turned and sprinted up the road, his form vanishing into the snowy forest. He left behind the only love he had ever known, in the midst of a crowd of Indian-hating white men—a betrayal so profound that even her father, Mata, would have condemned it.

Kane ran for miles into the uncharted mountains until exhaustion gripped him like a fist, eventually forcing him to rest. He returned to his human form and examined the bullet wounds: one in his arm and two on the side of his torso. Despite the chunks of flesh blasted away, he knew the injuries weren't life-threatening. He slopped up a muddy incline and sought shelter under a dug-out space with exposed roots, just enough to stay relatively dry.

His mind was in turmoil over the catastrophic events that had transpired in front of those despicable fur hunters.... and he had left his beautiful girl with them. The guilt tortured Kane, churning his stomach until he vomited.

The betrayal of the one person who had ever truly loved him shattered his soul into a thousand jagged pieces. Each fragment seemed to pulse with a searing pain, made even more unbearable by the dark shadow of Gideon and his relentless hunting party looming on the horizon. He could already feel the choking grip of dread, knowing that the story of what had transpired in the village would erupt with the ferocity of wildfire. Traders, ever eager to weave tales of the mysterious and the

extraordinary from the uncharted high country, would carry the story far and wide, fanning the flames of gossip and suspicion with their insatiable thirst for the bizarre.

Kane huddled under the roots, shivering from a mixture of cold and anguish.

His thoughts raced, haunted by the image of her lifeless body and the contemptuous faces of the men who surrounded her. The sleet pounded relentlessly, each ice shard a reminder of his failure and the constant threat he now faced. He had to keep moving, had to survive—not just for himself, but for the memory of the love he had lost in the midst of a crowd of hate.

Regaining his strength, Kane pushed further into the snow-capped mountains, determined to put as much distance as possible between himself and Gideon. Trudging through the snow, he heard something—a faint noise. He paused, thinking it might be brush falling under the weight of the snow, but he couldn't tell where it was coming from.

He strained his ears, the silence around him thick and oppressive, broken only by the faint rustling of the trees. Determined, he pressed on, each step deliberate and wary. Minutes ticked by, and then the silence shattered with a sudden, jarring crash. The sound was followed by the unmistakable crack of a small tree splintering under unseen pressure, a sharp, invasive noise that pierced the forest's stillness and set his heart racing.

A wave of nervousness washed over Kane as he searched for the source. His eyes widened in disbelief when a massive female grizzly bear with a set of twins emerged from the woodland. The bear stopped and stared at Kane, sniffing the air with her big brown nose. Then she let out a roar, not one of threat, but of recognition and acceptance.

Kane stood frozen, his heart pounding in his chest. The bear's eyes locked onto his, and he felt an uncanny connection, as if she sensed the turmoil within him. Her presence, formidable yet oddly comforting, brought a strange sense of peace.

The snow continued to fall, a steady rhythm that seemed to sync with his heartbeat. Kane knew he had to keep moving, but this encounter, this moment of mutual understanding with the great grizzly, gave him a renewed sense of purpose and strength.

As the mother bear trudged forward with her cubs padding closely in her wake, Kane felt an irresistible, primal pull to follow. The group moved through the dense forest, their breaths visible in the frosty air. After about thirty minutes of steady trekking, they arrived at a dilapidated shack, once a haven for fur traders and weary travelers seeking refuge from the bitter cold.

Despite the years of harsh winters that had battered it, the shack remained marginally habitable. Snow and ice had taken their toll, gnawing away at the wooden shingles clinging desperately to the roof. The structure stood as a weathered landmark, offering shelter against the relentless elements.

Opening the door, dust, thick cobwebs and empty food cans littered the table that accompanied a single chair. Kanes eyes glanced over to an open fire place and an

old rusty pot belly stove with a dinted well used kettle sitting upon it. Thankfully, whoever was there last might have been messy, but at least they had the sense to make sure there was plenty of firewood stacked in the corner.

Quickly, he grabbed some firewood and piled it into the potbelly stove, desperately searching for something to light it with as he stuffed kindling under the logs. Walking over to the stained washbasin, he found a box of friction matches placed carefully beside it.

“Thank Buddha,” Kane mumbled under his breath, glancing towards the heavens with his hands clasped together in a praying motion.

Steadily, the warmth of the fire began to comfort Kane’s cold bones and desolate emotions. He couldn’t shake the image of leaving Lone Bear with those vile fur traders.

“He must go back and see what they did with her body. But maybe that would be a bad idea, considering Gideon and his hunting party were hot on his trail,” he thought to himself.

"I'll stay here for a few days, then keep moving further into the high caps of the mountains," he resolved.

Looking further around the cabin, Kane discovered a dusty old chest. With a creak, he opened it to find warm clothes neatly folded inside. It was another blessing, as he had lost most of his clothes when he transformed into Shadow Bear in the village.

His knapsack was still intact, having mindfully carried it in his mouth as he fled like a coward.

After getting dressed, Kane filled the kettle with snow and placed it on the potbelly stove, eagerly anticipating the moment he could submerge his hands in the warm water to thaw them out. The one thing the cabin lacked was food, so once he was warm and comfortable, Kane ventured out into the forest in search of sustenance. He had not walked far when he saw a mother bear with her cubs scavenging the few wild berries that still clung desperately to their branches.

"Is this all there is?" he asked the bear. As though she understood him, she consciously led him to a trap that had snared a large jackrabbit by the foot. The animal squealed with panic as the bear approached, sensing its ultimate demise, but it was Kane who followed and grabbed the rabbit, instantly breaking its neck.

"Thank you again, Mrs. Grizzly Bear," he said, bowing to the majestic animal.

The bear replied with a resounding roar, echoing through the forest. Somehow, Kane thought he heard the faint whisper of the name *"Lone Bear"* in the powerful sound, but quickly dismissed it as his own guilty imagination.

After satisfying his essential needs—warmth, food, and quenching his thirst—Kane began to mentally dissect and question the accelerated aging and sudden demise of Lone Bear. He recalled her description of the green smoke that exploded in her face when she opened the human skin book. The image of the drawing of a haggard woman, made just days before her death, suddenly clicked in his mind, and with a jolt of realization, he knew it was his father who had gruesomely ended Lone Bear's life.

Grabbing the book, Kane stared at its cover, his grip tightening like a vice. His fingers dug into the skin, tearing it with his sharp fingernails as he growled with extreme anger. His voice deepened, eventually sounding like a wild beast unleashed.

"FATHER.... WHAT HAVE YOU DONE? I HATE YOU.... I DON'T WANT TO BE A PART OF THIS CRUEL MACABRE GAME. I DENOUNCE YOU, MY HERITAGE, AND MY ORDAINED DESTINY. YOU CAUSE NOTHING BUT PAIN AND

SUFFERING. LEAVE ME ALONE!" Kane screamed at the book, his voice bouncing off the walls with anguish and defiance. With a surge of anger, he hurled the book violently to the floor, slamming his massive foot down upon it.

Suddenly, the book burst open, revealing a perfectly round blue orb, about three times the size of a basketball, encased in a clear, glass-like shell. Inside, Kane observed a swirling, incandescently blue liquid substance that seemed to hover on the verge of boiling. It emitted a faint crackling sound, distinct from the hum of electricity, filling the air with an spectral energy.

The object radiated an unnerving aura, evoking a profound, unnatural anxiety that felt almost engineered, as if it were forcing an alien emotion directly into his psyche. At the heart of the swirling blue mass, Kane glimpsed a dazzling light, vibrant and intense, reminiscent of the sun at its pinnacle. In that instant, a wave of realization crashed over him—he was staring at the sky of his home, a gossamer portal leading to the dimension of his father, Lady Vixen, and Crowman. It was no mere oddity; it was a stargate, a gateway to another universe.

As Kane stared into the shimmering tunnel, he witnessed three imposing, faceless humanoid figures. Each stood about six feet tall and weighed approximately four hundred pounds. They emerged silently and with an air of steadfast intention, positioning themselves before him as though standing guard.

Kane felt the creatures' thoughts invading his mind, stirring the deepest and darkest corners of his terror, where something prowled, something lurked. It was elusive, manipulative, and violent, more haunting than haunted. The uncertainty and the intensity of the fear were exactly what the creatures wanted.

It was as if another reality was bleeding into his world, giving Kane unsettling glimpses of the universe next door. The boundaries between dimensions blurred, and he could sense the sinister presence of something far more malevolent than he could comprehend.

"YOU KILLED THE LOVE OF MY LIFE" Kane screamed at the three dark creatures. Swiftly, his father emerged from the portal, still carrying Ratikin on his shoulder.

Ratikin's grotesque human face twisted as he constantly chomped and gnashed his sharp, hideous teeth, adding a sinister edge to the already surreal scene.

"You disobeyed me, Shadow Bear. You went to the fort when I told you not to," his father said callously, devoid of empathy for his

son's grief and pain.

"I warned you there would be consequences, and ultimately, you caused the Indian woman's death."

He gestured toward the three dark creatures standing in silent attendance.

"These are my counselors," he said, his voice steady and hard.

"We have listened to your words. If you choose to renounce your heritage, your legacy, and me, we will be forced to strip you of your power and strength as Shadow Bear. You will remain immortal, but no longer as a man—your existence will be reduced to that of a spirit animal."

His father's voice thickened with stern finality.

"Your human emotions, inherited from your mother's side, are clouding your judgment. Think carefully. Once you disown your role as a leader in our universe, there will be no turning back."

"You promised me love and happiness, not endless rejection and ridicule, where I'm seen as nothing more than a freak and a monster!" Kane cried out, his voice cracking with raw, unfiltered anguish.

"I was beginning a new life with Lone Bear, and you tore that away from me! You've taken everything!"

"That was your choice," his father replied, his tone uncompromising.

"Do you think my words are hollow and without weight?"

Kane's voice trembled with desperation as he pleaded, "What are you? What am I?" His father's response came with a dark, intense gravity.

"You are, and I am, a skinwalker," he said, the words heavy with

a dark resonance.

"We are beings of inherent darkness, wielders of potent black magic," his father explained, his voice carrying a sinsiter chill.

"Our powers are derived from completing sinister rituals, including the murder of a family member and the consumption of their flesh. This is the path your earthly human father chose to access our world. His descent into black magic bound him to dark spirits, warping his mind and driving him to madness. This madness compelled him to kill your mother, his wife, after your birth. Through this act, he became one of us. He desires your presence here.... and so do I."

His father's gaze bore into Kane, a mix of authority and dark allure in his eyes. *"Do not forsake what is rightfully yours,"* he urged, his voice a haunting blend of command and seduction.

"Join us and embrace your heritage. This is where you truly belong."

Kane glared menacingly at his father's faceless form as Ratikin giggled and teased from the phantom's shoulder.

"Leave him be.... let him be alone.... he doesn't deserve to be with us," the nasty little rat tormented, its voice dripping with malice.

"No, I refuse to live a life steeped in evil, bound by rituals and spreading death and chaos," Kane declared, his voice adamant

"Perhaps that's acceptable to you, but I'm grateful for my mother's contribution to my life and the emotions of a human heart she gave me. It enables me to see clearly the curse that you and everything you stand for truly are."

"And I don't want to be a Buddhist either. All of my brothers have abandoned me because of what you've made me. Even within a faith that preaches love and kindness, I've received none of that at the monastery. It's all been a lie, and I've lost my faith. Everything I've known and loved has been stripped away from me. Now I have nothing left. I want nothing to do with you. You all sicken me."

Without a word, the three dark figures stepped back through the blue orb, leaving Kane's father lingering behind.

"Is this your final choice? You're giving up your princely status?" he asked one last time, his tone carrying a dark, almost sorrowful burden

"Yes, it is," Kane answered, sealing his fate.

In that instant, Kane's world turned upside down, unaware of the gravity of his choice that would eventually crash down on him. His father's form slowly dissipated into the ether, the shimmering orb collapsing inward until it vanished entirely, leaving Kane isolated in the oppressive stillness of the cabin. The air grew thick with an unsettling quiet, wrapping around him like a suffocating shroud, amplifying the loneliness that gnawed at his soul.

The next morning, when Kane awoke, an freakish curiosity spurred him to search for the human skin book. Panic surged through him when he discovered it was missing. It wasn't in the spot where he had left it after his interdimensional experience.

Frenzied, he turned his room upside down, lifting objects, overturning furniture, and searching every conceivable hiding place. At last, he spotted it in the far corner of the room. The book's cover, once a sickly yellow reminiscent of diseased flesh, had transformed into an ominous pitch black.

With trembling hands, he gingerly picked it up and examined it closely. As he attempted to open it, he discovered that the pages were sealed tight. The deformed belly button lock had melted and fused into the cover, its grotesque form now an inextricable part of the book. The once-movable lapel was now permanently sealed, rendering the book inaccessible and its secrets forever out of reach.

His portal to unimaginable power and grandeur had slammed shut, severing his link to the formidable strength and deep reserves of vigor he once had. Kane felt a profound loss, his vitality gradually seeping from his body as the reality of his diminished state set in.

With a surge of anger, Kane hurled the book back into the corner, his face twisted in disgust. Frustration gnawed at him, but he knew he had to find food. Resigned, he ventured outside. As he stepped onto the porch, he was startled to see the same mama bear and her two cubs patiently waiting for him.

"Do you want to be my friend?" he asked the bear with a touch of humor, his voice tinged with irony. Before he could step into the snow, the massive female bear dashed ahead and turned back, her eyes meeting his. It was as if she was beckoning him to follow her, a silent invitation that stirred something curious within him.

Walking for what seemed like an eternity, Kane followed the mother bear through the snow-covered wilderness. The journey was arduous, each step sinking deep into the drifts, his breath forming frosty clouds in the frigid air. At last, they arrived at a rocky lookout, the bear pausing as if to allow Kane to take in the view.

From this vantage point, Kane gazed down into the small valley below and recognized the fur traders' village. It was the same place he had fled from like a sissy just days before. As his eyes scanned the scene, they fell upon the people milling about in the streets. Among them, a familiar sight made his heart race: his mob of hunters. At the forefront was Gideon, clutching his grand staff, a symbol of authority and power.

They were engrossed in a deep conversation with a group of rugged men. A cold dread settled over Kane as he realized just how close they were, and the gravity of his predicament became starkly clear. The proximity heightened his anxiety, making the dire nature of his situation painfully apparent.

"They're finally here," Kane muttered to the bear, his voice tinged with a mix of fear and finality, as if she could grasp the magnitude of his words.

Without delay, Kane bolted back to his cabin, urgency propelling him through the snow.

His mind raced as he began crafting and setting up traps around his hideout, each one meticulously designed to annihilate his pursuers.

The forest resonated with the sounds of his frantic preparations. Each snap of a branch, the pounding of sticks with rocks, and the rustle of leaves became a testament to his relentless determination to protect himself.

Kane worked with a furious intensity, knowing that his life depended on the success of these deadly contraptions.

* * *

"Where the hell did you come from?" one of the fur traders

jeered, his eyes wide with disbelief as he gazed at Gideon, who stood at the forefront of the daunting group of men. Among them, Miko stood out, young and innocent amidst the hardened faces. "Did a large man pass through this village recently?" Gideon's voice cut through the murmurs of the crowd, commanding attention.

"Yeah, he did," another trader replied eagerly.

"He was carrying an old Indian woman who died in his arms while he begged for a doctor. Then, all of a sudden, he transformed into this beast—a massive bear. He looked terrified and bolted into the deep forest, clutching a knapsack in his mouth. We've had guards out every night since, but we haven't seen him.... and that was four days ago."

"Thank you. The sun is beginning to set, and the cold is settling in. Would it be feasible for us to find food and lodging for the night?" Gideon's voice carried a confident air, as though their welcome was already assured.

"We've traveled for days up here.... and I am an old man. We'll depart in the morning," he continued, his tone allowing no argument.

Without hesitation, several of the villagers guided Gideon and his companions to the local boarding house. Inside, a warm fire crackled, offering respite from the biting cold. The aroma of hot food filled the air, promising nourishment after their long journey. Beds awaited, offering a brief reprieve from the harsh wilderness.

Meanwhile, crouched behind a stack of barrels, Hiro observed from the shadows as Gideon and his men entered the hotel. Once they were safely inside, he moved swiftly and silently, slipping unnoticed through the building's entrance.

"Have you seen the strangers who just arrived in town? What a motley crew of characters. It was only a matter of time—someone was bound to come looking for that demon man. And did you catch the sight of the mix of oriental and Mexican fellows chasing him? I've never seen Mexicans join forces with foreigners like that before." the gossip spread like wildfire through the town. With each retelling, the tale grew in complexity and fascination, weaving a rich tapestry of fantastical details that captivated the imaginations of all who heard it.

Two rooms were allotted for the strangers: one for Gideon and Miko, and the other for Victor and Alejandro. Hiro stood outside, listening intently at the closed doors, trying to discern which room Gideon occupied. Once he identified it, he quietly approached the door where Victor and Alejandro stayed.

With careful precision, Hiro knocked three times, the sound just audible enough for the occupants inside to hear, but not loud enough to draw attention from Gideon or the curious Miko. Alejandro, cautious yet intrigued, gingerly opened the door wide enough to peer through a narrow crack. His jaw dropped in astonishment when he saw Hiro standing there, his demeanor both sheepish and motivated.

Instantly seizing Hiro's arm, Alejandro pulled him swiftly into the room and shut the door behind them, his expression a mix of concern and bewilderment.

He shot a brief, significant glance at Victor, silently conveying that Hiro's presence was both unexpected and potentially problematic, especially in light of Gideon's orders.

"What are you doing? You know you shouldn't be here,"

Alejandro questioned eagerly, his voice tinged with alarm.

"I've come too far to stay at the Fort like an invalid. I need to be part of Kane's final days. My injured arm won't stop me from doing what I'm destined to do—fight and

defeat the monster once and for all. I know Master Gideon won't be pleased, but now that I'm here, what can he do? I can still fight and I'll prove to be an asset, just wait and see," Hiro explained quietly but positively.

"Alright, Amigo, but I'm not the one who's going to break it to the old man. Tomorrow morning, you'll have to face Gideon if you want to stick with us. We've got a rough idea of the direction Kane headed, but our Indian tracker's heard the unsettling tales circulating in town about Kane's skin changing and transforming into a massive bear. "Now he's spooked, babbling about curses and absolutely refusing to venture any deeper into the wilderness," Victor grumbled, his deep, resonant voice thick with grave concern.

"I wouldn't want to be you tomorrow, Amigo, facing your serious and staunch Master Gideon. The old man's gonna throw a 'gan rabieta' (big tantrum)," Alejandro added with a chuckle, attempting to lighten the mood with a touch of humor.

In the early morning light, the snow swirled in a graceful ballet, choreographed by the gentle wind. The trees, freshly cloaked in white, stood like enchanted beings in the wintry landscape.

A few brave souls from the village had ventured out onto the streets, starting their daily routines despite the cold. They periodically blew into their cupped hands, seeking warmth from the biting cold that permeated the air.

Miko approached the door of the Mexicans' room and rapped lightly, the sound slightly audible over the whispering inside. Curious, he knocked again, louder this time, calling out to Alejandro. Unbeknownst to Miko, his insistence caught the attention of Gideon, who emerged from inside, drawn by the commotion and curious about the disturbance.

"What's going on? Why aren't they answering? We need to get moving," Gideon demanded impatiently.

"I can hear them, but there's someone else in there with them," Miko replied, pressing his ear against the door. He focused intently, picking up on the faint murmur of a third voice behind the closed barrier.

"Open up now!" Gideon ordered forcefully, banging his large staff against the door in frustration.

Slowly, the door creaked open, revealing Hiro standing there, his posture firm yet deferential, head bowed towards Gideon as if accepting the consequences of his bold decision.

At first, Gideon's eyes widened like an owl's, but his expression swiftly twisted into a mask of fury. He glared at Hiro, his scowl deepening with disappointment and anger. Without hesitation, he bellowed out Hiro's name.

"HIRO, you're constantly disobeying me! You should never have come on this mission with us!" His voice blaring down the hallway, sharp with frustration and betrayal.

Without another word, Gideon stormed back to his room, hastily gathering his belongings. He marched out of the boarding house in a huff, his steps heavy with

indignation. Miko hurried after him, mirroring his Master's brisk pace as if fleeing from imminent danger.

Alejandro and Hiro exchanged a tense glance as Victor packed his things. After a long moment, Victor pushed past them, frustration evident in his movements, and made his way out of the room, leaving Alejandro and Hiro standing there in silence.

"Gideon wait up. There's something else that won't sit well with you. Our Indian tracker refuses to go any further. He claims the higher lands are cursed, tangled in ancient legends of black magic and dark spirits. With the fresh snow covering Kane's tracks, finding him will be a challenge," Victor informed the old monk, with Miko standing by his side.

"I am a tracker. I've followed many animals and people through the snow in Japan," Miko interjected suddenly.

"Hai Miko can be our tracker. There's no other choice," Gideon agreed reluctantly.

As Alejandro and Hiro emerged from the boarding house, Gideon fixed a menacing stare on Hiro. Miko helped Gideon onto his horse, and the rest of the group mounted up, leaving Hiro standing there awaiting Gideon's command.

He steadied his mount and glared down at Hiro with intense disdain.

"You ride at the back of the pack. If you jeopardize the safety of anyone here, I will personally end you. You bring dishonor to Buddhism and the ninja way, and back in Japan, you'd be required to commit Seppuku. Stay out of my sight, Master Hiro," Gideon snapped sharply before urging his horse forward.

Meanwhile, Victor gathered additional supplies and collected information from villagers about the terrain ahead and the likely direction Kane might have taken.

* * *

Kane discovered an old, rusty bear trap abandoned by fur traders. Using his immense strength, he pried open the jaws and then hurried down the track leading to his cabin. There, he carefully buried the trap in the middle of the path, meticulously setting the trigger spring. He concealed the deadly snare with a layer of leaves and twigs, making it blend seamlessly with the forest floor.

To ensure his pursuers would approach exactly as he intended, Kane funneled the pathway. He blocked other openings with large branches he had broken off thick pine trees, forcing the group to take the treacherous path he had prepared. The stage was set for a lethal ambush, his cunning trap hidden in plain sight.

Kane also spent time sharpening the ends of pine branches, transforming them into deadly spears. He fashioned a catapult mechanism by fastening these spears to the ends of green, pliable branches, tied back with a trigger spring. Anyone who knocked over the strategically placed rock in their path would release the tension, sending the spears hurtling towards them with lethal force.

Moving further down the track, Kane hung the skeletons of dead animals in the trees, suspending their bones from branches. The macabre display served as a grisly reminder of imminent death, designed to instill shock and fear in his enemies even before they encountered his traps. The forest path became a gauntlet of terror, meticulously crafted to break the spirit of those who dared to pursue him.

Satisfied that his plan was in place, Kane retreated to his cabin and settled by the warmth of the pot-belly stove. He stoked the fire with an old poker, its rhythmic clinks and hisses adding a comforting crackle to the otherwise quiet room.

Despite severing his alliance with his father and emancipating himself from his lineage, he still possessed the power to transform into Shadow Bear. However, the transformation was no longer swift and effortless. His father's promise to strip away some of his strength was already manifesting, and Kane could feel the weakening process taking hold.

As he waited, the crackling fire cast flickering shadows around the room, a stark contrast to the cold, lethal traps awaiting his pursuers outside. His mind raced with the anticipation of the impending confrontation, his resolve hardening even as his physical strength ebbed. The duality of his existence, caught between human fragility and the primal power of Shadow Bear, simmered within him, fueling his determination to survive at any cost.

He sat and waited.

* * *

Gideon trailed behind Victor's horse, navigating through the dense forest where snow-laden branches drooped under the weight of snow. Miko followed closely, with Alejandro bringing up the rear. The villagers' directions had proven accurate, guiding Victor to a promising lead. Miko's keen eyes detected a well-used track ahead, suggesting recent activity.

The path led them to an area that appeared to have been freshly cleared, the snow disturbed and branches broken aside to create a passage. It was a subtle but unmistakable sign that someone had recently been through, likely Kane. The group pressed on, their senses heightened and weapons at the ready, as they ventured deeper into the heart of the wilderness.

Moving carefully around a cleared bend, the group unknowingly rode towards Kane's traps, drawing ever closer to his shack.

They recoiled in disgust as they entered a macabre corridor adorned with Kane's grim decorations. Low-lying branches were festooned with skulls and partially decaying limbs, some with rotting skin still clinging to the bone. The grisly sight filled the air with the stench of death, and the group felt a chill that had nothing to do with the winter cold. This grotesque display served as a stark warning of the horrors that

awaited them, heightening their sense of dread as they pressed on, every nerve on edge.

Victor's horse suddenly screamed in agony as its front leg triggered the hidden bear trap, the rusty, jagged jaws clamping down mercilessly. The horse bucked wildly, throwing Victor into the spiny shrubs.

Kane, inside his cabin, heard the cries of the injured horse and the subsequent gunshot as Victor ended its suffering. The sharp cracks vibrating through the forest.

"If Kane is around here, he would've heard those shots," Alejandro whispered, his voice tense.

"Si.... but I couldn't leave the animal to suffer and be at the mercy of bears and wolves. Besides, he already knows we're coming for him. Look at the welcoming pathway he's created for us" Victor justified, his voice firm but tinged with regret. "Now we know he has set traps. We must be close. Be very careful and vigilant," Gideon warned, his voice laced with trepidation as his eyes scanned the dense, misty white forest for any signs of movement. The air was thick with tension, each breath visible in the cold air as they moved forward with heightened caution, aware that danger lurked with every step.

As Victor motioned for everyone to dismount, the faint scent of pine-scented smoke drifted towards them, signaling a nearby fire.

"Kane is close by. The villagers mentioned a fur trader's outpost up here for travelers. That's where Kane is, just ahead," Victor whispered, pushing aside a branch to get a better view.

As he stepped forward, Victor inadvertently triggered Kane's trap—a rock that released a spring-loaded barrage of spear-laden branches. Sharp ends pierced Victor's upper leg, eliciting a cry of pain as he struggled to free himself from the green sticks lodged in his flesh.

"Kane!" he screamed, his voice filled with agony and fury.

From his porch, Kane observed the hunters emerging from the tree line. He walked toward them, beckoning with a mocking smile.

"Come on. You've come all this way. Why stop now?" he taunted, his voice carrying through the cold forest air. The stage was set for the long-awaited confrontation, tension crackling between them like the winter's frost.

Alejandro's hand tightened around his gun, ready to fire, but Gideon's restraining signal held him back. Stepping forward with measured composure, Gideon approached his nemesis, hoping to appeal to Kane's humanity and end the cycle of violence.

"Go on, Alejandro, shoot an unarmed man," Kane taunted, his voice edged with defiance.

"Kane, what has become of you?" Gideon implored, his voice carrying a mix of sincerity and subtle manipulation.

"I remember the mischievous boy who was eager to learn our sacred ways. You had the skill in ninjutsu to bring honor and prosperity to our monastery. Instead, you've chosen this remote hideaway, cut off from the comfort and support you once sought. Return with us. I promise you a fair trial at the monastery."

As Gideon approached, Kane finally saw the toll his actions had exacted on the old man's face. The scars and the loss of an eye were stark reminders of the violence and suffering inflicted upon Gideon. Kane felt a pang of remorse and guilt, seeing the physical evidence of the pain he had caused.

In turn, Gideon observed the deep scars on Kane's face, marks left by the fierce battle with Hiro. Each scar told a story of struggle and conflict, a testament to the path Kane had chosen and the hardships endured along the way. The wounds on Kane's face mirrored the internal turmoil and choices that had led him to this isolated existence.

"Hmmph, I don't believe you, Gideon. You've always hated me," Kane retorted bitterly, his voice tinged with accusation.

"I remember your devious scheme to expose me, to force my transformation in front of the Abbot. You endangered your friend's life just to elevate yourself to the position of supreme priest and scribe. You orchestrated a setup, drawing me and the Abbot into a confrontation under false pretenses."

As Kane spoke, the remaining men stepped fully into view, their faces reflecting a blend of curiosity and disbelief at the unfolding drama. His words lingered in the cold air, cutting through the silence and challenging Gideon's authority while exposing the deep-seated truths behind the old grievances.

"Maybe so," he retorted, his voice a low, seething growl. "But I was right, wasn't I? The monastery would never have accepted you once they learned what you truly are. A threat, always." Gideon's words cut through Kane like a blade, each syllable laden with bitter truth.

The weight of Gideon's accusation pressed heavily on Kane, the raw pain of the truth gnawing at his very soul. The stark reality of his existence became painfully clear: he had never truly belonged or fit in. The yearning for love and acceptance felt increasingly futile, like a distant dream forever out of reach. Allowing himself to be loved would mean endangering those closest to him, for he was a skin changer—a danger in every form he took.

In the tense silence that followed, Victor's impatience erupted in a sudden gunshot that shattered the air. The bullet tore through Kane's shoulder, a searing agony that convulsed his body. In that moment of excruciating pain, Kane's transformation began, his form twisting and contorting before their eyes. He channeled the torment, manifesting his altered self with a rapid, desperate intensity—his arms and mouth morphed, a terrifying visage though not fully complete, still imposing but not entirely bear-like.

Miko, Alejandro, Victor, and Hiro stood frozen in horror as Kane, transformed and frenzied, surged towards Gideon, his monstrous form ready to strike with deadly claws.

Gideon let out a piercing shriek as he saw the partially mutated bear lunging at him. Just as he raised his staff to strike at the beast, Hiro surged forward with fearless resolve. Ignoring the old monk, Hiro threw himself at Kane, his movements swift and determined. The blade Hiro wielded found its mark, slashing through Kane's wounded shoulder and cutting down his chest in a desperate bid to stop him.

Kane watched Hiro hurtling toward him, his mind racing as he braced himself for the impending attack. His retaliation was immediate and savage, a swift and brutal response to Hiro's desperate assault.

With a savage swipe of his claws, Kane struck Hiro with brutal force, sending him crashing sideways. As Hiro lay dying, his final words were directed at Kane with a burning intensity. "I may have hated Master Gideon," he gasped, "but I hate you more. Rot in hell, Kane."

Gideon, both astonished and deeply grateful, stood by, struck by the profound irony of the moment. He never imagined Hiro's life would end in such a manner, defending the very man he despised.

Meanwhile, Miko rushed to his beloved Master's side, his heart pounding with fear and urgency. He swiftly aided Gideon, guiding him to safety away from the unfolding carnage about to consume them all.

"Stay here, Master Gideon," Miko whispered urgently to the old man

"Where are you going, Miko....?" Gideon's call trailed off unanswered as Miko slipped away, swift and silent, disappearing around the back of the cabin. Kane's attention was fixed on Victor and Alejandro, his primal instincts guiding him.

Assessing the situation with heightened senses, Kane calculated that Alejandro, uninjured unlike Victor, presented the greater immediate threat.

It was as if fate had intervened—Victor's gun jammed at the crucial moment. The cold navy revolver's bolt refused to lock the cylinder properly, causing a critical timing issue. Unable to fire rapidly in double action, the wear on the bolt had accelerated, leaving him with a malfunctioning weapon when he needed it most.

Hampered by his injuries, Victor could only watch in helpless dread as Kane, the monstrous entity of terrifying legends, advanced menacingly toward Alejandro. The air grew thick with fear as Alejandro, paralyzed by terror, began to fire his gun erratically. His body shook uncontrollably, the relentless demon looming over him, poised to snuff out his life like a flickering candle.

With blood cascading down Kane's chest, tracing a vivid crimson path, he closed in on Alejandro, his presence casting a menacing shadow over the frozen ground. Just as fear reached its peak, a sudden, brilliant orb materialized—a portal from Kane's alternate universe.

A radiant white light erupted suddenly, engulfing Alejandro in its blinding brilliance. The intense flash was so sudden and overwhelming that it left him momentarily incapacitated, his vision obliterated. Just as quickly as it had appeared, the light

vanished, leaving a stunned Kane and a disoriented Alejandro in its wake. The intervention had been swift and decisive, its impact lingering in the stunned silence that followed.

Seizing the moment of distraction, Gideon cautiously maneuvered toward Miko's position behind the cabin, hoping to catch up with him undetected. As he carefully navigated the snow-covered terrain, his eyes caught sight of Victor, who was aiming his rifle with tense focus.

The gunshot echoed through the stillness as Victor's bullet found its mark, striking Kane's leg. Kane staggered, grappling to rise on his injured limb amongst the unforgiving snow.

With a final surge of primal strength, Kane lunged toward Victor, his inhuman speed closing in on the defiant Mexican. In a desperate bid to kill Kane, Victor drew his large hunting knife, driving it into Kane's abdomen with a fierce thrust. As he screamed, "You die today, demon!" his words were cut short. Kane's monstrous jaws clamped down with brutal force on Victor's skull, ending the confrontation with a ferocious bite.

The sharp fangs punctured bone and flesh, silencing Victor's screams in an instant as life ebbed from his body.

Inside the cabin, Miko cautiously had slipped through the back window and made his way to the small front one, where the grim scene outside unfolded before his eyes.

Alejandro, blinded by the sudden brilliance of the orb, sat in the snow, hands over his eyes, his anguished cries filling the air with a haunting moan.

As Miko peered out, his gaze shifted to the right. There stood Kane, towering over Victor's lifeless form, his massive chest heaving with exhaustion from the battle and the grievous wounds that marred him. In his pain-stricken haze, Kane's focus turned inward, consumed by the urgent need to tend to his injuries.

Unnoticed by Kane, Miko and Gideon's whereabouts slipped from his fractured awareness as he staggered back towards the cabin, each movement a testament to his dwindling strength and the toll of the savage conflict

Opening the door to the cabin with a heavy thud, Kane stumbled inside and collapsed onto the worn, creaking bed. Unaware of Miko's presence in the corner, holding the unsettling book wrapped in human skin, Kane began the agonizing transformation back to his human form. When his eyes met Miko's, recognition flashed across his face — his younger brother, an unexpected witness to his torment.

"Give it to me," Kane demanded, his voice still echoing with the deep growl of a bear. Miko hesitated, clutching the book with growing anxiety.

"Kane, what is this? Is this what transforms you into that.... demon?" His voice quivered with concern, probing for answers.

"I said give it to me," Kane growled again, his impatience mounting.

"I'll give it to you if you tell me what it is," Miko countered, his fear momentarily overshadowed by a desperate attempt to understand.

"You don't need to know anything," Kane retorted sharply. He rose from the bed with purpose, looming over Miko, intent on seizing the book. Quick thinking, Miko dodged aside and lunged for the pot belly stove in the corner, its iron door ajar, flames flickering within.

With a swift motion, Miko tossed the book into the heart of the fiery stove, where it landed with a soft thud, immediately catching flame. The pages curled and blackened as the fire eagerly consumed them, casting an eerie glow across the cabin.

Kane's scream tore through the cabin, raw and guttural, as he plunged his hands into the searing flames, snatching the burning book from the depths of the pot belly stove.

With frantic urgency, he beat down the last stubborn tongues of fire that clung to the ancestral book, his anguished cries slicing through the air. "No, no, no.... I need you back," he pleaded desperately, his voice breaking with sorrow and desperation as he crouched on the floor, his head bowed over the partially charred remains of his precious bible.

Unseen by Kane in his frenzied state, Miko approached silently from behind, gripping the fire-stoking iron with steely determination. Raising it high, he brought the rusted metal crashing down onto the back of Kane's skull in one swift, brutal motion. The impact reverberated through Kane's body, the iron embedding itself deep into flesh and bone, sending shockwaves of agony through him.

Kane dropped the now half-burnt book, his movements slowing as he turned to face Miko, his eyes wide with disbelief and pain. Blood trickled down his face, mingling with tears as he whispered his final words with a mix of resignation and betrayal, "Miko, my brother.... who would have thought it would be you."

With those haunting words, Kane's strength ebbed away, his body slumping to the floor in a final, silent surrender to the tumultuous events that had unfolded.

Miko gazed down at Kane, the figure who had once been feared and despised as the monstrous skin changer, leaving a trail of death and destruction across two countries, a legacy of ruin and shattered lives. With a heavy heart, he turned away from the fallen creature and strode purposefully to the cabin's front door.

Throwing it open, Miko called urgently for Gideon, his voice cutting through the chilling silence of the forest. At the same time, he rushed towards Alejandro, who remained huddled in the snow, his anguished cries carrying through the stillness. Alejandro's world had turned dark, his sight stolen by the brilliant orb, and now he clung to the icy ground, consumed by grief over the loss of his vision.

Gideon appeared on the cabin's porch, his voice filled with panic as he called out to Miko, who was crouched beside the distraught Alejandro, attempting to lift him up. "Where is Kane?" Gideon's question cut through the tense air.

"He's inside.....I killed him," Miko replied quietly, the weight of his actions settling heavily upon him.

"You did what needed to be done, my brave Miko. You'll be celebrated in Japan and at the monastery. Your courage will be remembered," Gideon reassured him, his voice firm with conviction, urging Miko to find peace in his decision.

"Let's get Alejandro inside the cabin. The warmth of the fire will help him dry off and recover. It's best if we stay here for a few days, to rest and recuperate after everything we've endured," Miko suggested, his newfound confidence evident in his tone.

Gideon nodded in agreement, offering his support as they carefully guided Alejandro toward the cabin. However, as they neared the verandah, a massive bear emerged from the cabin, its enormous form towering on all fours. At six feet high at the shoulder, its imposing stature cast a formidable shadow over the scene.

With a swift movement, the bear reared up on its hind legs, doubling its height to an intimidating twelve feet, unleashing a deafening roar that reverberated through the forest.

"STAY AWAY," the bear growled fiercely at Gideon and Miko,

its massive fangs and powerful jaws on full display. Meanwhile, Alejandro, still grappling with confusion and fear, cried out in panic, "What's happening? What was that?" His frantic blinded gaze darted around, searching for answers in the chaos.

The towering bear stood like a silent statue, its presence a majestic testament to a dimension steeped in darkness and solitude. Its eyes, deep and reflective, seemed to hold echoes of childhood days and tranquil memories from the sacred monastery in Japan. It paused for a moment, as if paying one final homage to the past before moving on.

In a final, earnst gesture, the bear turned and began its slow departure into the depths of the forest. Each deliberate step seemed to carry a sense of farewell, the rustling leaves and gentle breeze whispering their own quiet goodbyes. Sunlight filtered through the canopy, casting a warm, golden glow on the bear's fur as it vanished into the wilderness, embraced by the shadows of the trees.

Gideon, Miko, and Alejandro stood together in dignified silence, their hearts weighed down yet relieved by the bear's departure. The forest around them seemed to absorb the majestic creature's lingering presence, enveloping them in an atmosphere charged with both tranquility and a profound sense of loss.

Closing the cabin door behind them, Miko gently guided Gideon and Alejandro towards the warmth of the fire, helping them to dry off and settle in. As they gathered around Kane's lifeless body sprawled on the wooden floor, their eyes caught sight of something unexpected—words scratched into the floorboards nearby. It was as though the bear had left a puzzling message, just two words etched deeply into the wood: the name....Shadow Bear.

In that poignant moment, a silent understanding passed between them. They realized they had been forever changed by their encounter with the paranormal, woven into the fabric of nature's enduring mysteries.

They understood that they had just witnessed the birth of the legend of the Shadow Bear, a tale that would linger in their hearts and minds for years to come. It was a testament to the profound and inexplicable forces that shape their universe, leaving an enduring mark on their lives.

"I can't believe Hiro saved your life, Master Gideon. All these months, I've heard nothing but how much he despised you, and then he goes and saves your life," Miko remarked, hoping to catch Gideon's attention. But Gideon only grunted in response, his eyes glazed over, as if he were hypnotized.

Gideon shuffled over to the charred remains of the book, his heart pounding with anticipation. What secrets did it hold? What ancient knowledge waited to be deciphered? His fingers trembled as he picked it up, inspecting the damage.

The once delicate pages were now fused together, the original belly button opening sealed shut by intense heat. To access its contents, one would need to slice through the thick, blackened lapel band that secured the book from back to front, creating an impenetrable barrier.

He carefully placed the book inside Kane's old knapsack, his mind racing with anticipation. He reveled in the thought of the day he would spend hours delving into the mystical universal maps and formulas, exploring the secrets they held.

After spending two days in the secluded cabin, where they had hidden from the worst of the storm, the trio finally set out for the village. The journey back was fraught with the same treacherous weather, but Gideon barely noticed.

His thoughts were utterly consumed by the mysteries locked within the

human-skinned book. He clung to the hope that, once they reached the safety of the village, it would unveil its long-hidden secrets. The anticipation gnawed at him, as he envisioned the revelations that lay within its bewildering pages, promising to unlock profound and cryptic knowledge.

The following morning dawned clear and bright. Gideon rose early, dressed, and performed his ritualistic prayers and chanting, his voice a low murmur in the still air. With a sense of purpose, he grabbed the knapsack and the knife he had acquired earlier. Stepping outside, he found a sturdy bench bathed in sunlight and settled himself there, letting the warmth seep through his thick jacket, reviving his spirits.

He pulled the partially burnt book from its hiding place in the knapsack, its presence both a burden and a beacon of intrigue. With a steely purpose, he began sawing vigorously at the lapel band with the knife, the sound of the blade against the charred fabric sharp and relentless. Each stroke felt like a battle against the book's stubborn defiance, and he attacked it with the desperation of a man who believed his very life depended on it.

All of a sudden, the book screamed. Its high-pitched cry pierced the morning tranquility, stopping everyone in their tracks. Heads turned towards Gideon, who sat frozen in shock, the book clutched in his hands.

Miko stepped out of the hostel, making his way toward Gideon with a measured gait. But as he approached, he saw Gideon's eyes wide with horror, his feet beginning to solidify. The transformation inched up his legs with a cold, relentless inevitability.

"Master Gideon, what's happening to you?" Miko yelled, rushing to his master's side, panic etched deeply across his face.

As the petrification advanced, Gideon had just enough time to confront the gravity of his fate. "Give the book to me!" Miko screamed, his voice a frantic mix of fear and disbelief as he struggled to wrench the book from Gideon's firm grip.

"No, I want to uncover its secrets!" Gideon snapped, his voice seething with irrational possession.

"It's turning me into stone," Gideon said with a chilling calmness, despite the terror that gripped him. "The book has cursed me. This is the end for me. Goodbye, my friend."

Miko could only watch in helpless anguish as the transformation crept up Gideon's chest, then his arms, and finally his face. In mere moments, Gideon was entirely encased in stone, leaving behind a solid, immobile figure seated on the bench. The cursed book remained clutched in his rigid, stony hands, a grim testament to the fate that had befallen him.

The villagers stood in stunned silence, the eerie sound of the book's final scream lingering in the air. They gazed at the tragic monument of the old Buddhist priest, now a stone statue clutching the cursed book. The sight added a sinister layer to the already dark legend of the Shadow Bear.

Graphic stories of Gideon's fate quickly spread among the villagers, seeping into the valley, reaching the fort, Don Morales' ranch, and eventually San Francisco. Each retelling deepened the fear, leaving a permanent mark on anyone who heard the chilling accounts.

They spoke of the Shadow Bear, an ancient demon of forbidden knowledge, a skin changer said to curse anyone who dared venture into the high country. Gideon's transformation into stone confirmed their worst fears: the legend was real, and its power was not to be trifled with.

From that day forward, Gideon's immortalized statue sat permanently on the bench, a grim reminder of the perils of curiosity and the mystical dangers that lurked just beyond their understanding. The legend of the Shadow Bear grew, the tale of the old Buddhist priest's tragic fate forever entwined with the chilling myth, warning all who heard it to respect the unknown and to tread carefully when hiking through the forests.

Eventually, Miko and the blind Alejandro made their way back to Rancho Los Charro. Alejandro stayed at the ranch, with Don Morales promising Miko that he would take care of him in recognition of the loyalty and bravery he had shown for his boss.

Don Morales assigned one of his ranchers to escort Miko back to San Francisco, paying for his ticket on the ship that would take him home to Japan. As the ship

floated away from the American shore, Miko stood on the deck, watching the city slowly shrink into insignificance as they ventured further out to sea. His thoughts were consumed with the journey he had shared with his fallen brothers and the story he would tell the Abbot upon his return.

He had matured—not in physical size, but emotionally and with newfound wisdom. Miko understood that his responsibility now was to continue Gideon's legacy.

He embraced the role of the monastery's scribe, committing himself to the pursuit of knowledge and sharing his insights as a teacher of both his faith and the occult.

In doing so, he aimed to earn respect and become a revered and cherished member of the Buddhist order. The young monk had become an unlikely hero, stepping into a pivotal role that would shape the future of the monastery and its community.

Present Day

A group of young filmmakers unpacked their car, their faces shone with enthusiasm and anticipation after the long journey to the remote village nestled in the mountains. The legend of Shadow Bear loomed large in their minds, the very reason for their visit—to capture on film the terrifying truths behind the chilling tale and historic battle that had shaped the village's folklore for generations.

"Shane, bring the camera over here. Look, there's the infamous stone statue of Gideon holding the human skin book. Start rolling," Jennifer commanded, her voice carrying a blend of eagerness and professional readiness. She cleared her throat and adjusted her hair, preparing herself for the presentation.

The village's population hovered around 150 souls, with essentials like a post office and general store but no restaurants in sight. Despite its small size, the place exuded a quaint charm, although dominated by the solemn presence of its Civil War-era cemetery that occupied a significant portion of the town's 294 acres. "We're here today in the village where all the stories about the Shadow Bear converge," Jennifer announced proudly, her voice brimming with fascination and awe. "I'm standing right in front of Gideon's statue—the high priest—still clutching Kane's macabre human skin book. According to legend, this is the very spot where Gideon attempted to unlock the secrets of Kane's paranormal bible and was turned to stone, as if he had gazed directly into Medusa's eyes."

Some locals stood nearby, their curiosity aroused, watching the film crew with a mix of interest and wariness.

"I wouldn't be going up in those mountains if I were you, missy!" shouted one of the locals, his voice tinged with concern and a hint of a dire warning.

"If you're looking to find the Shadow Bear, you'll find him alright, but you won't come back. He's up there, just waiting for foolish people like yourself to venture into his territory. He'll rip your throat out. You mark my words," the old-timer cautioned, before he sauntered away, puffing on his pipe.

Jennifer exchanged a glance with Shane, the gravity of the information settling over them like a curtain. Despite the chilling tale, her determination to uncover the truth behind the legend only seemed to grow stronger.

"Don't pay any attention to him, Jen. They're all superstitious around here," Shane said with a zestful and hopeful tone as he lowered the camera.

"That's exactly why we're here, isn't it?"

The director and producer grabbed their backpacks, locking the car as the locals watched with shaking heads, disbelieving as they hiked up the road and vanished into the dense forest of the highlands.

Conversations with the locals had strengthend their expectation for ghostly sightings. Even though they didn't truly believe in ghosts, the prospect of capturing something creepy on film added to the authenticity of their documentary. As the sun began its descent, the group pitched their tents, struggling with the heavy cast-iron skillet Anthony had insisted on packing as they attempted to make a fire and cook dinner.

Their plan was simple: roam the woods with the filming gear and let fate guide their exploration. The atmosphere grew cooler as darkness settled, casting shadows that danced among the trees. Despite their initial bravado, the strange silence of the forest and the stories of local legends stirred a nervous energy among the filmmakers.

It may have been a full moon that night, but there was no evidence of it from their vantage point, obscured under a thick canopy of snow-laden trees. Their world was reduced to what their headlamp spotlights could reveal—twisting branches, scary shadows, and a carpet of undisturbed snow.

"Hello, ghosts?" Jennifer began tentatively, unsure of the proper way to address spiritual beings. Her voice sliced through the stillness of the night, mingling with the howling wind that rustled through the trees, while the camera captured the macabre scene.

Talking aloud to the unseen entities in the darkness began to unsettle them. Despite their skepticism, a palpable nervousness hung in the air, as if they half-expected an otherworldly response. The forest seemed to hold its breath, amplifying every rustle and creak, heightening their awareness of the mysterious unknown that encircled them.

After an hour of fruitless searching in the supernatural silence of the snow-covered forest, they retreated back to their campsite. Jennifer tried to reassure herself that "no news was good news"—not for the sake of their story, but because encountering the Shadow Bear would likely have resulted in frantic screams and desperate sprints.

Exhausted and disheartened, they crawled into their separate tents and called it a night. Jennifer couldn't tell what time it was when she suddenly snapped awake in the darkness. Weird but distinct crackling noises and a menacing, guttural grunting surrounded her tent. Regret washed over her for fully zipping up her shelter; she had no way of peering out to assess the situation.

If she mustered the courage to investigate, she would have to scramble out of her nylon sleeping bag, grope for the tent zipper, and burst out—potentially scaring off whatever lurked outside or, worse, alerting it to her presence. However, paralyzed with fear, she squeezed her eyes shut, pulled her sleeping bag over her head, and faked sleep, hoping whatever sinister presence was outside would pass by without incident.

Gradually, the piercing sound of a woman's anguished cries—reminiscent of a native wail—shattered the oppressive darkness, slicing through the stillness with a chilling intensity. The horrific echoes slashed through the trees, wrapping the night in a shroud of dread, leaving a deep, unsettling remorse in their wake. Everyone lay frozen within their sleeping bags, hearts pounding, as they strained desperately to identify the source of the bone-chilling sound.

The next morning, an unearthly silence enveloped the campsite. The group had vanished without a trace. Their tents stood empty, with belongings strewn about in disarray. The nylon flaps of the tent doors flapped eerily in the breeze, amplifying the unsettling emptiness left by their abrupt disappearance. The mystery of their fate remained shrouded in questions, with no logical answers in sight.

It was a chilling testament to the mysteries that still cursed those mountains—a stark reminder of the legend of Shadow Bear, untamed and unseen, whose presence appeared to linger in the whispering winds and the shadowed depths of the dense forest.....forever.

The End

www.ingramcontent.com/pod-product-compliance
Lightning Source LLC
Chambersburg PA
CBHW050837030726
47503CB00007BA/2214

9780975627358